ECHOES FROM THE PAST

RAIN TRUEAX

Echoes FROM THE PAST

Arizona Historicals Book 5

Introducing the Taggerts

is an original work of Rain Trueax.

ISBN: 978-1-943537-00-6
Paperback

Prepared and presented by:
Seven Oaks
Monmouth, Or.

120217 376
Personal Contact and
Rights Agreements : raintrueax@gmail.com

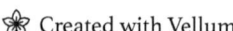 Created with Vellum

INTRODUCTION

This is the first romance for the Taggert brothers-- Vince, Jesse and Cole.

They had absolutely no reason to be together-- nothing in common-- except, oh maybe a few past lives where the passion was sizzling—with a minor complication—he always ended up dead. Pure coincidence. Couldn't happen again. Her fear that it could led her to try to convince him not to go with her on a potentially dangerous archaeological investigation to Central Arizona, where one of those lives had been haunting her dreams.

He knew, given his experiences, there were many ways he could end up dead, and he wasn't about to worry about dreams with no real bullets. He did know, however, that she could prove dangerous to him. He had never walked away from danger before and wasn't about to now.

1901, a new century and things should be less wild and woolly in Arizona. Very civilized, with only an occasional nightly shootout. Much safer—for some. Not so much for the son of an infamous outlaw family, who was falling in love with the one woman from whom he should have stayed many miles away. SHOULDS weren't in his vocabulary.

This western adventure takes these two unlikely lovers from Tucson, north into the Sierra Ancha, where answers and danger await. As the fifth Arizona historical, readers of the others will find some familiar characters.

CHAPTER 1

April 1901, Tucson, Arizona

Holly Jacobs looked at the mare Señor Perez had led from the stall. The hostler frowned as he studied her face. "You look frightened, señorita. Horse know this." She had hoped she was hiding her fear. "No, I am fine." She was lying, did not like lying and sucked in a breath.

Princess, a four-year old mare, had been purchased with the recommendation she was a reliable mount. She looked good. Light brown, strongly muscled, neither sway-backed, nor with damaged hocks, she was told she would make a good mount. Her mistake might have been to trust Clint Madison with finding a horse for her. One, she didn't want to owe him a favor. Two—what did he know about horses. He might be a good enough lawyer but that meant little where it came to evaluating a horse. She should have asked Ollie Oliver's opinion, but he had been so busy. No, this would be fine for her first time on the mare—hopefully, since it also was her first time with the new sidesaddle.

Taking lessons from Ollie, she had developed a reasonable amount of confidence while riding on the trails around his ranch. He though had always insisted that ladylike concerns were... Well the phrase he used wasn't one she was comfortable remembering. The long and short of it was-- ride astride until she had control of herself and the horse. Ollie had provided her with boys' britches and insisted she take her lessons astride. That was hardly proper when she was in Tucson. She could manage a sidesaddle. Ladies rode that way wearing proper riding skirts. How difficult could it be?

She stepped up on the block and situated herself on the saddle. Arranging her knee properly over the fixed head, her other leg under the leaping head, it felt right. This was going to be fine. She straightened her skirts before smiling and reaching for the reins from Señor Perez.

"You want I go with you?" he asked with that uneasy voice.

"That won't be necessary but gracias." She lightly touched her riding crop to Princess's rump, and the horse stepped out of the barn.

It had been several years, but she had ridden sidesaddle in the east. Never that far and never alone. She wanted this to be alone, to prove to herself that she could do it. If she couldn't do it, how could she get to her archaeological exploration on the Cibecue? She had to do it.

The roads leading from Tucson were full of other horsemen, people walking with burros, and heavily laden wagons. Past one home, small children jumped up and down laughing. No one paid her notice as she passed. With the smooth gait of Princess, her confidence grew.

She would take Princess out of town but not as far as Oracle. They didn't need a long ride. This was to put herself at ease and let her horse grow familiar with her. She smoothed her hand over the mare's neck. "We'll do fine, won't we," she said-- whether to reassure herself or the horse, she wasn't sure.

April was a delight on the desert with fields of colorful wildflowers. Even a prickly pear was coming into bloom. The breeze was faint, a lovely day for a ride with a sky full of fluffy clouds, passing in no hurry. She turned her mare to the north road and the traffic thinned out. Toward the mountains would be Ollie's ranch, but she wouldn't ride that far. Perhaps she'd take the sidesaddle and Princess to him for her next lesson. Rose, Ollie's wife, would enjoy seeing her riding like a lady.

After having ridden what she judged was about four miles beyond the outskirts of Tucson, she pulled on the left rein and turned Princess back toward the stable. It was then that the mare took it into her head to run. Trying to resist shrieking, which wouldn't be effective in stopping her, she pulled on the reins, but Princess had it in her head where she was going. The tightening bit wasn't changing her mind.

Holly's fear rose as she struggled to stay in the saddle. What would happen when they reached all those wagons, the burros, would Princess slow then? If she did, could Holly keep on her when she already felt unbalanced.

It was then that she heard the thunder of hooves, and a horse came alongside, the rider a stranger in dark garb. "You all right, ma'am" he yelled as he pulled his mount to match her horse's running gait.

"Do I look all right?" she yelled. She let out a shriek as he reached out a long arm and in seconds had pulled her from her saddle and had her in front of his. She felt even more frightened than she had when about to fall off her running horse.

He slowed his mount to a stop, gave her a cursory look, one that saw but didn't at the same time. "I need to get your horse. Can you stand?"

3

"If you put me down." She felt a mixture of fright, embarrassment, and shockingly anger.

He easily lowered her to her feet before he spurred his horse into a run that soon had him overtaking Princess. He reached out and grabbed the dangling rein, pulling the mare to him, and then slowing her enough to turn and bring her back to where Holly was dusting off her skirt even though it had yet to touch the road.

He leaned over his pommel as he studied her, and for the first time she got a good look at the tall man who had saved her from a bad fall or worse. "I... thank you," she said not feeling grateful even though she should.

When her gaze met his, she felt shocked at the handsome face—not young, not old, but an expression in those eyes that seemed older than the hills. She'd never understood what that meant, not until this moment.

His smile was crooked. "Riding sidesaddle seems a little stupid to me, if you'll pardon my saying it."

"It's what ladies do," she protested tightening her lips.

"Not those with the sense they were born with and who don't want to break their fool necks."

She didn't like him, but she would behave properly even if he didn't. "I don't know why she ran off with me," she managed, working to avoid the fuming words coming to mind. Good thing she had been raised polite—even if he clearly had had no such training.

Holly did not consider herself vain, but men generally responded to her looks. Her blonde hair, slim body, and finely boned face led to expected smiles and compliments. This man didn't see her as a beautiful woman or even as a woman. His expression had the same disapproval he might have shown a disobedient child

Determined to hide her irritation, as she was never rude—

4

especially not when someone had done her a major favor, she managed a smile that she hoped was grateful—even while she felt anything but.

"I truly appreciate your help." She guessed her tone didn't sound contrite when she saw his smirk.

"That skirt could get caught by the wind?"

"No, hardly any breeze."

"You ridden her many times?"

"This is our first."

"And you started to gallop her but lost control?"

"No, I never intended... We had just turned back to the stable."

His smile didn't change. "You need somebody to ride her who knows how to handle a horse and teach her when she wants to go home, she can't race to do it."

"I've been taking lessons," she protested and couldn't stop the resentful tone.

"Whoever it was should have taught you about horses and barns. Next time you take her out, when you turn her toward her stall and oats, keep a better grip on the reins. Are you afraid to ride her now?"

"No." She looked around for a big rock to help her mount. He leaped from his horse, and she saw he was even taller than he had looked. "I'll lift you up," he said as he moved to her side.

She wanted to say no. She didn't want him touching her again. She still remembered how his powerful arm and hand had felt as he had reached out and lifted her from her saddle as though she had weighed nothing. She had no choice. She could never get up without help. She nodded with more irritation than she had a right to feel. "Will she run off again," she asked as she arranged herself on the saddle.

"I'll stay with you until you are back to the barn."

"I have her in a stable," she said forcing a smile. How could she repay him? Oddly enough, she felt more like giving him a slap. He had treated her as though she was a novice, a child, an inexperienced... Well, she was where it came to a horse.

With seemingly one fast step, he was back in his saddle and rode alongside her. It helped her to gain back the confidence she had lost. At the stable, she didn't object when he dismounted and lifted her down.

"I would like to give you a reward," she said. "I don't have money with me but if you..."

He stopped her with a raised hand. "No reward needed, ma'am." The sarcastic look was back. She wished she hadn't noticed how handsome he was. He wasn't young. There were lines on his cheek, and she saw around his eyes-- eyes used to looking toward the sun too often.

"I insist," she said.

"You can insist all you want, but I'm not taking money for doing what anyone would do in that situation."

Before she could argue, Perez came out from the stable. "You are back soon," he said as he took Princess' reins. He looked up then at the man who had remounted his horse. "I know you?" he asked.

"Antonio?"

Perez grinned. "Sí."

"Good to see you again." He tipped his hat and looked back at Holly. "Good day, ma'am. Consider riding astride next time. Ladies do many foolish things to be proper. It isn't much help in avoiding a broken neck." With that, he rode off without a backward glance.

She gritted her teeth against that desire to say something cutting—even if he couldn't hear. He made it difficult to remain a lady. "You seemed to know him. Who is that man?" she asked Perez as he led her horse back into the stable.

"Used to be a padre."

"A priest?" That didn't seem possible. The man had had a hard look to him. She had felt his cartridge belt against her body as he had lifted her in front of him. Where many men wore holsters, not many wore them low enough to need to be tied down as his had been.

"No, a padre. He is not now though." He led Princess into her stall and pulled off the saddle, which he carried to the saddle room.

"I want to care for Princess," she said as he removed the horse's bridle. She needed to learn to do all these things. Perez handed her a curry brush. After she had brushed the mare's coat for what she felt were sufficient minutes, she found a portion of oats to feed her.

At the gate, she turned and looked into the mare's eyes, petting her forehead, unsure what would make her happy. Maybe the swishing tail meant the same as it would in a dog. The horse had a pretty face, a lighter brown than the rest of her. Watching her now, the mare had one ear forward and the other moving as though trying to hear something.

"When she wags her tail, is that that the same as a dog?" she asked Perez, who was cleaning the nearby stall.

He shook his head. "Flies bother her. The ears though, that's what tells you a horse is listening. If they are back, she's angry." He studied her a moment. "She is trying to figure you out."

"Me too."

She smiled then and walked from the stable to her cottage. The ride hadn't gone well. On the other hand, she has survived. Maybe Ollie and the stranger had been right. She should stop worrying about being a lady and ride astride. She didn't have the natural balance and ease in the saddle of her friend, Grace. She could learn to handle a horse though. She would learn.

Vince Taggert drew his horse up to the hitching rail in front of Sicilla's General Store. He grinned, as he saw an automobile working its way down the street, startling his horse as well as all the burros and horses on Main Street.

He shook his head as the funny little horseless carriage managed to get past him and turn the corner. It would never catch on—too unreliable. He thought about lighting a cigarette but decided to go inside first.

The building was cool. Goods lined two sides with clearly a feminine and a masculine division of merchandise.

"Damnitall," Del Sicilla said as he came out from behind a counter. "John Damian. How the hell are you?"

Vince reached out to take his hand and then Connie Sicilla emerged from the other side to give him a big hug. "Welcome, friend."

"How about a drink?" Del suggested and ushered Vince back into their living quarters. In moments, the two were seated at the kitchen table and sipping good bourbon.

"Been awhile. What brings you back?" Del asked.

Connie entered, went to the stove, poured hot water into a tea pot before she sat at the table, her eyes on Vince. "It is good to see you. I didn't think you'd be here so soon... John."

He grinned watching her over the rim of his glass. "What, you don't like the name?"

"It would be fine for some men." She smiled with that witchy look she used when she wanted.

"It seemed a good idea. Do you know my real name since you know it's not John Damian?"

"No, but you never felt like a John to me."

8

"Ever think about telling your husband?" Del asked with a teasing grin. He turned his gaze on Vince. "If it's not John, what is it?"

"Vince... Vincent Taggert."

Although Connie didn't react to it, Del did. "One of the Taggerts?"

She looked at her husband. "That has significance?"

Vince nodded. "In some places it does."

Del sucked in a breath and let it out loudly. "So you were trying to avoid..." He didn't go on.

"All right," Connie said with exasperation. "I may lay claim to being a psychic of sorts, but I am not a mind reader." She gave a little laugh. "Explain."

"Not too complicated. I come from a family known for robbery, killing and scaring others into obeying whatever they demand. It began with my grandfather, Josiah, and his brothers... although likely further back."

"You are confusing me."

Vince smiled but felt no humor. "Most of the Taggert brand came from Kansas, Missouri, and Wyoming. No reason you'd hear about them down here. At least it's what I once thought." He looked at Del. "How do you come to know the name?"

"We've lived a lot of places, and gambling halls tend to gossip as much as a church full of women," Del said with a chuckle.

When Connie still looked perplexed, Vince said, "I've spent over twenty-five years trying to get away from that name."

"And gave up?" Del asked.

He shrugged. "In the end, it went with me name or not."

Del shook his head. "How'd you end up back here--right now?"

"The letter."

"I wrote him," Connie said. "I didn't think you'd be here this fast though."

Now it was Del's turn to look confounded as he turned back to his wife. "Why?"

"And how did you know where I was?" Vince asked. He had mulled over the answer to that question as he had ridden south.

"You and Sam kept in touch."

"Now and again."

"When he and Abigail were in town, I asked if she knew how I could reach you. She didn't, but Sam overheard and asked why. He accepted my reason, and told me what he had last heard. I had no idea if you would still be there, of course. As to why, I argued with them over that."

"Sam and Abby?"

"No."

Vince leaned back in his chair and studied her. "Then who?"

"The voices." She smiled sheepishly. "I was worried about a friend and a proposed journey she is going to take. I felt concern as to the reliability of her friends. I asked the other side for whether it was safe and what to do. You kept coming up although it wasn't by name. It was the man in black, the man with the gun. I knew who they meant."

"You think this friend needed a man with a gun?"

She flushed. "I wasn't sure why you were their answer. I remembered though how you stood up for us when we were in Sutter Creek, and the mob was going to... well attack me for being a witch, or so they feared."

"I also remember how brave you and Del were. I doubt you needed me."

Connie shook her head. "That day you saved us from who

knows what end. I also saw that while people respected you, stood back from you, you were also a man who wouldn't use a weapon-- if he didn't have to. That was maybe why they... wanted you. Or maybe not."

"You aren't making much sense, sweetheart," Del said.

Vince shook his head. "Seems a roundabout way to get help. Did you try warning your friend?"

"I did. She is stubborn. When she gets her mind made up, she goes straight for it. In this case, however, she has a good reason, one that I respect. Knowing that didn't worry me any the less."

"It can't be Abigail. Who then?" Vince asked.

Connie shook her head. "Holly Jacobs."

"The name doesn't ring a bell."

"She isn't from here. She arrived in Tucson to visit Grace. That was November of '99."

"She needs a gun hand why?"

Connie sighed. "I don't know that she needs that. She needs a guardian angel." She smiled then and levelly met his gaze.

"I am no angel, ma'am."

"You were to us that night."

"Well, don't mistake me for one. I may not be an outlaw, but many of the trappings that come with the Taggert name belong to me too. My weapons have gotten used a lot more than I could wish. I was in Sheridan because they offered me the job as deputy. I tried it, and it worked for awhile."

"They fired you?" Del asked.

"In a manner of speaking. The main problems in town had been straightened out." Or killed. "When a Colt is no longer needed, a man carrying it isn't either—especially after someone told who my family was."

"You ever try being a minister again?" Del asked. His

expression seemed more contemplative than Vince would have expected.

"It seems I'm not much good at turning the other cheek." He smiled.

"There is an irony about this. Happens there is another Taggert in town." Del's words were succinct and his lips tight. It was Vince's turn to be taken aback, and he waited for the rest. "He was at the Pedrales last night. I heard his name from Ridge. He is also a man who stands out in a crowd—or maybe makes a crowd stand back. Ridge warned him to cause no trouble there, fingering his shotgun when he said it. Taggert only smiled with a look that is a lot like yours. I never thought about it at the time, but you two resemble each other. He's not as broad in the shoulders but tall with the same dark hair, rugged features."

"You get a first name?" He could hope they weren't closely related.

"He didn't offer it that I heard. I should add he had two hard cases with him. Maybe they were his brothers, but they didn't look like him—one sandy haired, mean eyes, short. The other middle height, balding young—a face nobody'd remember."

Vince smiled. "If you weren't a gambler whose business it was to remember."

Del nodded with an acknowledging grin. "Or a store-keeper. Anyway, those two use their guns a lot would be my guess. Not cowboys or storekeepers, if you get my drift."

Vince let out a breath. "The other mention what he was here for?"

"He was quiet, didn't say much, not the kind of man folks ask questions of."

"Great." He barely knew his three half-brothers. He had left home as early as he could get away. When he'd gone, the oldest would have been eight. Vince had taken off without even saying good-bye as he had believed it was the only way he'd get free. Asa, Cole and Jesse were vague memories. The one he remembered most was the oldest, Asa. Even at eight he had shown a cruel streak.

There'd on been one brief encounter, five years earlier, where he'd seen Asa and Cole. Asa might've grown to a man, but inside, clearly he hadn't changed. Cole gave away nothing of the man he was. Growing up with a father like theirs wasn't likely to be encouragement to become good men. If one of his brothers was in Tucson, he guessed he was about to find out which way the twig had been bent.

"Will you have supper with us?" Connie asked.

He shook his head. "Thanks, but I want to get my horse stabled, a hotel room and eat in town. The Rainbow still open?"

Del nodded. "You are welcome to bunk here."

"No, it should be a hotel, but I'll be back in the morning and... hear more about this problem. Any chance that in your shelves you have a suit and white shirt, maybe string tie?" He smiled at Connie as she nodded and led him to the store to show him a black suit that fortunately fit even his shoulders perfectly.

As he walked out of the store, he was aware Connie was still staring at him thoughtfully. He didn't want to know what she saw. There was no chance in hell that he'd ask her for one of her readings. He already knew his fate.

CHAPTER 2

Holly stalked into her house feeling as though she wanted to kick something. She was annoyed at her behavior toward the stranger, who well might have saved her life. He had struck her wrong though. He had had such an officious way of speaking. A tone of voice that said he was used to giving orders and expecting to have them obeyed. How dare he claim a woman should not ride sidesaddle?

It was even more annoying how handsome he was. Why did the one man who she personally found attractive have to be such a dictatorial despot? As she went upstairs to change out of her riding clothes, she worked to put her irritation from her. Using common sense generally worked. Her fear had been transferred to unjustified anger against a man she didn't even know. Except, those eyes...

Using the fresh water and bowl from her dresser, she washed and then put on a light green, cotton dress before hurrying back to the kitchen where she smelled something good cooking.

When she had purchased the home, from her older friend,

Rose, she had quickly found herself a good cook—that not being one of her own skills. Song not only was a wonderful cook, but she had become a friend as well. The dishes she prepared were heavy on vegetables, poultry, fish, and any seafood that had arrived at the markets. She arrived punctually at noon, prepared Chinese dishes, some that took hours to cook, and left for her own home, to allow Holly to serve herself. The arrangement suited both women.

"Would you like tea? I have some ready," Song asked with a smile.

"I would love it." Anything to soothe her frayed nerves. She invited Song to join her, and the two sat at the table. "How was your day?" she asked the older woman.

"Before I came, I went to the gardens, and found fresh carrots, lettuce, green onions, bok choy, and sugar peas. Thanks to the chicken I bought two days ago, I am fixing you my favorite soup, egg flower. Very delicious."

"It smells wonderful." She sipped her tea. Song seemed disturbed. She wondered if she could guess the reason. "How is your son?"

Song shook her head and let out a sigh. "Zian is a stubborn young man. What I want, he does not. Sometimes he listens to his grandfather. Mostly not. He has refused taking a wife. Now he wishes to be called Sam."

"I suppose that fits in better with those he works."

"Perhaps, but it angers his grandfather, who has said he will send for a wife for him. Zian or rather Sam, says no." Her laugh showed no humor.

"He doesn't want to garden and sell produce?"

Song shook her head. "I am not sure what he wants to do. It is worrisome for an old woman."

Holly laughed. "You aren't old. You hardly look a day over twenty."

"I am many days over twenty," Song said, but Holly could tell she was pleased. The truth was that she didn't look much over thirty. Her hair was coal black, and her figure as slim as Holly's own. "Is Mr. Madison coming to dinner tonight?" Song asked.

"No, I have work to do."

Song giggled. "I would imagine he asked."

"He understands."

"That man wants to marry you. I can tell."

"I have told him it won't happen. I am marrying no man—ever. I saw what happened to my mother when my father ruled her life. I don't need a man for anything."

"What about for having children?" Song's smile was sly.

"It would be unfair to a child. My work is my child. I can't imagine any family understanding my desire to go off and dig in the dirt." She laughed and took another sip of the flavorful tea. "What kind is this?" she asked.

"Finally, it arrived today-- Qilan."

"I like it very much. It has a sweet but faintly nutty flavor."

"I agree. How did your ride go with your new horse?"

Holly sighed. "Do we need to talk about it?"

Song laughed. "Of course not."

"I was raised to be a lady but... there are times I am not so sure it's worth it. Riding sidesaddle reminded me today." She managed a laugh. "If I was a natural horsewoman like Grace, I suppose it'd be easier; but then Grace generally rides astride. On a ranch, far from town, nobody cares. I thought in town, I should look like a lady. Some of the neighbors seem a bit suspicious of me anyway, as a woman living alone and running her own business." Appearing to be a lady, whether she saw herself as one or not, could be protective—if she didn't break her neck first.

Song studied her a moment before she said, "In my

culture, in China, women of the higher classes, all had their feet bound into tiny, childlike feet. It began when they were small children."

"I have read of that."

"My father was a man who looked ahead. He believed that the end of the Opium War would lead to killings and even more repressions. His family was wealthy, but he said it would not stay so. He took what he could-- and my mother. Many men back then did not take their wives, but they had only recently married. He knew he would never go back. Had he stayed, most probably I would have been one with those tiny feet, where I would hobble now like an old lady. Instead, I was born in San Francisco. I am glad the wealth we might have had was left behind for freedom and choices here."

Song had never spoken so much of her own story. Holly didn't know what to say and put out her hand to stroke the older woman's. "I am fortunate you came to Tucson. You are a chef worthy of the finest restaurants."

That pleased Song. "My husband thought we would find a better life here. His father, Wei Chen had come and said the land was good, the needs great, and he believed a living could be made, not great like gold but good. Instead, Lin grew sick and died, my son and I were taken in by Lin's father. Still, I regret nothing. I would not have liked crippled feet." She smiled.

"I understand. And also, the lesson you shared. Quit trying to ride sidesaddle to look like a lady and maybe end up crippling myself."

Song smiled. "If the shoe fits." She smiled more broadly.

Holly laughed. She had another issue that she needed to discuss. "In a month, I will be going north to the site where I plan to do an archaeological investigation. I would like you to come with me, to cook for myself, and the small crew. I plan to take a wagon with supplies, which would mean a small cook stove and two tents. Your wages for the time we are there will be more than here. I will though offer you the option of staying here. I will pay you the wages you now receive even though I am not here. This isn't magnanimous of me, as I want you to be here when I return." She smiled. "You could even live in the extra bedroom here if you would like that during the months I most likely will be gone."

"If I go, I would not have to ride a horse?"

"No, you could ride in the wagon. You would cook for more people though than you do now but less complicated—no gourmet expected. The menu would be your choice."

Song licked her lips. Her expression grew thoughtful. "How long will you be gone?"

"I plan until September, but I am unsure. It will depend on what I find." She knew what she hoped that would be, but it was not based on scientific methods.

"Will it be dangerous, this journey?"

"Ollie says it will. I don't know. I will establish a base camp once I get to the proper site. I have written permission from the Apache nation as the probable sites are all on their land. I will admit though there was some resistance. They told me that not all liked the idea of my digging there even though the ruins are not likely to be of their ancestors."

"So some might cause trouble?"

"I don't expect that but will be prepared should problems arise. I plan to hire six to help with the excavations, some of whom will be familiar with firearms. I am a good shot— although on skeet and targets, not animals of any sort. There is an unknown factor to this kind of trip. I have to admit that it'll probably be safer for you here."

"Less interesting though. I will think about it. When do I have to tell you?"

"Take your time and be sure. I won't leave until sometime in the first week of May, but, of course, if you don't want to come, the sooner you can tell me the better. I will try to arrange for another cook." She smiled. "That person won't be as good as you, but I will find someone. Don't be concerned about that."

Song nodded. "I will tell you as soon as I can." She laughed then. "And, I think that is Mr. Madison I see walking up the walk."

Holly groaned but went to get the door.

Satisfied with the quality of the stable and the feed it offered, Vince gave Jupiter a good brushing, several forks of the available hay, and most popular of all, oats, before he headed for the nearest hotel, the San Xavier.

"I need a room with a bath and hot water," he told the clerk as he signed the register for the first time using his real name.

The clerk looked him up and down, taking in the dusty and rough clothes. "Not cheap."

He laid out enough bills to cover it, and the clerk nodded. He turned the register around, glanced at the name, but paid it no mind as he added a number behind it. "How many days?"

"I'll pay for two to start."

The clerk handed him a key. "First door at the top of the stairs. Hot water might still be there this early."

In his room, Vince stripped off his clothes as he filled the tub. Before he stepped into it, he set his cigarettes, matches and revolver on the nearby stand. He appreciated that the tub allowed him to face the door. He didn't expect trouble but naked in a tub wasn't where he wanted to find it either.

The water wasn't exactly hot, but the warmest he had in

months. Sheridan had fewer luxuries, not to mention his own quarters had been the back of the jail, with any possible bath only above the barbershop.

Leaning back, he considered his day. He hadn't expected to have to deal with family. It had to be coincidence if one of his brothers was here. He thought back as to the possibility he had told anyone in Sheridan where he was heading. He hadn't, not even the hostler when he had picked up Jupiter. It had to be chance, which didn't answer the question as to why he and his friends had come.

Lighting a cigarette, he had his first smoke of the day. Drawing it deeply into his lungs he thought about what was the smart thing to do. Why would he start being smart now? He chuckled silently. Nothing in his life had gone the way he might've hoped or planned. He'd quit looking for answers to life years earlier. They weren't going to be found in Tucson. Trouble was more likely.

Almost five years it had been since he received a letter at one of those places along his route. His stepmother was grievously ill. That woman had been good to him. She'd taken a motherless boy into her heart and raised him with her own sons as though he was also hers. Knowing she was ill, he'd headed straight for the Vernal ranch.

When he'd ridden up, the old man had been sitting in a rocker on the porch. As soon as Vince had dismounted, he had lit into him with a string of obscenities regarding what a useless son he had been. He didn't try to argue and waited it out.

"She's dead," finally his father had said. It was then that two men had emerged from the house. He'd last seen his brothers as children. He would not have known them if he'd come across them in town or maybe he would as both were dark like him, carrying their father's rugged features.

"You come back hoping to inherit something?" the shorter of the two had asked with a snide smile as he had moved forward to lean on the porch. He had rested his hand on the butt of his revolver. The other hadn't been wearing a gun and said nothing.

"I had hoped she would still be alive."

"Wal, she ain't. You're too late." The man lit a cigarette.

"Are you Asa?" He still had the mean eyes.

"I am."

"Where is she buried?"

The other said. "In Vernal's cemetery-- three weeks ago."

Vince had remounted, rode back to the small community, and to the cemetery where he found her marker and the freshly turned grave. "Valerie Taggert, beloved wife of Jeremiah." That was a sad joke. He doubted his pa loved anyone, certainly not his sons. He didn't ever remember a tender touch or kind word.

He had knelt by the grave with his hat off as he thought of the woman who had given him the only kindness he'd known from family. When they had come through, his father's uncles hadn't been any gentler than his father. Ruthless men who found fists and guns the best lessons for children or others.

Not so, with his step-mother, Valerie Rasmussen Taggert, who had taught her boys to read despite Jeremiah's snort of disdain. She had used a worn Bible, and he had learned the words along with the stories of Noah and David, men who nobly stood up for what was right. She had mentioned these patriarchs were some foolish about women, but where it came to doing right, they found a way despite obstacles.

She had planted in Vince the desire to be a pastor before he had come to know he was cut all wrong for it. Once he had hoped it would make up for what his family was. Or maybe he hoped it would make up for the darkness he knew to be in his own soul.

In the cemetery, that day he had knelt for long moments before he realized he was not alone. His two brothers were watching from their horses. "He said to bring you back," Asa said with a snide smile.

"Think you can do it?" he had asked as Asa dismounted.

"Slung over your horse. Oh yeah, I can do it." He had laughed as he moved toward Vince with his fists raised. The fight hadn't lasted long. Vince hadn't only learned to use his guns but also his fists. His brother hadn't expected the blows he received and soon crumbled.

Vince had then turned to the brother who hadn't dismounted, nothing of what he was thinking showed on his face. "You want to bring me back?" Vince had asked.

The smile was crooked. "Not particularly." He looked toward Asa who was groaning on the ground.

"Which one are you?"

"Cole."

"Jesse doing all right?" he asked as he mounted Jupiter.

"As good as can be expected, I reckon. He doesn't come to the ranch anymore than he has to, works for a neighbor."

"Tell Asa, when he comes around, that I want nothing from him or any of you. Leave me alone."

"You leaving again?"

"Yep." Vince had mounted and ridden off. He hadn't looked back. Family they might have been, but none he wanted even to know. Now he had to face one of the tree, with no idea what kind of man he would be anymore than he'd known that day in the cemetery.

Two hours later, he had shaved off his bristle, and dressed in the new clothes. He brushed off his black hat enough that when he looked at himself in the mirror, he looked respectable. Nothing could be done about his scuffed boots. He'd deal with them later if he stayed in Tucson long enough for it to matter.

As far as he knew, Tucson hadn't yet gone to the no guns within the city limits of some other western towns. If that had changed, he'd find out soon enough as he belted back on his Colt before walking downstairs and heading for restaurant. He might as well get a good meal before he faced the reason his relative was in town.

In the restaurant, he found a table, studied the menu. A waitress came up with a pad.

"Steak, rare," he said. "Do you have a red wine?"

She listed off the choices. Tucson was coming up in the world. He chose a Bordeaux. It had been longer than his last bath since he'd had a good wine.

An hour later, he had polished off a salad, steak, potato, and two glasses of the wine, which if not great, was at least acceptable. He lit a cigarette as he looked around at the other customers. Most were well dressed. It appeared Tucson was growing in wealth if this establishment was any indicator.

The waitress returned. "Would you like dessert?" He shook his head, and when he saw the bill, he handed her the right number of bills plus a generous tip. her smile widened for the first time since she had served him. "Thank you, sir. Enjoy your cigarette."

He strolled outside and looked toward the Pedrales down the street. Tucson's streetlights had come on. The street was dimly lit with more foot traffic and fewer wagons or burros. The train pulled into town, and he watched as passengers disembarked. Yes, Tucson was growing. It might not have been Arizona's capitol, but it was going to be a city someday worth living around or even in— for those who liked the desert.

The sheriff walked down the boardwalk and not surprisingly stopped beside him. "You in town for long?" he asked. They neither looked at each other but watched the passengers being met or hurrying off.

Vince took a long draw on the cigarette and let the smoke out. "I take it you read the hotel register."

"I did. By the way, my name is Adams."

"You already know mine."

"I also checked. No warrants out on you."

"Which means I am welcome to stay in town as long as I want," Vince said with a derisive smile.

"Of course. Or until you get in trouble."

"You know about another Taggert being here too." It wasn't a question.

"Yep. The other one is Cole. No warrants on him either."

"That so of my father, Jeremiah, Asa, or Jesse?"

"No reason to look them up. You here for trouble?"

"Why would you ask that?"

"Logical question given your kin. Of course, a man like you doesn't have to look for it. It finds him. I like a nice quiet town. It helps me keep my job."

"I understand."

"If Cord O'Brian hadn't stood up for you last time, I might've took a different view of you sticking around."

"I appreciate that. I am not sure how long I'll be here anyway." He never stayed too long anywhere or hadn't until he'd taken the deputy's job in Sheridan. That had been the limit at two and a half years.

"You here on a job?"

For the first time Vince turned to look into the sheriff's eyes. He looked to be close to his own age. The years hadn't been any kinder to him than Vince's own forty-one had been to him. "I'm not a bounty hunter if that's your question," he said. "As for my brother, I don't know."

"There are reasons some kinds show up here, those who aren't cowboys or don't work as a clerk or driving a rig."

"Robbing a bank?"

"That's always possible but men robbing a bank don't go drinking and talking."

"If you were hoping for answers from me, I haven't seen my brother in five years."

"He's got a hard edge to him, though he ain't caused no trouble. Still, him showing up here and hanging around with gunnies." He chuckled. "Both called Smith. It didn't look good."

"Ah ha. I understand. You already know why he's here, don't you?"

"I asked a few questions. They came down from Utah. Why do men like that travel and then hang around, I asked myself. Turns out that one of the Smiths talks too much when he's in his cups. They're here for a job all right—to kill Ryker."

"Sam Ryker?"

"Yep."

Vince felt a cold chill. "Sam's ranch is at least half a day's hard ride from here."

"When they asked around, they got lucky. Ryker is due in with a herd. He's bringing it up end of the week. You being a friend of his and his brother, Cord's, I figured you might be interested."

Vince drew heavily on the cigarette before tossing it to the dirt and grinding it out with his boot. "Drunks often talk. Doesn't have to mean anything," he said when he could steady his voice. A hit on Sam would be as if a hit at Vince himself.

"Not always. Sometimes, it's the only warning I get." Vince

ground his teeth as he considered the implications. "You know, although men like Ryker always have enemies, he's not likely to be expecting trouble after a drive. He'd be vulnerable, maybe not as fast as usual. Good time for pushing him to a fight where he will lose. One more thing—word is that he's bringing his son with him."

"He's old enough, I guess."

"Sixteen."

At sixteen, Vince had been on his own for two years. David was old enough, and the risks grew if this was why Cole and his friends were in town. Damn.

"You may be able to find out if that is why he's here... before Ryker is," Adams suggested.

"Oh, you can count on that."

CHAPTER 3

With Clint Madison dawdling in her parlor and wanting her to tell him more about her ride on Princess, Holly was more displeased when Gabe showed up for their scheduled appointment. Her plans for being effective were being effectively blown apart. She cursed her lack of firmness in making Clint leave.

The lawyer had not taken her hints that she was busy and then had suggested her dinner smelled delicious. How could she send him away without feeding him? Graciousness demanded feeding even unexpected visitors. She found herself more and more annoyed at trying to be proper, gracious, or a lady. Maybe she wasn't cut out to be one.

"Am I late?" Gabe asked as he entered the parlor, and then looked from her to Clint who had arisen.

"I am sorry. I evidently am interrupting something." Clint's smile showed no concern that he had.

"Actually, you are. A business meeting," Holly retorted feeling increasing irritation.

"I could leave." He didn't head for the door, and the smile didn't go away.

"It relates to my trip," she said when she saw he would wait until she said what she had no doubt he had guessed.

"To the Cibecue," Clint said and smiled at Gabe.

"As you know."

"I also know Mr. Oliver suggested it's a poor idea. Why can't you do your archaeological excavating around here?" The way he said it showed he clearly meant playing with dirt. She had had all she was willing to take before she began using a few words ladies never used. She had been to college. She certainly did know them.

She walked to the door and opened it. "Good night, Clint."

His smile did not disappear, but he did walk through the doorway, standing where she could not close it. "I was on my way out anyway. I needed to talk to Mr. Oliver about a matter."

"I will be the one to tell him my business-- when I have the details finalized," she said working to find a well-mannered smile.

"Of course. I meant another matter." He looked then at Gabe. "Goodnight and good luck."

When the door had closed, Gabe's expression was perplexed. "What was that supposed to mean?"

"I suppose that you will convince me to play in the dirt outside of Tucson, perhaps at the Romero Ruins."

"That won't do for you though, will it?" Gabe said with a smile. He was taller than she but not as tall as his brother Rafe. His dark complexion and high cheekbones would have revealed his Yaqui heritage if she hadn't already known.

"It will not do for me," she agreed. "Would you like a glass of wine?"

He shook his head. "I have a ritual tomorrow. Another time." Knowing he was an elder and did the Deer Dance,

Holly respected his dedication. His sister-in-law, Grace, had told her that he was thought to have seatakaa energy, which meant spiritual powers, although she had never quite understood what all that involved.

"Have you had any luck in finding workers for the summer?"

"It's proving to not be easy," he said moving with her to sit on the sofa. "Some consider that land to be cursed. Others fear the Apache, despite their leaders agreeing, will cause trouble. I will keep looking. You need five besides me, is that correct?"

She nodded, pressing her lips more tightly together as she tried to think what she could do to make this happen. She had already offered more money than most would for what would be three or four months work. She wanted trustworthy workers—most especially not those who would take a job but disappear before the work was finished. She was not naive and understood some might prove dangerous to a woman once away from the security of town.

"Don't worry," he said, flashing a confident smile. "I will keep trying to find the right ones. I won't let you down."

"For yourself, you are not worried about the things they are?"

His smile changed into something that went beyond humor to confidence and inner wisdom. "I have things I must learn also—just as you do. This is important for my growth."

She had one last concern for him. She did not want it to hurt his life. "Can you be gone for so long? I know you have tribal responsibilities."

"My uncle has always been there when I am not. Yes, I can do it. As I said, don't worry. You look tired, chiquita. I should take my leave now." He rose as she nodded her agreement. "Did you get the map for me?" he asked as he walked to the door.

"Oh, yes. I meant to give that to you." She hurried into the dining room where she had piled supplies, dug through some papers and handed him one of the maps.

"Good. I am not familiar with that region, but my father is. I will talk to him tomorrow regarding what to expect. He may even have some possible workers for us."

"Would you like to stay for dinner?"

"Some other time."

"Thank you again." She was relieved when she closed the door and finally she was alone. For the first time that day, she felt relief wash over her. Although she did well with people, she needed times of solitude. Lately, with gathering supplies and trying to put together this venture, she had had few such opportunities to stop and reflect.

She ate, read a few of her manuals, then locked the doors and turned off the lights before going up to her bedroom. Although Rose, its previous owner, had slept on the main floor, Holly much preferred the second. She liked how the breezes could blow through opposite windows, bringing the scents of the desert to her nights.

Undressing in the dark, she put on a light nightgown before pulling back the covers to lie on her bed. She stilled her breathing and looked up at the sky through the open window. April, for a desert, could be surprisingly cold at night, but this year she had already been able to sleep with the windows open.

Although they were not yet installed, she had ordered screening, which would keep out the bats that had occasionally flitted inside after insects. She didn't mind bats—at least not the ones that didn't swoop low over her head. Still, she'd be happy when the screens were in place.

The stars were particularly vibrant with a new moon. Various patterns came into view, most vivid was Orion and his sword—a warrior in the sky. Soon she would be seeing them from the Cibecue.

She thought back over her day and the negative experience with Princess. She supposed the stranger had been right—even if curtly said. She had been foolish to ride her for the first time with the sidesaddle when she was not that comfortable riding even astride. She had believed it would work out, as she equally believed going to the Cibecue would.

She tended to jump into things, often without thinking enough as to the consequences. She had been assured by others that it was a character flaw. Perhaps, but it also gotten her to where she was—a woman willing to step out on her own, hire a crew, and investigate the unknown—even more when it was the unknown within her own soul and a journey that, in many ways, would be a solitary one.

In her dreams, she had seen the dwellings she sought. Although the name of the place had never been in her dreams, she had found it through reading the works of Adolph Bandelier. An ethnographer, he had explored the region and written detailed descriptions of the various prehistoric dwellings found there. From his words, she had believed the Cibecue would be where the homes would be waiting.

Or they would not. That was the issue for her. In some ways, she as much hoped the dreams had been silly and not some true view into the past. They had things to them that very much made her not want to find they had been of real events. When she finally reached the room, when the pot was not in the corner, when the grave didn't exist, maybe then she could put away the dreams as childish and not of meaning. The man, with the dark intense eyes, he wouldn't have ever been real.

Vince entered the Pedrales, scanning the room to see if his brother was already there. He recognized no one except the bartender. Ridge grinned at him. "Damian, glad to see ya again. Been awhile." He poured him a shot glass of the whiskey that Ridge remembered he had liked.

"I have a confession to make," he said after he slugged the whiskey and put the glass in place for another pour.

"Hope it ain't nothin' illegal," Ridge said with a grin as he poured himself a whiskey at the same time.

"No, but might be something you won't like hearing."

"I hear a lot of that. Shoot."

Vince considered a moment but there was no point in beating around the bush. "I made up the name John Damian. Seemed a good name for a pastor. Better than mine... Vince Taggert."

"Whoa." Ridge gave him a second look and then shook his head with a grin. "Kind of odd you wearing the collar considering from where you come." He stopped and grinned. "I heard about your family for years. Famous as the Dalton and Youngers, least if you lived in Kansas before and after the war."

Vince sipped the whiskey. "Infamous is a better word."

"Ruthless is what I heard especially the old man. Josiah, wasn't it?"

"My grandfather."

"He was a jayhawker, wasn't he?"

He nodded. "Among other things when he could make money from them."

"Ain't heard much about him for years, but he did cut a wide swathe at one time."

"His brother, Jericho killed him in '62."

"God, a brother. Can't trust nobody can ya. Speaking of that, there's another Taggert in town too. Coincidental, ain't it?"

"I heard."

"Now that I think on it, he looks some like you."

"We got a mark on us all right."

"I didn't mean it bad or nothing."

"Well, it has been bad."

"Your pa still alive? Jeremiah, right? He had some gun fights that ended up with most dead except him. He killed by a brother too?"

"Likely would have, except he didn't have any."

"Hell of a life, ain't it?" Ridge poured him another shot. "Looks like you could use it."

Vince pulled a cigarette from his pocket and lit it, drawing in the smoke for the likely only peace that he'd find that night.

"The other Taggert been in tonight?"

"Nah, but he come in late last night; so might be he'll yet be. How do ya figure you never ended up like the rest of your tribe?"

"I did have a mother." He smiled at Ridge through the smoke.

"Well, I'll be damned. Likely would, o' course, but jest never figured that."

"That I had a mother?"

Ridge chuckled. "I can see why you wanted to change the name, assumin' you didn't want constant fights."

"It seemed smart—at the time."

"And now it don't?"

"It was catching up with me anyway."

"That fella, he one of the mean Taggerts? I heard about them."

"I've been wondering that myself. I left home pretty young. To be honest, don't know a hell of a lot about him. He evidently is my brother, Cole."

Ridge snorted. "Guess you're figurin' to find out."

Vince nodded.

"Wal, he's quiet, but he's traveling with real hard cases." He moved to the other end of the bar to pour drinks for two new arrivals.

When he returned, Vince picked up the bottle. "If he comes in, tell him where I am." He motioned with his thumb to the one where his back could be against the wall. He put a five on the bar.

Ridge counted out the change for him. "I don't want no trouble in here."

"Me either." Vince smiled with the first real humor he'd felt all night. He didn't usually want trouble, but the sheriff had been right. It had a way of finding him. He needed to know why Cole was in Tucson. If he didn't show up at the Pedrales, he'd go looking.

At the table, he poured himself another whiskey, which he intended to nurse. He would need a clear head. He watched as men came and went. Some gathered at a poker table. Ridge had a new Faro dealer. Vince considered that a fool's game unless the player was the house. As the night went on, the laughter and talking grew louder. Smoke clouded the air, including from Vince's cigarettes.

The doves wandered down and back up with customers. One, a little younger than the rest, came to Vince's table. "You want some company?" she asked with a smile that he supposed she judged to be seductive.

He shook his head. "Not tonight." She smiled again and left. He wondered how a girl like her had ended up in her business, but then remembered his own life and took another sip of the whiskey.

Two hours later, he was about to move to another bar when he saw a tall dark-haired man enter. He'd toughened some since the last time he'd seen him but no mistaking the

Taggert brand. Ridge had been right about the two walking beside him. Vince watched as Ridge told Cole where he was. Cole turned then and looked at him a long moment before picking up his beer and crossing the room.

"Didn't expect to see you here," Cole said as he sat down.

"Who are your friends?" Vince asked looking from one tough to the other. They looked like the kind who got hired for the dirty work nobody else wanted to do—the ones good people didn't like being around. He understood that. Good folks didn't much like to be around him either once they knew what he could do with a gun.

"This is Brody." He gestured, "and he's Jackson."

"Pa's crew?"

"He doesn't have a crew these days."

"Can you and I talk alone, or are they here to keep an eye on you?" he asked with a hard cut to his voice, lighting another cigarette.

"You're as feisty as ever," Cole said but smiled and told the two to give them room. Their frowns said they didn't like it, but they left.

"So you didn't know I'd be here," Vince said.

"Nope."

"But you are here for a reason."

"Could be."

"Like a job?"

"Define job."

"You know what I mean."

Cole smiled crookedly but said nothing. Vince waited. He also kept his eyes on the toughs, who had moved to a table across the room but were watching them.

"A month ago," Cole said finally, "this fellow came out to the ranch. He said he'd been told Pa was a man who could remove a man who needed removing. His boss had been

35

trying to get a ranch. South of Tucson. The owner wouldn't sell. And..."

"Ryker." It wasn't a question.

"So you already know."

"Part of it. I want the rest."

"Pa went on about how Ryker was a no account. Pa had his own grudge as he'd done him wrong once—or so he said."

"And you got the job."

"I was along to be sure it got done. Brody is the one with the gun and the job. He's fast—real fast."

Vince worked to control his anger. "You won't be killing Ryker."

"Like I said, I won't. Brody will."

"He won't either. Sam Ryker is my friend. The best friend I have ever had or will have."

Cole looked honestly surprised. If the word honest fit him. By this time, Vince wasn't sure. "Well, that does complicate it. Pa didn't know, did he?"

Vince drew on his cigarette. "Maybe. Maybe not, but you know now."

"You'll side him then."

Vince nodded. "In a manner of speaking."

"You'd be smart to not get mixed in this. Pa is already mad at you."

"I am aware. You know what kind of man he is."

"Do you know? You left home pretty early."

"He has a reputation."

"Those things aren't always earned."

"From all I know. His was. Now I am wondering who you are."

Cole's smile was cynical. "A little late to wonder about that, isn't it?"

"If money is keeping you doing his crooked deals, I can

give you enough for a new start. You follow his orders, and I'll be paying for your burial." He didn't want to kill Cole. He didn't want to risk being killed himself, but nobody was going to take out Sam Ryker.

Cole considered that with a small smile, but he didn't answer the question. "He's followed you all your life. Did you know that? He knew when you tried to be a pastor."

"No. I suppose he thought that was funny."

"Not so much. Ma was proud."

"She hear it didn't stick?"

"Pa always knew."

"Get away from him."

"You suddenly care what I do?" Cole's smile was tight.

"You are my brother."

"Half, and it seems you forgot that for a lot of years."

Vince gave him that. "Regardless of that or the past. I don't want to kill you now, but Brody and Jackson are not taking out Ryker. I'll make sure of that tonight."

"You'd kill your flesh and blood to save a friend?"

"Blood doesn't always mean much. Sam is closer to me than anybody in this world."

"I admired you once, Vince. You left without a word. Not hard to see you don't value blood kin." Cole's jaw clenched.

"You were a child. I was in no position to take you even if you'd wanted to go. You could have left yourself later."

"Could I? And leave her?"

"What about after she died?"

Cole shrugged. "There were reasons."

"What?"

"Pa needed me."

"Did he?"

"I thought so."

"To be a robber and thief?"

"You make a lot of assumptions, don't you?"

"Sometimes." Vince smiled.

"I didn't join the family business. We had the ranch too. A few cattle on hardscrabble land. It kept us fed—not always that easy."

Vince hadn't thought about that. All he'd known is he had to escape. He should have thought more about his family, his three younger brothers. When he had left, he'd shut that part of his life behind. He'd gotten good at shutting away what he couldn't have or shouldn't want.

"That last day when I left, Ma came out of the house," Vince said still remembering how she had looked. She had always been pretty, even aging as she was beginning to do. "She handed me an envelope and said open it when I was a long, long way off. She turned then and ran back in.

"A good-bye letter?" Cole asked with cynicism. "You know, Pa raged around the house. He tried to find you but lost your trail then. Of course, he picked it up later, time after time, like the wolf he is."

"When I left, I used the streams, the tricks I'd been taught by the best—him. I wrapped my horse's hooves to keep from leaving tracks across the places I knew they would show up."

"It worked. Ma never said anything about talking to you that day. Not a word."

"He'd have beaten her if he had known what she did."

"I saw her slap him more than once. Never him her," Cole said with another of those sardonic smiles.

Vince remembered that too. She did have a fiery temper for such a sweet face. "After I'd gotten far enough to feel safe, I opened the envelope. No words, but she had shoved bills in it-- $104." Vince felt a surge of emotion as he remembered. He knew what putting together that kind of money had cost her.

"It seems she wanted to help you." Cole's expression darkened.

"She did. It was enough to get a start. I worked a couple of cattle drives for more money, traded my horse in for a stronger one. Then I got the idea of being a minister, as a way to pay back to Ma for being how she had been to a motherless boy."

"She was a good woman."

"She taught me right even if it didn't take."

"Looks like being a minister didn't take either. You look more like a slick gambler today."

Vince had to smile. Not too far off. "No, it didn't take. I used a gun to solve a problem. It was then I knew I wasn't cut out for it. I'd always use the gun." He looked then at his younger brother. "How many men have you killed, Cole?"

"Why?"

"How many?"

"None that I know of anyway."

"In robberies?"

"I told you. I don't do those. It takes a gun."

"You're wearing one now."

"Not planning on using it though."

Vince thought about the brothers. "And Jesse?"

"No robberies. He's slow or did you remember that either?" His tone was harsh.

"Slow with a gun?"

Cole smiled at that. "No, fast with a gun but slow to think or talk. Something not right there, or so Mama always said when she told me to be nice to him."

"I remember he rode horses early."

"He can train any horse, wild as the wind or broken by some rotten human, and have it eating out of his hand. His problem is words. He doesn't use them if he doesn't have to. That day you came to see Ma's grave, he was working for Barkers. I reckon he does anything to stay away from us and be with animals."

"So he's got no record?"

"You are mixing us up with Pa or his uncles. Asa too. Too bad you never knew your brothers. You might've found some could be friends too."

Vince ignored the sarcasm. "You came here on a job requiring a gun."

"I told you I was only to see it got done. And it was to be a fair fight. Pa said Ryker would be easy to push into one. This wasn't to be a shot in the dark. No murder."

"Other than someone so fast he knew he couldn't be beat."

"Other than that."

Vince smiled the cold one. He knew what he was going to do. He stubbed out his cigarette. "Well, Cole, you can side Brody and Jackson. If you do, you'll be facing me, and you better be ready to use your gun because I will be."

"I'm your brother." Again, it sounded more a question than the statement it was.

"They're not killing Ryker. And I am not waiting for him to come to town to stop them."

"Then you might be the one dead. Brody is the fastest man with a gun I know."

Vince felt at peace with his decision-- as he always had when he knew what he was going to do and there was no going back. "Sam is coming to town with his son. It won't only be him killed if there is shooting. This is going down tonight, and it's up to you with who you side." Vince rose pushing back his chair and loosening his revolver. He already knew it was ready to fire. "You have a choice, Cole. If you're not with me, then you better step out of the way."

"You going to kill him in cold blood? You'd be arrested."

"I won't have to. Look at Brody's face. He's salivating."

He walked across the room unsure where his brother would stand in what was to come. He stopped in front of the two men's table. "I need to talk to you-- outside," he said gesturing to the door.

Brody smiled. "Just talk?" He had the snake eyes that Vince had seen in other killers. Jackson was of a different stripe. Eager to do wrong but not so eager to stand up to someone else's bullets.

"I ain't got no quarrel with you," Jackson said.

"I know who ya are," Brody said with a satisfied smirk. "No mistaking who you are. Maybe I can make some more money on the deal by taking you out."

"Maybe." Vince smiled coldly. "Outside."

In a few moments, they were on the street, and others had moved away. Jackson was beside Brody, but it was clear that he wanted no part of this. Vince glanced at him but kept his eye on Brody. "Either of you can ride north tonight." He flipped his coat behind his Colt.

Jackson looked beyond Vince to Cole who had stayed on the boardwalk. He nodded and then stepped away from Brody. "I am out of this. I'll be heading north."

"I ain't goin' nowhere, you bastard," Brody said.

Vince did not like his uncertainty as to where Cole would stand in the fight. His brother hadn't committed to anything. He had to forget about that now and deal with Brody, who was eager to shoot. If Jackson didn't draw his gun, he'd let him go.

He saw the moment Brody decided to draw and had his own gun out at the same time. As he fired, he heard a shot whiz past his shoulder. Brody staggered but didn't fall. Vince shot again.

CHAPTER 4

Holly woke with a scream. She quickly stifled it with her fist. The dream. She cursed the dream as she sat up. It was as though something violent and frightening had entered her room and taken hold of her. She turned on the light. It was midnight. The bewitching hour.

After the kind of fear that had her heart racing, sleep wouldn't be easy to find. She pulled on a robe and headed for the kitchen where she heated milk. The only time she liked milk was warmed and in the middle of the night.

As with the other times, he had been in the dream. Taller than her people, he had come as a trader. Where her family had round, smooth faces, his was craggy and dark, a hawk-like nose. From the first moment, he had seen her, his eyes spoke to her. In the beginning, he could not communicate with language, at least not a language made up of words.

She didn't want to think about the dreams, but it was midnight and there was nothing to prevent them from filling her imagination. Some were violent. They weren't all. Sometimes the events were peaceful as he began to learn her tongue. He was a trader and indicated he had come from far to the north with intricately carved bones and baskets tighter than their own. He had feathers such as she'd never seen. Initially, her father had liked him and encouraged him to stay. What the trader wanted was turquoise, which her people mined for ornaments.

Then what he had wanted was her. In each dream, at least at first, her family had been friendly and welcoming to the trader. He had a facility with weapons that they needed. He had used a spear with deadly precision but even more valuable was his skill with bow and arrow. Her people had seen the advantage of a man who could stand against their enemies, those who killed for only amusement.

As she sipped her milk, she tried to reason through from where the dreams had come. For twelve years, she'd had them coming to her with no warning of which night. No dream ever had all the pieces of the story, but slowly she had put them together. Always they were near or in a set of buildings under the protection of a cliff.

Within those buildings had been one room that had been her family home. Her people lived a simple life. She had ground pine nuts for food, scraped hides, dug roots, and sometimes watched her mother create drawings on the cliff walls. Her mother was a wise woman.

As Holly had later gained an education, she had come to believe the mother in the dreams had been a shaman of some sort. It seemed to be unusual but accepted.

The nightmare did not come with each dream. It had this night, and she still felt shaky from remembering it. It repeated something she had seen before. In front of her eyes, she saw the man she loved struck by a spear. She saw the pain in his eyes, heard his cry and then saw him fall before the light went out of his eyes. Although she had wakened this night with a scream at his death, in some of the dreams, she had seen herself burying him. Always she had wakened filled with the horror that the one she loved was dead, and she was alone.

The same man had come in other dreams, in other places, not only in cliff dwellings. Sometimes they lived in towns or even once by a sea. One way or the other, they always ended the same. Whatever culture they were living in, whoever the hidden enemies had been, always it was the same. He died before her eyes.

Walking back upstairs, still not sleepy, she tried to bring other thoughts to her memories. She was horrified to realize the first image was that of the man who had saved her life, those intense eyes. She forced the image away. Not him. Please, not him.

"I was hoping you'd not cause me grief," Sheriff Adams said to Vince even as he looked down at the body of the man who had been called Brody.

"He went for his hogleg first," Ridge said. "I saw it. He was looking for trouble, and he found it."

"Where's the other one?" Adams asked now looking at Vince.

"He rode out," Vince said.

Adams looked beyond him to his brother. "And you didn't go with him?"

"No," Cole said.

"You going to cause trouble?"

Cole shook his head.

His brother had stayed out of it. Afterward, he had said nothing but seemed pale, maybe shaken by the sudden delivery of death. In some ways, Vince envied him an emotional reaction to violence. For him, when it came, it was always the same. He was cold as ice and felt nothing afterward. A human should feel something when they took a life, but he'd trained himself not to feel. It came in handy and yet...

Adams sighed. "Looks like we'll have one less useless human being. Self-defense, and don't need no judge."

The four men walked back into the Pedrales where Ridge poured them each a shot. Vince was tired enough that he didn't want the whiskey, but he took it anyway.

Cole slugged the whiskey before he let out a breath and said, "I'm going to bed. Been a long day." He had said nothing about the shooting beyond his answers to Adams.

"You heading north in the morning?" the sheriff asked.

Cole shook his head. "No. If anyone wants me, I have a room at the Continental." With that, he was gone.

"You look spent yourself," Ridge said. "There's nothing more to do here."

"You saved me trouble as I see it," Adams said. "You might've bought more yourself though. Jackson is likely heading straight back to your pa. You know that."

Vince smiled. "You are pretty sharp for a sheriff."

"I work at it. Helps to stay alive."

"It was a combination of reasons that brought those three to town."

"Ryker is still at risk."

"Most likely. I am trying to figure out who would pay for a killing to get the Circle R."

"That's what it was about?"

"It doesn't make sense, but it's what Cole was told."

"When Jackson tells him what you did to Brody, your name could go to the top of that list."

Vince smiled coldly. "It likely never was too far down."

"It might be smart if you move on."

"I don't disagree, but I'll talk to Sam first. You said he's due Friday or thereabouts."

"Yep." Adams nodded. "Seems reasonable. I'll take care of this."

Back in his hotel room, Vince stripped and laid on the bed, as he ran back over this night. Who was out to get Sam's ranch? Was it that simple? It was illegal to pay for a murder but paying someone to start a fight, would that also be considered a crime? More importantly, would killing Brody stop whoever was behind it? It seemed unlikely. That kind of money didn't usually stop until it got what it wanted.

He thought then about the shooting. He reached for his cigarettes and lit one, watching the smoke curl toward the ceiling. He supposed that he should have felt remorse. He didn't. Most likely, his soul was already dead, only waiting for his body to join it. He had never killed except in self-defense. Tonight though, he had made a choice to take Brody out. It was as close to murder as he ever wanted to get. He smiled into the darkness. Connie wanted an angel. Well, he was an angel all right, an angel of death. With no regrets, he knew he would do it again, until he was killed himself—the inevitable end to a life like his.

He had little to show for his forty-one years—just an ability with a gun. Seven, now eight men, would still be walking around but for him. He could see their faces as he stared at the ceiling with the lights reflected from outside and mingling with the smoke. Ghosts of the dead didn't trouble him. They couldn't hurt him, but they were there, waiting for their revenge. It would come. Until then, he wouldn't think about it. He had one goal in mind—make sure Sam Ryker stayed alive and that meant-- find out who wanted it otherwise.

First thing in the morning, right after breakfast, he'd go to the Sicillas and talk to Connie about the reason for her letter, but he didn't see her having any need for him that was going to take priority over Sam. He stubbed out the cigarette and was almost instantly asleep.

As Holly drank coffee and nibbled on toast, she considered her plans for the day. After sleeping restlessly, she was eager to get the rest of her supplies and leave Tucson for the north. Problems remained. She needed more men. Would Song want to come?

She had ordered clothing from one of Siclla's catalogs. No lightweight cotton would hold up to the demands of excavations. Besides boy's pants, she had ordered a heavy cotton, divided skirt. It would look proper and yet enable her to move freely. She had also sent for laced leather boots, which went almost to her knee. That offered protection, she hoped, from the rattlesnakes she was likely to encounter.

With a bit of luck, her order would be there along with the medicinals she planned to bring. She had accumulated the needed trowels, shovels, tarps, small and large picks. Excavating a site required extensive note taking, and she had a stack of blank notebooks waiting for drawings and details. More than half of what she needed was piled on and around her dining room table.

Putting on the hated corset, as well as several petticoats, before she dropped the plain gray dress over her shoulders and buttoned herself into it, she thought about how odd Connie had been each time she had talked about the trip. Had she gotten some sort of premonition or was it because Ollie was so against her going? From the time she had first mentioned the Cibecue, Rose's husband had tried to talk her out of it.

47

There was no talking her out of it. Her answers were there. Nowhere else would do. The descriptions she had read of the land fit what she had seen in her dreams. It would lie in a valley where cliffs rose up on each side. Below the valley was a river or maybe creek. There were rolling hills, but some plateaus, which had allowed them to raise corn and squash.

She had only to close her eyes to see the trees along the rock lined stream-- cottonwoods, willows, scrub oak, but above had been manzanita, juniper, and pines. It was a pretty land if one liked wilderness of the high desert sort. In dreams, she had seen it repeatedly. Soon it would be reality.

Walking to Sicilla's store, she enjoyed the fresh morning air. The scents of breakfasts being cooking mingled with the dusty smells of the desert. She had traveled quite a lot, but until Tucson, no place had seemed home-- not Chicago, not where she had attended schools. She had only found home when she got off the train to visit Grace. At first, she expected the feeling would not last. It had.

The Sicillas' doors were already open. Holly walked in with a smile, which was instantly lost when she saw the tall man talking to Connie. The two turned to look when she had stopped through the doorway. Connie smiled broadly. His face was dour. She couldn't imagine him smiling-- other than maybe as he squashed a spider.

"Holly," Connie said as she pulled her into a hug to draw her forward.

"Is my order ready?" she asked, avoiding looking at him. He hadn't moved from where he was standing, arms crossed over his chest. Even though clean shaven and now wearing a suit and white shirt, he looked as disreputable as when he had pulled her from her runaway horse. He was wearing a gun only partly hidden by a broadcloth jacket.

"Some came in. I want you to meet someone." She pulled

Holly to the last place she wanted to be. "Holly, this is Vince Taggert. Vince, Holly Jacobs is who I was telling you about."

The smile on his face looked as unreal as she was sure hers did. "Glad to meet you," he said with apparently no sincerity. He didn't put out his hand, and she was glad. She'd not willingly touch him again, not even to be polite.

"How about you both come into the kitchen. I had something I wanted to explain to Vince, and now that you're here, you can hear it also."

Reluctantly, Holly followed Connie, all too aware of the tall man right behind her. Something about the sound of his boots on the wooden floor annoyed her, but then almost everything about him irritated her. She wondered if he would tell Connie how he saved her. She wished she had waited until later to come to the store. Then he'd have been gone, and she'd have been spared the awkwardness.

In the kitchen, Connie motioned for them to sit as she poured hot water into a tea pot. "I think you will like this one," she said as she brought the pot and three cups back to the table for the tea to steep.

"Where's Del?" he asked as he turned a chair and straddled it, leaning his elbows on its back.

"He was going to the river to bring back fresh greens. He gets restless and a ride in the morning helps."

"If my supplies aren't ready, I can come back," Holly said wanting anything more than to be across the table from that man.

"First drink some tea, while I explain why I asked Vince to come to Tucson," Connie said with another of those smiles that always made Holly wonder what she saw that she did not.

"You asked *him* to come?" she asked without modulating her tone. She knew the *him* had come out with unmasked annoyance. She glanced over to see him watching her with a faint smile.

"I wrote him." Connie turned to Vince. "Holly is why I wrote you."

Vince's smile of amusement broadened. Holly's annoyance grew. "I am having a hard time understanding why," he said.

"Holly is an anthropologist, an archaeologist. She is about to go on an excavation into the Cibecue area."

"Cibecue huh." He turned that cold stare onto Holly then. "You know much about that country?"

"Enough," she said tilting her chin up with an expression that she hoped would stop his smile. It did not.

"Nobody with a brain would think that's a smart place to go pot hunting."

If she had been annoyed before, she was close to infuriated now. "Archaeology is not about pot hunting, Mr. Taggert."

"Tell that to the Wetherhills." He snickered.

"So you are not totally ignorant about the science," she snapped.

"Not where it comes to making money."

"Archaeology is about discovery. It is not about making money."

"Ah and who pays for the digs?"

"Well, benefactors or universities."

His smile broadened. "Money."

"In some cases. I am, however, funding my own."

This time he laughed. It sounded genuinely amused. It made her more annoyed and convinced she never wanted to see him again. "You are funding it because those with more sense wouldn't."

She felt as though the top of her head was going to explode. "I did not ask anyone else."

50

"Children," Connie said as she poured the tea. "Drink some tea and calm down a bit."

"I don't see why you'd ask him to come for me," she said turning to Connie. She wasn't annoyed with her, but she was genuinely mystified.

"Because the voices told me he was needed by you."

Holly knew Connie believed that she communicated with the other side. She was unwilling to insult such a nice person, even in this situation where those possible voices were interfering with her business—when she had not requested such help.

"Even if I needed help," she said, when she saw no one else was going to speak. "Why would it be him?" If she had been less polite, she'd have pointed at him as she said it.

"He's the man in black. He is the one who can help you find what you want and bring you safely back from where you are going."

"I hardly think so."

She looked over and saw he was staring at the teapot and not looking at either of them. "Even if that was so," he said finally, "another problem arose last night which means I couldn't do it—even if Miss Jacobs was of a mind that I was needed."

"Which she is not," Holly retorted. She didn't want to look at him but something drew her. The handsome face had not been her imagination. He had one of those faces that suggested strength and structure. She was unsure why she felt so annoyed by that—except he had seen her at her worst. She was being unfair to use that as a way to find fault with him. For heaven's sake, he might have saved her life or at least from serious injury. She sucked in a reluctant breath of acknowledgement that she was being unfair. "I am sure though," she said, "if I needed such a man, he would be fine."

She had thought she said it graciously, but his chuckle said he had seen right through her.

"Here's the thing," he said looking at Connie now. "Someone hired men to kill Sam Ryker. I learned about it last night from my brother, who had been one of those men."

"My God," Connie said with shock in her voice that went beyond the words. "Last night. The shooting?"

He nodded.

"At midnight?" Holly asked before she could hold back the words.

"Gossip spreads fast," he said but offered no information as to when. He didn't need to. "The sheriff suggested I leave town, but I am waiting until Sam arrives on Friday. After that, I need to be sure he's safe."

Connie nodded. "I understand that, but..." She hesitated. "I know you don't believe in my gifts but would either of you mind if, while we are together, I consulted those on the other side regarding this issue."

"It won't change anything," Holly said at the same time Vince said it.

Connie smiled. "But you don't either one mind?"

"You can do it, but..." Holly stopped.

"I know, you won't believe what I hear. I understand, but I would like you to let me do it."

"Fine," Vince said and Holly nodded.

"Please, all I ask from you both is that you let me hold your hands as I try to contact the other side."

Holly looked over at Vince and saw his clear reluctance but like she, he put out his hand for Connie lightly to grasp. Holly felt grateful the older woman didn't request she take Vince's hand. Even if she felt she'd been unfair, she didn't want to touch him. She was unsure why she was so repelled at the thought, but she remembered too forcefully how it had felt the few moments he had held her in his arms before he had lowered her to the ground and ridden off to get her horse. Whatever that had been, she didn't want to experience its powerful energy again.

"All right," Connie said, bowing her head. "Just close your eyes. I don't ask you to try and hear anything but let me see what I can get."

The minutes, where Connie was trying to reach whatever it was she thought spoke to her, seemed to go on forever. The room was silent except for the sound of their breathing. With her eyes closed, Holly saw again the man in the ruins. Was he trying to come to her in some kind of séance? She didn't want that. She wanted him to be a figment of her imagination. She squeezed her eyes more tightly closed and thought of other things, of tea, of roses, of her home, anything but those eyes looking at her and then the moment they went dead.

She felt relieved when Connie sighed and released her hand, apparently Vince's at the same time. She doubted Connie had received any sort of messages. She wasn't about to tell her what she had seen. It had no meaning.

CHAPTER 5

C onnie's face was somber as she looked from one to the other. "I requested information on Sam as well as Holly since they are both problems for you, Vince."

His smile was crooked. "Only one of which is my business."

"All right... for now." Connie looked at Holly also. "I won't force either of you to hear what I was told. Do you wish to know?"

"You actually heard something?" Holly asked. When Connie nodded, she said, "Of course, you can tell me." It wouldn't change anything. It was not as though she would believe it had meaning.

"Sure, I am fine with it too," Vince said, his own face showing a similar disbelief.

Connie looked at Vince first. "Sam's enemy is female and not young. Her hate for him showed up as a flame. I think that the ranch is subterfuge, an excuse. This is not about land. She didn't come to me, but someone else did, someone who gave me the images. He came across as masculine, and he wanted

Sam to have the ranch. He is delighted with how he has worked it and made it into a real family home. It has made him happy. He is trying to help Sam and the ones he loves-- from the other side."

"What other side?" Vince asked even though Holly felt from his expression that he only wanted to hear Connie say it.

Connie only smiled at him. "The entity who came to me is a man Sam knew. He is a gentleman, and he only passed recently and yet... He is surprisingly adept at coming through. I would guess he has had many lifetimes—perhaps with Sam. He is the one who made sure Sam could own the ranch. I think the woman had some connection to him, but it was vague what he was trying to tell me. I saw that letter B, which might mean her name. Beside it was a long knife."

"She then is the one who paid to get Sam dead?" Vince asked, his tone one of skepticism.

"Symbols are hard to interpret. I think though the knife meant B was using a deadly tool. When you talk to Sam, perhaps he will know more."

"You understand what Sam means to me, don't you."

"I have seen and understood your love for him. I can't tell you what to do." She looked then at Holly. "You wondered why I would ask this man to come here to help you."

"I did and do."

"First let me tell you what I saw when I turned my questions to you. What you are looking for is buried in the corner of a room. The sun never strikes the corner where it is waiting, has waited many years." She closed her eyes. "It is large but a plain pot, reddish, like sunset colors on the outside and gray inside. It had objects inside, but I didn't see what."

Holly felt a chill pass through her. "A room?" Maybe Connie wasn't saying what she thought.

"The room is made of square stones, reddish also. When you find this pot, you will find some of your answers."

"So it is about pots," Vince said. Holly looked up expecting to see a smirk on his face but that wasn't the expression. It was more one of sympathetic understanding. Why would he understand?

"My interest is discovery," Holly said with the first genuine smile she had ever given him.

"All right," Vince said looking back at Connie. "I already told you I can't do it but why me on this?" Holly wished she could read his expression. It was a mix of contemplative and resigned.

"It is dangerous where she needs to go. Unlike Ollie, I think she does need to go there. But she will need someone who can protect her... maybe even from one of those traveling with her."

"You are trying to scare me," Holly said staring at Connie.

"No, to warn you. You are trying to enter into something that has been closed to you. There was a reason it was closed. Are you sure you are ready?"

Holly knew Connie had not meant the question literally, but she decided it would be how she would take it. It seemed safer. "Well, not yet. I don't have the men I will need. Gabe though is working on that."

"Gabe Cordova?" Vince asked, as he finally reached for his tea.

"Yes, he thinks he can get me dependable men."

"What about Clint Madison?" Connie asked.

"Why would you mention him?"

"He's made no secret of his interest in you."

Holly frowned. "He is not going. He has work here."

"Clint is a handsome man."

"Is that important?"

Connie chuckled. "No, it is not, but doesn't he want to marry you? This by the way is not from the other side, but my own observations the times I have seen him with you."

"Wanting and happening are two different things. I have told you all that I do not want to marry anyone."

"Wise choice," Vince said almost under his breath.

"Meaning I'd be a poor choice as a wife," Holly retorted glaring at him again. Any brief good feelings toward him vanished.

"No, meaning marriage is not good for women." His smile was that crooked one that was almost endearing-- if such a tough looking man could ever look endearing.

"So who besides Gabriel?" Connie asked.

"I asked Song to come along to cook, but she will have to think about it. She seems uneasy about her son right now. It seems Zian now wants to be called Sam."

Connie smiled. "It is the age where young men decide on their identity. He's over twenty isn't he?"

"I think twenty-one."

"Maybe he would like to go."

"I hadn't thought of that, but it might be a bad idea. If he's looking for excitement, a boring dig would be the last place he'd enjoy."

"Boring?" Vince asked.

"Tedious. You don't only dig up artifacts if you want to make discoveries. You note the layers of soil to approximate the time they were placed there based on what else you see. Middens are another place to go slowly, where you find the garbage from that culture, and learn things about what they ate, if they hunted big animals or small, their pottery, even broken weapons. If human remains are there, it tells you more about who these people were. None of that is discovered by pot hunters. They tear apart the ground, do not take notations and destroy the opportunity for a future generation to learn anything."

His smile seemed genuine. "You are passionate about it."

"I am."

Vince turned back to Connie. "What did you see that worried you regarding her going to the Cibecue?"

"You know I saw something?"

"I wouldn't use the word know, but you aren't the type of woman to panic. I remember that about you from California." He smiled. "So what led you to go looking at what the other side thought about this and then to write me?"

From the time Vince had seen the beautiful blonde walk into Sicilla's store, he had known he was in trouble. Mostly, he had avoided women in his life, and that not because he didn't like them but more because he couldn't afford emotional connections to anyone.

After he had pulled her from her run away horse, he'd purposed not to think of her. He'd nearly cursed when he saw her walk through the door in all that lush beauty. He would have made quick excuses to leave. No luck. For the moment, there was no escape. All too soon, he had found himself sitting across from her, watching her expressive face as she listened to Connie

Sam needed his help. He would refuse Connie. That had sounded easy until he thought about that innocent beauty coming across those like his family or the renegades who frequented the shadowy places. If she had seemed a foolish young woman, he might still have found it easy to say no. She clearly was not. She had more intelligence than he'd expected —stubbornness too.

Connie watched him with the thoughtful expression he'd seen so often on her face. Although he had mixed feelings about what she saw, he had to admit that sometimes it did seem to be coming from more than her imagination.

"I wrote my letter to you because I had had a vision," Connie said finally. "The images were vague, but they were violent. You weren't in it, Vince, and yet you were. I saw it in a different time. Death was there. Violence. A reckoning of some sort. Perhaps neither of you believe in reincarnation, but if you did, it might make understanding this easier."

Vince saw shock on Holly's beautiful face. "Can you describe where this happened that you saw?" she asked with a strained sound to her voice.

"It wasn't today. I didn't see it for our time, but what I think I was seeing might have been a pattern frequently happening at that place. Perhaps it is a place that has known tragedy again and again. I saw one of those times." She turned her intense gaze onto Holly. "I still wish, like Ollie, that you wouldn't go. I have come to care for you in the short time we have been acquainted, but at the same time, I understand something has to be resolved for you. It seems it can only happen there, at that place. After that violent vision, the voices came and told me that you needed the man in black." She looked then at Vince. "I knew it was you because of how you saved us that time."

"I didn't save you."

Connie smiled. "I know better. You stepped in, at risk of your own life. Had you not, it could have meant an end to my life and Del's."

Vince heard the step at the door. With his back to it, because of Holly's taking the side he would have preferred, he had straddled the chair, to give him a quicker potential reaction. How he had felt, as he turned, that instant where he didn't know if danger was there, made him aware how he had come to live his life always as predator or prey.

59

"I heard about last night," Del said as he moved to the cupboard and brought out a whiskey bottle. "Want a drink?"

"Too early for me," Vince said.

"Not for me." Del had a sick smile as he poured himself a shot. "There was trouble down at the gardens." He looked then at Connie. "A shooting. Nobody killed in that one, but it riled up the place. Lots of talk, most of which I didn't understand."

"I hope it wasn't Song's son, Zian," Holly said. "She has been concerned for his misdirection."

"No, it was Fong Bai. Some of the white boys came down to have a little fun. Five of them. They used their fists on those they came across. Fong came out with his gun, fired some shots in the air. The boys hit for town and the sheriff. He arrived this morning to arrest Fong."

"For what?"

"Don't ask me. I don't think he'll hold him long. He only wanted to appease those who think there have been too many guns are going off recently." He gave Vince a pointed look.

Vince smiled. "I already told the sheriff, I'd leave after I talk to Sam."

"I would like to hear more about what happened last night," Holly said in a level tone that said she was working to keep it that way. Her gaze was on Vince.

"I killed a man," Vince said.

"My God."

"Not usually." He smiled. He was beginning to find he liked her, which he didn't want to do.

"The sheriff said it was a fair fight," Del offered and refilled his glass before sitting at the table.

When they heard the bell chime of a customer from the store, Connie reluctantly left.

"What happened exactly? I do think I have a right to ask if you were going to be a bodyguard for me."

"I thought you said you didn't want one," Vince said smiling with more reluctance. There was a bigger risk than guns where it came to this woman. He couldn't have her. He wasn't at all sure he wouldn't want her. He didn't like wanting what he couldn't have.

"Well, Connie said I might need one. So tell me."

"My brother told me what two men had planned for Sam Ryker when he arrived in town with a herd on Friday. I could not let that happen. One of the men fancied himself good with a gun. Men like that don't take much encouragement to take on someone like me. We went outside. I gave the second one and my brother a choice—join in or stay out. They stayed out. Brody wanted another notch on his gun. He missed. I didn't."

"Guess he wasn't as fast as he thought," Del said.

"As you well know, it's not so much who's fastest with something like that. It's mostly about firing too fast and missing."

She slumped in her chair. "That's terrible. You might've been killed."

"That's the usual outcome of men shooting at each other—for one at least."

"You seem so calm about it." She looked at him now as though he frightened her. Maybe that was for the best.

"Not my first time at it," he said as coldly as he could. He didn't want to be her bodyguard, didn't want to care what happened to her.

"But never when it wasn't a fair fight," Del said sipping his second drink more slowly. "I asked around about last night and more than a few remembered stories about John Damian being fast with a gun."

"A true character endorsement," Vince said cynically.

"Who is John Damian?" Holly asked now with confusion in those beautiful blue eyes.

"Me. I might as well tell you all of it not that it matters since you don't want me around anyway. I was born into a family crooked as the day is long. My grandfather, his brothers, my father and at least one of my brothers. A lot of this went down in Kansas in the jayhawker days. It let a lot of men profit from robbing trains or banks and even be seen as heroes to the locals. My father took his family to Utah, but he didn't stop being a road agent or hadn't when I left home. Turns out there is no warrant out for him; so guess so far he's avoided being caught at it. I have three brothers I barely know. One though is mean as a snake."

"The other two?"

"Not sure yet. For a lot of years, I took a different name to try and get away from who I was." He knew his smile was mocking. "I realized recently it didn't work. I brought me with me. No use running any more."

"Oh." Her voice had grown small. He imagined she could hardly wait to get away from him. On that note, he rose. "I better go check on the brother who came with the man I killed. I sent him off last night to get over the vapors."

"Vapors?" Holly looked confused again.

"He was not feeling well."

"I want to get this straight," Del said. "Downtown, they said your brother was with the jasper, who tried to kill you and planned to kill Sam."

"He was."

"Can you trust him?"

"I plan to find out."

"Not knowing, you are willing to keep him near?" It was Holly who asked what he knew was the logical question.

He turned to look at her. Again, her beauty nearly took his breath away. He had to work to remember what she had asked. "Yes," he said finally.

She stared at him and then smiled. "Well, I understand that." He wondered for a moment if she was being sarcastic but then saw she was not.

"Good luck with your excavations," he said as he turned to the door.

"Wait." She rose and came to him. "Would you consider coming by my house to talk about it more? Not to be a body-guard, you understand, but to let me know what I might need in one."

Nothing she could have asked would have shocked him more. He looked into those big eyes trying to decide what was behind the request.

She smiled. "You said something that made me believe you have been to the Cibecue country. I have some maps. It might help to hear what you know."

He felt a nearly overwhelming urge to kiss those full lips. He needed to stay a long way away from this woman. To be around her would be stupid. "All right. When would you like?"

Her smile widened. She clearly had no idea what she did to a man with that smile. "Come to dinner tonight. I live in the home that Rose Redman used to have. Are you familiar with its address?"

He nodded.

"Six?"

"All right." He walked out the door feeling more stunned than after he'd faced Brody with the gun. He had the feeling, as he stepped into the sunlight, that she was more dangerous to him.

Holly looked back at Connie who had entered the room but only watched. "What?" She bit her lip. She knew what. Something had changed in how she saw Vince Taggert. There was a pull toward him, which she couldn't explain. Maybe the extreme antipathy she had felt earlier was the same energy while protectively she had resisted it. Whatever it was, it was overwhelming all her other senses.

Del went back to tend the store, but Connie stayed. "He is a powerful man, isn't he?"

"I've never met anyone like him."

"He has come to Tucson a few times. Often on his way through to see Sam Ryker. Every time I have felt the same force field around him. Very powerful aura."

"What is an aura?"

"The energy that surrounds us and sometimes it can be seen in colors."

"You see them?"

"Sometimes."

"And his is..."

Connie smiled. "I'd rather tell you yours."

"All right. What is mine?"

"Red, orange and with some purple to the left edge."

Holly smiled. "Fits holly berries I guess. Does it have a meaning?"

"Passion, strong feelings and someone who will act on those feelings."

"Sometimes," Holly agreed. "I am thinking that Mr. Taggert's power is why you thought he could help me succeed at the ruins." It wasn't a question.

"I listen to the inner voice most especially when I have asked a question. I knew he could use a gun. I also believed he would not use it if he didn't have to. Warriors like that are not common."

"In my world, warriors haven't been, that is for certain," Holly said taking a sip of her now nearly cold tea.

"Would you like a reading from me now?" Connie asked. "You never have wanted that and feel free to say no."

"What kind?" Holly still had little faith in such and yet... Connie had seen some of what she had in her dreams. How had she done that?

"Tarot. I like it best as the cards help to make things clearer. Visions are so filled with imagery that sometimes they are hard to interpret."

"What would be the purpose?"

"Possibly the kind of journey you are going on."

That sounded safe. Moments later, they were sitting back at the kitchen table. Del went out to manage the store, and they were left in the quiet. Holly could still feel the energy that Vince had left behind.

After shuffling and cutting the deck several times, Connie asked, "How many times shall I cut it?"

"Three."

In moments, she had laid out three cards. "Interesting but also reassuring to me," Connie said. She explained the cards. One was a woman on a throne. "She represents that you have within you all you need for your journey." She pointed to another card and it showed two people in a canoe with swords in the bow.

"Another indicator that you are on a journey that requires weapons. What you will find is yet to be known but again I believe that it shows you have the strength do what is required. This last card is another woman on a throne but it represents choice." She shook her head. "I haven't seen this card often in a reading. It suggests that you have been a follower but you are going to break away from this and find your own path." Connie smiled. "It's might be a spiritual path, possibly a hidden secret, but you are going to find your answers and what you do, on the journey, will impact the rest of your life."

"In a good way?" Holly asked still unsure how much she believed in any of this.

"I think it is-- considering what you are attempting. It says that you will succeed. You may not know all that is ahead for you but given the other two cards, you will find your answers."

"And Vince?" She could not believe she had asked that.

"He has never wanted a reading from me. Because of how he saved my life and even more Del's, I believe he is the kind of man to step in and help even those he may not know. A loyal man. But..."

"The but is?"

"He is fatalistic if I can use that word. I think... I cannot do a reading for him but can do one for what you need to know about him. Would you like that?"

"I... I guess I would."

Again, the cards were shuffled and laid out. "Interesting... Well, you know he's a man of power and here it is with the King on a throne with a sword. He can think clearly and rapidly. The next card represents losses. I believe it represents the losses he's experienced. All of his life. But the third card..." She smiled. "It is growth and encouragement. It also involves change. What was-- is not what will be."

"I am confused by that."

"Are you thinking of asking him to go with you to the Cibecue?"

"I don't think so."

"Why not?"

She couldn't explain that. Despite the positive reading, that Connie thought she saw for him, Holly was beginning to sense something else. Maybe the warrior in her dream was... No, that could not be. She wished she had not invited him to dinner.

CHAPTER 6

Heading for Cole's hotel, Vince did not have to go inside to find him. He was sitting in one of the chairs out front. He looked grim as he watched Vince approach. Vince dropped into the chair next to him. Saying nothing, he lit a cigarette.

"Are you mad at me?" Cole asked finally.

"For what?"

"You know for what."

"This isn't about being mad," Vince said as he drew deeply of the smoke before releasing it. "I am trying to figure out who you are." He looked over at his brother trying to read the answer in his face. It wasn't there. Maybe the fact that it was his little brother made it impossible for him to be objective. He found it interesting that Cole wasn't wearing a gun. Most men had one somewhere but dressed as he was, Cole wasn't wearing a hide-out either.

"Let me know when you figure it out." Cole's lips were set.

Vince looked away, trying to find the right words. Out on

the street wagons were passing. Two women crossed the street in a hurry to get to wherever they were bound.

"It's you who has to figure it out, Cole."

"What is it you want to know?"

"The big one is-- are you likely to shoot me in the back?"

"I don't shoot anybody in the back." Cole's voice sounded exasperated.

This was getting him nowhere. Facing his own complex set of problems, Vince had decided what he needed was taking Jupiter out for a ride. He wanted to get away from people and clear his head. He hadn't planned to take anyone along. Impulsively, he changed his mind and asked Cole if he'd like to come. Maybe out there, he'd find the answer to who this brother was.

"Where?"

"Does it matter?"

"No, guess not. All right."

An hour later, Vince had changed out of his suit into the clothing he'd worn riding into Tucson and with Cole was riding past Steam Pump Ranch. Beyond, he turned his horse off the main road onto one that wasn't much more than a trail. On the hills, wildflowers were in full bloom with vibrant colors. The lower elevations showed them fading, a reminder of the heat to come.

"Pretty out here. I like desert," Cole said as they turned their horses into a small canyon guarded by tall saguaros on all sides but with willows in the bottom where the cattle trail kept it open for their horses. Jupiter tried to break into a gallop that Vince pulled back to a trot. This was no place to go for a run. His gelding didn't care much for Cole's horse. The two were jockeying for who was to be in the lead whenever the trail narrowed to where they could not walk side by side.

"Where does this lead?" Cole asked as the rocky walls grew

taller and the canyon more narrow. Vince had forgotten how far it was to the place he remembered.

"Eventually out the other side and drains off the mountain. We won't go that far."

"So, where are we going?"

"Where we can talk. And I'll show you something I thought you might like."

"Nobody lives up this way. Man could be killed here and nobody would find the body," Cole observed and looked over at Vince with raised brows.

Vince smiled but found no humor in what his brother had implied. They had both obviously lived too long with those where that exactly was what they might do. "If you were concerned about that, why didn't you wear your gun?"

Cole's smile was impossible to read. "Wouldn't have done me any good if I had. And if somebody else comes along who's dangerous, you can do the shooting for both of us."

"Yet, you did think I might kill you out here?"

Cole shrugged.

"If I'd wanted to kill you, I'd have pushed you to be with Brody last night. I wouldn't do it out here."

"Maybe. The truth is I don't know you anymore than you know me."

Vince couldn't argue with that. As they rounded a bend in the canyon, he saw what he'd been looking for. He nudged Jupiter to step up some slick rock. On the other side, the canyon walls receded as the canyon broadened. He pointed to the huge boulder and pulled Jupiter to a halt.

"We'll ground rein and let them graze here." There was green grass and even a trickle of water from the last storm. When they dismounted, he noted with approval that Cole also rode with a hackamore. It meant his brother was a good rider who cared about his mount.

"What is this?" Cole asked as they walked closer to the rock where shapes had been carved into its side.

"Petroglyphs. Apparently, there was once one of those stone and clay village nearby. A few ruins are still there. From what I've been told, they are the ones who put these drawings onto cliffs and boulders all around the valley. Some are weathered away or destroyed in flashfloods." The boulder's most impressive image was of a giant owl, stylized but clearly an owl.

"The Apache or Pima didn't make them?"

"Older than that. These were ones here a long time ago, and they left. The O'odham called them Hohokam. It means those who have gone."

"Who are the O'odham?"

"Whites call them Papago or Pima but it's what they call themselves."

"Never seen anything like them. I suppose they'd be in Utah canyons too. I never looked," Cole said studying the symbols.

"They are all across the Southwest. Man likes to leave his mark."

"You know what they mean?"

"Nope." Vince moved back to sit on a big rock from where he could see the owl rock as he had come to call it. "Not sure if anybody today knows for sure."

"You've been a lot of places, haven't you, Vince?" Cole sat beside him looking at the ancient markings

"I've traveled a lot, yes. You didn't?"

"No." There was a brief silence. "You ever been married?"

Vince shook his head. "I haven't had a life to offer a woman."

"Yourself."

Vince gave a laugh and lit a cigarette. "Not much of a

bargain. I won't live to be an old man. I am surprised I have lived to be as old as I am."

Cole pointed to a snake undulating its way across the sandy canyon floor. "Rattler. You going to kill it?"

"Why?"

"It could kill us."

"It isn't interested in us. Look, it's hunting. Let it be."

"Last night, you killed a man without much thought."

"Oh, I thought about it. He was going to try to kill someone I love."

"I am trying to understand you as much as you said you are me."

"Well, you can know one thing about me. I don't believe violence is the answer to everything."

Cole snorted. "Before this, the last time I saw you, you were taking on Asa with your fists."

"He was the one coming after me if you remember."

"You didn't seem to mind bashing him into the ground."

"Once a man takes a stand that involves using fists or guns, he better not second guess it. It's a good way to get killed."

"You've killed enough to know." It wasn't a question.

"Yeah, but never set out to do any." He smiled. "Well, maybe Brody but that's because of who he was sent to kill. None of the ones I faced in a fight were like that rattler, minding their own business."

"You are confusing the hell out of me."

"I have a question for you."

"Shoot." Cole grinned. "Not literally, of course."

"Last night the shooting shook you. I saw it. Yet, you didn't seem scared. What was it?"

"I've had some experiences with shooting... and death." His smile changed into the cold one. Vince waited but Cole offered no more.

71

"You felt bad I killed Brody?"

He shook his head. "Not that so much. That was how it was going to be—even if it had been Ryker. I heard he's good with a gun too. Brody was on his way to where he ended up."

"Where we all do."

"Don't get philosophical on me, Vince. It doesn't suit you." Cole smiled with that strange one that had Vince trying to read but giving up. He noticed then that his brother was looking at the canyon rim where a small javelina herd was moving along and eating prickly pear, butting each other. A family.

"I may not know much, but I know you need to get away from Pa and Asa if you want to live a long life," Vince said. "Stick with them and you'll end in chains in Yuma or in the ground."

"You might be right... How about if I trail along with you awhile?"

"Why?"

"Maybe I want to see what makes you tick." Cole gave a little laugh. "Like you are wondering about me."

"It's not so safe to be with me."

"I figured that part out."

"I have made my share of enemies through the years. Brody will add to it."

"Because of his rep?"

"It can work that way. Although, usually I can avoid that sort of trouble. But sometimes I can't walk away."

Cole stared at the petroglyph. "Owls are bad luck."

Vince drew in the smoke and resisted laughing. "And you were calling me philosophical."

Cole gave a little laugh. "Maybe it's the place... a place of death."

"Life is about death," Vince said and then laughed. "Maybe I will blame it on the place. You got a woman, Cole?"

"No. Not saying I've never been with one but not the kind I'd want to call mine. Sure didn't want a whore for a wife." His laugh showed no humor.

"How about Asa and Jesse? Last time I was back, when Ma had died, I didn't stay long enough to see if there was a woman around."

"Not Jesse. The folks kept him out of school, afraid he'd be bullied and maybe worse."

"Worse?"

"Folks like Jesse sometimes get locked up."

"He's not crazy, is he?"

"No, just slow. But about the women, because of how he looks, handsome devil, he had girls coming around. He didn't give them any encouragement. He works with the horses and cattle, good with animals. Animals love Jesse."

"How about Asa?"

"He had a woman, but she left him, left Utah without saying where she went. My guess is he was mean to her like to everybody else. Since then, he sticks to whores. They don't mind when he beats them up... if he pays them enough."

"He was a mean bastard even when little," Vince said as he took another deep draw on the cigarette before throwing it to the dust and grinding it out with his boot.

"He hasn't changed. So, what are you doing next?" Cole asked. "I meant it. I'd like to go with you."

"I am not sure. I have a kind of business meeting tonight. Then tomorrow Sam should be in Tucson with his herd. I'll know better after I talk to him."

Cole stared at the sandy floor of the canyon without looking up. "I'm sorry I was part of trying to see him killed.

When I think about it, I don't know what the hell I was thinking."

"Especially for a man who claims to not like guns or killing."

"Yeah." He let out a breath and shook his head. "Especially for that sort."

"I'll think on you coming with me."

"After you figure out where you head next?"

"Yeah." He stared at the owl figure on the rock. Maybe it was a symbol of death. Maybe he had come to this place because of his own nature being drawn to death. He wasn't a man often to look inside, but when he did, he could see himself as someone, who believed his end would be violent and not that far in the future. He had never expected to get to his forties. By all the laws of luck, he should not have and yet, here he was.

"That business meeting," Cole said interrupting his musings. "Want me to come along... wearing a gun this time?" He smiled. "Yes, I know how to use them if I need to."

"No guns needed for this one and no." He would go to help her with her maps, tell her what he knew about the Cibecue, maybe encourage her to find other places to explore that were safer. Beyond that, he'd never see her again—if he wanted to stay alive himself.

Helping Song prepare a special dinner for her guest, Holly grimaced as she saw the all too pretty, Clint Madison walking up the path to her home. When she growled, Song laughed. "That one can't stay away," she teased.

Holly went to answer the door only because she did not think he would believe she wasn't home. The delicious smells of food being prepared would give her away. Song had prepared some of Holly's own favorite dishes. They would either finish cooking by six or be easy to heat back up when Vince Taggert arrived.

"Good afternoon," Clint said as he removed his hat and stepped inside.

"I am busy. What can I do for you?" she asked not moving toward the parlor until she had no choice as he had settled onto the sofa.

"I want to talk about your archaeological trip."

"What is there to say?"

"I can't have you going off by yourself."

"I won't be by myself. Gabe is rounding up reliable men for me. Song told me she will come as the cook."

"Count me into your six needed men. My conscience simply cannot let you go without me."

She hadn't expected that. "How about your clients?" she asked as she tried to think of a polite reason to refuse him.

"I arranged with James Angus to take over while I am gone."

"I can't ask this of you."

"You aren't. I am telling you."

"Clint, a dig is a boring and tedious string of days even if there are discoveries. So much must be cataloged. It is digging in dirt literally." Pointedly, she looked down at his suit.

"I have other clothing. You knew I went to Cuba with Rafe and the Rough Riders."

"I understood you did not see action there."

"Not of my doing. I was ready but was needed more in other ways. I can help with the record keeping, but I have a strong back and can dig with the best of them." He smiled with those flashing white teeth. She saw he was determined. He seemed so soft to her. Only a year older than her, he seemed in many ways younger but that was foolish thinking.

"All right," she said finally. "But I am going to be the boss of this excavation. I hope that is clear." He seemed like the sort who would take that over if he could.

"Of course." His smile broadened. She wondered what there was about him that made her not trust his good intentions. Handsome, smooth, but with an underlying energy that had made her uneasy from the first time she had met him. She couldn't imagine he'd last long on the Cibecue, and so she smiled also. He'd be gone before the first week was out.

"Something smells good," he said sniffing expressively.

"I must ask you to leave now. I have a dinner guest tonight." It wasn't the only reason, but it sounded more polite than the real one. It also was more apt to get him to leave.

He rose and smiled. "Let me know when you plan to head north."

"Of course."

Closing the door, she felt annoyed that she had not told him no. She had no good excuse for her reluctance to see him come with her. Maybe she should have let Connie give her a reading for who Clinton Madison was. Handsome barrister or something more, something far less than the gentleman he appeared. She was annoyed at herself again for even considering the question. She had made a mistake by allowing him to come with her to a wilderness and a place many claimed would be dangerous.

A few minutes before six, she heard the knock. At the door, she saw he was wearing the suit, white shirt, and had freshly shaved. Taking off his hat, he smiled as she ushered him inside. "Something smells good," he said. He was also wearing the tied-down holstered revolver.

76

"You won't find enemies here, Mr. Taggert," she said looking pointedly at the cartridge belt.

He gave her a contemplative look but took her less than subtle hint, removed the gun, and laid it on the side table by her door. "Better?" he asked with a smile.

"Much. I hope you like Chinese food. Song can fix other things, but her Chinese dishes are sublime."

"That sounds very good." He followed her into the kitchen where she had set a table since the dining room was piled high with supplies.

"Would you like a glass of white wine?"

When he nodded, she poured one for each of them. Handing him his, their fingers brushed, and she felt a disturbing and almost elemental pull.

He lifted the glass. "To my lovely hostess," he said as he took a sip. "A mellow chardonnay. Very nice."

"I would like to take credit for the meal," she said gesturing toward the stove and counter as she lit the candles. "Wei Song prepared it all with my minor aid. I am not much of a cook, I am afraid."

"No one can do all things."

"I like to try."

He smiled again. "I can believe that."

"I hope that was a compliment." She wasn't sure it had been.

"I meant it that way. I admire your drive and even spunk with wanting to go to the middle of nowhere and excavate a prehistoric dwelling. There are places much closer, of course."

"I did know that." She managed to resist making it sound snippy.

"All right, I give up for now anyway. What are the dishes Song prepared?"

"Why don't you sit at the table, and I will serve you." Even as she said the words, she felt a kind of excitement growing inside. She had no idea what the proximity to Vince Taggert was doing to her, but she had never felt anything like it. Angry at him or attracted, there was no denying its power.

He gave her a look, something in his eyes seemed a mix of amusement, but what else she wasn't sure. He obeyed though, and she brought over the dishes. They were colorful, and the scents had her ravenous.

"Fried rice and chow mein, of course, you are familiar with." He nodded, not looking at the dishes but into her eyes. She forced her own gaze away and came back with more dishes. "Wontons, Gong Bao Chicken, and spring rolls finish out the menu."

"My God," he said his tone saying he was impressed, and now his gaze had turned to the food. "I haven't seen finer in San Francisco."

She smiled as she sat across from him at her own plate. "Have you spent much time there?" she asked as she handed him the first of the dishes and then served herself.

"Not a lot at any one time. I am in and out on business."

"What kind of business are you engaged in that would take you there."

"A trader, ma'am. I buy merchandise there that can be sold for much more in states farther from the ocean."

She felt a shiver that seemed to go clear through her. She had to work to school her voice. "You are an entrepreneur, then."

"A fancy word for a trader, but yes." He took his first bite of the Gong Bao Chicken, and she saw the pleasure on his face. "I am a simple trader. I bring Navajo turquoise jewelry to the city, finely woven rugs, beads, sometimes even pottery. People in the Bay area pay more for it than it would bring here. It benefits the tribes and myself, of course." He smiled again.

"You talk like an educated man and yet, you said your family is one of outlaws." She took a sip of her wine.

"I left home early and set out to learn what I needed to make my way. A salesman has to be able to sell."

"Some of what you do though has involved the gun you were wearing when you arrived."

His smile was the crooked one that she had seen before-- which had almost melted her heart. It was no less devastating across the dinner table in candlelight. Shockingly, she realized she wanted something from Vince Taggert that she'd never imagined wanting from a man. She fought the feelings away. She wished she could have stayed angry at him. It seemed safer. He instilled emotions in her, and none were halfway.

"Yes, some has involved a gun."

"But you don't use it in a business."

"Except when I worked for two and a half years as a deputy in Sheridan. My gun then was mostly a way to do the job and stay alive."

She began to eat and kept their conversation to small talk, the wildflowers on the desert, what the weather had been or would be, anything but what she was feeling. She had to work to keep eating even with such succulent flavors. The man across from her had an energy she could not identify. It both frightened and fascinated her.

Shaking his head at yet more food, he put down his fork. "Your dinner was delicious. Thank you very much for inviting me. I know you wanted information, but this wasn't necessary to get it."

"Perhaps this was my way of thanking you for saving my life the first day we met."

"Was it?"

It was her turn to smile. "No, I only wanted to... Well, I

hoped you would enjoy Song's cooking. She has agreed to go with me to the Cibecue."

"Some men don't enjoy light fare like this."

"She can cook anything. This happens to be what I prefer, and I thought you might." She wasn't sure why she had added that. She had had no way to know what he might've preferred in foods. She didn't know him at all. Even as she thought it, she knew she was lying to herself. She did know him and knew him all too well—as well as where any association with him would end.

CHAPTER 7

W hen Holly asked Vince to go into the parlor, and she would bring in their after dinner coffee, he agreed. Anything but continue sitting across from her at the table. If he had been attracted to her before, the feelings had only grown stronger. She was a gorgeous woman but wearing a burgundy gown with her blonde hair piled high on her head, she was the most beautiful thing he'd ever seen. He didn't belong anywhere near her.

She brought the coffee in on a tray, sat on the sofa beside him, and handed him a cup. This was a life such as he'd never known. As a trader he interacted in the stores, warehouses but never on a personal level. It certainly was nothing like his growing up years.

"You said you were familiar with the Cibecue," she said.

"I have specifically been there twice, traveled through the region more times. I haven't liked it much and spent as little time there as was needed."

"Why not? I have heard it's beautiful there."

"It is beautiful."

"Then why?"

"You know how the natives feel about it."

"I've heard stories, of course."

"It's where the dead are. Navajo don't like anything to do with the dead. Death potentially leaves behind chindi. Those ruins are bad luck to enter as who can know if someone died there."

"Are you part Indian?"

He shook his head as he sipped his coffee. "Not in the flesh anyway," he said with that mocking smile she'd seen before. "But I share their aversion to that region."

"But you said you know about it."

"Let's go look at your maps."

She smiled and led him into the dining room. She had spread her best map out on the table on top of several boxes. "I think this map is pretty accurate."

He studied it. Outside the sun was setting; so Holly turned on the lights and waited for him to say something. He looked at her thoughtfully and then pointed to a curve of the map. "This is above the Salt River. You can see by this map how the creek curves around and has a serpentine path it follows. You go above a waterfall, about here."

"I heard about the waterfall. Have you been there?"

He nodded. "It's pretty but deadly during the rainy season as you never know if water will come down in a torrent. If you believe your dwellings are on the Cibecue, you would have to go way around to come in from above or have your main camp below the falls where you'd have to climb the cliff to get the likeliest ruins. That would be difficult either way." He pointed to another spot. "Here it is fairly level and you could form a base camp. It will require though every day going above through this narrow slot." He pointed again.

"Perhaps a base camp below and smaller camps for a few days above?" she asked.

"You could do that. It's beautiful. No denying that. Clear green pools and they grow deeper as the canyon narrows. There are large boulders that add to its beauty. It is a special place but also vulnerable."

"Vulnerable to what?"

"Attack."

"Why would anyone attack us? The Apache leaders gave me permission to do this."

He shrugged. "There are always renegades in any society, and the leaders don't speak for everyone in the tribe," he said. "When you have a tall cliff like that, someone can be up there and even push off boulders. Gunshots could start rockslides. I am not saying any of it would happen. I am saying if it did, it wouldn't go well for the ones below."

"If you dislike it so much there, why did you go? It doesn't seem it'd be a direct route from the reservations to San Francisco."

"My last time on the Cibecue, I was on a hunt," he said looking up from the map. "I might as well tell you as if I don't you'll think it's worse than it was. I had been trading with one of the Dinè."

"Dinè?"

"What the Navajo call themselves. Alfred Yazzie had become a friend. He was murdered. The trail was clear. His family could not go after the killer, I could."

"For revenge?" She didn't like anything about this.

"For a reckoning. The man headed down the Cibecue. I didn't catch up with him until he reached the Salt."

"And you murdered him then?"

"He took a shot at me. Made it a good one. My shot in return was better."

"His was a good one?"

"He shot from ambush. Rifle. I'd show you the scar but you being a lady, you will have to take my word for it." He pointed to his leg, high up and not far below his hip.

"You could have been killed." She hated that thought even more than the idea of his hunting down a murderer.

"It came close and laid me up for a week. But it also made my friendship even stronger with the Yazzie clan. I still trade with them. Or did before I took the job of sheriff... That worked out worse than the trading, which I will be going back to once I assure myself Sam is safe."

"It appears you are a loyal friend."

"Sometimes. Anyway back to your map." He pointed to another spot. "This is where the Cibecue massacre happened. Cavalry and Apache killed a medicine man. Who did what is up for debate still today. Anyway another bad medicine place."

"Not near the ruins though."

"Not too close." He pointed again. "Here is where I saw the largest one. It was several stories, in relatively good shape. Are you aware there are ruins in most of the canyons around there?"

"I did know that."

"Then why the Cibecue?"

"It was a place to start more than anything. So you have actually never gone into any of the rooms to look around—not even out of curiosity?"

"No.

"Because they had bad karma?" She studied his face as he considered her question.

"Maybe for me." His smile was tight. "I play my hunches,

and my hunch is I should stay out. I can trade enough with what is legally attained without risking that."

"Archaeologists can't worry about that sort of superstition," she said knowing that she was trying to keep him there, extend their conversation. What on earth was this all about?

"Perhaps they should." He softened the words with a smile.

"Would you like a glass of red wine?" she asked. When he nodded, she told him to make himself comfortable in the parlor while she got it.

In the kitchen, opening the wine, she was glad he had said he would not go on the trip. If such places were bad luck for him, he should stay far away.

On the other hand, it wasn't bad luck for them to sit together in the parlor and... She returned and handed him a glass. She could have sat across from him but again sat on the sofa—although not too close.

"It looks like it was a beautiful sunset," she said as the glow slowly faded in the west.

"Another day," he said taking a sip of the wine. She liked his hands. They were large, like the rest of him, but the fingers were straight. When he used them to gesture, the hands had a kind of grace she would not have expected on such a large man. She supposed it made him fast with a gun. She wished she had not thought of that.

She worked to find something commonplace to say. It had to be nothing like what she was thinking, which was wondering how those hands would feel on her skin. "I like how days end here, so often with those marvelous sunsets," she managed to say-- in what she hoped was a neutral tone.

"The last time I was in Tucson, you weren't here."

"That must have been before November 1899. Grace Cordova and I went to school together. She studied architecture and I anthropology. Do you know Grace?"

"A little. I mostly have been in and out of Tucson. Cord's daughter, right?"

"Yes, and Sam's niece."

He smiled. "That's right. Brothers who didn't know they were." He stared into his glass.

"And now you have a brother here."

"For awhile."

"I have a sister who still lives in Chicago."

"Are you close?"

She shook her head. "We don't know each other well. Lily is younger by three years. I was sent off to the proper boarding school and then college. I think in temperament that she is more like our mother-- certainly closer to her before she died. Since he never had a son, Father groomed me to take over the businesses."

"It seems fathers tend to hope for that from firstborns."

She nodded. "Lily is a painter and gifted. Mostly portraits, but she sets them in landscapes, beautiful, even enigmatic sometimes. She captures the soul of her subjects."

"It is nice you are proud of her."

"I suppose I haven't told her enough, but I am. We haven't been close, but we also don't hate each other... at least anymore. There was a time..." She hesitated. "If your brother came here to kill Sam, can you trust him?"

"Good question. I am hoping to figure that out."

"I wish you well with it then. When you leave, where will you go?"

"Eager to get rid of me?" he asked, those dark eyes seeming to see right into her.

"You were the one who said the sheriff asked you to leave."

He raised his eyebrows. "It was suggested. I will decide after I talk to Sam. Somebody wanted him killed enough to

86

pay for it. I would like to know if he has an idea who. At least he'll be warned now."

"I've only met him briefly but liked him." She took a sip of her wine. Until she had come to Tucson, she'd never known men like Sam Ryker or Vince Taggert. Even Ollie had been a breed apart from the men she'd known in Chicago, from her own father.

Her father had never treated her mother well or for that matter her younger sister. It wasn't abusive with any of them, at least she didn't think, but more a mix of too many expectations, sadly expressed disappointments, followed by benign neglect. She wasn't glad he was dead, but she did feel a weight had lifted.

"How are you coming with acquiring your crew?" he asked.

She made a face. "I do have one more. Clint Madison said he will go."

"Sounds like you don't much cotton to that idea."

"My tone gave me away, huh?"

"And expression."

She didn't want him reading any of her expressions. She was feeling something she didn't remotely want him to guess. This was like nothing she'd known. She felt a desire to reach over and touch him. Ridiculous. How could she even imagine such a thing? She forced her thoughts to what he had said.

"I don't have a reason for not wanting him to come. He's tried to help me since I arrived. He would probably be a help." She sucked in a breath and sipped more of her wine before she set her glass on the small table.

She was aware his arm was resting on the back of the sofa. There were hairs on the back of his hand. She wondered if his chest was hairy.

He touched her hair with a finger. "So soft," he said in not much more than a whisper. She felt an almost uncontrollable urge to turn her head enough to capture his hand against her shoulder. This was all wrong, and yet she didn't want him to stop. She had to fight to keep her hands primly placed on her lap.

He dropped his hand. "I should go," he said but didn't rise.

"I uh appreciate the information you gave me regarding the Cibecue." She had to struggle for words that would not reveal what she was thinking.

"I wish you well with your venture. Thank you for the dinner tonight." He did rise then. She smiled but said nothing as she followed him to the door where he belted back on his gun, tying it down, before settling his hat on his head. He turned to face her. "I still wish you'd think twice about going up there."

"I need to go. I am sure it will be fine. Only this one summer."

He opened the door, turning to look at her. "Then I hope you find what you are looking for." For a moment, she thought he meant to say something but then was out the door and gone.

An hour later, Holly lay on her bed but found sleep impossible. Her thoughts were filled with turmoil. For one thing, as sure as she'd ever been of anything, she had known this man before they met in Tucson. He was the one in her dreams night after night. The same and not the same. If she had doubted reincarnation before, she did no longer.

It was the eyes. His eyes were the same as she had seen in dream after dream since she'd turned thirteen. It did not appear that he shared her memories. Good. The last thing she wanted now was for him to come with her to the Cibecue. In the morning, she would visit the Cordovas and try again to make Gabe see how important it was for him to find a crew to go with her. Maybe she didn't need six men.

The one man she didn't want with her would be the one she'd seen die in so many dreams. She would wish him well, but they needed to part and never see each other again.

Despite that sensible logic, all she could think was how much she had wanted to touch him, to feel his lips against hers. What would his kiss be like? Gentle and sweet or hot and fiery? Her body grew warm thinking about what it might feel like to touch Vince places she'd never imagined a woman would touch a man. The scar high on his thigh, what did that look like? You fool, she told herself, angry at the same time she felt incredibly heated.

She had to take deep breaths to calm down. What would those supple fingers feel like if they were touching her breasts, her belly? Foolishness. A man like him would never want a woman like her. She was inexperienced, naive even in the ways of the world. He would want a stronger woman. In many ways, he intimidated her merely in looking at her. How would she ever get control of that?

"All right," she whispered to the darkness, "this is logical and sensible. He won't come with me. I won't go to him." The connection though felt so strong, like nothing she'd ever imagined possible. She was dangerous to him. Let him live out his life without dying at her feet.

She wondered if Connie had known about their connection, and if it had been the real reason, that she had written Vince. If the psychic had, she didn't believe she would have seen the violent end that always came when they were together. Connie would never have lured a man to his death.

At the Pedrales, Vince took a whiskey bottle and shot glass to a table. He didn't often get drunk, but he was in the mood for exactly that. Cole came to the table with an empty glass, sat down, and poured himself a shot. "You look mad at the world," he said.

"Good guess." He noted Cole was again wearing a gun but not tied down. He had no better idea who Cole was or what he really wanted.

Before he could say more, Sheriff Adams came through the swinging door and straight for him. He saw the bottle, turned and went to the bar for a glass. "There was a reward on Brody," he said as Vince poured whiskey into his glass.

"For what?" Vince lit a cigarette.

"From the railroad. A thousand bucks. I won't have it until Monday, but it's yours."

"Hell." He wasn't a bounty hunter but had never turned down manna when it came from heaven—or from wherever.

"Something like that," Adams said with a grin.

"Guess I don't have to leave town right away."

"Nope. Although on the off chance his partner shows up back here, you might be smarter if you do. From his description, I'd say his name is Lloyd Jackson. Five hundred on him too." He looked then at Cole. "How about you? Any reward out on you?"

"Not that I know of."

"I looked through the stack of posters and didn't see your face. If I had, I'd not be asking." He looked back at Vince. "One of your brothers though might've had his face on one. Looked like you but described him as shorter, stockier. Al Smith."

"Creative. Wanted for what?" Vince asked.

"Robbing a train. Seems to be a lucrative trade for a few."

Vince drew on the cigarette. "If you can call it a trade."

"Well, I just wanted to tell you about the money." He slugged his whiskey and was gone.

"Did you know they were wanted?" Vince asked his brother.

"No. They worked out of Vernal and went out with Asa sometimes. Pa sent for them. Maybe he knew."

"It might pay you in the future to consider who you ride with."

Cole's smile was strange, in a knowing sort of way that surprised Vince. "I did. That's why I am going with you."

"Despite the risks."

"Yep, how'd your business meeting go?"

"Well enough."

"What will you do with the money?"

"Put it in the bank, I guess. You have any money, Cole?" he asked as he poured himself another shot.

"Not much."

"Skills?"

"Some, I can drive a herd, brand, castrate, shoe a horse, cut down a tree, chop it up, rig a pack, follow a track, build a cabin. Survival mostly-- not the type to earn a lot of money."

"When did Pa put cattle on the ranch? I don't remember any growing up."

"Not enough grass to handle many, but it has kept us fed."

"So Pa isn't in on the train robbing?"

"He's getting old, Vince."

"Aren't we all?"

"Yeah, I've thought about that. I never have found the thing I most wanted to do. I wondered about you sometimes— whether you'd found it. I didn't know how to get in touch with you."

"I admit I didn't want to come back. It didn't seem there was a reason. I should have thought of my brothers."

"If I ride with you for awhile, I'll earn my way—and not by robbing."

"Can you read and write? Tally up numbers?"

"I don't read Shakespeare," Cole said with a grin, "but I can get through a book, and yes, arithmetic is important in keeping a ranch afloat too."

"Good then." The whiskey was beginning to make him feel mellower. He had lost the desire to get drunk. The morning after was never worth it. He had to figure out what he should do next.

"After you talk to Ryker, you going down to his ranch with him?" Cole asked. "If it's a big one, think he'd hire me? Guess not since I just came here to kill him." He smiled that cynical one that said he saw the humor in places others didn't.

"Not if he's smart, and he is. Did you hear the name of the person who put up the bounty on him?"

"It was a woman but never a name. The man she sent called her the madam. Madam wouldn't like this or that. I didn't know. Maybe a whore?"

"Maybe." But unlikely. He remembered Connie's seeing the problem being a woman with the initial B. Maybe Sam would make sense out of it. He hoped whoever had been after the ranch hadn't hired more than his pa to make sure of Ryker's death.

He walked slowly back to his hotel room, the night air blowing any remnants of the whiskey from his brain. The night with Holly had been too good. The best he'd known in years. The best he'd known ever. She wasn't for him, but she made him want things he'd thought he'd put out of his mind, living like a monk as he mostly had been.

In his room, he stripped. Lying on the bed, he found himself unable to sleep. Having dinner with her had been a mistake. He couldn't be near her and not act on what he wanted. It would be a matter of when not if—unless she pushed him away. She was an innocent, likely waiting for the right man, the fenced yard. It wasn't him.

Connie had wanted him to help her. The cost would be higher than Connie knew. It wouldn't work. Holly wouldn't want him telling her what to do. She'd think she knew it all and end up getting herself killed. That beautiful body would be broken from a fall or poisoned by a rattler—human or otherwise.

He couldn't let himself think of that. If he did, he'd find himself up there with her and dead or worse. He felt half mad at Connie for bringing him here. He knew she had meant well, but she also had had no idea what she was asking... or had she.

Morning came after a restless night. Vince dressed in his rough clothes and headed down for a quick breakfast. He had decided to ride out south of town to meet up with Sam before he got to Tucson. He wasn't sure what that would gain other than helping ease his own restlessness.

He had barely finished his second cup of coffee when Cole came in the cafe. "What's the plan for today?" his brother asked ordering his own breakfast.

"You need a bath," Vince said as he rubbed his own bristly jaw.

Cole chuckled. "Where'd I get one if I was to believe you."

"Above the barbershop while I get a shave and then you do."

"Shave? Damnitall, Vince. What's up? Or you thinking I need to be clean shaven and washed up to meet my maker, and Ryker is going to make sure that's sooner than later?" he chuckled.

"Maybe I want you looking more reputable when you meet him so he'll be less inclined to do that." Vince smirked.

An hour later, both men were clean shaven with hair trimmed and standing back on the street. Looking out at the town, Vince felt less eager to ride south to meet Sam. He walked out toward the corrals where the cattle would be brought and leaned on the wooden panels as he lit a cigarette.

"You figure he'll be in today?" Cole asked.

"Or tomorrow."

"And then what?"

"And then we'll see. I think though I better meet Sam without you there."

Cole's smile was crooked, but he nodded and left.

Vince wondered then where Holly was, and it made him mad the instant he thought it. Thinking of her led to a swelling in his groin. He needed to ride out of town and get a long way from her. Maybe he should go down to Sam's ranch. Working cattle might help to work out whatever the hell was going on with him. Sam could get a chance to see if Cole was good with cattle. Maybe it's what he'd do...

CHAPTER 8

J ust past noon, leaning his elbows on the top rail of the corral and smoking his next to last cigarette, Vince saw the dust of a trail herd approaching. He smiled as he thought about seeing his old friend. Then he remembered he had something to tell him-- not only about the threat to Sam's life, but also about his own name. He didn't look forward to either.

The herd came into town at a relaxed pace and seemed resigned to entering the corral. There were five drovers. It wasn't until they closed the corral gates that Vince realized two of them were women. Abby and Alice had come along for the drive. He was more than ever glad he had killed Brody.

"Damn it all," Sam said as he leaped from his horse, as agile as the first time Vince had seen him. "What the hell are you doing here?" He reached out and grabbed Vince in a bear hug. Sam was the same height as Vince although even broader of shoulder. Both were powerful men. He proved it by lifting Vince into the air.

When he could breathe, Vince laughed. "What kind of welcome is that?"

Abby threw herself off her horse and ran to give Vince another big hug. "Wonderful to see you."

He looked up at Alice who was still in the saddle. Even at thirteen, it was obvious she was going to be the beauty her mother was, with the same head of curly auburn hair. "Who the hell is this lady?" he asked with a laugh.

"Uncle John," she said with a big smile.

Vince sighed and looked at Sam. "I need to talk to you," he said.

Sam frowned at the somber tone. "All right." He looked back at the tall youth who had ridden up. "Dave, you and Joe take care of things here, all right?"

"Sure, Pa."

In moments, Sam had stalked with Vince to a corner where it was quiet enough to be heard over the bellowing cattle. "What's the problem?"

"Two things. First is my name is not John Damian. I am Vince Taggert." No point in delaying the thing he most hated to say.

Sam stared blankly before he sucked in a breath. "I know the Taggert name. Your family?"

He nodded.

"Why didn't you tell me before? It's not like you haven't had time."

Vince drew on the last of his cigarette. "Because I didn't want to be Vince Taggert."

"You could have trusted me."

"I did. It wasn't about you. It was about me."

Sam considered that before he grabbed the cigarette from Vince and took a long draw. "I don't smoke anymore... as an example for Dave."

"Good. It's a lousy habit."

"Let me get this straight. Your father is Jeremiah?" He let out the smoke.

"Yes."

"Damn, there is more, isn't there?"

Vince nodded, took the cigarette back, and sucked in the smoke before he let it out. Too bad it didn't help. "Someone wants you dead."

Sam laughed and gave him that sarcastic smile he'd seen so often on the rugged face. "Tell me something new."

"This one involves money."

Abby came up behind him. "Is there a problem?" she asked.

"Sounds like it. In the meantime, meet Vince Taggert."

Abby looked at him, her doe-like, exotic eyes narrowed. "Explain."

"Can we take care of the cattle first? It's a long story," Vince said dropping the cigarette to the dust and grinding it out with his boot. "Where are you four staying?"

"With Ollie and Rose, of course," Abby said.

"Then I will come up this evening after supper and explain the whole thing. Might as well be when Ollie hears it too."

"Come up for supper," Abby said. "I know you and believe you had a good reason for the name. It's not as though this changes who you are—our good friend."

"You feel that way too?" Vince asked meeting Sam's hard gaze.

"Let's talk tonight." He turned then and headed for the buyers who had arrived.

Sam was a hard man but a fair one. Vince knew he'd not like any part of what he had to tell him. Even more, he would not like knowing Vince had killed to protect him. No more lies. Whatever the end of any of this, he was going to live with his real name—for as long as he had to live anyway. Someday it would be the one on his marker—if he even had one.

At the Cordova's, Holly learned nothing regarding an increase to her crew. Gabe was gone working for one of the local ranchers. She wondered if even he would come in the end.

Gabe's mother, Maria handed her a cup of tea. "You look sad," she commented as she sipped her own.

"No. Well, maybe worried. I am concerned at getting everything ready to go north by the end of the month."

"Gabriel will help you. I know he will."

"It's not his problem." She didn't want to bring pressure on Gabe from his mother.

The door opened and Rose walked through. "Good to see you." She hugged Holly and Maria. "I didn't expect you to be here."

"I am still trying to get my crew together." She wondered if Rose was as disapproving of her venture as her husband, Ollie.

"Very exciting," Rose said answering that question. "I wish I could go with you. I'd love to explore old ruins, such as I've heard those are. Royce though is too young to spend a summer up in rattlesnake heaven." She grinned. "Not that our home is much less. I had to kill one this morning with a shovel. I hate doing it, but with an active child and his dog, I can't take the risk."

"Predators sometimes must be killed. Even when one values all of life," Maria agreed.

Rose nodded. "I don't like it when I have to do it. Ollie was out though taking a horse to the Davidsons."

"I should go and let you two visit," Holly said, wondering if Gabe did not come through, where could she find reliable men to go north. She was beginning to consider taking even unreliable ones. She knew how to shoot if required.

"Why don't you come up to the house for supper tonight," Rose suggested before Holly got out the door. "Sam and Abby are arriving today."

"I guess I could do that. I would love seeing them again. Did their children come?"

Rose laughed. "I expect them. They are not such children anymore. David might end up taller than Sam. Alice is looking more like a woman every day. They grow up so fast."

"I'd like to see them. Can I bring something?"

"Not a thing. I have it in hand." Rose smiled. In her early sixties, Rose was as vibrant as a woman much younger. Of course, some of that had happened after her recent marriage to Ollie.

Holly grinned. "I will be there. Six?"

"Perfect although if you come earlier, that's good too. Feel free to bring guests. As many as you wish. I am slow cooking a huge roast in the fire pit Ollie made for us. It should be tender and delicious. I wish Maria and Raul would be there."

"I have Anita's four tonight," Maria said. "They are wonderful children but way too spirited to behave for an evening with friends."

"There will be other times." Rose's face glowed with the joy she always showed when she feeding others. It was a sensation Holly felt when digging in the dirt and finding something from the past that opened up understanding to those who had come before.

Rose turned to Holly. "Will you be riding your new horse up?"

"Maybe." She hadn't gotten back on Princess since she had lost control of the mare. She was unsure how comfortable she would be if she did. Not sidesaddle whatever she chose. Maybe she'd hire a driver to bring her out. "I'll be there though," she said with a parting smile, as she walked out the door.

She walked back to her home, grinding her teeth as she saw Clint sitting on her front porch chair. "I didn't expect you," she said.

"I needed to be sure you understood that I meant it when I said I am going with you north. What date are you leaving?"

"I have been told it could be dangerous," she said as she let him into the house. Fragrant odors came from the kitchen. She wondered if what Song was cooking would transport to Rose's.

"Which is why I will come."

She gave up arguing with him. She didn't have anyone else she could be sure would come. Except Song, unless she backed out when she saw the crew was not to be what she had been led to believe.

Clint followed her into the kitchen where Song was rolling out dough. "Hello, Mr. Madison," she said.

"Clint, please."

"I won't be here for dinner tonight," Holly said as she took the cup of tea Song handed her.

"Dinner invitation?" Song asked smiling at Clint.

"Rose and Ollie. Sam is in town with Abby. I guess their children too. Although it seems they are not such children anymore."

"They grow up; so fast." Her face darkened. "I would like to ask a favor."

"Of course, ask."

"Could Zian come with us?"

"Would he want to?"

"I am not sure. I wanted to talk to you first. He fights with his grandfather. He will get in trouble if he stays here. I would like him to find other answers than his friends, who seem to be looking for trouble."

Holly had her doubts about whether an excavation would help with that, but she smiled. "Of course, he can come. He's old enough to be a help. I would, of course, pay him if he wants to work." That would give her three of her crew.

Song handed Clint a cup of tea. "He's strong and tall. I know he would work." Song smiled. "He needs a purpose that isn't involving a gun."

"Guns don't lead to a good end," Clint said as he took a sip of the tea.

"I know that much," Song said, "but he doesn't believe it right now. Sometimes the white boys come out to cause trouble, to make fun of the Chinese with their pigtails. Zian is going to strike back the wrong time and..."

"Definitely bring him," Holly said. She was determined she would go even if she could not get all the people she needed. It would be all right. She had a purpose, and that would make it all right.

"When are you leaving?" Clint asked.

"With the full moon. May 3."

He smiled at that. "Superstition?"

"Perhaps but I thought a full moon would be good for night camps. Besides, isn't it supposed to be a good time for starting things?"

"Or is that a new moon?" His smile widened.

"If you don't want to come, you don't have to."

"I do want to. Can I come tonight with you to the Olivers?"

She wished she could refuse him, but if she couldn't stand him for one evening, months on the Cibecue would be impossible. "Of course. Rose said to bring anyone I came across."

He finished his tea. "I'll be back with a buggy to escort you up." He looked over then at Song. "Are you coming also?"

She shook her head. "I am going home to convince Zian he needs to do this." She took a determined breath. "I know I can make him see the wisdom of it. Of course, the money might help." She smiled.

Holly wasn't sure Song believed it. She added her own smile to give encouragement. They both needed all of that they could get.

To clear his head before facing Sam at the Oliver ranch, Vince took his gelding out for a run up one of Tucson's broad washes. He let his horse run all out, to feel the wind whistle past, the pull of the mighty muscles as he leaned low to get the maximum speed.

After a few miles, he slowed Jupiter and turned him back toward the mountain and Ollie and Rose's home. This wasn't going to be fun. He supposed Ollie would be angry with him too.

Never one to put off a problem, he got to the ranch ahead of the time he'd been told the meal would be served. If they wanted him to leave, he would do it. He put his gelding in the corral with the other horses. He didn't have to knock as Ollie and Sam were waiting for him on the front porch. Gabriel Cordova sat on a bench.

Ollie handed Vince a glass of whiskey. "I hear ya got a story to tell," he said with a smile.

Sam looked as irritated as he had earlier.

"My name is not Damian. It's Vince Taggert."

The older man grinned. "Already knew it."

Sam turned on him. "You knew it and never told me?"

"Now, that's obvious, ain't it, boy," he said.

"How did you know?" Vince felt flummoxed. Ollie had never once given it away, not in all the years he'd known him.

"Remember that day in Tombstone when ya stepped in and saved Sam's life." He gave his old boss one of his gimlet eyed looks. "I told ya then I thought I knew ya, but I couldn't place it how. It was ridin' back to the ranch that I remembered. It was '77, I think, that I seen ya in a gunfight in Abilene. Ya wasn't much more than a kid, still usin' yore old man's name. This fella had been laughin' at a cripple. When he kicked him, you stepped in before anybody else could and gave him a solid kick that sent him sprawling. You asked how'd you like that? The galoot pulled out his hogleg. Fast as greased lightnin' was what I saw that day when ya plugged him. Ya ain't never stopped steppin' in, have ya?"

Vince took a gulp of the whiskey as he thought back to that day. "So all the time, you knew."

Ollie nodded.

"Why didn't you tell me?" Sam asked still sounding annoyed but less than he had.

"Man wants to change his ways, get away from a rotten family, who am I to say something. It wasn't my business or yours either, for that matter." He gave him one of those parent looks that had Sam smiling and shaking his head even before Ollie added the finishing touch. "You also got two names, ya know—Sam Ryker O'Brian."

"All right, I get it." He turned then to Vince. "I thought we were friends."

"We were. Still are on my end. Sam, you are the best friend I ever had."

Sam swallowed hard and let out a breath. "I've been acting like a horse's hind-end. Nothing new for me, of course." He managed a laugh. "Who am I to try and say a man can't change."

"I'd like to say I have," Vince said, "but not..." He stopped as he heard a buggy pulling up behind him. Normally, he never had his back to a road but because it had been Sam and Ollie, he'd broken a cardinal rule of survival. When he turned to see who it was, he tightened his mouth. Holly was arriving-- driven by the lawyer, Madison.

He watched as Madison lifted her down, and the two walked toward the adobe. "Where can I put the buggy?" Madison asked.

Ollie took him while Holly stepped onto the porch. Her gaze went from Gabe who had arisen back to Vince. Before she could say more than hello, Rose had come out and pulled her into the house. Gabe followed.

Just as well, as anything that came to Vince's mind to say would have been cold and unfriendly. He had thought she didn't want anything to do with the shyster.

"Don't think much of him, do you?" Sam asked with a grin.

"He's all right." He had to work to manage the words.

"You think a lot of her though. I saw that look in your eyes."

"Imagined you mean."

Sam chuckled and refilled both their glasses from the bottle. "Sure I am. But, all right, for now. Tell me the rest of it."

Before he could start, Clint and Ollie were back. Vince wasn't eager to say what he had to with the lawyer listening, but there was no option. Ollie poured Madison a drink and refilled his own. There was no point in trying to sugarcoat it. Madison was going nowhere. He might as well tell him too.

"As I told you, someone has offered money to see you dead." He reached for his cigarettes and lit one, taking a long draw.

"Reasons given?"

"A man came to the ranch in Vernal. From the sounds of it only hired to find a gunman. Cole said the reason he gave is his employer wants the Circle R. He also said our pa didn't like you, and it's why he took the job."

Sam smiled. "Well, I likely know who was behind it. Remember how I bought the ranch?"

"Marius Gray."

Sam nodded. "He sold it to me cheap. Of course, with Geronimo still out there, it was country that had less value than today. Still, he wanted me to have it. He said I was as close to him as the son he never had. He left only when he knew his wife, who hated the remoteness, wasn't coming back. The first letter came six months ago. Marius had died. A wasting disease the letter said. It was from a lawyer asking for his client to buy the ranch. His client was Breanna Gray Osbourne."

"His widow?"

"Divorcee. She remarried years ago. Michael Osbourne."

"Why would she want the ranch now if she hated it before?" Vince asked as he remembered the B Connie had seen with a knife.

"Money, maybe. It's worth a lot more today than back then. There is another factor... A second letter came shortly after from a different lawyer to inform me that Marius had left me everything he had. There were no details but sounded like it would amount to a lot."

"Ya never told me that," Ollie said shaking his head.

"Wasn't your business," Sam said with a laugh. "I hadn't decided if I'd even take it. I don't know why he would have done it."

"Wal, it makes sense now that she'd be wantin' you dead."

"And why she'd hold a grudge. How about Jeremiah. What was the grudge? Cole said he had one but not what."

"Long time ago. I'd have figured he'd have forgotten, and it was indirect. I never actually met him. I did meet his men. This was... hmmm I guess in '75 or maybe a year earlier. Time gets away from me. I was a shave-tail. Ollie was off on a drive. I'd gotten laid up."

"Shot is what he's sayin'." Ollie chuckled.

"Yeah, and Taggert's men came into Ellsworth. It was booming then, big herds coming through. They started talking in the saloon about taking the herd Ollie was ramroding." Sam looked at his old friend. "I had a little conversation with them about finding a new line of work. It didn't go well." He shrugged.

"So you took out part of his crew." That would make sense.

"Seven actually. It was a fair fight, and in that case, it wasn't only me. Ellsworth was a rough town in those years, and the locals had formed a vigilante group. Three of them saw what was happening and stepped in. It was over fast. Everybody knew how to shoot. I got hit in the other leg." His smile was wry.

"I was still at the ranch then. It was '74," Vince said. "I remember the aftermath but had no idea you were involved. Pa was ready to chew nails and beat anybody who got close. Not long after, I left." He drew heavily on his cigarette before Sam took it from him.

"You all have had quite a violent history," Madison said. "I just went to college and to work."

"Better way to live," Vince said with reluctance. He didn't like saying anything positive about the barrister. Still, if he had less killing in his past... No sense thinking about that-- it wasn't the way it had gone. Can't go backward and going forward didn't look like it had a lot of change in it.

"Is Rafe going to be here tonight?" Madison asked.

Ollie shook his head. "Donny's got the sniffles. They didn't want him out."

Rose came to the door. "You gentlemen wash up. Supper is about ready."

106

After washing up at the pump, Vince stepped back to let the others go in first. He took a last drag on his cigarette before grinding it out. He had thought facing Sam would be the hardest. He had been wrong. Hardest would be going into that house and seeing Holly again-- another man at her side.

CHAPTER 9

Holly helped Rose put the dishes on the long wooden table. Her answers from Gabe regarding the crew were disappointing. The Yaquis were superstitious about going into the ruins. Gabe was fine with it, but he had yet to find others. She guessed she would have to go without the crew she had hoped. Money could not buy everything.

When Vince walked through the door, hat off and gun left on the table along with Sam's, she felt her heart begin to pound. He was a striking man, no denying that, but her reaction went way beyond the high cheekbones, dark eyes and black hair. Although he had not dressed in the suit, he was wearing a clean shirt and had shaved sometime that day. She realized she was observing every detail of him when she saw Sam watching her with speculation in his intense blue eyes.

Within moments, they were all seated at the table, and Rose had said grace. Holly hadn't intended to sit across from Vince, but she was. She tried to still her hand from shaking. Clint was at her right and Abigail at her left. It took all her effort to listen to what Abigail was saying.

"Tell us more about this archaeological venture of yours," she asked. "Alice is interested in science." Her look-alike daughter was looking on with interest.

She explained a little of what such an exploration involved. "Nothing about this one though is going as I had hoped," she finished.

"Have you been on others?"

"Short ones. The longest was for one summer, I was in a class that was exploring a culture of mound builders near Collinsville, Illinois. These large mounds were likely built for ceremonial or burial purposes, out of soil but shaped rather like pyramids—although may predate the Egyptian ones. That is still to be proven."

"How fascinating."

"It was a limited excavation, but we did validate the earlier belief that more than 20,000 people lived near it. It was a surprisingly advanced culture. I say surprising because of the European belief that such cultures didn't exist here in America."

"Is that kind of thing what you hope to learn when you go to the Cibecue country?" Alice asked between bites of food.

"She danged well should not go there," Ollie said giving her that look she had seen too often since she first broached the plan to him.

"It is the region where I am sure I do need to go," she said. "I admit though it's been a struggle to get a crew large enough."

"How many do you need?" Abigail asked. She turned then to Ollie. "And why shouldn't she go?"

"Dangerous country is why. Bad enough that alone but add a beautiful woman and just plumb foolish."

Holly stopped herself from saying what she was thinking. She could not resist glancing at Vince. He had given her basically the same advice. He wasn't looking at her though but at Clint who was smiling. "I will be with her to protect her."

"Oh, that'll go well," Vince said with a wry smile. "Who protects her from you?"

Clint's smile widened. "I won't take that as an insult."

"Wise choice," Sam said with one of those laughs that said more than the chuckle. Clint looked away.

"What makes it dangerous?" Alice asked.

"You name it, and it's got it," Ollie said. "Predators of all sorts. Rattlers. Human and otherwise. The Apache or Navajo neither one like someone going into these places."

"I have permission—signed by tribal leaders," Holly insisted. She had heard all of this and believed it was true. It wasn't going to stop her. She only had to get a crew. Vince's gaze had turned to her. She couldn't read the expression in his eyes.

"I think it sounds exciting," Alice said.

"Danger can seem that way," Abigail said contemplatively.

"I think it can be done safely, or I'd not do it," Holly said. "I would never ask others to enter into risk." Her gaze never left Vince's eyes.

"It's a few months," Clint said. "We will go well armed--in case."

"Like you know a lot about that," Vince said with an ironic smile.

"Some." Clint looked back down at his plate. "Whatever your opinion might be about it, I will be there for her."

"I will also," said Gabe from down the table.

"I'd go if not for Royce," Ollie said. Holly understood that. His seven year-old grandson, who had come to live with him when his mother died, was young for spending a summer in such a place.

"You don't need to," Holly said. "I am sure I can find a crew. I merely must look other places.

"How about us?" The question came from Abigail.

"What are you talking about?" Sam sputtered.

"We could do it for a summer. You can see Alice is interested. I bet Dave would like it too."

The youth nodded and then said, "I would like it. I have never seen that country."

Sam snickered. "You'd like anything that got you off the ranch."

"Is that a problem?" David asked with a laugh that already sounded a lot like his father's.

"How long would this be for?" Sam asked. To Holly's surprise, it appeared he was considering it.

"I had planned to bring enough supplies for two months, see how it had gone and resupply as we see what is needed. It could be through the summer though."

"Resupply from Globe?"

"Or Show Low." She nodded. "I would though listen to others who can more assess what is best. Although I know about the archaeology part, I have never planned a venture this size."

She looked back then to Vince and smiled. "I will have enough now that you won't worry."

"I won't because I am coming."

She blanched. "You can see I don't need you to come."

"You and I need to talk." There was that dictatorial tone she remembered from when he had pulled her from her runaway horse. She felt uneasy but nodded. The conversation then drifted in various directions until she helped clear the table.

When she looked up, he was watching her from the doorway. "All right," she said and followed him outside. Clint had disappeared into the parlor with the gentlemen for brandy and cigars. David, although too young for either, had followed them.

Outside, the air was fresh and clear, the stars highly visible overhead.

"What did you want to say that others couldn't hear?" she asked when he stopped her at the corrals and turned to face her.

"They could have. I thought you might prefer they not."

"Why?"

"For this." He reached out and pulled her to him. She never even thought of resisting as he put his arms around her and bent to claim her lips. The kiss was like none she'd known as she felt herself melt into his body in a way that went beyond the physical. Warmth surged through her. She wanted the kiss to last forever. What was this?

"You weren't supposed to do that," she said with a smile, when he finally released her and stepped back.

"On that we agree." His smile was self-mocking. The half moon was rising. The light of it gave his face an eerie glow, almost otherworldly.

"We agreed before that you would not go with me to the Cibecue."

"It hadn't gotten to that point. Connie wanted me to do it, but you and I had never gotten specific regarding it."

"It would be a bad idea."

He smiled again. "Probably but I'm going to do it."

"You know you shouldn't, Vince." It was the first time she had used his name. It rolled off her lips as though she had used it hundreds of times.

"I know that too, but I am going. There is one condition."

"You are so dictatorial."

He laughed. "Sometimes. This though is where you will agree, or I will do everything I can to stop your going at all. And I have more influence in that than you might imagine."

"I am listening."

"You are boss of the digging. I am boss of security."

"What does that mean?"

"It means where we camp, traveling to and from it, the guns, the things you want to do that I say are not safe. You listen to me."

"Of course, I'd listen." She didn't like even saying that.

"More than listen. Obey."

Never in her life had she imagined hearing a man say that word and her not becoming infuriated. Instead, she felt heated in a different way. "I don't believe you'd shut down this whole venture for that."

"Believe it. This is going to be more dangerous than you can imagine right now. If you can't listen to commonsense, it would be even worse."

"I do understand its danger." She wasn't willing to tell him about the dreams.

"Then you understand it's not a world you know anything about. I have been there, can help you, but I won't do it if you are going to risk your life or others out of stubbornness."

"You make me so mad." She felt like yelling at him.

"I know."

"All right, but tell me this-- why did you kiss me?"

"It was what I wanted to do all night."

"And you always do what you want?"

He shook his head. "No, not always. A kiss though isn't much to give a man, who you might be asking to die for you."

She shuddered. "If you think that, I don't want you to come." She already knew she should not want him to come--

and yet, she did. She very much did. They had a history up there. Did it have to end as it had? No, that was silly superstition. Except she wasn't sure it was. How could she explain the dreams and then here he was. He might not know it, but she did.

"Are you ready to go home?" Clint's voice interrupted whatever he might have said as they both turned toward him.

"I should. I'll just say goodnight to Rose and Ollie. Be right back."

"I'll get the buggy," Clint said, "and meet you here."

At the house, she saw Abigail first. "I wanted to tell you how much I appreciated your offering to come to the Cibecue with me. I won't hold you to it though when you talk it over as a family." She smiled.

The older woman laughed. "Once he gets used to the idea, Sam will love it. I think it will be good for our family. We'll send Joe back to the ranch. There are enough men there to do what needs doing. Dave is getting restless, needs an adventure, and Alice has to decide what she wants. She has spent some time with Grace, and is already thinking she'd like to also go to college."

"That's wonderful. I didn't want you to feel pressured by a momentary impulse."

"We won't, but thanks. We will stop by to talk to you more about what we need to do to prepare."

Vince lit a cigarette and watched the buggy head down the lane. "You going to do anything about it?" Sam asked as he came to stand beside the corral with him.

Vince handed him the cigarette. "Not much I can do."

"Sure there is."

"What have I got to offer a woman like that?"

Sam snickered and took a long draw on the cigarette before handing it back. "The same thing any man has to offer a woman, but isn't that decision up to her?"

"She already knows she can do better. You actually going with her?"

Sam leaned his elbows on the corral. "My family is going. You heard them, and I am not about to let them go without me."

"I don't trust Madison."

"With reason?"

"With jealousy." He smiled with a self-acknowledgement. "I wasn't going to go."

"What changed your mind? Holly? or Clint?" Sam chuckled as he took back the cigarette for a long satisfying draw.

"Or you. Until we get this thing resolved with whoever is out to kill you, I am going to be your shadow."

"Finish the story from earlier about ones who came to kill me."

"Nothing significant was left out." He smoked a moment before he said, "Well, there was a shooting." He had leaned his elbows on the top rail also as he smoked.

"And?"

"And nothing. I killed a man. He was the one I saw as most dangerous. I let one of them go and, of course, my brother. Cole stayed out of it. I am still though trying to figure him out."

"Is he a back shooter?"

"I don't think so, but I've asked myself that question. He's a bit of a lone wolf is what it seems. He came with the two, and the plan was for one of them to brace you when you got to town. Brody was hot to kill. It didn't take much to get him to take me on first."

Sam let out a breath. "I won't say thank you."

"I didn't expect you would."

"Don't like another man stomping my snakes."

"I know." Vince smirked. "I also got a thousand dollars for doing it—when I go pick it up."

"He was wanted?"

"Adams told me the next day. Too bad I let the other one go. Adams thinks he was worth five hundred." He laughed. "Jackson, the other, will head right back to Pa. I don't know if I could have pushed him to fight me. He backed off though, and I couldn't just shoot a man down."

"No."

"So, I am glad you decided to go to this thing with Holly. It gives her the crew she needs and keeps you out of where the ones looking to kill you can find you."

"It might be Breanna won't go on with it anyway. She's an old woman now. Bitter but then she always was."

"What about the man she married?"

"I guess I should find out more about him."

"I'll talk to Adams about it. I know how you dislike all sheriffs with the exception of Cord when he was one."

"Didn't much care for it even then, but a brother is a brother, even one I didn't know was until years later. it's why I understand how you feel about Cole. You have other brothers though."

"Yeah, and one of them I don't have questions about. Asa was always mean as a rabid skunk and not because he had to but because he liked it. There's another, Jesse, but I haven't seen him since he was a child. They are half-brothers, like you with Cord but different—no closeness."

"Maybe." Sam took the cigarette again. "I will get an

agency to do some looking into Osbourne. It didn't matter to me before. Now it does."

"You smoking, Dad?" David asked as he came out of the dark.

"Bad habit, son." Sam smiled and handed the cigarette back to Vince.

"I tried it. Bull gave me one. Near coughed myself to death."

"Don't tell your mother about Bull. She'd not take well to that."

"And don't smoke," Vince said. "Lousy habit."

"Why do you do it?"

"I should break the habit. Maybe I will... sometime."

David chuckled. His voice had deepened from the last time Vince had seen him. "So you aren't really Uncle John," he said.

"Nope. Uncle Vince."

"Going to change it again?"

"Nope."

David looked then to his father. "We actually going to go on this archaeology whatever it is?"

"You said you'd like to."

"I never figured you'd agree. I thought the ranch was every-thing to you."

"No, Dave. It's not everything. You, your sister, and mother are everything." He smiled then. "Well, along with this galoot, Ollie, my brother, yeah a few others."

As Vince rode back to Tucson, he felt relieved that the old ease had returned between Sam and him. He had hidden his name, but Sam had accepted the reasons. Hearing Sam say he cared for him had given him a warm glow.

He thought then about the brother he was coming to know.

117

Could he trust him? Maybe and maybe not. Cole thought deeper than he had expected, but that might mean he was playing a role.

Riding past Holly's home, the lights were out. He didn't see a buggy. He hoped that meant all had gone well, and she was safely in bed.

At the stable, he gave Jupiter a good brushing, the oats he expected, forked in some fresh hay, while he told him what a good horse he had been.

Back at his hotel, he didn't have to wonder what Cole was doing. He was waiting in one of the chairs on the porch. "I thought you'd be back earlier," his brother said without rising as he watched him in that contemplative way.

"What'd you want?" Vince dropped into the chair alongside his. Two men sat at the other end of the porch. They looked asleep.

"Nothing, but I was worried about you."

Vince didn't like hearing that. He didn't want anybody worrying about him. Connections weakened a man, made him vulnerable. A caring man turned his back at the wrong time. He ended up dead. Still, learning to care for no one had been a steeper price than he'd realized. Seeing Sam with his family had made him more aware of what he had given up with his nomadic and dangerous life.

"Are we leaving Tucson after you get that reward money on Monday?" Cole asked.

"No. You can go when you want. I will be hanging around here until next week."

"Why?"

He wished he knew if he could trust Cole. He had to start somewhere. "I am going on an archaeology trip."

"Pot hunting?"

"I don't think so. Anyway it will last maybe through the summer."

"What about me?"

"What do you want to do? You can get a job here and wait until I return."

"Can't I go with you?"

"From what she said, it'll be hot and dusty work. In my opinion, add to it dangerous."

"A woman? That's the business the other night."

"More or less."

"I'd like to go. Never been around one of those. Might be educational." Again, that enigmatic smile.

Vince considered that. With his uncertainty regarding Cole's character was he better off leaving him where he might let his father and brothers know where he was-- or even more potentially deadly, tell them where Sam was. Or was he better off taking him and worrying about his back?

Finally, he nodded. One way or the other Cole could follow. Better, he be with him. "You'd have to do what Miss Jacobs said. It's science. She seems to know her stuff."

"Sounds good to me. I haven't had much schooling."

"Except the school of hard knocks," Vince said.

Cole laughed in that sarcastic way. "Except that."

Vince headed for his hotel room. He didn't necessarily believe Cole, but he realized that he wanted to. The idea of having a brother was surprisingly appealing to him, but if he was wrong about his brother's intentions, it could be a fatal mistake.

CHAPTER 10

Vernal, Utah

J eremiah Taggert looked up from the cowhide he was tanning to see Jackson come riding into the ranch yard. Where in blazes were Cole and Brody? He couldn't afford another foul up. It seemed the story of his life lately had been nothing but mistakes. The agreement to kill Sam Ryker wasn't one of those. Or had it been?

"What the hell happened?" he yelled at the spent man.

Jackson dismounted and stepped onto the wooden porch. "Your son is what happened."

"Cole?" He felt mystified at that. But then Cole always had him uncertain as to who the hell he was.

"Vince."

"Vince? I thought he was in Wyoming." He snickered at that. He had done what it took to let the right people know Vince's real name and get him out of that misspent hellhole, ending the ridiculous job as a sheriff. He had thought it would bring him home. What would that take?

"Vince was in Tucson and didn't take kindly to the idea of anybody killing Ryker. He got Brody to call him out, and he shot him dead."

Jeremiah had to suppress the smile. That boy had gumption. Damnitall, he needed him. He had counted on his first born someday to take over. He needed him, and what did he do—run off and only come back to see Valerie's grave.

"Vince is fast, Mr. Taggert. Real fast."

"Didn't kill you."

"He ain't a polecat, like some we both know, pardon me saying. Said he'd let me off if I was to leave. He didn't have to say it twice."

"Where's Cole then?"

"He stayed, I guess. I didn't stick around to find out."

"Hellation." He had to think about that. A weakness. Could it be exploited?

"What'd I hear?" Asa asked coming out from the house with a sour look on his face.

"Brody is dead," Jeremiah said. "Vince killed him."

Asa sneered. "I shoulda killed that bastard when he come to the ranch. Where is he now?"

Jeremiah sucked in a breath, lit a cigar, savoring the smoke. "I need to think," he said. "For now nobody do nothing."

Asa chuckled. "Don't take too long. I might not wait." He went back in the house.

Jeremiah saddled his gelding, Blasted, and rode to Vernal. He'd kept his reputation clean in Utah. Any jobs had been pulled away from his nest. It didn't matter. Someday they'd come after him. The world was changing. He gnashed his teeth. He needed Vince. He'd know what to do.

For awhile, a bank robbery now and again, one train holdup, it worked. Now the Pinkertons were on it. He'd heard they nearly got Butch. Miner was still in prison. The world was changing, and he didn't know what to do to fit in.

He cursed Valerie, who had turned his son against him. He thought about visiting her grave, but if he did, it'd be to curse her for what she did to him. Marry him, make him want her more than any woman he'd ever known. Then nothing he ever did satisfied her. Didn't like him robbing banks or trains. How the hell did she figure he paid for the food she ate? On that hardscrabble ranch, barely enough grass to feed a few cows. Cole had tried to make it pay, but the land wasn't good enough.

At the bar, he tied Blasted to the rail and went through the doors in a mood to slam somebody into the ground. Wasn't much fun being an old man. Sixty-one and too old to have the fun he used to. Too old for a woman or getting drunk. At the bar, he ordered a shot of whiskey and sat at one of the tables. When one of the girls came over, he whisked her off. He needed to think.

Sam Ryker deserved to be killed. He was as much an outlaw as Jeremiah. Why did Vince have to interfere? He ground his teeth with irritation. Tucson, huh. He ran his fingers over the butt of his revolver. The reason Asa, who was more rattler than human, hadn't killed Jeremiah was his uncertainty of how fast his pa was. He smirked. It'd been a few years since he'd had to prove it. Once he'd been as fast as Vince evidently was. No longer.

If he hoped to get the money for the killing, he couldn't send anybody else to do it. He'd go. he'd take his rattler son, the slow-witted one, and two others. That should do it. He smiled as he imagined the fight that had cost Brody his life. Not bad, son. Not bad. Now all he had to do was find a way to turn Vince back to him. There was still money to be made. He needed a strong right hand. He didn't have it, but he would.

Tucson

After a week-end of putting together supplies, Holly had called and sent word to her crew that she would like them to come to her home in the afternoon for some explanations as to what they could expect the work to be. A week and a half remained to get everything together. She would need it all.

Song had arrived earlier to prepare the evening meal. Zian would come with the others. She had only met him a few times. She hoped to gauge how seriously he would take the work. To avoid people going and then quitting, she would try to convey to them how hot, dusty and exhausting such an exploration of prehistoric sites could be. Anyone looking for excitement would be happier changing his or her mind.

Before the first arrived, Del was at the door. "I was picking up a shipment for us and saw this." He waved his hand toward the wagon.

When she saw what it was, she grew excited. "Thank you so much." The boxes were of two cases of dry plates, a case of development chemicals, a box with camera, tripod, hood, and another with dark room trays. She felt relieved they had arrived. She had begun to worry. Although photographs were not essential, they added a significant dimension to the reports she would write. They also added a level of work that likely only she could do.

In the field, developing would have to be done at night. If she took photos, every night she'd be developing the images or she'd lose them. She had taken classes at the university, but there had always been a professor to assist. Now she'd be on her own. She hoped the instructions with the camera would have needed details.

She followed Del to the wagon. He carried up the heaviest box, while she brought the lightest. When they were inside, she thanked him again.

"Would you like tea before you head back to Connie?"

"Actually I would. I was curious when I saw the boxes were camera gear. How does that fit into the work?"

She led him back to the kitchen. "Cameras are useful for documentation. There are times, say like with human remains, where you don't want to disturb them but would like a record of their positioning and any items with them."

"And the position matters why?" He sat and took the cup from her.

"It is one way to determine to which cultural group they belonged and even what period of time. For most of these regions, the current inhabitants came after the cliff dwellers had been gone, sometimes long gone. There are, of course, myths but how much of them are based on facts, real historic events. That is what an archaeologist hopes to learn. Burials vary quite a lot."

"You expect to find graveyards there?"

"Not in graveyards like we have, of course. The practices vary. Some though could be... grouped together." She tried to repress her shudder. Del's quizzical look said she had not succeeded. She carried a visual image from her dreams. She wanted to remove it from her life. Forcing a smile, she sipped her tea. On the Cibecue, she would know how accurate her dreams had been. The coming summer could provide her personal peace of mind. She hoped.

When the Rykers arrived, Del left but not before quick smiles and handshakes all around. "I made tea," she said. "Also lemonade. I'd like to wait for the others to arrive before I start to explain what I thought you would need to know."

Half an hour later, Zian, Clint and then Gabe arrived,

which left Vince. She was about to start without him when he came to the door with a man who, although narrower in build, resembled him.

"My brother Cole would like to work for you," he said as they entered the house.

"On the archaeology or security?"

"He'll be working for you. Archaeology."

She smiled at Cole and offered her hand. "Glad to have you join us. We can use all the help we can get." She led them back to the kitchen. Vince and Sam leaned against the counter, while the others sat at the long table. In moments, they all had a glass or cup; then looked at her expectantly.

"I believed you all would like to know more about what you will be doing." She felt nervous and tried to keep her eyes away from Vince. What must he think about all of this? Being a trader, he was more familiar than she, regarding the tribes in the region they would be going. He was probably more used to speaking to others explaining what he wanted. She would do the best she could.

"There are theories I have had about the people who lived in Central Arizona, well, for that matter, all prehistoric peoples in the United States. This trip will not be for taking away pots, art, or the tools we find." She smiled at Gabe as she knew that had been a concern of his.

"I have permission to take back a few objects that might be needed for proof of my theories and that will be all. I am privately funding this expedition, which means there is no university or organization, like the Smithsonian behind it. I deliberately chose this route rather than applying places where I might be forced to follow their procedures, some of which I disapprove of."

"What did that mean?" Vince asked. He had crossed one ankle over the other, looked relaxed; but since he'd left his gun on the side table by the door, she knew him well enough by now to know he probably was not.

"Many museums are more interested in acquiring items than documenting their grouping, possible dating, or even where they were found. I am interested in finding answers, not objects.

"The only place I applied for a permit was the Apache nation. These ruins are on their land although there is no reason for them to believe they have a relationship to those living there when the dwellings were built. Their permission came with a request that we leave things as we find them. The objects we document, when significant, will be reburied to protect them. With the few exceptions, I mentioned earlier, all I will be taking are notes, photographs, and drawings. Are any of you gifted in art?"

Abigail pointed to Alice. "She is. I am good at note taking. I guess I should have suggested Joe stay instead of sending him back to the ranch. He's the artist, and he's been teaching Alice. She has a talent for it."

"Wonderful. Now, I need to be sure everyone understands that an exploration like this will not be exciting or filled with momentous discoveries. Small things are what often tell the story. It will involved labeling what is found, those few things we would take need to be documented, and they will frankly not look at all thrilling. Each day can be backbreaking. Fingernails break if we had them. Blisters are worn until fingers grow calloused. The basic tools are pick, shovel, trowel, and knife. Sleeping will be in tents or out in the open. Song will prepare food for us, but it will be simple, easy to prepare dishes. Hearty food but nothing gourmet."

"More exactly, what are the things you hope to prove?" Gabe asked.

"That the people back then were more connected to each

other than has been believed. Trading may have involved not simply those in Mexico but also the Pacific Northwest."

"Montezuma in any of this?" Vince asked with a smile that suggested he found that amusing.

"You have then heard the stories," she threw back at him.

"Anybody, who has spent time with the tribes, especially those in New Mexico, the pueblo dwellers, will have heard their shamen tell the stories of when he came north to visit his descendents. Or even better-- came as a god. Some call him Push-a-ya or Pose-yemo. The tribes vary for the myths, but it all comes down to what the white man calls Montezuma."

Gabe gaze turned to Vince. "Myths are often true."

Vince nodded. "They can be... in a limited manner of speaking, but trying to prove that he was ever there is like Coronado leaving behind gold. He came through that region too... if you believe the stories."

"Gold." That captured David's interest.

"That rumor, with no proof, has damaged many sites," she said, shooting a glare at Vince. "It is an important reason to get to sites like the ones on the Cibecue, which have been mostly untouched. There it might be possible to find definitive evidence helping us better understand the people who built these dwellings."

Vince smiled at her glare.

"Surely you don't believe in gold being buried some-where," she said.

"About as much as I believe in men becoming gods. As to whether the leader of the Aztecs came to Arizona or New Mexico, I have no reason to believe or disbelieve."

"What about the trading that may have mixed together cultures in unexpected ways." She studied him trying to see if he remembered any of what she did. Did he have dreams? Was his being a trader today because he had been one nearly a thousand years earlier? Foolishness. She shook her head. She was out to prove a cultural truth by the artifacts left behind. None of this was her. Her dreams would be proven meaning-less—echoes from a past that never existed at least for her soul.

"Humans, in a tribe or not, still move around," he said his gaze meeting hers. "It's a free world, at least for some." The crooked smile was back.

She worked to concentrate as she explained some of the processes that they would use, the way they would divide a site and then label what they found. Most of it would make more sense when they were actually there.

"What about the dead?" Gabe asked taking a sip of the lemonade.

"We will probably find bodies. We will be respectful of them. It's why I wanted the camera."

"You know how to use it?" Clint asked.

"I've had classes." Which she hoped would be enough.

"Are you saying we can't keep what we find?" Zian asked.

"I am paying you well to leave what you find where it is— after noting its location and what was around it. You will each have one notebook-- more if you fill the first. There will be some small samples, but nothing a museum would pay to acquire. Sorry. This is about culturally looking into a people, who have gone but left behind evidence of who they were." She wondered if that made sense to any of them.

"I think it's going to be fascinating," Alice said as they all rose at the end of the meeting.

"I agree," she said. "There can be some interesting things at these sites and then, of course, the petroglyphs."

At the door, she stopped Vince as he was buckling on his cartridge belt. "Could you remain a few minutes?" she asked as the others exited.

He nodded. "Cole, I'll meet you for dinner in an hour at the Paradise Cafe." His brother nodded and left.

"What did you want?" Vince asked as she closed the door after virtually pushing Clint and Gabe out.

"I thought we should discuss the security aspects." It wasn't the whole truth. She wanted more time with him. "Song prepared something I can heat up if you can stay for supper, but I guess that won't work since you just said you would have it with Cole."

"No, it won't." His smile was reflective. "Maybe tomorrow."

"Good. Tomorrow, come in late afternoon. We can discuss plans, and you can have dinner with me. I know you like to eat what Song prepares." She wished she could have interpreted that enigmatic smile when he nodded. Regretfully, she watched him walk out the door.

When they spoke of security, she should urge him not to come. She understood, probably even better than he, what the risks would be for him specifically. Despite what she knew, what she wanted was very different. She was barely willing to let herself think of what she wanted.

Absentmindedly, she took the knife on the table and slit open the first of the camera boxes. On top was the manual. She would need to practice in the morning to be sure she could make it worth the difficulty of carting it safely to the site. She thought then of what she should photograph and smiled.

She realized, with almost a bolt of insight, that she didn't just want his photograph. It was a shock as she accepted what she did want. The question was—did she have the courage to make it happen. It would take more courage than going to the Cibecue.

After dinner, which was adequate with meatloaf and mashed

potatoes, Vince and Cole walked to the Pedrales where they brought a bottle and two glasses to a table. Vince poured them each a shot.

"You want to talk about it?" Cole asked as Vince took a sip of the whiskey and then pulled out a cigarette and lit it.

"What?"

"You know what. That woman."

"There's nothing to say."

"I saw it. She looked at you for approval of everything she said. The only time you weren't watching her was when you were checking out the two jaspers, who would like to be in your boots."

"I thought you didn't know much about women."

"I said I haven't had any I wanted to keep, not that I'd never known any. You know what's up with her too. What are you going to do about it?"

"Help her get through this summer, find what she's looking for, get her safely back here before I head north, and deal with Pa."

"Hmmm. Planning to die?"

"Maybe."

"Back to the woman. Forget Pa. Marry her."

Vince snorted. "She wouldn't have me."

"How do you know? Did you ask?"

"Cole, I won't be getting married ever."

"She's got money."

"Is that supposed to be a factor?"

"I never knew it to be a problem."

"It puts us on two different levels. So does her education. Not to mention she's too young. She'd not have me even if I were so inclined. But even more than that-- it'd never work if she would. She and I come from two different worlds. Those kinds of worlds don't mix."

'They will this summer. You could have her if you wanted."

"Change the subject. This is going nowhere."

"I don't think you should go see Pa."

"Not much better." Vince smiled. "Do you have anything upbeat to talk about?"

"Well... I liked what she said about going to the ruins. You ever been in any of them?"

"Not in but I've seen them."

"I like the idea of finding out about a people we never knew. Maybe they are more like us than we imagine. You ever think that way, Vince?"

"You are sounding more and more like a philosopher, Cole."

"You making fun of me?"

"Nah." He looked up then as Sam came through the door, looked around and then came to them. Before he sat down, he went back to the bar to pick up a shot glass, which Vince then filled.

"Not bad," Sam said as he sipped it. "Thought I might find you here."

"Any special reason?"

"Needed to get out of the house. Is that good enough?"

Vince smiled as he took a long draw on the cigarette before offering the pack to Sam. He shook his head with a regretful expression. "It's a bad example for Dave."

"True."

Sam laughed and then took one of the cigarettes. "My life though is full of those. He better find his own path."

"He looks like a strong kid. He will." Vince looked around the room. He had situated himself so that his back was against the wall. Sam then had taken the other seat, one Vince doubted he liked much more than he ever did.

Sam smiled. "I think of that too and yeah... I am counting

on you being my back. Hickok needed that in Deadwood that day, didn't he?"

Vince nodded. "I almost met him. He was in Elsworth before I was though. Heard talk of him. Nobody ever agreed what he was."

"Sounds about right," Sam said taking a big draw on the cigarette, letting out the smoke with a sigh of satisfaction. "You don't smoke, Cole?" he asked looking at him.

"Never took it up. Couldn't afford it."

"Smoking takes away a man's wind," Sam agreed but didn't stub out the cigarette.

"How'd you know I was thinking about having your back to the door?" Vince asked pouring himself another shot.

"It was on your face. I also notice you almost never do it. Me either... unless I am sitting with someone I trust."

Vince smiled. "I am glad you trust me after the lie."

"It wasn't one that mattered. Those are about who we really are. You didn't hide that."

"No, I didn't."

"It's what matters the most." Sam then turned to Cole. "I don't know you."

"Just that I'm Vince's brother."

"Yep and considering the rest of his family, that doesn't tell me much."

Cole's smile was ironic. "No, it wouldn't."

"Can he trust you?"

"Would you believe what I said?"

"I shouldn't since you evidently came to Tucson to kill me."

"It could look that way," Cole acknowledged.

"How else could it look?"

Vince smiled. Not hard to know why Sam had shown up. It wasn't accidental or casual. It came after he found out Cole was going to be on the crew. He was going to assess the risk. If there was one, Cole wouldn't live out the night. Vince trusted Sam's judgment as much or more than anyone in the world. It would answer his own questions.

"I came to Tucson to see you got into a gunfight where you ended up dead. I don't blame you for distrusting me," Cole said finally.

Sam stared at him through the smoke and sipped his whiskey. "You're right."

"What do you want from me now? A pound of flesh. Take it."

"I don't kill anybody in cold blood."

"Guess you and Vince are a lot alike."

Sam's smile was cold. "He's like my brother. Anybody wants to hurt him, and they go through me."

Cole chuckled.

"You thought that was funny?" Sam asked coldly.

"I thought it was familiar. I ran into it the night I saw Vince again. Pretty much what he said and did."

"In a fight, you'd not have been given a chance to stay out. I might've killed all three of you. He could be soft, and the evidence is he let you go."

"I wouldn't count on it," Vince retorted.

This time it was Sam's turn to laugh. "I won't. So back to you, Cole. Are you a danger to Vince?"

"Would you believe me?"

"Try me."

"I've never shot anybody in the back, which I reckon is your concern."

"There's always a first time."

Cole considered that. "I'd need a lot of motivation."

"Like money?"

"Survival."

Sam smiled, chugged the last of his whiskey, and rose. "All right." With that, he was gone.

"Looked for a little like he came to kill me," Cole said as he sipped the whiskey with a reflective expression on his face.

"He came to decide if that's what was needed."

Cole smiled for the first time. "Surprisingly, I like him. Glad you didn't let Brody kill him."

"It wouldn't have been as easy as he maybe thought."

"I see that."

CHAPTER 11

Vince had his own chores to get things ready for going north with Holly's crew. In the morning, he used the bounty money to order two new '94 Winchesters and five boxes of cartridges, plus 5 boxes of 45 Colts. Sam would have a good rifle. As far as he could tell, Cole had no interest in guns, and the rifle he had showed it. Whether he was a decent shot was hard to say, but when a man hesitated in using a weapon when needed, he often was better not having one at all. He didn't know about Clint or Gabe. Extra weapons could be important if things went wrong—something that happened too often in his experience.

"How long before they are here?" he asked Del when he walked him out of the store.

"Two days. Prescott or Phoenix will have them. You need a slicker or anything?"

"I'm fine."

"You keep an eye on that gal, won't you?"

"Holly?"

"Yeah. Connie and I have gotten real fond of her. She's got something going on, not sure what."

"I'll do my best."

Del nodded. "You're a good man."

Vince smiled. "Not so much, but I will do my best."

Two hours later, he had cleaned up, changed into a white shirt and vest before he walked up to Holly's home. Knocking on her door, he hoped she wasn't going to argue with him about guns or the rest of the things he felt would keep them all safe —if anything could.

When she opened the door, she smiled broadly. Her hair was pulled back and tied with a dark ribbon. The blonde mass hung down her back. Her green dress was a plain cotton.

Because he knew it made her uneasy, he took off his cartridge belt and revolver, placing them on the table. He hoped she would not expect him to go unarmed when they went north. It wasn't happening.

"How would you feel about discussing this in the back-yard?" she asked, sky blue eyes on him. He tried to read her expression but failed. In moments, she had led him into the yard. "It's such a wonderful day. Soon it'll be too hot to do this. Lemonade?"

"Sure."

The yard was full of colorful flowers, shaded by a large cottonwood tree. She gestured toward two chairs with a small table between them. When he sat, she went inside and came back with a tray, pitcher, glasses, and a plate of sugar cookies.

"I love this season in Tucson," she said as she filled the glasses. "Still some wildflowers, cactus blooming. Not sizzling hot. Perfect."

"It is nice," he said thinking it wasn't the only thing perfect, as he found it hard to take his eyes from her. She bloomed with her own glow that he guessed must be due to the coming trip. She seemed excited, even eager. Her enthusiasm led to his smile.

"Where do you call home now?" she asked, handing him a glass.

"Nowhere. I was born in Kansas, raised in Utah but for a lot of years, I've just moved around." The lemonade was perfect, tart and not too sweet. He supposed Song made it. A good cook would be a plus for this venture.

"I was born in Chicago. I could hardly wait to leave. Boarding school, college, and then here. I call this home now--a feeling I never really had before."

"How are things progressing in terms of getting all your equipment together?" he asked mostly because all the things he was thinking he shouldn't say.

"I do have one problem." She smiled. Again, he wished he could read the expression in those clear blue eyes. "I was hoping you'd help me with it."

"And?"

"The camera." She gestured toward where he now saw the black box, on a tripod, with its eye pointing directly at their chairs.

"You can't make it work?" He knew nothing about cameras and tried to think who would.

Her smile was amused. "I can, but I need a subject. I need to make sure it works before we go north."

"You don't mean..." He had never had his photograph taken. There had once been a man who had suggested he'd like to take some photos of him. He let him quickly under-stand the error of his thinking.

"I was hoping you would agree. I could then develop them and be sure I was doing it right."

"Why not photograph a flower?" He was uneasy at the idea of her taking a photo of him. He didn't know why. It was innocent enough.

"Not as challenging." She smiled sweetly. "Nor as interesting. Please, let me take your picture."

He let out a breath that he hadn't realized he was holding. It seemed foolish to say no. "All right," he said finally. He knew his reluctance had to show in his voice. It didn't deter her.

"Oh good." She quickly rose and headed for the camera where she thrust what looked like a slim box into the back. "This is the emulsion plate. It will be what the image forms on. That is, if this goes right." She looked up from her camera to study him. "Do you suppose you could kind of sprawl a little on the chair. Sort of spread your legs like you were before I suggested this, and you froze." She smiled.

He realized his breath was coming a little more quickly. Damn, he had thought they were going to be discussing guns. What was this? He did as she asked though. She studied him, with a surprising intensity. He supposed it was her challenge as a photographer—not that he had any reason to know. Then she moved to stand in front of him. "Your shirt looks well... a little uncomfortable. Do you mind?"

Before he could respond, she had moved between his spread legs and was unbuttoning the top buttons of his shirt. Her fingers brushed against his skin. She opened the shirt farther down than he felt a photograph needed. "What the hell?" he asked but she was already back at the camera. With the shirt spread apart, he felt the breeze on his skin, as though it was touching him. Everything about what was happening was making him increasingly uncomfortable.

She bent over the camera and positioned it. He was relieved when he heard the click. She quickly drew the plate out and inserted another. "You can't mean to take a second one?" he said starting to rise before she was back beside him.

"I would like to but let's try standing for this one. You know a different sort of lighting and background." She pulled him up and brought him to the cottonwood. Now he towered over her and was aware of her physical nearness in a way that had him breathing faster. Her innocence was going to kill him.

She took hold of his arms and moved him back against the trunk of the tree. "If you kind of leaned one shoulder against it," she suggested as she pressed her hand against his waist and moved him where she had indicated.

"Holly..."

She was gone and back at the camera, now moving the tripod and again pointing it at him. With the lens on him, he felt a strange sort of vulnerability-- even more than the times he'd had a gun pointed at him.

"You know," he managed, "some Indian tribes think having their picture taken steals their souls."

"Superstition, of course," she said. "Now stand still." Again, she snapped the button and took out the plate.

He moved away from the tree, but she wasn't done with him. "I was thinking if you moved to the sunny spot where I can better judge how it works there, you know with different light." She came to him again and reached for his shirt, freeing more buttons. "I think the vest should go." Before he could think of an argument, she had slid it from his shoulders.

"Perfect," she said stepping back and surveying her work with that strange smile. "Now, just let your hands go free at your side. Oh wait." She was back again and this time unbuttoning the cuffs of his shirt. "If they were folded up," and she was soon doing just that until his sleeves were at his elbows. "That looks more relaxed."

Damn, he was anything but relaxed when she again

centered the camera's eye on him. He let out a breath wishing he had a cigarette or a shot of whiskey. When the camera clicked, he sucked in a breath. "I should go," he said, but she was back.

"I am such a fraud," she whispered and this time she was putting her hands on his chest. "I wanted the photos but not for practice. I wanted them... I want..."

He had taken all he could. Before she could finish, he pulled her into his arms. He bent his head as she lifted her face to him. He pushed his tongue against her lips, spreading them and then delving within her sweet warmth. He felt her shock but then her quick response as she tentatively moved her tongue against his and then into his mouth. He moved his hands down her back, cradling her buttocks, thrusting her against his growing hardness.

"Do you know what you're doing here?" he asked as she shoved his shirt off his shoulders to hang from his pants.

Instead of answering, she pulled his head down for another kiss, this one deeper and more intense than the one before. His hardness against his jeans was becoming almost painful. If she didn't know, she was going to put him through hell.

"Beautiful," he whispered, when the kiss broke again, "you can't do this to me."

"Not out here anyway. The yard is fenced, but it's not... private enough." He looked into her eyes then and saw that she knew exactly what she was doing. Maybe she wasn't the innocent he had assumed. If it was what she wanted, he no longer felt capable of saying no.

In moments, he had followed her up the stairs to her bedroom. She turned then and smiled, that little girl smile that had him wondering if she was ready for what would come next. Before he could ask, she had pulled his shirt from his pants, letting it fall to the floor, and was running her fingers over his chest. She moved to his belly and touched the ridges before she got to his pants and undid the first button.

"Let's take this slow," he whispered as he moved her to the bed, sat her down, and began working on her buttons. There were a lot of them. As he undid each one, he touched and caressed her skin. Under the bodice, she had a cotton chemise, and he pushed that from her shoulders to reveal her breasts. They were as perfectly shaped as a woman's could be. He sucked on each nipple, bringing them to erect nubbins.

He unfastened more buttons and pushed her dress from her leaving her in a thin slip and pantalets. "You are so beautiful," he whispered as he caressed her breasts moving down to finally strip her and leave her gorgeous body open to him. "You sure you want this?" he asked even though he could see how flushed she was. He didn't need to touch her intimately to know she was aroused.

"More than you could know," she murmured. She pushed him onto his back and unbuttoned more of his pant's buttons. When his erection sprang free, she studied it with a fixed smile before she pulled his pants down. He pulled off his boots and stood for her to look at him, giving her every chance to say no.

She smiled and drew him back to the bed. Lying beside her, skin to skin, he had to get control of himself or this would be over before she got her satisfaction. It had been a long time since he'd made love, and he was more aroused than he ever remembered.

When she would have touched him again, her fingers on the line of hair that led to where he was painfully hard, he took her wrists and held them over her head. He had no idea how many lovers she had had, but he wasn't about to disappoint her. He worked to get his own body under control as he set out to drive her insane with desire.

He'd been taught by the best and that back when he had been little more than a boy. The whores his father had brought to him had told him what a woman wanted. Even when he'd been too young to have been sure it was what he wanted, he had been unable to say no. He was grateful now for the instruction as he played with her and had her writhing with desire and need.

"You want me," he whispered. She was hot and ready for him. He needed to move on this or he'd be going off without her.

"So much. Take me now, Ka-tah-yang," she whispered as he spread her legs and moved over her.

He positioned himself to enter her-- thrusting forward only to run into an unexpected barrier. He looked at her with shock, but she had her hands on his buttocks. Even if he had been able to say no, it was too late, and he thrust deeper, past the barrier, and then held himself still, aware of her warmth engulfing him.

"Are you hurt?" he asked trying to steady his breath and avoid going farther.

"Oh no, so good. Feels so good. She thrust up against him and then he lost all control as he went into her again and again, keeping himself back from his own release until he heard her cry out. When he let go, his body convulsed with a more powerful climax than he'd ever known.

He collapsed to the side, pulling her with him, still inside her. Her arms were around him. It was then that he realized tears were running down her cheeks. "I am sorry," he managed even though he knew she had wanted all that they had done.

"Those aren't sad tears," she whispered as she kissed his

chest, then took one of his nipples into her mouth. "Those are tears of joy."

"I didn't realize you hadn't done this before."

"Not in this lifetime," she said and he felt her smile against his skin.

"I am sorry, or I'd not have..."

"Good, because I wanted you to. I am twenty-five years old, Vince. My friends in school, some had lovers, but I didn't want them, didn't want it to be that way for me."

"You know I am not the marrying kind." He didn't want to hurt her.

Her laugh startled him. "Neither am I," she said and laughed again. "Does this mean we have to marry?"

"Not in my world."

"Not with the modern woman either. I didn't seduce you to get you to marry me."

He realized now that she had seduced him. She had known what she wanted before he had. "Why did you then?"

She lay back flat and put an arm under her head. Her blonde hair was now spread across the pillow. So soft, as he'd felt that first day. "I didn't want us to do this the first time up there. And I knew we would be doing it sometime, somewhere. I wanted it to be here and now. I set out to make it happen." Her smile was teasing. "I thought it might be the only way I could have you." Well, that spun his world upside down.

He lay on his back and laughed. Then turned back onto his side, one elbow under him as he looked at her naked body, so beautiful, so perfect and so full now with the flush of lovemaking. He ran his hand down her hip and then to her thigh. "And when did you decide this?" He wanted to take her again. Would she be too sore?

"It might have been from the first time I saw you. After I

got over being furious that you saved my life. It was for certain the first time I looked in your eyes, the night you came here for dinner. I can't say why, but I knew it had to be you."

"What about getting pregnant?" It hadn't been a thought in his head when he entered her, but it was now.

"Another reason why now was best," she said. "I just had my time. It is safe."

"Then..."

She turned toward him and put her hand on him, instantly causing the proof of his being ready again to be evident.

"What does this mean to you?" he asked with his last sane thought.

"That I wanted it to be you and now. There might not be a tomorrow for either of us. Now is all we have, isn't it?"

He couldn't deny it. Maybe she was as fatalistic as he was. He didn't care as he took her nipple into his mouth and began to suck. This was a gift, one he'd never imagined receiving. It wouldn't last, but he also wanted this moment.

Hours later, Holly woke. Vince was sprawled naked beside her, one of his legs thrown over her thighs. She smiled. It had been an impulse to use the camera to play with him, to tease him, to make him want her. She had wanted him wanting her so much that he wouldn't be able to say no, that he would be unable to resist. Maybe it had been a foolish thing for her to do, shocking even, but given the dreams she had had, she understood how little time they might have. She would take every moment she could have.

She realized then he was watching her. "When we made love, you called me Kata-yang or something like that," he said. "Is that someone you love?"

"Loved," she said, unaware she had used the word that had

been in her dream. She wasn't even sure she had said it right as the dream was so uncertain where it came to words. In that lifetime, he and she had communicated more by sign language than words. She had thought it meant he was her love.

"He's dead?"

"Let's get up. Would you like the dinner I promised you?" She smiled. Song had prepared food. She saw he wasn't satisfied with her evasion, but he let it go as they dressed.

Downstairs she heated up rice, chow mein, and spring rolls. "There is white wine in the refrigerator. Would you pour us some?"

He nodded. She knew he felt as mystified as in some ways she was. When he handed her the wine, she wished she could find words to explain what hadn't been an impulse, but was instead fated. It had been right for them to make love now, this day, this time. No games. It was what it was. He would not marry her. That was fine with her. She had no intention of marrying.

Making love had been better than she had expected. Some of the girls she had known said it was fine, if a man knew how to do it. She guessed, he obviously knew how to do it. Smiling, she put the food and soy sauce on the table even as she felt it was so strange to do such routine things when her day had been anything but routine.

"Can you spend the night?" she asked as they ate.

"I should not. Not if we want to keep what happened today a secret."

"I suppose that would be best." How did he see what had happened? Two souls came together in a fiery collision. She didn't want to keep any part of it a secret. She wanted to shout it to the skies. She recognized that was not intelligent. An archaeological excavation required people to work closely together. She and Vince would have to be careful.

She remembered then the plates. She needed to develop them. Of course, she needed to be sure she did it right, but there was more than that. They might be all she could keep of him. "I should go get the plates," she said rising, hardly having eaten. "They need to be developed tonight."

"Do you need my help?"

"Not all. I suppose, your going would be best."

He rose. He hadn't eaten much more than she. "I want you to know... this was special for me." He hesitated. "That word doesn't do it justice. It went beyond anything I have known. I know it was this one time, with no promises, but..."

She stopped him by putting her hands over his lips. "Can't we see what happens? Of course, on the Cibecue, we can't... well, not with others so close, but do we have to plan out what comes next?"

"When it's over, when you are back safely in your home, I will have to head north." He walked to the hall and picked up his belt and holster as he turned to look at her.

"You won't ever come back to Tucson?" she asked as she reached up to button his shirt to the place it had been when she had begun stripping him.

"I don't know. Let's take it as it happens. I will help you get what you want, keep you safe." He laughed then. "We did forget to talk about that."

"Blame me," she teased as she touched his cheek and then let her hand drop. "I have no regrets. I hope you don't either."

"No. I didn't expect it. It was a gift though. He buckled the cartridge belt around his hips, tying down the holster. "Maybe we can talk about the security tomorrow."

"We don't need to," she said. "I trust you with that. I am arranging for a wagon and a team. I am not sure where we can camp, but I guess I don't need to know, do I?"

He smiled then. "No, you don't." He bent then and kissed

her lightly on the lips. He lifted his head. "If you need me, I am at the San Xavier. Leave a message or... Well, I'll be back whenever you need me."

She watched him walk off. She would need him for the rest of her life. She closed the door and headed for the plates. She tried to remember the steps that would be required to develop them into something that would last... forever. yes, think of the work. If she did that, she could manage.

An hour later, she had the negatives drying. She sipped a glass of wine as she waited remembering what it had been like slowly to see his face appear in the liquid. She was unsure how many hours she had sat looking at the final images. There was him sprawled in the wooden chair looking at ease when she remembered he had been anything but.

He had had no idea she had intended to seduce him from the moment she had seen him at the door. No, from way before. From the moment, she had had half a chance. It was going to happen between them. She would waste no time with what was proper—never again. She no longer cared about proper.

Making love to him had been better than she had imagined. They had made love three times, learning as they went each other's bodies. Each time had been better. She did feel some soreness. There had been a little bleeding, but nothing that hadn't been worth what she had experienced.

Ka-tah-yang she had called him in the height of her emotion. The trader had used it. In her dreams, she had thought it meant lover, beloved, something like that. He was all of that. She had never actually believed in love at first sight. This was not. It was lovers rejoined.

Hours later, lying in her bed, Holly stared up at the moon. It was high in the sky, not yet full. The patterns she could see reminded her of the ancient Aztec myth that she had studied in college. Coyolxauhqui, the moon goddess, ever to be in the moon as a punishment.

Staring at the golden orb, she could almost see the shapes that had been in the artifact she had viewed years before. The traveling exhibit had illustrated how a mythology worked into the physicality of a culture. Sometimes the stories were mixed into the art, often quite cruel when they involved the Aztec culture.

Was she the woman who would be cut in pieces? Destroyed by her love? Or was it her lover? There was no answer to that. She could only go forward. On the Cibecue, she would find her answers. Except, was the price going to be higher than she was willing to pay?

CHAPTER 12

The dream was the most violent she had had in months. The worse part had been that the face no longer was the man from long ago. It was Vince's. She had seen him near her. He smiled. Hearing something, he had turned. There were shots, he had out his gun, then staggered, falling back against a rock. She had bent to him, uncaring for her own life. His eyes were open and staring. He was dead.

Her scream wakened her. Eyes open, staring into the darkness, she had been relieved the night was still. It hadn't happened. He wasn't dead. He could not go with her to the Cibecue. Fate waited for him there. She had to stop him.

In the morning, Holly made coffee. She was torn by conflicting emotions. She wanted him up there in the place they had known joy. If he came, it would be to his doom. She had to stop him.

Sipping the coffee, she considered how she would do it. He was a stubborn man. She hadn't known him long, but she knew that. What he set out to do, he would finish. It would take harsh, even brutal words to turn him from his path.

Knowing what she had to do, she rang the hotel. "Can you get a message to Vince Taggert?" she asked the clerk.

"You're in luck," the man said and she heard his raised voice. "Taggert. Call for you."

In moments, it was Vince's deep voice, sounding a little surprised when he heard her voice. "Can you come here today?" she asked. She would not tell him this over the phone. She knew now how she would convince him not to go. It had to be done in person.

"I was on my way to breakfast with Cole."

"Come right after, please?"

"Sure."

After she hung up the phone, she felt almost sick. She went back to the counter to look at the negatives. She had these. They were all she would ever have. One way or another, she would keep him alive.

Less than an hour later, she heard the knock at her door. She was eager to get this over. He'd never forgive her. That didn't matter as much as keeping him alive.

To her annoyance, it wasn't Vince but Clint Madison. "I thought I should check in to see how things were going," he said. She stood in the doorway, not wanting him inside.

"It is fine, but I am busy, Clint. I would invite you in, but I have a business meeting soon."

"Oh." His tone was disappointed. He turned then as she looked beyond him to see Vince walking up.

"Good morning, Taggert," Clint said with a polite, disinterested tone.

"How are you?"

"You must be her business meeting."

Vince looked beyond him to Holly standing in the door. His gaze met hers. "Could be."

"We should get to it," she said before she reached out and

pulled Vince past Clint, into the house, and shut the door firmly.

"Would you like coffee?" she asked trying to keep her voice level.

"Sure."

In a few moments, they were seated across from each other in the kitchen. He took a sip of the coffee, those dark eyes on her but giving away none of his thoughts.

"I do not want you to come with me to the Cibecue," she said. There was only one way to do this and it was quick and brutal.

"And the reason being?"

"We made love. You seduced me into it. I should not have let you." She rose and walked to the counter, not looking at him. "It changed everything. I don't want you on the excavation where others would know. It was a mistake. I am going to fix it."

There was a moment of silence and then a laugh.

She looked at him with shock. "I mean it."

He smiled and rose to come to her. "I know. Now tell me the real reason you don't want me there."

"I did."

He shook his head and pulled her into his arms. "No, you didn't. You are also a terrible liar. I believe you don't want me there. Now tell me why."

She could not stop the tears. He pulled her back to the table, sat on the chair again, and drew her onto his lap. His arms around her increased the fervor of her tears. When she finally could stop, she sniffled and looked up at him. "I am sorry."

"It's all right." His tone was warm and caring. It was all she could do not to cry again. "Tell me everything."

"You will die up there."

"And you know this why?"

"You will think I am idiotic."

He tilted her head up where she was looking directly into his eyes. "Tell me anyway. I will listen."

"Can we... go outside?"

"Sure although let's not get distracted this time by me seducing you." His smile was humorous. "I want to hear all of this and from the beginning."

They sat on the same chairs they had before they had made love. The air was warm but not hot and overhead two cardinals were dancing over the branches with their unique melodic song.

"No delaying, Holly. I need to know what is going on."

She sniffled and couldn't look at him. He would think she was insane. Maybe she was.

"Since I was thirteen, I have dreamed of the ruin I expect to find there. I dreamed of another lifetime lived there. In the dream, there was a girl with a family. They grew some crops, lived in a three story building with twenty or so other people. One day, from the west, a stranger arrived. He was taller than us, his features more... rugged. We knew he had come from a long way. What he wanted was to trade. He brought with him trade goods, carved bone and wood items. His tongue was strange even though he spoke several languages. To begin he used sign language to get us to understand what he wanted."

She looked to see what he made of that. "Go on," he said watching her with those dark eyes, the ones she had seen through many lifetimes.

"The man, he and I... well, we were attracted to each other. My family did not mind because the trader was also a warrior. He carried a bow and arrows. We had never had anything like that as our men used axes and spears. There had been threats... Well, the community wanted him to stay. He could help us against the ones we knew were attacking other villages."

"And you saw this place, these people repeatedly."

She nodded. "Over the years, there would be pieces of it and eventually I put the whole thing together. It got to where I could hardly understand what had been happening in my real life and what was in the dream."

"And this ruin is where you want to go."

"Yes."

"Tell me the rest."

"The trader and I... we fell in love."

"He's why you called me Kata-yang when we made love."

"Yes."

"There is more." He reached out and drew her from her chair to settle her onto his lap. She stroked his neck with her fingers. She liked sitting on his lap. She had never done it before with any man, not even her father. It gave her a feeling of empowerment to be connected to this man in such an intimate way. He was so strong. Maybe it would be different, but no, the dream man had also been powerful.

"I watched the man I loved being killed, time and again. A spear through his heart." She suppressed the tears. "I saw his dead eyes looking up at me. We buried him. I have since buried him again and again."

"And despite that, the violence there, you wanted to go back." It wasn't a question.

"I wanted to know if it was true. There would be things there that could confirm that my dream had a physical reality behind it."

"Reincarnation." It wasn't a question.

"Yes or was it all imagination? If when I am there, I don't see the ruin as I remember it, if there is not a pot in the back of one room, a pot with items in it, which we left maybe when we had to abandon our home, if..." She had to struggle to get the words out. "If there isn't a grave where it would be under the manzanita trees."

"You will think it only a dream."

"And if it's all there, than I will believe there was such a life, and I lived it."

"There are other possible reasons for such a dream. Maybe you are feeling past life energies but not from one you lived, but instead from one that existed."

She sniffled. "I suppose." She did not believe it, not with it being so vivid.

"You think I was the man." It wasn't a question.

"I knew it the first night you came to the house. It's your eyes. But... it wasn't until last night that I dreamed it was you being killed up there. It wasn't the man this time. It was you."

"And it's why you don't want me going."

"It will be your doom." She felt his hand stroking soothingly down her back.

"It takes a lot to kill me."

"It can be done though."

"Anyone can die."

"In the dream last night, you and I were together. You heard a sound and turned, the bullet struck you in the chest. You fell. Your eyes were dead. All the life had gone from them. It had been the same with the trader." She began to cry again.

"All right." His hands stroked her hair. She had pulled it back with combs but it hung down her back. He tangled his fingers in it. It was soothing to her shattered emotions to be petted by him.

"You can't go," she said when she could. "You understand why now."

"I understand your fear. But I will go, and we will face this together. If this was a past life, not sure I believe in such, but if it was, why don't we make it right this time."

"What does that mean?"

"We go up there, find what you need, and we both walk away alive and by choice. You aren't driven out, and I am not killed."

"But..." His fingers on her lips stopped her words.

"You don't think I'd let you go there alone, do you? Even if you had meant it about the lovemaking being the reason, I would have gone. I won't let you go into that region without me. This will not be on you whatever happens."

"I don't want you to die."

He brushed a tear from her cheek. "Neither do I."

"Then you must stay away from the Cibecue."

He shook his head. "No, I don't, but we will both go knowing more. We may not be able to have a happily ever after, but for this summer, we will be a team."

She began to cry again. He held her, not saying anything, softly stroking her hair. When she finally could stop, she whispered, "Do you want to make love?"

He kissed her forehead. "I will always want to do that, but we aren't going to. Not now anyway."

"Why not?" she sniffled and raised her head to stare into his face. He had such a wonderful face, those bones, the strong nose and most of all that kissable mouth. She wanted his body, wanted him, wanted all they could have.

"Because you are stressed. I have things to do. And if we are going to be a team, let's make it one of friends."

"I can't believe I heard you say that."

He laughed. "Me neither. Now I have a few things I want us to do before we go north. One of which is to assure myself you can handle your horse. If you can't, we are getting you another."

He was so arrogant. So pushy. Even when she knew he was right, that annoyed her—at the same time it attracted her. "All right," she agreed reluctantly. "I will need to get changed if you mean to do it today."

"I do, and I mean for you to ride astride. No riding skirt. I need to see how you handle a horse, and I want to know your horse better. That means, you ride Jupiter, and I'll take your mare."

"Why?"

"That thing she pulled with running when you hadn't given her the signal, she might do it again. I want to know."

"Shouldn't I ride her?"

He grinned and lifted her into his arms as he rose. "No, I should do it. You get changed into britches. I'll be back in half an hour with both horses."

She opened the door and he carried her into the house. His arms were so strong, so firm, so... "You sure you don't want to make love instead?" she asked as he set her on her feet.

"Positive."

"I could seduce you," she suggested.

He laughed. "I am more onto you now. It won't be so easy."

"I might like to try."

"And someday I might like you to try but not today. I like your neck as it is and don't want it broken by the wrong horse. Get ready." He kissed her forehead again and was out the door before she could think of another argument.

At the stable, Vince saddled both their horses, adjusting Princess's stirrups to his long legs. Before he could ride the mare out of the barn, Cole showed up. "Where are you going?"

"Taking a ride with Holly. I need you to head to Sicilla's and see if our order came in?"

"What order?"

"Does that matter?"

"No. You already paid for it?"

"I did. Take the boxes to my hotel. And to satisfy your curiosity, it is two rifles and plenty of cartridges."

"You expecting trouble?"

"I always expect trouble."

With that he rode to Holly's home and was satisfied that when she came out to meet him, she was wearing the britches he had suggested. She wore a sensible brimmed hat with all that beautiful blonde hair stuffed up inside. God, she looked good with the pants. He almost changed his mind about her offer to make love. Almost.

He dismounted and tied the horses' reins to the front fence. "You sure I shouldn't ride Princess," she asked as she looked at his big gelding.

"Later." He lifted her into the saddle and then adjusted the stirrups to the proper length. "Did Ollie tell you how to put your boots in the stirrups?"

"Heel down, and only my toe in the stirrup."

"Good. Too far in and you could be dragged if you were thrown. Form the habit even with a horse like Jupiter."

"Did you name him?"

"Nah, I'd have called him something like Brownie. Now, he will do whatever you want. He wants to do that, but don't send him mixed signals."

"Which means?"

"Don't sit all stiff in the saddle or yank on the reins when you don't mean it. Try to relax."

She managed a small smile. "It's not easy. I am not like Abby or Grace, easy in the saddle. I did a lot more buggy riding than horseback in my life."

"And maybe you will need to ride the wagon heading

north, but let's see how much of your nervousness is not getting a feel for the horse, and how much is Princess not being a stable mount."

"Is it safe for you to ride her?" she asked.

"Lady, you do find a lot to worry about," he observed as he mounted Princess.

"Might as well know it now," she admitted.

"Okay, let's get started."

"Where are we going, not that it matters."

"How about Sabino? Have you been out there much?"

"A few times."

"Give him a nudge in the side, just enough to tell him what you want." When she touched the heel of her boot to Jupiter, he responded with a nice walk. Perfect.

Vince had confidence in his horse but realized he was more worried about her on him than he had expected. This was not good. He knew a man should never care too much about another. It could get him killed. Except, it was too late for him where it came to this woman. Knowing it could never work between them, didn't change a thing where it came to what he felt. Hopefully, after the summer, he would be able to go away and not spend his life mourning over what he couldn't have.

Princess was jitterier than he liked, but she was responsive to his slightest movement. High spirited, maybe a little nervous, but then she had probably gotten a scare too when she had started to run and had Holly picked from her saddle.

Looking over he saw Holly was stiff. "You need to relax," he said.

"How can I? I am on a horse that is so tall." She managed a smile, and he gave her full credit for the attempt.

"What's the worst that could happen?"

"I'd fall off."

"If you do, roll with it. No reason to get hurt by falling off a horse... well, unless you land on a big rock." He did see a few of those alongside the dirt road as they headed east to Sabino.

"I don't have a feel for this."

"You don't have to. You need to understand that a horse, like Jupiter, wants to please you. He is waiting for you to tell him how. Sending mixed signals confuses horses." He tried to think how to get her to relax. Most of his best ideas were impossible.

"How far should we go this first time?" she asked obviously eager to turn around.

"Look around you, beautiful. See that cactus over there. Brilliant red, a barrel and in bloom already."

She looked over and for the first time had a real smile. "Yes, and beyond the saguaro too."

"The desert is a garden."

"I can tell you are a salesman," she said as she began to sit more easily on the horse.

"Traders have to be."

"You really don't have a home?"

"Why would I need one? The sky is my roof, the ground my bed. I can build a fire and cook a meal, be gone in the morning."

"What about when it rains?"

"One benefit of deserts."

"You don't use even a tent?"

"What for? I have a tarp if it's needed and can rig up a temporary shelter." In the right locations anyway.

"What about when a storm turns violent and there is lightning?"

He laughed then and shook his head. "I try to stay out of gullies and high places and take my chances. So far so good."

"I can't imagine living that way."

RAIN TRUEAX

"You don't need to. I suppose you grew up in a mansion."

"I guess you'd call it that. My father was a banker, who owned several. He never enjoyed anything he had though, not anything. It was never enough."

"Sad."

"Which proved to me that money doesn't solve anything. Although I admit it's handy for something like this, where I can afford to do this trek and not have to ask someone else to fund it or control it."

"It may not solve everything, but it gives some security."

"You don't have security or money?"

"I didn't say that. I actually do have some money in a bank account. Trading can be lucrative, and the way I do it has low costs attached. I don't though have the kind of money you grew up with."

"It wasn't all that perfect a life. My father got his money from my mother when they married. He mistreated her, and she lost control of her wealth through the laws that favor a man with marriage."

"So it's why you didn't want to marry."

"Some of it. I have seen other reasons. Some states do let a woman control her own estate when she marries, but other places don't even let her control her income if she works as a waitress. It's all under the man's power."

"Geesus, you are a little bitter there, aren't you?" He was purposing to keep the conversation going in a way that took her mind off the horse and onto something else. He could see her relaxing, and Jupiter liked it a lot better than the tight hand on the reins.

"Actually, as much as he could be, my father was good to me. I was the one he counted on to take it all over. I have a sister, Lily. She got the worst of it. Father saw me as the intelligent one and his heir for the businesses. Lily was the one to take care of him and run the household staff. It didn't make it easy for Lily or me."

"I didn't have much family life but the one good thing in it was my stepmother. She's the one who taught me to read and about the Bible. Seeing what she went through has made me understand why a woman would reject marriage."

"I guess it depends on the man. Some are selfish bastards. Sorry for the word."

He grinned. "No, it fits. I guess all men can be. Not saying I am an exception either."

"You are trying to help your brother, Sam, me. You do sound like an exception."

"Don't count on it." He laughed. "You are doing much better in the saddle. Remember don't pull on the reins. You confuse him. One hand on your thigh and the other firmly holding the reins but not pulling on them. You use them when you want to encourage him to do something. He's trained to a hackamore, not what I put on him today for you, but I use it. He knows what I want by the light touch of the reins and how I lean."

"Did you train him?"

"To that. He had a good temperament. Okay, pull Jupiter to the side of the road and stop him. Good. Stay here. I need to find out something about your mare. Keep the reins firmly in hand. Don't let him turn to go with us. Princess and I are going for a lesson."

He turned the mare back toward the town to see what she would do. When she started to pick up her pace, without his signal, he leaned back and talked to her, pulling on the reins and turning her to the left and circling. When she obeyed that, he pulled her to a stop and then back toward Holly. Almost there, he turned Princess again. This time she walked. "Good girl," he said as he patted her neck.

Bringing her back to where Holly and Jupiter waited, he said, "I think she will be okay when you get easier with her. She is nervous, but the longer she's ridden, the better that will go. How do you feel about doing some trotting?"

"I guess." She sounded uneasy, but he felt the sooner she rode at a faster pace, the more confidence she would have in herself and the horse. When they began a slow trot, he saw she had been trained to use her knees correctly.

"You actually have a good seat," he complimented her. Jupiter had a better gait than Princess, but she wasn't rough to ride. "Want to go faster?"

"Do I have to?" she gave a nervous laugh.

"No, but the sooner you ride him at a run, the better you will feel. The road ahead is clear. Give him a stronger nudge with your heels and lean forward, let him go. When you want to stop, pull back a little on the reins and straighten a little. He will get the message. Remember to ride with your knees. You are meant to be on this horse, and he wants to please you."

As she obeyed and Jupiter took off, he gave Princess a kick to stay with them. She wasn't as big a horse as Jupiter, so it required him riding her faster. When Holly pulled Jupiter to a slow walk, he made Princess circle and then brought her alongside the gelding. "How was that?" he asked.

She laughed. "Better than I expected." She stroked Jupiter's neck. "Good horse," she crooned.

"See how well he responds," Vince said. "He'll follow you anywhere when you treat him right."

'Does it work with men?" she asked with that teasing smile.

"You already know it does."

"Handy to keep in mind." Her smile turned sensual. "You don't mean we can't make love before the end of the summer."

He did, but he doubted he could stick to it when she said it

162

in that tone. "I don't want to get you pregnant," he said as he let out a breath.

"I don't either."

As they rode back into town, he wondered if Sicilla's sold condoms. He hoped Holly wasn't reading his mind. He had used them before when he wasn't that sure about the health of his partners. Mostly he had only had sex with whores with a few exceptions of women who had come onto him and made it clear they knew what they were getting—which was a man who would ride off sooner than later. His life was too filled with risks and the need to move on. He'd tried many things in life. What he had never tried was staying when it meant one woman. It's something he would never know.

He felt angry at his thinking. It was how it had to be. He had things to do. She did too. There was no room for anything between them. He wouldn't buy the condom. It would make weakness too easy. What he had to do was stay away as much as he could until they headed north—and then sheer numbers would protect him from his own weakness.

CHAPTER 13

Vernal, Utah

Jeremiah sent Jesse to town for the two men he wanted. Two days earlier, he had sent Asa on an errand that should keep him away long enough. He had did decided that he didn't want him going on this one.

He was in his bedroom, stuffing clothing into a bag when he heard the outside door slam. Asa stood in the door. "Why didn't you tell me about this?"

"I thought you were gone."

"I am going with you. I know what you are up to."

Not all of it. Jeremiah suppressed a smile. He didn't trust this son. He liked to kill too much. He would never understand why it had gone that way. It seemed to have been the case from the beginning.

"I don't need you this time," Jeremiah said. "You keep an eye on the ranch while I'm gone."

Asa's smile was snide. "You can argue all you want old

man, but unless you are ready to take me on with your Colt, I am going."

Jeremiah considered that. When he'd been a younger man, he might've considered it. Now he was sixty-one and couldn't likely take Asa, who had practiced with guns since he had gotten old enough to heft one.

"All right. But you do what I tell you when we get to Tucson."

"Sure." Jeremiah didn't miss the sneer. He sighed as he shoved the last shirt into the bag and closed it. Vince could take care of Asa. Once he got his oldest son back into the saddle with him, it would all be better.

He had lost his purpose. It hadn't begun with Valerie's death but after that, he'd felt lost. He missed her. God, how he missed her. She was so beautiful, but why was he never enough for her? Why had she sickened and then died. He was sure she had come to hate him and yet she never left. She stayed with him and the boys.

He forced her from his mind. When he had his ramrod, then he'd be fine. He could do what he needed to do. It was like the story she'd read them about the true son. Vincent was his oldest, flesh of his flesh in a way none others had been.

Maybe it was because of how much he had adored Agatha —his tall, beautiful Amazon of a wife. Why did she have to die bearing his son? Agatha had been the one to laugh and ride with him—his true partner. Valerie, a delicate flower, the love of his life, was also never satisfied with anything he did.

He sighed. Always it went that way, round in circles.

"What are you thinking, old man?" Asa asked as they walked out of the house.

"Looking forward to being on a horse again." He didn't look at Asa.

"How many men we taking?"

"Besides you and Jesse, just Brewster and Boggs."

"Ain't Brewster getting kinda old? Why not Jackson?"

"He won't go. I talked to him. He said if Vince saw him again, he'd kill him."

Asa snorted. "We'll see about that. I'll take out Ryker, and then we can get paid off."

Jeremiah nodded as he began saddling his gelding. "Mrs. Osbourne will be in Tucson. Her agent told me we'd get paid there. We will have to go out to the Ryker ranch now, but that's all right. You'll take Jesse, Brewster and Boggs to do that."

Asa swung into the saddle. "Why not you too?"

"I'll wait in Tucson in case you miss him."

They rode out the gate. They would pick up supplies in Vernal. Jeremiah didn't figure to make this a fast ride down. He had been soft, not on horseback enough. He'd need to limber up. Asa would be biting at the bit, but he knew how to slow him down. His saddlebags held four bottles of whiskey. He grinned. Nothing about what was going to happen would be like Asa would be expecting.

Tucson. Yep, all he needed was his good right arm. When he had him, it'd be back like it was. Agatha's son wouldn't disappoint him as the other three had.

Tucson

"Are you sure we can leave in two days?" Abby asked as she helped Rose and Holly with the evening meal at Rose and Ollie's home.

"Everything is ready. I will know for sure when the rest of the crew arrives, but I see no reason to wait. May 1 should be perfect. The sooner we get there, the better."

166

"It will help with Sam. He's restless whenever he's not active."

Rose took a large ham from the oven. "I will miss you all. It will be so quiet here."

"Royce keeps you busy," Abby said.

Rose grinned. "And Ollie." Her smile widened.

"You two are so perfect together," Holly said. "I knew you would be."

"You were right."

Hearing horses outside, Holly felt a jolt that she hoped she had suppressed. Her disappointment rose when it was not him. Vince had not been near her alone, since their horseback ride. When he did come for any needed business, it was with Cole.

When she told him it was going to take two wagons, he had argued that it made the expedition look more important, potentially drawing trouble to it. Her point had been there was no way to have the tents, blankets, clothing, cooking gear, equipment for the dig itself, and enough food in only one wagon-- not for eleven people, some who would be working hard and need hearty meals.

Tonight, she would suggest moving up the date of leaving. She hoped it would work for everyone. Well, except for Vince. She still hoped he would change his mind. It was unlikely, but the way he had been avoiding her, perhaps he already had.

An hour later, the dinner had been consumed. Everyone but Vince had arrived. Cole had said his brother would be late. Sitting on the porch with Abby and Alice, she saw him riding up. Even if she hadn't recognized his face, she could never mistake the hell for leather way he rode. It was no surprise he was friends with Sam, who had the same way with a horse.

Pulling up by the corral, Vince talked to Sam who had come down and then the two walked up to the house.

"Sorry," he said to Rose. "Sheriff Adams asked me to give him a hand. I couldn't hardly say no."

"Doing what?" Ollie asked as he handed Vince a glass of beer. "Cold even," the older man said with a grin.

"It is." He took a big sip and smiled. "How'd you pull that off?"

Holly couldn't take her gaze from him, but he didn't look at her. He looked tired, as though he was worn to the bone, thinner than he had been. What had he been doing?

"Idle hands are the devil's work," Sam chuckled.

"He didn't have anything else to do; so he got the keg and the ice." Ollie laughed. "Be good when he gets going. Edgy as they come, waitin' around."

"There is no reason to wait," Holly said. "We have all the supplies. I think we should go Wednesday. We are all edgy."

"Sounds good to me," Clint said from where he was leaning back against the wall with his own cold beer.

With everyone talking at once, asking what they needed to do at the last minute, she watched Vince even as she answered questions. Something seemed wrong, but he wasn't addressing it.

She rose and walked to him. "I will need to talk to you tonight. Can you come by the house?"

For the first time, his gaze was on her, his eyes glittering. "What time?"

"When you leave here. I am going now."

"You come with Madison?"

"I rode Princess and came with nobody. You did a good job with her. She is a different horse. I was surprised that one such ride did so much."

His smile was tired. "I might've taken her out a time or two or three this week."

"Might've?"

"Did."

She knew then what she was going to do. He did care about her. He had worn himself out fighting it, but he did care. When he came by the house, she'd fix the problem between them. She didn't disagree regarding a future together. It wasn't in the cards. It didn't take a Tarot reading by Connie to tell her that, but they could fix the karma that had ruined other lifetimes. "I will see you later then," she said and walked into the house to tell Rose she was leaving.

Clint waylaid her on the way back out. "Can I see you home?"

"Not necessary," she said and glanced over to see Vince's gaze on them before she turned back to Clint. "I hope you can leave your clients without them turning to other lawyers. If you have had any second thoughts on coming for the whole time, I will understand."

"None and Angus will look after any problems. I'll be back in Globe a time or two to check for wires if there are questions. I am looking forward to time in the mountains with you."

Gabe came to stand with them. "And with me, of course, compadre."

Clint managed a smile. "Of course."

Holly smiled her good bye, walked down to the corral, and slid her skirt off to reveal her pants. She bundled the skirt into a saddlebag, tightened the cinch, and mounted Princess, feeling more and more secure.

Princess responded well as they headed back to town. The idea that Vince had taken her mare out, making sure of her dependability warmed her heart. He had done it all with no seeking of thanks. While he might not see himself as a noble man, she knew he was and on levels, which men like Clint Madison would never reach. Vince was a man who would do whatever it took to protect those he loved. If she had wanted to marry, it would have been a man like him. Marriage wasn't right for her, but she would be his lover. He would come to accept that.

Because having children wasn't something she saw for herself, she had visited Sicilla's store and bought something she had been told about in college. A condom. Connie had smiled at the purchase. She reminded Holly that they could be reused but not more than a few times. Holly had purchased four. It would be a long time in the mountains. While it would not be easy to find time alone, once Vince understood how it was going to be, they would find a way. Then there were her safe times. She was pretty regular and knew based on the lunar cycles when it would be safe.

At the stable, she tended to Princess and gave her a fork of fresh hay before she headed back to her home. Probably, she should not feel as confident as she was about how it would be. She and Vince barely knew each other in this lifetime, but the soul connection, that was what made her confident of the man, of their love. He would be her lover for as long as it was possible. If that was morally wrong in the eyes of some, she could live with that too. She knew what mattered most-- making it right this time. Perhaps they'd get a future lifetime where it could be for the two of them.

It was almost an hour later when the knock came at her door. She had changed into one of her light cotton dresses, wearing nothing under it. When she opened the door, she was not surprised to see Cole beside him.

She smiled. "I am so sorry, Cole, but I need to talk to Vince alone."

"My brother can hear whatever you have to say," Vince said with tension in his voice.

"Everything?" Her smile broadened as he whitened.

"All right, Cole, see you in the morning." He let out a breath and walked into the house as she shut the door.

He left his gun on the table by the door before walking into the parlor. He chose the straight chair to sit. Her smile widened. He was so determined, but this was a battle he needed to lose for both their sakes.

"So what's up?" he asked with that muscle jumping in his jaw.

"I hope you soon," she said as she stood in front of him and began unbuttoning her dress.

His mouth dropped open. "Holly?"

She let the dress fall to her feet revealing her nude body. "Yes?"

Before he could move, she settled onto his lap. "We can't do this," he said, but she felt of his growing bulge and knew they could and would.

"Oh, but we can, and we will be doing it again and again. You don't get the whole say in this."

"It's not like you can force me." His smile showed his acknowledgement of where this was going.

"I won't need to." She bent and claimed his lips as his hands stroked over her body, pulling her more tightly against him. She kissed him with her mouth open and his tongue thrust into hers. She turned in his arms and began to unbutton his shirt brushing it off his shoulders and down his arms. She so loved his muscular chest, that smattering of hair between those exciting male nipples. She never knew how stimulating a man's chest could be. She bent to tease his nipples into tight little nubs.

He rose with her in his arms as he took her up the stairs to her bedroom. He laid her on the bed and began stripping off his clothing. The gleam in his eyes told her all she needed to know about why he had stayed away. Before he came back to the bed, he reached into his pocket and took out a small package, which she recognized. He came back to the bed. "You know what it is?" he asked, with a crooked smile, as he unwrapped the rubber condom.

She laughed as she took it from him. "I should. I bought us four of them. I didn't figure out how they worked though. I counted on you for that."

"It's pretty obvious. And... from Sicillas?"

She laughed and nodded. "They must have found it funny. I got mine from Connie."

"And I bought mine from Del."

Taking hold of him, she took her time slipping the thin sheath on, tightening it at the root. "I guess it will take away some feeling."

"I think I have enough to not worry about that."

An hour later, after he had assured her he would be back, he had taken care of Jupiter in her stable and returned to strip and lie on the bed with her. She reached over and began touching him. Her gaze was intent as she looked at him more intimately than anyone ever had. He was fully erect, but when he reached for her, she stopped him. "Let me play for awhile, please."

He lay back as she ran her fingers down his side. "This was the wound, wasn't it?" she asked as she came to the scar high on his thigh.

"Not pretty."

"It could have been fatal."

"It almost was."

She kissed the scar as she stroked, running her fingers over the points that caused him to writhe. "Do you like this?" she whispered as she found a particularly arousing spot. As she moved down his body, her long hair touched him intimately. Repeatedly, she brought him almost to the brink and then pulled back to touch another place. She pushed his legs apart and ran her hands up his inner thigh. Never quite touching where he wanted most.

"God," he groaned finally, at the feeling of her fingers on his rod. His erection grew until it was almost felt painful.

"Goddess," she corrected as she used her mouth to bring him to a climax that filled his whole body before it finally left him feeling limp as a wet cloth. Breathing hard, he lay, wondering how in the hell she had learned to do that to a man.

"It must be other lifetimes," she answered, without his having voiced the question, as she kissed his neck. "It appears that while riding a horse may not be one of my talents, this might be. You cannot begin to know how many things I want to do to you."

He laughed and sighed with recognition of his fate. "You know why I stayed away," he said when he could speak with any coherence.

"You thought it would be best for me."

"And me. It's too late to worry about that now though."

"You could only keep yourself from doing this if you were at a distance."

He nodded. Near her, he would want her naked and in his arms. Near her, he would never be able to say no to what his body wanted even while his brain argued against it.

"It's not wrong for us," she whispered kissing his shoulder.

"It is more than wrong. It's dangerous."

"Because of my dreams."

He shook his head. "No, it's because of who I am."

"Let's worry about it tomorrow someday."

"It's not smart." He knew that.

"You cannot believe how little I care about what is smart. I am not going to use my head where it comes to you. You need to stop thinking so much. I don't care who knows about us. You need to let go of that also."

He let out a breath and wished for a cigarette. He shouldn't smoke in her house.

"Want some whiskey before we go back to sleep?" she asked. "I stuck a bottle up here for whenever you came back. I also have an ashtray. I figured you'd still have that nasty habit."

"Who are you?" he asked but he didn't need to ask as he bent to his shirt pocket and pulled out the cigarettes. "You want one?" he asked as he lit his.

"I tried it once with some girlfriends. It didn't take."

"Better that way. I should break the habit."

"You will... in time." He lay back on the bed, one arm under his head and the other holding the cigarette as he smoked. He had done everything he could to stay away, kept busy not only with her horse but other jobs, finally helping the sheriff on two arrests that he had believed could be dangerous. He'd ridden out into the desert, stretching both Jupiter's and his own legs. Nothing in the end had been enough. If she crooked her beautiful finger, he'd come running. He was as much her slave as if there'd been a collar around his neck.

"You aren't happy," she said as she ran a finger lightly around one of his nipples.

"It doesn't matter."

"It does. Tell me. Share it with me. I told you."

"You already know it can't be between us."

"Maybe when it comes to forever, but it can very much be an us for a time. Do we have to look into the future for what might or might not be? We can make it right by how honest we are with each other. We know what's coming. We never knew before. And when we say good-bye, it won't be with bitterness or loss but because it's the right thing."

"You have been thinking this out." He smiled crookedly as he took another long drag on the cigarette.

"Give me enough time, and I can think anything out. I might've let this go until after the dig... well, buying the condoms said I didn't intend to, but when I saw you tonight, I didn't think you were making either of us happy."

"I wanted to do what was best." He stubbed out the cigarette in the ashtray before reaching to turn off the light.

"You are."

With morning, she fixed him a breakfast of scrambled eggs, bacon, toast and coffee. "Don't think I can cook," she teased as they ate. "This is the sum of my skills in the kitchen."

"There are more important talents," he said with a grin as he sipped the coffee. "And you make a good cup of coffee. Strong enough but not too strong."

"How about you?" Can you cook?"

"I do a mean plate of trout over a campfire, rabbit if i get lucky enough to shoot one and have even cooked a rattler. Not bad but not like chicken in my opinion."

"Campfire cooking could come in handy."

"For a man on the move, it's essential."

"Song will do ours but not sure how good she is with a campfire, which is why we are taking the small stove for cooking and also why we need two wagons."

"I still don't like that."

"I know, but is it such a problem?"

"Like I said, it draws more attention. When we go through Globe, some, who haven't seen us before, will notice and wonder what we are up to."

"Why does it matter?"

"Depends on who does the wondering. There are many stories about buried treasure in the mountains. Not only Coronado but other Spanish expeditions, hidden goldmines."

"And we might look like we are out to find treasure."

He nodded and ate a strip of bacon. "You know the potential of trouble up could come from more than those out to steal gold. The Apaches, those who roam the mountains often alone, they may not trust an expedition like ours with so many people."

"Eleven is a lot?"

"And yet not enough. Drifters, whoever they are, are always looking for the easy dollar. We could look like that with two wagons, horses and mules—not to mention four women, all good looking."

"You are trying to worry me." She took another bite of her eggs.

"You didn't figure this would be easy."

"I was thinking though mostly in facing past life karma." She smiled with some obvious effort.

He reached out and took her hand, stroking it lightly. "There are even more reasons to be concerned-- my family."

"I thought they lived in Utah."

"Jackson, who I didn't kill, likely went back with the story of what happened. It could bring them or even Brody's friends, if he had any, back to Tucson for revenge."

"Now you are worrying me."

"You need to be aware. There is also, whoever hired Brody to kill Sam. They could still be out there—although more likely to show up here than along the Salt... I hope."

"Sounds like the dig is the least of our problems," she said licking her lips nervously.

"It's your problem. I will deal with the others. Well, with Sam's help."

"You don't count on Gabe or Clint?"

He snorted. "Do you?"

"Not Clint."

"Why did you let him come then?"

"I didn't really. I didn't say no because I didn't have a reason. You don't think he is dangerous though, do you?"

"Mostly just useless." He laughed. She went back to the stove for the pot to refill their cups.

"And Cole?" she asked.

He drew in a breath on that question, taking a sip of coffee before he tried to answer. "I would like to know. But Sam is aware of that situation. I hope Cole means what he says but..."

"He's your brother."

He nodded. "A brother I don't know. I left home at fourteen. Cole was a child. Growing up with our pa is no recommendation, but he did have Valerie at least."

"Your stepmother?"

"A good woman who urged me to get out of there."

"But not Cole?"

His smile was thoughtful. "I don't know. Maybe the fact that I wasn't her son made it easier to let me go... Maybe she wasn't all I thought she was."

"That can happen."

"Anyway, about Cole. I won't trust him too much—for now. So don't worry about that."

She smiled and moved to sit on the chair next to him. She took his free hand into hers and brought it to her lips. The kiss was soft, innocent and had him instantly hardening.

Blue eyes wide, she met his gaze. "It will be different this time." She smiled, but he thought it took some effort.

"Well, the end you told me about didn't sound good, so it

better be." He smiled as he drew her onto his lap and kissed her deeply and thoroughly.

As she cleared the table, he remembered what he hadn't told her. She wasn't the only one who had now seen that other lifetime. "Holly, come back for a minute."

She turned to look at him. "All right, what?"

"I wasn't sure I'd tell you but..."

"We said we'd be honest."

He nodded. "I took a lot of rides out onto the desert to try and stay away from you."

"I figured that much."

"On one of them, I visited a boulder up a nearby canyon where there are petroglyphs. One of them is of a big owl."

"I have heard of it."

He let out a breath. "I ground reined Jupiter and sat on a nearby rock, staring at it. I am not sure where my mind was or how long I was there, but... I saw something that was not real. A woman seemed to appear in front of me."

"A vision."

"Maybe." He smiled. "Or ghost. She was beautiful with coal black hair, full lips. She was not looking at me but at a man who also appeared. He put his arms out to hold her but then the whole image exploded, shattered. I blinked, trying to clear my head and looked around. The canyon was quiet, no explosions— that weren't in my head. I heard mourning doves, a cardinal in a mesquite, Jupiter moving and eating grass. I can't explain what I saw or heard. Nothing was there."

"Maybe it was us."

"I don't know but I believe we do have to see this through."

She settled back onto his lap and put her arms around his neck. "I believe what you told me. We can change it."

He gave a little laugh. "You didn't used to be so certain."

"No, but we weren't together then. Now we are. We can

break the curse. I feel sure that there was one and not only that lifetime."

"You saw others?"

"Less pieces of them but yes. And it seemed we were fated."

"Maybe this time too." He didn't still believe in life after life, but had no idea what to make of any of it.

"Last time... all the times, we didn't know what we'd face. We do now."

He held her and only hoped she was right. For the first time he did believe they had to go there, both of them. Something needed to be settled. Maybe it was only his own lifetime of guns and death. Perhaps the reckoning was for him. Whatever the case, it would be changed up there. One way or the other.

CHAPTER 14

The next morning, with wagons packed the night before, Holly and Vince walked to the stable to hitch up the mules and saddle their own horses. Cole arrived early enough to help with the traces. He proved to be of more use than Vince had expected.

When Song and Zian arrived, Vince learned that Zian could ride and had him saddle one of the four spare horses. He loosely tied the other three to the back of the wagons. It was not until they were ready to pull out that Gabe and Clint arrived from different directions.

"Have you ever driven a team?" he asked Clint.

The lawyer gave him a considering look. "Just buggies."

"I have," Cole said.

"Then you take the first wagon. We will need to trade off with drivers. Clint, if it's all right with you, ride with him, tie your horse on behind. Let Cole teach you what it takes to handle a team.

"I've driven wagons," Gabe offered.

Vince looked at Song. "You ride with him then." He smiled then and looked at Holly. "Ready?"

"You're the boss—well, of this at least," she said with the smile that had him wishing they were alone. "You tell me."

"Then head 'em out. We'll stop at Steam Pump, water the horses and meet Rykers there."

An hour later, with the whole crew heading north, Vince brought up the rear where he could see how it was all going-- especially Holly with her mare. Riding beside Abby and Alice, she seemed increasingly at ease in the saddle.

Although he had brought the four spare horses, he counted on the mules to get their wagons to Globe where they would exchange them for fresh mules, picking these four up on their way back. Some of this was counting on luck, with no wheel problems or an animal going lame. He only hoped he had remembered everything needed if it did.

"You worried?" Gabe asked as he came alongside him. He was riding a pinto that looked to have plenty of go in him.

"No more than usual."

"You look worried."

Vince smiled with recognition that he was right. "A lot can always go wrong."

"Spirit says it will."

Vince turned to study his face. "The other side tell you that?"

"Nah," Gabe said with a laugh as he met his gaze, "my papa."

"Raul would know."

"He didn't want me going."

"Why did you then?"

"Stories I heard about the ancestors." When he caught Vince's skeptical look, he nodded. "I understand your doubt."

RAIN TRUEAX

"The stories regarded the people who lived in those dwellings?" he asked. He had a lot less doubt than once would have been true.

"Perhaps."

David had ridden alongside and was listening but saying nothing.

"Superstitions against visiting them?" Vince asked.

"Not many Indians like being where the dead are. Bad karma." Gabe chuckled.

"How many Yaquis know Buddhist teachings?" he asked with a laugh.

"Those with a sister-in-law who got an education," Gabe said flashing a broader smile.

"Pa wants me to go to college. Ridiculous idea. I know all I need to know for what I want," David said. "I want to live like you, Uncle..." He hesitated. "Vince."

"My way is a bad way. It's more what happens when everything else goes wrong. Get an education first, then decide. You are lucky you have that option," Vince said.

He glanced back at Gabe. He had barely met the man other than briefly once with is brother, Rafe. He was interested in knowing to what level he could trust him or his wisdom. "So what will you be looking for on the Cibecue? I gather it's not pots."

Gabe chuckled. "It would be bad juju to take them from a place like that."

"Grace teach you that one too?" Vince asked.

"What's it mean?" Dave asked.

"See, that's why you need an education," Vince said with a laugh.

"Do you know?" Dave asked.

"I do. The word came with slaves from West Africa. I didn't

learn it from a book though, but a man whose family had been slaves."

"And it means?" Dave asked with increased interest.

"Bad juju would be objects or actions that bring bad luck."

Gabe nodded. "The belief is not just that of witches but those peoples who live close to the earth, who follow earth religions, they know it. And fear of juju is not why I don't look for objects there."

"You going to tell us your reason?" Vince asked.

"Are you familiar with the Yaqui ways of spirituality?"

"Only a little. Although I have been a trader with many tribes, I have worked little in Southern Arizona or Mexico."

"Yaquis believe in five separate worlds. There is the desert world, the mystical one, the flower world, the dream world, and finally the night world. We progress through those worlds... or seek to. We grow in our understanding as we do. Have you heard the word seatakaa?"

"No."

"Seatakaa is the energy of the heart. Some are born with it. Those who have it are protected—unless the person turns to evil. It can be lost through bad deeds. Some say they can then never gain it back."

"And this connects how with the Cibecue?"

"Not it so much." When he saw the look Vince gave him, he smiled again. "I am not trying to be confusing. This may not be easy to understand. Dreams are a part of seatakaa. Are you following me more now? That fourth world, the dream world."

Now he got it. "Then it's about Holly?"

"In a manner of speaking."

"I don't understand what the seatakaa is," David said with enthusiasm. "Is it something someone other than a Yaqui might have?"

"Perhaps. I do not know. Let me give you an example of a dream that has seatakaa. Suppose you climb a pole, a very high pole only you walked up it. When you realize you are very high. You will die if you fall, but you cannot stay there. The one with seatakaa would fall but then walk away. The dream shows he has it. However, it is in living where he must prove it. Those with seatakaa flourish in even difficult times. They survive when others would not."

"So the dream world taken into the real world is your interest now." It came together for him, and he knew why Gabe had been quiet during all meetings—other than concern for no damage being done. Gabe was not drawn to Holly romantically but for the other thing, the one he had evidently sensed. Vince knew she had told no one her motivations for going to these ruins, unless she had Connie. Gabe knew it by other means.

"Yes."

"Have you talked to Holly about this?"

"No, but I knew she wanted something much bigger than whether tribes traded with each other. The truth she seeks is much more than that." Gabe looked at Vince, his eyes speculative. "You know this too, don't you?"

Vince shifted his gaze to where Holly and Abby were riding. Holly laughed at something. He liked watching her ride and trusted more in her ability to handle her horse.

"You'll need to ask her about that. I need to check ahead. Talk to you later." With that, he nudged Jupiter in the side. As he came up alongside Holly, he said, "I'll be riding ahead. I need to find us a campsite for tonight." She nodded, with that smile that melted his heart.

As he took off at a fast trot, he was not surprised to find Sam at his side.

"It's over a hundred miles to Globe. You figure three nights camping and then a night there with a hotel at least for the women?" Sam asked.

"It might work that way. Although, I am not wanting to spend longer in Globe than we have to."

"The reason being?"

"You know what it is. That kind of trouble we don't need."

Sam stared at the distant ridges. "It could happen anyway."

"I don't want to invite it. Before we arrive, we need to make sure everybody knows no talking about where we are going. The wrong ones hearing will assume it's about gold."

Sam nodded. "I saw you talking to Cordova. Dave looks interested in him."

"He's looking for where he fits in life. It's the age."

"I had hoped that'd be the Circle R."

"It might yet be. He needs to test things out."

"He admires you."

Vince snorted. "Because he doesn't know me as well as he does you."

"It's tough raising a boy to a man," Sam said finally.

"You and I just jumped right in."

"I had hoped he'd have it easier. A lot got killed doing what we did before they reached manhood."

"It was different for us. Neither of us had a father there or in my case, to admire. Dave doesn't know what a benefit he has. He'll figure it out."

Sam shrugged. "I hope so. Damn, let's let these horses run it off."

Vince chuckled. "If you'd have gelded Zeus, like you should have, he'd not be so edgy with Princess in heat."

"Like I said, we'll run it off. I'll make sure he doesn't get near her tonight. Wearing him out with a run will help."

Within moments, they had let their horses out to a full gallop and were thundering down the road. The few wagons they passed easily let them split and go around. It was after maybe seven miles of hard riding, that Vince slowed Jupiter to a trot. They rode then without words, each always scanning the higher ground, never relaxing or ignoring any possible warning signs.

"I like the looks of that." Vince gestured toward a broad, open space above the San Pedro. There was enough flat ground for a tent, water for the animals, and even some grass, which would save the oats for drier camps. Although it wasn't a full twenty-five miles from Tucson, it was worth stopping earlier for the grass. It would also serve to break-in the crew and give their bodies a chance to adjust to future long days on the road.

By the time, the others had reached the site, he and Sam had gathered stones and built a fire and dragged over a fallen cottonwood to make a bench. An hour later, they had the live-stock secured, had set up a tent for the women, and had eaten the first meal of the trail.

"This wasn't as hard as I had thought it might be," Holly said as she settled next to Vince on the log.

"Tomorrow will be a longer day but also pretty level country."

Clint was watching them from across the fire. Vince saw jealousy in the lawyer's eyes at Holly's easy familiarity with him. He hoped that wasn't going to create a problem. A distraction was in order.

"I brought two extra rifles," Vince said. "What kind of rifle do you own, Madison?"

"Winchester 73."

"I also have the older Winchester," Cole offered.

"Gabe?"

"Spencer. It's an older model though."

"Gentlemen, come on over to the second wagon. I want to show you something."

Using the tailgate, Vince unwrapped the new rifles. He held up one for them to look at. "I know Sam has his own '94."

"How'd you know that?" Sam asked with a grin.

"Because I never knew you not to have the best gun out there. And this is it."

"Nice looking weapon." Gabe lifted it to his shoulder and did an imaginary sighting.

"How about we take these down to the river where we can try them," Vince suggested. His reasons were not only to check the guns again, as he already had, but to judge how good a shot each man was before it became an issue.

"Abby has a fine rifle too," Sam said. "She's got a good eye. Alice too."

Vince hadn't thought of the possibility that Holly would also want to shoot and quickly remedied his mistake with the ladies. Sending the men ahead with the rifles, he went back to the campfire. "Any of you want to try out the new Winchester?" He said it gesturing to the others while looking at Holly.

"I would," Alice said.

"It's good to know how to shoot," he said again directed at Holly.

"I don't need practice," Holly said. "I'll help Song clean up if you want to go, Abby."

Down at the river with Abby and Alice, they all took turns shooting at branches on the other side of the river. Vince's purpose was to assess, who got the new guns if they ran into trouble. The Rykers were all good with them, but they also had fine rifles. Gabe and Zian hit their marks or near enough. Clint was a lousy shot. Cole's shots were surprisingly good, but Vince hadn't forgotten his dislike of guns. If they had need of marksmen, he'd let both of them keep their older rifles.

Back at the campfire, Song brought out the bottle of whiskey. "Do you gentlemen, who are of age, want a drink?" She smiled and poured some in several of the tin cups.

Sam sat beside Vince. "So what'd you figure?"

"What you did. Good to know your ladies are dead-eyes."

"Need it that way where we live." Sam sipped the whiskey. "Smooth."

"Ollie suggested the brand," Holly sat on Vince's other side.

"He was right."

Abby cuddled next to Sam. "I like being out like this."

"Even though we sleep apart?" Sam asked with a teasing smile. The moon was just rising.

"That is a drawback. Maybe we could all sleep out."

Song shook her head. "Me, I like tents, and no rattlesnakes in bed with me."

"We could all sleep close together," Holly said leaning against Vince's shoulder. When Vince looked down at her, she was smiling up at him. She ran her fingertips over his cheek. "You need a shave."

"Barber in Globe." Obviously, she had meant what she said about not caring who knew about her feelings for him.

"That is a long way off." He looked down at her. It was a long way, going to seem too long—the summer even more so. He had liked sleeping with her. He had never slept with a woman before, hadn't known he'd like it.

"I want that rifle," Alice said as she settled on the other side of Abby. "It was a beauty."

"At the end of the summer, you'll have earned enough to buy one," Holly said.

"You mean we also get paid?"

"Of course."

"Wow." She looked at her father. "You don't pay us."

"Of course, he does," Abby said. "You get room and board."

Alice groaned.

CHAPTER 15

For Holly, the next days were a mix of learning to drive a team, which Vince insisted they each needed to try, riding Princess, nights slept with the women when she wanted to be beside Vince, and eagerness mixed with dread over finally being on her way to the Cibecue.

At the Gila River, Vince warned them to keep their horses on the road bed. "It's solid but there's quicksand around here." He had looked upriver and nodded. "The river is low. That'll help when we get to the Salt, where it's likely how it'll be too."

"Why?" she asked, finding every part of the venture interesting. She was hungry to learn more about how he made decisions, what was important to consider, how he weighed each element. Someday she might have to do this by herself. She didn't much like that idea when she thought of it.

"One road snakes above the Salt. Generally fifty feet or so above. It's rough, a lot of up and down over every arroyo and can be washed out. If we can take the wagons up the right or left side of the river, it will mean less miles and easier. Can't do it in high water though."

Arriving in Globe, they took the wagons to the livery stable and arranged for all the animals to be fed and kept overnight while they checked into the hotel, taking rooms for the women.

Happily, for Holly, she and Abby each had one to themselves with Alice sharing with Song. The privacy meant Vince might come to her. She was sure Abby hoped for the same with Sam. They had even found the rooms offered baths to be brought to them. She took a long time soaking in hers with her mind on a lot more than the joy of warm water and being clean again.

She knew Vince had watched her on the seemingly endless days and nights on the road. It might be difficult though, since the men were bunking in the stable with the horses and wagon. It hadn't been a shortage of rooms but Vince's concern at leaving the wagons unguarded. The men had taken a turn at the barbershop for shaves and use of the upstairs bathtubs.

It was after midnight, and she had given up on his arriving, when she heard the light tap at the door. She rushed to it but had the sense to ask first who it was. When she heard his voice, she had pulled it open and him in before he could say more than his name.

"Mmmmm," she whispered as he bent and claimed her lips. "I didn't know if you could come."

"I can't. I can't stay either."

"Oh," she smiled. "I like the shave." She ran her fingers over his cheek. "I guess we better make the most of what time we have." She began stripping off his clothing as he lifted her nightgown from her.

An hour later, they lay in the bed, cradled in each other's arms. "Do you really have to go back?"

He kissed her forehead. "I should not have even come." He smiled. "I made the others promise to stay with the wagon, but I can't count on that. They wanted to hit the bar even with the bottle I left them."

"And the problem with the bar is?"

"Drunks talk."

"Oh, but I don't want you to leave me," she said as he rose and began dressing.

"Me either. But there are things we both have to do that we may not want." Fully dressed, cartridge belt again at his waist, he sat back on the edge of the bed, running his hand along the curve of her hip. "Did you know that Gabe is interested in your dreams?"

"Not really. I guess he has asked a few questions but... Why do you think he is?"

"What they might prove, or so he said."

"He wants to be a holy man. I think they have resisted taking him the last step."

"Do you know why?"

"Grace said he had been envious and even gotten into a fight with Rafe over his jealousy of him. I think he wanted Grace... or maybe it was a brother thing."

"Spiritual power can be positive or negative."

"I am not familiar with the Yaqui religion," she said as she took his hand and kissed each finger.

"It sounds like they believe in a kind of enlightenment but as something someone is born with. You may have it. Your dreams show you that you are connected to more than most."

"Maybe."

"He's hoping up there will prove something about life and death. That's what I think."

"I am hoping, after it doesn't end the same way, that those dreams will never come again."

"So no more dreams?" He smiled

"Oh, I want dreams but new ones... like ones where we do what we just did." He felt her smile against his hand.

"I have to go. Lock your door." He bent, claimed her lips and then was out the door.

She did as he asked with the lock and then lay back on the bed, feeling the relaxation that had always come after sex with him. Now though, she felt something new. She wanted to sleep with him and not only for a night. She smiled as she stared at the ceiling. Maybe a better dream would show her how that could be.

Vince headed back to the stable only to find Cole and Clint were gone. David and Zian were sleeping under the wagon. "Damn it to hell, where'd they go?" he growled at Gabe who had been sitting on one of the feed barrels.

"You need to ask?"

"No, I guess I don't." He stared toward the brightly lit and noisy bar two blocks down from the stable. "All right, I'll be back. Tell Sam where I am if he gets back." Gabe grinned.

Vince checked the load in his gun before he pushed open the bar doors. Five men were playing cards at a table to his left. The bar was crowded with the usual laughter and loud voices. To the right, he saw Cole, Clint, and two men he didn't know. A bottle was on the table. Cole was the only one who looked sober as he looked up when Vince strode to the table, trying to suppress the angry words he felt like yelling. "I thought you were guarding the wagon," he managed in a level tone.

"You didn't stay with it," Clint said with a grin. "Wonder why not."

"Time to go back." He gritted his teeth and sucked in the angry breath.

"Don't have to do what you say," Clint slurred.

"You agreed to take orders when you came on this." He glanced then at the other two. They were drunk and both armed. "You had a job, and I told you not to leave the stable, to stay out of bars."

"Man's got a right to a drink," Clint said. "You are not my boss."

"You're right. You're heading home tomorrow."

"You can't fire me. Holly is the only one that can do that," he sneered.

Vince grabbed his shirt and yanked him out of his chair. "Guess you will find out," he said.

When Clint reached his hand out to strike him, Vince slammed his right fist into his face and his left into his belly. The softer man doubled and fell to the floor. Maybe he should have goaded him into a gunfight. It might have been better in the long run, but he wasn't going to kill a man for being weak.

"You have an opinion on this?" he asked Cole as he glared at his brother.

"No. Want me to help you drag him out of here?"

A man with a badge appeared at the door. "Any trouble here?" he asked looking from Vince to the man now snoring on the floor.

Sam stood in the door behind him. "Don't look like it to me." He had that hard smile Vince had seen before when he was about to launch into a fight and wanted to do it.

The marshal looked from one to the other and then smiled. "Want me to lock this one up for the night? Looks like an unruly drunk to me."

Vince smiled. "It would help. I'll be by to collect him at first light." He and Sam carried Clint to the jail where they deposited him on a bunk to snore loudly.

Out in the night air, Cole was waiting. "He was going. I figured I should go along to keep an eye on him. It wasn't like I had the authority to tell him no."

"Did he tell anybody anything about us and where we are going?"

"Not when he was with me. He went to the bar once but not long enough to say much if he did."

"All right." Vince looked at Sam, the moon's glow highlighting his face. "I guess it is what it is."

Sam's smile gleamed. "It usually is."

"You want to go back and see if they told anybody where we are going?"

"Sure, I can always use a drink." An hour later, he was back where Vince was trying to sleep at the front of the stable.

Sam grabbed a blanket and lay down beside him. "Maybe or maybe not," he said.

Vince cursed. "Not like we can kill them all."

"I planted a few false trails. The jaspers he was drinking with seemed the most interested."

"What'd you tell them?"

"That we were on our way to Snowflake, maybe would be buying a ranch up there."

"That might work."

Sam nodded as he closed his eyes.

Vince lay awake thinking. There was nothing he could do about Madison's big mouth. He'd get rid of him in the morning. Taking him or leaving him, unless he killed him, neither would be a good solution. He wouldn't kill someone without a fair fight, and Madison would never give him that. What he didn't want was him at his back. The man's jealousy had gone way out of control.

In the morning, he went to the cafe where he had seen his ladies heading.

Holly smiled brightly at him as he entered. "Oh good," she said, "you can have breakfast with us."

"Not this time. I need to talk to you."

She didn't argue and followed him outside.

"The short of it is—I fired Clint last night."

"With reason?"

"Yes."

"Will he be dangerous to you whether he stays with us or goes?"

"Possibly but we can't afford to have him along. He threw a punch at me, maybe talked in the bar. He is a liability. I don't want him with us."

She studied his face. "So here or in Tucson, neither is a good option."

"I can't shoot him down-- much as I might like."

"No, firing is all you can do. I did promise him wages for the summer's work." She delved into her pocket and came out with a wad of bills. She peeled off one for him. Twenty should be enough."

"You are okay with this then. I know you originally wanted him."

"He pushed himself onto me. I think you are right about his character. I worry that it might not be safe for you to fire him. Maybe I should do it; so he won't have any doubts that it's coming from me."

He appreciated that, but it wasn't how it would be. "I'll do it."

She pulled his head down for a quick kiss. "All right, I

agreed you'd be the boss of all but the excavation itself. You think he should not be with us. Whether he later causes us trouble or not, I think you are right. He should go."

"Good. I might even get back for breakfast." He turned then and headed for the jail.

Inside the small office, the marshal opened the door to the jail cells. Clint was sitting on the cot still behind bars.

"You had no right to get me arrested. You were the one who hit me. You should be in here."

Vince handed him the double-sawbuck. "Your horse will be at the stable when you get out. Get back to Tucson."

"Holly agreed?" Clint looked at the bill with surprise.

The marshal stood in the door. "Want me to hold him a couple of days?" he asked with a grin. Apparently, he didn't think much of the tinhorn either.

"That would help," Vince said.

"You can't do this to me," Madison said with rage in his face.

"There are other choices," Vince said. "You want to face me on the street with a gun?"

"No."

"Then go back to Tucson and forget anything you knew about us. If I see you again, before I get back there, you won't have a choice about using your pistol."

Madison started to say something but slammed his mouth shut.

An hour later, Holly was wearing a pair of gloves and driving a team with David as her teacher. "No," the youth instructed, "don't pull on the reins that way." He took them from her. "Like this."

They had left Globe with fresh teams of mules. All their horses were still in good enough shape that they either were ridden or tied on behind the wagons. Vince rode alongside her wagon. She knew it was to be sure these mules were trained enough to be trustworthy. The wagon behind was being driven by Cole with Song the one learning how to handle them.

Mostly the route was level with buttes on both sides, wildflowers in various places, but nothing to distract her from the concerns she felt. She wasn't sorry Clint was no longer with them, but she also worried that he would yet prove to be a problem. He didn't seem the kind of man to follow them or shoot someone from ambush. From what Vince had told her, he wasn't that good a shot anyway. Still, it worried her.

She blamed herself for not being more firm with a no, when he first said he wanted to come. She still wasn't sure about the why of his desire to come along. She suspected he was more interested in her fortune than her. Maybe Clint wanted more wealth than his law practice could afford him.

They gave the animals a break for lunch but then pushed on. This time Vince had Zian learning to drive a team and Abby took the other. She needed no instruction.

Freed from driving the wagon, Holly rode beside him. "Where will we stop tonight?" she asked as the sun began heading down in the sky.

"From what I remember, a bit off the road, there is an old mining camp about three miles ahead. There used to be quite a few small mines in these hills. Most either petered out or never developed into much."

"A mining camp with buildings?"

"Not worth much for shelter, but yes. More likely homes for rattlers and varmints."

"Did Clint threaten you?" She couldn't resist asking what worried her most.

"You need something new to worry about?" he asked with that teasing smile that made her forget her concern.

"I like to know what is going to be a problem."

"I am not worried about him, if that's your concern. I told him if I saw him up here, I'd kill him. Hopefully he believed me."

"Would you do that?"

"I don't say what I don't mean."

She had to digest that. "Not in cold blood though."

"No, I'd make him draw on me. Let's forget it. He won't be coming—at least not by himself. He'd have to hire a gang. Does he have that kind of money?"

She shook her head. "You know, I was thinking about that this morning. I think he actually was interested in my money more than me. I don't quite know what to think of him, but my greatest attraction was probably the fortune I inherited." She glanced over to see what he thought about that. Was her money a barrier between them? She knew it wouldn't be an inducement because she knew the kind of man he was.

"You underestimate your desirability, beautiful," he said with that crooked smile that had her heart melting.

"You think I am desirable?"

He laughed. "Do you have to ask?"

"A woman likes to hear such from her lover."

"Ah, so you want compliments. Well, I've never wanted a woman as much as you. You also are the most beautiful woman I ever saw and even more so when you are handling a team of mules and gritting your teeth against a few choice expressions."

"I don't use choice expressions," she retorted with indignation.

"You should learn a few. Comes in handy when handling a

team." She looked over with a skeptical look to see his amusement.

"Will we have a chance to be alone tonight?" She was thinking of a few things she'd like to do to him that needed there to be no audience.

"Unlikely, pretty close quarters. Maybe when we finally hit the Cibecue country, there will be more chance. What'd you have in mind?" His smile was that enticing one.

"It's a surprise." She wasn't sure she actually had such in her arsenal. Maybe she should talk to Abby, who doubtless knew a lot more about seducing a man, considering their eighteen year marriage. They even still seemed happy, which was a bit amazing to Holly. Maybe though, the marriages she had seen were based around money. That obviously had nothing to do with the Rykers. She frowned. A private moment with Abby was about as unlikely as one with Vince.

"You have a conniving look in your eyes," he said with a chuckle.

"I do?" She tried for innocence.

"You definitely do."

"You should worry," she said lifting her chin in the air. "Worry a lot. I will have you on your knees sooner or later."

His laughter rang out. "We'll see who ends up on their knees."

She grinned. That sounded good to her too.

The mining camp was still where Vince had expected. The buildings were deteriorating but a hundred feet off the road. Song immediately set about preparing their meal as the others unsaddled and unhitched the animals. Vince created a primitive but effective rope corral. With dried grass, a portion of the oats they had brought, sufficient water from the small creek, their animals would not be testing its limits.

Holly and Alice headed for the most upright of the buildings. "There are actual walls," Alice said at the open door before her father stopped her and went in first.

One gunshot and then he was back. "When it quits twitching, I'll remove it. Otherwise, the room looks fine, no rodent holes. Stay away from it. They can sometimes still bite when dead."

With a dirt floor and a roof partially gone, it was not a lot of shelter but better than they'd had. There were walls. With the door closed, snakes wouldn't find it so easy to access. It would be easier than setting up the tent and she would like the openness better. "I claim this for the ladies," she said as she headed back to the wagon to gather the quilts and blankets.

Two hours later, the women had gone into their cabin, the starry sky overhead. A nearly full moon was peeking up over the mountain ridge. Quickly they stripped off britches or skirts, having gotten used to sleeping in their underwear instead of nightgowns. Sleeping four abreast, Holly took one outer side and Abigail the other.

"Tomorrow we head into the canyon," Alice said. "Papa said it's steep. I wonder if it will be dangerous for the wagons."

"You do think ahead," Holly said. She had worried some about that herself. She patted her hand out for Song's arm beside her. "How are you faring with meals to fix every night after traveling all day?"

"It's different and good. I hope it will be good for Zian. That's my main concern."

"It is for us with our children," Abby said. "He seems like a nice young man."

"He's cute," Alice observed.

Holly laughed.

"Do not tell him that," Song said. "He has big head already."

"I wouldn't dream of telling him." Holly could hear the embarrassment in the girl's voice. She hadn't thought of the possibility that Alice would get a crush on Zian, but now that she thought about it, it seemed quite possible. He was tall, slender but muscular and handsome. Also, way too old for her to get any silly ideas.

Not that she was a paragon where it came to silly ideas about older men. She wondered how old Vince was, but it didn't matter. She was in love with him. The number of years he had lived had nothing to do with it. Or maybe they did, and she liked it that he was a strong, experienced man. She enjoyed breaking down his barriers, getting past all that strength to where he softened... well all but in one area. She suppressed her giggle.

Outside Sam and Vince were having their last cigarettes down by the makeshift horse corral. The others had already gotten into their bedrolls.

"What way you figure to handle this tomorrow?" Sam asked taking a long drag on the cigarette he had bummed off Vince.

"I'll take the lead wagon. You take the second."

"Good."

"You know I worried some we might run into another crew sent by my pa when we got this far. I sure don't want to see them tomorrow before we get to the river. I thought I'd send the others ahead of us with Gabe hanging behind keeping an eye on the opposite rim. He's got the best eye for shooting if it came to it."

Sam smiled, his teeth flashing white in the rising moonlight. "Think positive, friend."

"I am. So having Gabe with the gun and maybe Zian, except I don't know if he'd be comfortable shooting anyone."

"You think Gabe would be?"

"If he knew it had to be."

"Why not your brother?"

"He doesn't like guns. I don't know what that's about. He'd hesitate though, and that's not a time I want a man hesitating."

Sam chuckled. "Then have Abby stay with him."

"True. With you vulnerable on a wagon seat, she would not hesitate."

"That why you wanted me to handle the other team?"

"Nah. It was your strong arms and way animals. I think Gabe will be enough. I don't really expect anybody over there."

They smoked in silence.

"Sam, why didn't you take your father's name, once you knew?"

"Brothers and fathers on your mind?"

Vince took a long drag on the cigarette. "Some."

"Ryker was my mother's people. By the time, I found out Cord and I had the same father, I was pretty used to it and didn't have a reason to change. Our father was a son of a bitch from all Cord said. O'Brian didn't mean anything to me personally."

"Blood."

"You worried about blood when you finally face your pa and brothers?"

"Where it comes to my brothers, that's likely with Asa. The one I don't know about is Jesse. Cole said he's slow but not with a gun. He'd be thirty-three or so."

"And your pa?"

"He was tough. Guess he's old now. I last saw him in '96. He cursed me as an unfit son."

"Not hard to see why you picked another name to get away from them."

"Didn't do any good. Can't run from some things—especially not who you are inside."

"You worry about that?" Sam asked with his usual perceptive insight.

"You don't?"

Sam chuckled. "Not admitting anything. Bad enough the way Abby digs in. Not about to let you start."

"I remember the first time we met."

"Me too. I thought you were one of those sky pilots who'd preach a sermon at the least excuse."

"Standing in Boot Hill, trying to figure out how to comfort the ones left behind when I didn't know them or the one who'd died."

Sam chuckled. "Didn't imagine then you were good with a gun."

"I'd put it behind me."

"Good thing for me it wasn't too far behind. Guess it ruined your life there though. That was what... eighteen years ago. You were not much more than a kid."

"We were both pretty young."

"More alike than I knew then though."

Vince nodded staring out at the dark sky. Maybe that alikeness is why they had bonded through all the years.

"In Tucson, you said I was the best friend you ever had," Sam said looking at Vince.

"It is true."

"And it's mutual. It's a lot of why I am glad we are doing this together."

"You kind of got stuck into it with your family."

"Not so much. I saw the way you looked at that little gal. I knew you'd be going, no matter what you said. I could have said no to the family. It wasn't just for them that I didn't."

"You son of a bitch," Vince said, humorously shaking his head.

"You too, buddy." They both laughed.

CHAPTER 16

Tucson, Arizona

Riding into Tucson, Jeremiah was shocked at how much it had changed since his last time there. That had to be in '84 or thereabouts. Years got away from him. He knew Cordell O'Brian had been the marshal. Tough bastard and nobody he had wanted to run up against. He'd stayed overnight and ridden on.

"We going to a hotel?" Jesse asked. He was looking around uneasily. Jesse didn't like people.

"Of course," Asa said ignoring his little brother's concerns. "And then hit the Pedrales."

"You been here before?" Jesse asked.

"Couple of years ago." Asa's smile was mean. "Just a little job." He glanced over at Jeremiah. "I did take a few you didn't get first."

Jeremiah shrugged. He didn't care. On the long ride south, most of which they had kept to the roads least traveled and to the east of the state, he'd more and more become convinced he needed his second eldest dead. It was going to be him or Asa. The only reason they hadn't already braced each other is Asa hadn't decided that he needed to. It wouldn't take long before he'd want his old man out of the way. Better Jeremiah picked the time and place.

He had his boys stable their horses while he arranged for two rooms at the Continental—Jesse and Asa could share one. He could afford that for a few nights. Longer, once it was only him.

The last word he'd had for Mrs. Osbourne is she'd arrive on the train the next day. She'd be at the San Xavier and suggested he talk to her there after she'd had time to rest. Other than knowing that she was a woman who didn't mind paying for murder, he had no idea what to expect. A viper for certain. Rich most probably. Neither was bad. He headed for the barbershop for a shave and bath.

After a good night's sleep, having skipped the bars where he knew at least one of his sons likely would not have, Jeremiah went to the corner cafe for a quiet breakfast. He was less than pleased when Asa and Jesse showed up before he'd done more than get his first sip of coffee.

"Ryker ain't in Tucson or at his ranch," Asa said. He glanced up as the waitress appeared. "Just coffee," he said.

"Who told you?" Jeremiah asked.

"At the Pedrales, we ran into a guy. Clint Madison. He ain't happy at all with Ryker or Vince." When the coffee arrived, Asa drank half the cup without coming up for air. Hard night, Jeremiah guessed resisting the grin.

"So who is this Madsion?"

"Lawyer, two-bit shyster most likely, but you need to talk to him."

Something about this didn't smell right. "Mrs. Osbourne arrives at eleven. I am meeting her train."

Asa guffawed. "That why ya got cleaned up?"

"We already blew it once. Gotta make a good impression if we want her to have faith in us now. Doesn't sound like you trust Madison." He sipped his coffee, studying his son.

"No reason to."

Jeremiah looked Jesse. "You have an opinion on this?" His youngest shook his head. No surprise. If he did, he wouldn't share it with Asa listening. "Where are Boggs and Brewster?"

"Hung over." Jesse did volunteer that. When the waitress returned with Jeremiah's order, Jesse looked at it and said he'd take the same.

"Why didn't this mouthpiece tell you where you can find him?" Jeremiah asked as he ate.

Asa shrugged. "He wants something more, but not like I had any money to give him last night."

"Did you set up a time?"

"Sooner the better. He has an office."

Jeremiah cursed under his breath but nodded. If he did it fast, it'd be over before the train arrived. He could send his boys off after Ryker and have time to maybe even court Mrs. Osbourne. That might prove more profitable than a shooting. Ryker was good with a gun though. Maybe he'd get rid of Asa without having to do it. A definite consideration.

Half an hour later, the three of them walked into a law office a block back from the main streets. A little shabby but that wasn't a surprise since the man was selling information, not busy in a courtroom.

"So you are Vince's father," Madison said as he ushered the three of them into an inner office. There had been no receptionist out front. Another indicator that this mouthpiece had fallen on hard times.

"You know my son?"

"You all resemble each other. Your hair is graying now but

looks thick. Your sons are all black-haired, hawk like faces." He looked up then at Jesse. "He's a big one." Jeremiah waited. "Cole went with Vince—and they are both with Ryker."

Jeremiah let out a hiss. "So where are they? And why did they leave Tucson?"

"I'll answer your second question. It's an archaeology excavation."

"This is making no sense. What would Vince know about archaeology?"

"I am giving you no more information. To have me tell you where they went, I want something in return."

"How much?"

"Not money. I want to go. You are out to get Ryker. Your son said as much last night. I can help you get there but will only do so if you take me."

Jeremiah leaned back in his chair. It wouldn't be hard to get the information from the lawyer. He looked soft. It might be better though to learn more about his motives.

"Why do you want to go?" Madison was not a man to trust. And for him to say that, given his life, that was saying a lot. He had dealt with many dishonest, crooked men. This one was of the cowardly rat variety. Never know what a man would get from rats. He looked over at Asa and saw his son understood the caliber of the lawyer.

"There is a woman with him... er them. I have an interest in her."

"Then why aren't you with her instead of here?"

"I had clients here."

Jeremiah resisted the smile. He knew a lie when he heard it. "We will need to get together supplies. I have someone coming into town today. I'll get back to you on timing."

As he walked back out, he spit on the road. "Sleazy little man," he said as he lit a cigar.

"But he knows what we need," Asa said.

"I don't see Vince trusting him."

"Yeah, Mr. Wonderful. Sure, he'd never misjudge a man." Asa snorted.

"All right, get together supplies. I am not anxious to get back on a horse right away." Damn, it was no fun getting old.

"We take him with us?" Asa asked with that look in his eyes that said he knew all that Jeremiah did. They didn't need to take the lawyer to get what he knew.

"Why not?" Jeremiah said with a grin as he blew out the smoke.

Salt River Canyon

"Oh my," Holly said as she looked into the canyon. Vince knew what she was feeling. It was an awesome sight the first time. Her gaze scanned to the opposite canyon wall. It was made up of various bands of color and different sorts of rock. The river far below seemed tiny, the trees along its banks-- no more than weeds. The road wound in a serpentine pattern as it worked its way to the bottom. Her face whitened. She was seeing what anyone would—what would happen if a wagon went over the side. It would be a long drop.

Vince smiled. "It's deep all right. What you want is west of us, down that river. See how low its flow is. We will have no problem taking the wagons down the rocky beach along the right and then maybe left depending on what the floods have done."

"It seems dangerous to me to get the wagons down. Maybe we should pack the supplies on horses."

"The wagons can make it with an experienced driver. This

is a wagon road." He pulled on gloves as he walked to the lead wagon.

"You are taking one down?"

"And Sam the other. You and the rest will go down first. Except for Gabe. I want him up here behind us. He'll come down last with the extra horses on a string."

"Why?" she asked, after less than a moment's hesitation. She wasn't the type not to want to know everything, but he'd try anyway.

"I'm the boss. Remember?"

"Does that mean you won't tell me why?"

He lifted his brows. "You can walk or ride down. Which way makes you feel more comfortable?"

"I guess my mare is steady enough on her feet."

"You'll be riding Jupiter. He's steadier."

"You are being bossy today."

His smile widened. "Been deprived lately of something important. Makes me cranky."

"Whose fault is that?" She gave him a saucy smile.

"I plan to fix it soon."

"Good, then you have to get safely to the bottom."

"In my plan."

Sam walked up. "We need to get going. I want off this rim before dark." Vince looked back to the road where Song and her son had begun walking down. Alice, Abby, and David were on horseback.

"Me too." He walked Holly back to Jupiter and lifted her onto his back. "Trust him," he said as he patted her leg and watched as she began down. He and Sam would wait until they were halfway to the bottom before they started. The wagons would to go slower—if all went well.

He and Sam smoked, as they watched the crew's progress. Gabe stood to one side sipping water from his canteen. He had his gelding tied to a nearby juniper. The other horses were on a string behind him. He was to wait until the wagons were nearly on the floor of the canyon before he came down. "You think somebody might take a shot at you on the way down?" he asked for the fourth time since breakfast.

"If they did, we won't be able to protect ourselves as we go down."

"But..."

"I should have told you this earlier. There is money out on Sam's head."

Gabe let out a puff of disbelief. "A bounty?"

Not a legal one."

"You expect someone might be over there waiting?"

"Unlikely, but not impossible. We are most vulnerable on the way down. Shooting off a rifle with a mule, that already doesn't like the road ahead, could be more at risk than someone shooting us."

"All right. I got that. I'll watch for movement over there and shine on metal. Nobody will get a shot off at either of you." He took the new rifle from its scabbard.

"Thanks." The others were far enough down. They could start. Vince took one last puff on his cigarette, ground out the butt. Should be interesting.

Sam walked with him to their wagons. "You ever drive a wagon down a road this steep?" he asked taking one last drag on his own cigarette.

"Nope but I've driven lots of wagons."

"I have too but not this road. Any tips?"

"Don't ride the brake." He laughed.

"Don't upset the mules would be good too." Sam chuckled.

Climbing up on the seat, Vince took the reins in his left hand, lightly flicked them, and moved his right boot to the brake. The mules started down the road with a sureness to their hooves that was reassuring. He concentrated on being sure the wagon was to the inside and no big rocks were in the way.

They slowly moved eastward on a gentle down slope as they got their feel for the track. After the first hairpin to the left, the road ran flatter for a couple of hundred yards before it began a long straight drop to the northwest with nothing to the side but air. He felt some confidence as he remembered testing the brake linkage from the foot pedal under his boot to the lever shaft that rotated the new, rear oak brake shoes he had installed at the livery in Globe.

No wild gusts of wind and no shooting, and they might make it down without a rodeo. At the second reversal, the road was narrow. A steep drop of 50 feet separated the load from a sheer drop to the rocks and water below. Then, the second most likely disaster point was past.

At the third reversal, it was all rock and sloping into the canyon. No place to go if a mule slipped or a spoke cracked with the side loads. The last turn was a pleasure as he saw everybody smiling ahead. With Sam right behind him, this was good day.

With a quick kiss for him, and a relieved smile as they unhitched the mules, Holly helped get the food out of the wagon. Dave and Zian carried the cook stove to the fire they had built.

Sam and Vince stood smoking a cigarette as Gabe rode up. When Vince offered him one, he took it. "Sacred smoke," he said with a grin. "Now, tell me more about this unsavory agreement."

Vince told him as much as he knew. When he finished, Gabe looked at Sam. "You should look more scared."

Sam's smile was humorous. "It's not like it's new to me."

Vince agreed. "Had someone out to kill him when I met him. He has a knack."

"This one was not my fault."

"Were the others?" Gabe asked with an answering smile.

Sam put out his hand with a twisting movement. "Sometimes."

"Who should I be looking for then?" Gabe asked turning to Vince. "In case, I wanted to keep him around for awhile."

"Somebody who looks like me would be a good start. Besides Cole, I have two brothers and a father who used to look a lot like me. Guess he's gotten old now though, maybe a little decrepit." He could hope. He snickered.

"We all have brothers then where it's not always been an easy road," Gabe observed with another long, appreciative draw on the cigarette.

"Cord and I never even knew each other 'til we were long grown. We fought plenty since." Sam grinned.

"Cord is salt of the earth," Vince said.

"On that we agree. So is Rafe."

"Sometimes that can be hard to live up to," Gabe said staring into the growing darkness. "When you know you'll never be the man your older brother is. Not a good feeling."

"I'd know about that one," Cole said. He had been standing back in the shadows where Vince had not seen him. "Oh, and I was supposed to tell you-- supper's ready."

After they had eaten and the ladies cleaned the dishes, Vince pulled Holly to him where he had his back leaned against a log. "Tell me more about this place we are looking for," he said.

"It's more open as a valley than this. The cliffs are on both sides but the bottom had ground for a garden."

"I thought this was an archaeological exploration," David said,

"It is, but it is based on both what I have read from Bande-lier and his travels as well as..." She hesitated. "Dreams —mine."

"Bandelier?"

"Adolph Bandelier. He is an ethnographer, who traveled the Southwest, describing all the prehistoric ruins he was told were there. He wrote a book with their descriptions. An elder of the Jemez told him what they believed happened to the people who were here first."

"Those who lived in these deserted buildings?" David asked.

She nodded. "There are, of course, different opinions. The only certainty is that they were occupied and then abandoned. The elder told Bandelier that the survivors ended up at his village. Others believe they went south."

"The Aztec," Vince said.

"Yes, but it's not been proven. The connection of the tribes throughout the Americas is what might be proven by archaeology."

"But you have more to prove, don't you?" Gabe spoke up.

"Perhaps but that is what I am looking to for in a scientific sense. The connections to tribes as far up as the Pacific North-west and Canada could be proven by artifacts that were traded."

"Tell us more about the dream," Abby said. "I am inter-ested in that because I sometimes have powerful dreams... or so I think."

Holly explained the basic images she had seen, the pot buried at the back of the small room.

"That's all to it?" Abby asked. Holly could hear the skepti-cism in her voice. She had not wanted to talk about the trader, but she supposed she had to. She described the way she saw the man arrive and his expertise with weapons, then finally how he had been killed.

"The closer we get to the place, the more I wonder about the things I didn't get from the dream," she said in conclusion. "For instance, I assumed it was marauders but I don't actually have a clear sense of who used the spear to kill him."

"This is fascinating," Alice said with excitement. "I had no idea we were out to solve two mysteries—one historical and the other spiritual."

"Buddhists believe in reincarnation," Song said. She rarely talked when the group was together, but it appeared the story also excited her interest. "I wonder if any of us were there also, back in that lifetime. Maybe we all were. Some believe we come again and again in soul families, I think that would be the best way to describe it."

When Sam chuckled, Abby sent him a look of remonstrance. "You can't possibly not believe in it."

"Dust to dust is what I believe," he said with that smirk that had Abby growling at him.

"How do you explain us?"

"Oh, baby," he said with a laugh. "I can easily explain my end of that." His grin was a little softer.

Vince tightened his arm around Holly. "I am interested now in what you saw in terms of terrain. We can work out who was there or not later." He smiled. "Tell me what we will be looking for."

"There are tall canyon walls like these but not so tight. There is a wonderful vista from the rooms." She closed her eyes trying to remember. "I think there is a creek below, which is why I thought the Cibecue, but I suppose there are others."

"There are. And if the canyon you are looking for is not narrow, a slot canyon, then it's not likely to be the lower

Cibecue. It requires wading up it in places. The upper has less of the canyon feel as it broadens way out."

"You have been there?" Gabe asked.

"Yes." He rubbed his fingers lightly along Holly's arm. "The first time, I had come with Cho Nah, a White Mountain elder. He had to give permission for me to trade with the tribe. We had come down mostly for the Salt Banks."

"What are they?" David asked.

"Three miles down the Salt from Cibecue Creek are a series of salt springs with massive, beautiful formations, like the kind in some caves. The colors are more varied and intense than you see here. Orange, red, and dark green. It's sacred, and the Apache get salt from there as well as go there to perform rituals."

"I have heard of that place," Gabe said. "Why would he take a white man there?"

"It was a test. I understood the reason. You know how often the Apache have been cheated."

"And all the tribes," Gabe acknowledged.

"Cho Nah wanted to know if he could trust me. He suggested the two of us go off for a few days to hunt, and he would show me the salt springs. I knew what he was doing but decided to go anyway."

"Anyway?" Holly asked.

Gabe was the one who chuckled. "If the ancient ones had answered you could not, what would have happened?"

"I wasn't worried."

"You had a lot of trust in him," David said. With the fire burning in the center of their circle, the faces lit by it, it was a time for ghost stories.

"You are still here. Guess he heard the right message," Sam said.

"I trade and don't cheat. I was interested in their bead

work. Once we got past the test, we went up to the falls. They are beautiful, drop probably sixty feet. In August, they were booming. There is a pool below that is deep enough to swim during the monsoons. We did."

"It sounds beautiful. I'd love to go there... with you, you know for rituals," Holly said. He saw in her eyes what she had in mind. He liked the idea too.

"The Cibecue is beautiful, but I am thinking what you might be looking for is up Canyon Creek. There are ruins. The Apache don't go there much."

"Because?"

"Death isn't something they like being around either." He smiled though no one else did.

CHAPTER 17

Tucson

Opening his hotel room, feeling spent, Jeremiah was unsure what he thought of Mrs. Osbourne. The lady, and he used the term loosely, was nothing like he had expected. Beautiful even though older, with the bone structure that would last. He had expected her to be an easterner, which she was. But she was tougher looking than he thought folks back there would be—especially ladies of wealth. He could easily imagine the woman, whom he had sat across at dinner, ordering a murder. What he still didn't grasp is why. She was no rancher. Why did she want the Circle R?

She had been surprisingly understanding about the failure of their first attempt on Ryker. When he had explained they would have to head north to get him if she wanted it done soon, she had smiled with that look which made him wonder again—who was she?

Although she had been well groomed and dressed, he noted the material in her gown had been repaired and not by a seamstress. Fine cloth but not new. Her hair was obviously hennaed but not by a professional either. He knew what that should look like from the few proper ladies he'd been around —usually when on the wrong side of a gun.

The woman had smiled but revealed nothing about herself, beyond what he already knew. Although her speech had been fine, an education somewhere back there, he had a feeling much harder words lurked right under the surface. He saw it in her eyes.

He lay in bed staring up at the ceiling as the streetlights bounced patterns off passing wagons. He was concerned equally about Asa, who was clearly up to something, but he had admitted nothing when he had seen him after his dinner with Mrs. Osbourne. Asa had instead talked about heading north, killing Ryker and claiming the reward. He had not mentioned Vince at all. Did he expect Vince to remain disinterested in any attempt to murder Ryker? Unlikely.

He thought then of his youngest son. A man never had a more beautiful son than Jesse. Even as a baby he'd been so beautiful that it took everyone's breath away, but he didn't talk until late. When he did, it was with few words. He took a lot more time than most would to answer any question. The boy had avoided him as much as possible. Strong, fast, coordinated, but something wasn't right with his head. It wasn't only the headaches that dogged him, but his inability to reason things out—even simple things could stump him, and he'd close down.

Both he and Valerie had worried, as mental illness had been a factor in his father's abrupt end. Jesse though had a sweetness that didn't seem anything like Josiah. It was Asa who more resembled that. Still, Jeremiah knew what happened to the mentally ill, how they were treated, and he went out of his way to be sure no one could accuse it in his son.

Those were all reasons that Jeremiah needed Vince. He had it all, the coordination, the brains. He would be his right hand. He knew who his oldest could be for him but how to turn him that way. Jeremiah might have considered praying for God's help to get his first born back, but he was well aware he'd passed over that bridge long ago.

Mrs. Osbourne had asked him to join her for breakfast. He'd most likely find himself paying for that too. She had manipulated him into paying for their dinner by waiting and smiling that tiny smile. Didn't rich people pay for the meals they ate, or was that how they stayed rich?

Because he could not read the woman, before he had gone back to his room, he had stopped by the Pedrales to tell Asa and Jesse to join them for breakfast. Asa might be mean as a snake, but he might recognize who Mrs. Osbourne was under the ruffles.

In the morning, when he walked into the Rainbow cafe, he saw she was already there. The surprise was so were his sons. He sat on the remaining chair and signaled to the waitress for coffee, then looked back at them scanning from one face to the other before he settled on hers.

"Did you have a good sleep?" he asked her after he had his coffee.

"It was a bit noisy but fine." Again there was that insincere smile.

"I take you don't like Tucson much."

"It's all right, but nowhere I would choose to be, of course, when there are better choices."

"I am surprised then that you want the Circle R." That had been a bone that he'd wrestled with from the start.

"I don't want it to keep it. I want what is fair."

"Ryker cheated Breanna's husband out of the ranch," Asa said lifting his cup for more coffee.

Jeremiah didn't miss the use of her name. She hadn't invited him to use her given name. Guess she had a thing for young dogs, not old ones. He grinned at the thought. The waitress was back to take their order. Jesse hadn't looked at the menu ordering what Jeremiah had. He knew why, that his youngest couldn't read, but it was depressing to him.

When the server had gone, Breanna Osbourne said, "Marius was gullible. He wanted Mr. Ryker to have the ranch and sold it to him at a foolish price." She grimaced.

"There is more to this, isn't there?" Jeremiah said resisting the impulse to get up and walk out before eating. He was a snake sometimes, but this woman was clearly a viper.

"There is another aspect to this. My husband..."

He stopped her by raising his hand. "I had the impression you had remarried. Was I wrong?"

"Where did you get that information?"

"From your name. I have sources for information, and I find all I can on any job we take. Ryker's ranch was owned by a Marius Gray before he bought it. Unless you went back to a maiden name after you divorced him, it appears you have a husband."

"Did. He is also dead." She gave a sad little smile.

Asa put out his hand to where hers rested on the table. "So sorry for your losses, Breanna."

Jeremiah found that an interesting gesture also. Who was playing who with those two? "So you believe Ryker's widow will sell you the ranch at a low price where you can then resell it," Jeremiah said making sure he had it straight.

"There is that, of course, but also..." She sniffled. On a young woman, it might've been attractive—not so much on an aging whore. He was pretty sure now what she had been and probably still was. "My first husband left a will which named Sam Ryker as his beneficiary. Again, ridiculous, but he had come to have a fondness for the man. I had no idea of its existence, of course, until I went to the lawyer after Marius' death. There is a codicil."

Jeremiah resisted the smile. Now he got it.

"If Mr. Ryker is dead and cannot claim the bequest, it falls to me."

"Who deserves it," Asa said stroking her hand again.

"Yes, I was after all his wife at one time. What was Ryker to him?" She almost snarled it out.

Fortunately, their order arrived, and Jeremiah was spared saying anything. As he ate, he again had to suppress a smile. Asa wasn't as good a judge of people as he had always thought. That was actually not a bad thing. The problem he saw was, although Breanna Osbourne might get the money her ex-husband had left, there was no way to be sure she'd actually pay for the murder of Ryker. He had a decided feeling she would not. So they would do the killing, take the risk, and she'd move onto another sucker. Sweet. Now how could he use what he knew?

After breakfast, Breanna went back to her hotel. Jesse went to make sure their horses were being cared for. Asa asked to talk to him Jeremiah lit a cigar and waited for what he expected would come next. It didn't take long.

"I want to go after Ryker."

"Seems like a plan. Take Jesse, Brewster, and Boggs. I would only slow you down."

From his expression, Asa didn't like that idea. Jeremiah decided to reassure him. "I have no interest in the widow if that worries you. She's clearly got her eye on you anyway."

Asa smiled. "She is a beautiful woman."

"Agreed. So, leave in the morning."

"Sooner I go, the sooner I am back with the news that the lady wants to hear."

"True. The mouthpiece ready?"

"He will be." Asa sneered.

"Fine. I'll see if I can scratch up some jobs for us when you get back."

"We won't need them when we get her reward."

Jeremiah resisted the snort. It was one of those days he had to show self control—never his long suit. "Good luck, son," he said suppressing his smile.

An hour later, Jesse came to the bar where Jeremiah was nursing a whiskey. "What went wrong?" he asked his youngest.

"Nothing."

"When is Asa leaving then?"

A muscle twitched in Jesse's jaw. "He left."

Jeremiah sucked on that idea. He saw that Jesse was in no mood to give him answers. "You want to gamble for awhile?" He slid a twenty dollar bill on the table.

Jesse looked at it and then up. "You said gambling is stupid." The word rolled almost angrily off his lips.

"It's not a good idea as a general rule. Better ways to make money. House always wins, but I am in a good mood today." He rose then. "Have some fun, then meet me for supper at around six back at the hotel."

"With Mrs. Osbourne?"

"No, just the two of us." He could not afford to keep paying for her meals. Besides something was up with Jesse. He knew from experience that it wasn't easy to get anything out of him. When his son had relaxed a little, he'd give it a try.

He supposed he was an unnatural father not to be concerned he might never see Asa again. Except, that son was dangerous to him. If someone else took care of that problem, good. If Ryker was killed, Vince would come back through Tucson to help the family get home.

He knew, once he saw his eldest and could talk to him that he could convince him to come back to him. He was good at convincing when he wanted. He'd handled it badly before, been upset over losing Valerie, and snarled at Vince. He knew better ways to bring his son back under his wing.

Salt River Canyon

Vince rode Jupiter ahead of the wagons as they headed down the Salt. Rivers changed all the time, and he had no way to knowing whether there would be problems ahead. If they were fortunate, they could camp where Cibecue Creek ran into the Salt. It had had a wide beach. The mules needed a break. One had been favoring one leg. He'd have to find what was wrong. The next day, he'd ride downriver with Holly to see if Canyon Creek looked more like the general location to start looking for her ruins.

The canyon walls loomed over him, and he could not help but remember his first time riding this way. He had known he was taking a risk to go with Cho Nah, who he let ride behind him—something he almost never did with a virtual stranger. How did he know what words the old man would hear from his ancestors? He didn't. But he trusted in the elder's good nature and his own honesty. Maybe, because of his family, the whites didn't see him as a good man, but the tribes judged him for who he was and what he did.

When they had arrived at the salt springs, Cho Nah had told him to remove his weapon. Vince recognized what that meant, but he did it, putting the belt over his saddle before he walked down to the river with the Apache beside him.

At the bank, Cho Nah had said he should take off his boots and shirt, then kneel. He had done that with the Apache dancing around him. He had waited unsure how long it would take. Had it been an hour or more? When the dancing and chanting had stopped, Cho Nah was behind him. He had waited in the silence of the canyon, only ravens overhead screaming a warning. The touch on his right shoulder had come first and then his left. Still he had waited until he had been told to rise. He still remembered the words.

"You are honorable man. They say to trust you." The old man was grinning broadly. Vince had managed a smile also. He knew how close he had come to death. It wasn't the first time. It was, however, the only time he had accepted someone else's decree for whether he would die. Something in this ritual or experience had gone beyond the ability to trade with the tribe for why he had done it. He had wanted to be acknowledged and respected. It was something he would not find from his own people; so he had sought to find it elsewhere.

The canyon was much as he remembered. Wildflowers bloomed in crevasses. Here and there small springs fell in tiny rivulets to the river below. There were willow and cottonwood trees, some had been upended by the last major flood. Wherever they camped, if it was to be for the summer, they would need to stay well above the rivers and creeks. This country was hard on those who got careless.

When Vince got to the mouth of Cibecue Creek, he was relieved to find the desired camping spot. There was even fresh grass that the horses and mules would appreciate. This would provide the right spot until they found the ruin fitting Holly's dream—if it was possible. Anywhere else was unlikely to be this good for water and some forage, an area the animals were likely to remain without rope fences.

He dismounted and let Jupiter graze a bit as he studied the nearby cliffs. Nothing looked apt to crumble, a concern in canyons like these. There were many ways to die, under tons of rock wasn't one he would choose.

Lighting a cigarette, he let himself think about his life. He rarely looked back or forward. It was enough to live the day. He had some money in a bank. No home. No family of his own. He was forty-one years old. Strong, muscular, he could work all day when need be. That wasn't going to last. He would be old and then what would it all have meant?

Taking a long draw on the cigarette, he didn't find the relief he often had with the smoke. It was not a good thing to think deeply—not when a man had no choice.

Except, did he have a choice, one he wasn't willing to look at? No, he had been right. Holly made him want things he had no right to want. He had to keep on the course he had set, which meant someday he'd be the one killed. Sooner maybe than he'd wish.

Hell, not good to start thinking.

By the time the wagons had reached the beach, he had built a fire circle and with Jupiter's help, dragged logs to form seats around it. He liked the setup as a place to protect. It would not be easy for anyone to come on them when they didn't see them first. Of course, he had the advantage in wagons being noisy but even a horseman would be heard before he could get within gunshot. His smile was grim as he acknowledged that he was again thinking like prey.

Holly felt both excited and scared. She was close to her dream. She felt it. If not up Cibecue Creek as she had originally expected, it was near. She could feel the energy of the home she had lived in. It had been different then, but she had been in this very spot. She was not sure how she had been here. Maybe it had been for the salt or even the waterfall which she could almost see in her mind's eye. Could it have been for something else nearby, something her people had also needed?

After they had prepared a simple meal, she dropped onto the log, as tired as the others looked. They were all ready to lie on the beach or wash in the pool a little upstream from their camp.

Everyone knew about her and Vince. Could they go off together? She glanced over at Abby who was brushing and then braiding Alice's hair. This trip had given her a chance to get to know her and even Song in a different way. They had more interest in the mystical than Holly had expected. She had thought others would find her dreams ridiculous, but they had not. They had also had experiences. Maybe many humans did, but they didn't share them with each other.

"Your thoughts go deep," Gabe said as he came to sit beside her.

"You were interested in the dreams, but you never told me," she said as she watched Vince working with one of the mule's hooves with his knife. He was bent over the hoof while Sam held the animal's head. Vince had rolled up his sleeves and his forearm was muscular as he strained with whatever he was doing. When they released the mule, it walked off with a huff. Sam and he laughed.

"I wanted to know more about how you were going to handle it. How seriously you took it. I thought it might've been a game for you."

"And now you don't think so?"

"No."

"I might not be logical about it though." She was having a hard time finding her professional balance. She had trained to explore what had been left behind for answers as to whom a people had been; however, she had been driven to do this exploration for something personal. It had become even more personal once she met Vince.

"You two look deep in plotting," Vince said as he and Sam walked up.

"We are," Gabe said. "Dream plotting."

Vince laughed and sat on the other side of Holly. She felt his presence as though he had touched her even when he hadn't. "Where do we camp tomorrow?" she asked anxious now to reach what had been her home in another lifetime. She was increasingly sure of it.

"Here."

"What?"

"For a day and maybe two, the wagons need to be where they are. It's been a hard week. We will move on when we know if we have another good campsite."

"I want to move on," she said hoping she had controlled the demanding tone she was feeling.

"Hell, I don't want to hear this," Sam said with a laugh and left to find his family. Gabe chuckled and agreed.

Alone, Holly wanted to rephrase what she had said, but she wanted to get to where they were going. Before she could find a way to achieve both her goals, Vince said, "That mule had a bad hoof. The animal and our horses need a day's rest, maybe more. If you kill off your mules, your expedition is done. When we go downriver, the way will be harder, it winds around like a snake. Rockier shores and places we may have to go to the hills, which won't be fun. You might be able to smell the country you want, and if you were a crow, you could get there without much trouble. You are not."

She clenched her jaw against her retort. Knowing, that he was right and she effectively ignorant about what they were doing, did not help. "All right," she said resentfully.

"You are a scientist, aren't you?"

She resented the condescending tone, but she nodded.

"The people you are interested in finding knew this area. They came down for the salt. There is something else near the salt. I haven't been there but there is a vein of quality turquoise."

"So that's why you want to delay. You want to take turquoise."

He gave her one of those looks and rose from the log. "When you want to talk sensibly, let me know." He stalked off.

She felt like crying or yelling. Maybe both. As she struggled to get control of her wayward emotions, Gabe came back. "He was right. You know that." Tears rolled down her cheeks. Gabe's arm went around her shoulders. "We're all tired. A rest here will be good."

She sighed. "We're so close, and I so much want to..."

"I know. Prove what you have been dreaming had a purpose."

She nodded.

"Then trust the man you said would be the boss. You know he'd never take anything from the Apache lands."

She knew that too and was angry with herself for even suggesting it. "I will say I am sorry."

"Good idea as soon as he gets back."

"Back?" She looked around but didn't see him.

"He just went up Cibecue to check it out."

"Why would he do that?" Stupid woman to ask someone else that question. She knew the answer.

"Because he wants to be sure it's safe for others to travel up it. You do know this country has wolf, bear and cougar in it—

not to mention human predators. Not far from here, when my brother came with Grace, he was nearly killed by a cougar attack."

"I'm a fool."

Gabe grinned. "No, only a woman anxious to prove her truth. It will come. I have a question for you."

"All right."

"You think that trader was Vince, don't you?"

"Yes." She more than thought it. She knew it, but in her heart, not where she could prove it.

"And you loved him then."

"Yes." She felt the tears start again.

"If it was him, then he knows this country too—in his instincts whether he's had dreams. Trust that."

She brushed away tears. "You are so wise."

"Seatakaa," he said with a smile. "I want to think anyway."

"It seems like it to me. All right, I will try to be more mature about this." It wouldn't be easy, but she would try. She would apologize to Vince whenever he gave her a chance. She understood how insulting her accusation had been especially to a man who had worked hard to earn the respect of others. She felt furious with herself. Grow up.

CHAPTER 18

I t was dark when Vince returned to the camp. The fire was
dying down and only one person was up. Holly. He didn't
want to face her but maybe they needed to get this out. She
was leaning back against the log and looked up when he came
into the firelight.

"I wondered if you would come back tonight," she said in a
low voice.

"I thought about not."

She rose and took his hand, pulling him downstream to
where they had argued. In the dim light, he could see the
bedrolls. Both of theirs. He looked at her then. "And?"

"Everybody already knows we are lovers, well except
maybe Zian, Alice and David. I don't mean for us to do
anything anyway. Can we sleep together? Will you let me apologize to you?"

"I understood how you felt." He wanted to, but she had cut
deeper than she knew.

"I don't. I had no reason to say what I did. I know you

wouldn't take anything that didn't belong to you. I know you respect the Apache. I was a fool."

Seeing the tears reflected on her lashes, he pulled her into his arms. "We're all stressed."

"You have so much on your mind, and I understand it's not only here but the risk to Sam and your family reentering your life." She burrowed her head into his chest.

He let out a breath. He pulled her to the blankets to lie beside him. She had set them up, so one could be under and one over them. He put his arm around her and cuddled her against his side.

"It's you too," he said finally. "I want this to be what you want."

"I know. I am sorry I said that. Please forgive me."

"It's forgotten."

"Not by me. I never want to hurt you."

He kissed her hair and then stared up at the sky. The stars were intense at this elevation and away from other lights, less dust in the air. The moon just peeking over the ridge, it was still almost full. The light slowly bathed the canyon walls with an eerie sort of pattern. As much as he knew Holly had needed to come, for him it was presenting a much more difficult journey. He didn't have her dreams or memories of living here in another lifetime. Yet, there was a kind of energy that seemed both threatening and welcoming.

Had that trader been like him, a man without a home? Had he come to this place and thought he had found a home before it all fell apart? The thoughts had all come down hard on him when he had waded and clambered over the rocks to reach the falls.

"Did you make it to the falls?" she asked kissing his chest where the shirt was open.

"Yes, it's beautiful up there but a rough hike, not sure you'll want to do it."

"I do want to. I need to relax more. I am pushing too hard. We have the whole summer for the exploration of the ruins. I don't know why I have felt such pressure."

He understood better than she imagined. He felt it too. Maybe they all did.

"Do you know the patterns on the moon have a story?" she asked kissing his neck.

"You know it, I take it." He smiled.

"I do. The images on the moon are of the Aztec moon goddess. It's not a happy story." She began unbuttoning his shirt.

"They usually aren't," he said beginning to wish the moon wasn't so full, coating the world with light, as she was making him want her in a way that was not about to be satisfied this night.

She put her fingers over his lips. "Want to hear the story?"

"I am trying to decide. Will it make it any harder to sleep than what you are doing to me right now?"

She tucked her fingers inside his shirt, stroking down his belly. "Maybe."

"I hope this one doesn't relate to us."

"I don't think so although... anyway, the Aztec goddesses name was Coyolxauhqui, which means golden bells. She was the daughter of Coatlicue, who was the earth goddess. Coyolxauhqui had a rather strong sense of her own right and wrong, which wasn't necessarily obedient. Maybe it does relate."

She ran her fingers along one muscle ridge and over to his side. He sucked in a breath trying to get control of his body's response to her play.

"She encouraged her four hundred brothers and sisters to kill their mother because she had been dishonored. In retribution, I guess, her brother cut off her head and threw it into the sky, along with parts of her body to form the moon. It's why we see the patterns in a full moon. There are some impressive Aztec engravings that illustrate it with the severed breasts most prominent."

"They are fond of breasts. That's not hard to understand," he observed as he felt her fingers moving below the line of his pants. "Holly."

"It's not like I couldn't you know... It might take off the tension some." She smiled against his neck as she delved lower.

He took hold of her exploring hand and brought it back to safe territory. "I have a better idea. Tomorrow, we will get away, the two of us. Instead of going up Cibecue Creek with the others, we will take an amble with the horses, and see if we can scout out a good camping site downstream."

"Oh," she said with some reluctance in her voice, "you mean I have to stop playing with you."

He smiled. "Only until tomorrow morning."

"I'd like to also see the falls." He saw her smile in the moonlight.

"No reason you can't. I think that mule will need two days if we don't want to risk laming him. So you'll have your chance... after you've worked off some of this steam."

She laughed. "It might take a lot to work it off," she warned.

"It might. I think I am up to it. Figuratively speaking, of course."

"Oh, I hope so. I do hope so." With that, she cuddled down against him. The last thing he felt, before falling asleep, was her pulling the blanket over them.

Tucson

To avoid the widow Osbourne, Jeremiah took Jesse to a restaurant in a less desirable part of Tucson. He asked him nothing to begin, letting his son feel at ease and that he wasn't going to pump him. Of course, he was. When they had finished their meal, he smiled. "Want a piece of pie, Jess?"

His son looked at him, a wary expression in his eyes.

"Just apple. You like apple?"

"Not now."

Evidently bribery wouldn't work. "All right, you know what I want. There is a reason you didn't go with Asa, isn't there?" Jesse had a sweetness to his face even with the probing look he had turned onto Jeremiah. "I want to know why you didn't want to go?"

"Just didn't." His son rose and Jeremiah followed him from the restaurant. He had rarely seen Jesse smoke, but now he leaned against the post supporting the roof and took out a cigarette. He was stressing but from what?

"You might as well tell me the truth. I will find out."

Jesse lit the cigarette and stared into the street. Tucson was only starting to come alive with the saloons lit up and more and more men pouring into them.

"Jess, you can tell me. You can trust me. I am your father." Jeremiah knew he was no great shakes as a father, but he also felt a sympathy for his youngest as he could see how troubled he was. He was not sure what had gone wrong with his son's mind but from birth, a difficult birth, he had been slow. He was so powerful looking, a face that gave no clue to what was wrong inside. A gentle giant with a loving spirit. Jesse hadn't known a lot of love in his life—mostly it had been he and his mother trying to protect him from the world. It made him feel guilty to push him now, but he had to know what Asa was up to.

"Let's hear it. Were you afraid to go?"

Jesse smiled at that as he smoked. "No."

"Then tell me why you did not want to go."

"Asa hates Vince."

Jeremiah felt a shock wave go through him. "Why?" he managed to ask without giving away his reaction—he hoped anyway. Jesse shrugged without answering. "His hate of Vince means what exactly?" But he already knew what it meant. He should have thought of it himself. "What did he tell you that he planned that you wanted no part of?"

Jesse blew the smoke out. "Nothing."

"But you know something."

He nodded. "It's Vince he wants dead more than Ryker."

Jeremiah considered the words. Sometimes slow though he might be, Jesse knew things. It wasn't hard to put it together, and he should have seen it himself. Sure, Asa wanted the widow's money, but he also wanted to kill his brother. He couldn't take both Ryker and Vince; so that meant he would bushwhack one.

"He has to beat Vince, doesn't he?"

Jesse smoked but finally nodded.

Asa would want to kill Vince in a fight, convinced he could take him. To do that, he had to kill Ryker first. Killing Ryker where it would hurt Vince and then seeing Vince be beaten and die, that is the only thing that would satisfy Asa's nature.

"I didn't want to kill Asa," Jesse said without looking at his father.

"Of course, you didn't. You should though have told me right away." He didn't blame Jesse that he hadn't. He had no reason to trust any in his family, least of all his father. Damn, he didn't want to get back on a horse, but he needed to warn

Vince-- if he could get there in time. If he warned him, he'd think more kindly of him. Except, where the hell was he?

"Did Asa give you any clue where they would be heading?"

"No, just that he was meeting Madison at Oracle."

That made sense. Asa didn't want to be seen leaving with the barrister because he was going to kill him as soon as he knew where to find Ryker and Vince. From Oracle, they were bound to go to Globe. They might delay there in the bars. Would Asa be in a hurry? With the softer lawyer along, they might lay over a day. It might give him a chance to get to Asa before he found Vince. Except where?

"Let's go to the Pedrales," he said to Jesse. "I feel like a whiskey. How about you?"

Jesse nodded.

Cibecue Creek

Waking in Vince's arms seemed the best possible way to Holly until Alice looked down on them. "Breakfast is ready," she said with one of those looks that only a young girl can give. Holly knew about that because of her own curiosity at that age, something that didn't get satisfied until many years later, over ten actually.

"We slept in," Holly said before Alice ran back to the campfire.

"Guess she'll wonder," Vince said as he buttoned his shirt before sitting.

"Maybe." She rose straightening her heavy cotton skirt. She had purchased it, which she had split in two. It looked like a skirt but functioned as pants and looked more proper—as if anyone cared.

She looked down at him. "You still plan on us riding downriver?"

"After sleeping next to you all night," he said with one of his smiles, "you better believe it."

She patted one of her deep pockets. "I brought condoms."

"Good."

She walked up to the camp wondering what the others would think of her sleeping next to Vince. If they thought anything, they didn't voice it.

An hour later, they had all eaten and were sipping their coffee. She helped Abby and Song clean the tin plates and listened as the plans for the day were discussed.

"I could ride with you to look for another campsite," Cole suggested when Vince told them what he and Holly were going to do.

Vince lit a cigarette. "You need to stick around here to guard the camp. I don't want anyone stealing our horses or mules."

Cole looked to the canyon rim. "You think we're being watched?"

Vince blew out the smoke. "Want to see their tracks? Nothing happens on their land that they don't know. They have had an eye on us since we got to the Salt."

"You expect trouble?"

Vince shrugged. "They know we have a permit to be here. Some of them may just want to sure we mean right by them. Don't be quick to shoot. But stay alert to what's around."

"What about that turquoise?" David asked. "Can we explore that if we don't take any?"

"It's up the side of a cliff, requires some clambering. Why don't you save that until I am with you? Going up the Cibecue though to see the falls will not need me."

"I don't want to go," Song said. "I will stay here and make bread."

"You sure?" Holly asked. "I don't want you always working."

"I won't be. The bread will have to rise. I don't care to scramble over rocks. I did enough of that when young." She grinned.

"Is the pool deep enough for swimming?" Alice asked.

"If you don't worry about bumping your knees in a few places. It's wide but shallow except where the water pounds down." He looked then up at Sam who was watching him. "You go armed, of course."

"Of course."

An hour later, Vince and Holly headed downstream, while the others had begun their hike up the creek. She admired the beauty of the canyon. In places the walls came down almost to the river, the formations always were interesting, sometimes almost columnar. She watched as a cardinal swooped overhead and landed in a nearby cottonwood. In moments, she heard the song and an answer.

"How long ago were you here?" she asked.

He considered that a moment. "My first time was in '87. I had gotten into trading at that time mostly with the Pueblo people, the Navajo with their rugs. I came down this way to Fort Apache and asked around. It's when I met Cho Nah."

"Was it dangerous still?" She had little knowledge about when the wars had been fought.

"No more than anywhere. If I had been dishonest though, my first trip here would have been my last."

"You would have been murdered."

"Executed more accurately describes how it'd have been seen."

"Why did you take that kind of risk?"

"I was interested in trading but even more in the Apache culture. They had stood up against the whole United States a long time. They are a proud people. I guess I was curious."

"And willing to risk your life to satisfy that curiosity?"

He laughed, his gaze scanning the walls high above them. "I wasn't planning to take it that far. I had met Cho Nah and felt he was honorable. I knew my intentions were. I trusted him."

"Did you come back?"

"Only the time I told you about, the hunt. Otherwise, coming through the general region on my way elsewhere."

She was silent a moment as the river did another switchback and the horses had to pick their way to solid ground. When it was flat again, she debated whether to ask him the other thing that had been on her mind since they had left the camp.

"Do you think Song is interested in Cole?"

He snorted. "I hadn't thought about it."

"But now that you have."

"It's not my business."

"Typical male answer." She glanced over to see his amused smile. "She is older than him. Would age matter?" she asked more interested in how he saw age and how it might impact them.

"Maybe."

"If he and she got together, he'd then stay in Tucson." She liked that idea because then it would bring Vince back—at least she hoped it would.

"Why don't you concentrate on your own problem," he

suggested with one of those grins that had her thinking about a soft sandy beach and no scouting for ruins.

"What is my problem?" she asked with what she hoped was a smile to match his own.

He pointed ahead, and she saw the beach. Tucked back in an alcove, cottonwoods for shade and brush for screening. "Looks like a good place for the horses to graze for a bit. What do you think?"

She smiled but didn't answer. He already knew what she thought.

CHAPTER 19

As Vince took care of the horses, Holly walked to the river. It was almost green but didn't look unclean. Maybe the color came from the shale, sandstone and mineral laden rocks around it.

"Look to your right," he said as he came up behind her. That was when she saw the beautiful shapes and colors. It looked much like the inside of a cave with stalagmites and shapes formed in ways not usually seen.

"This is the salt springs?" she asked as they walked down toward them. The curve of the river blocked their access to reaching them.

He nodded. "When we leave, we will have to cross the river right above here on solid sandstone. You can see them even better from the other side."

"Is that the Apache sacred place over there?"

"And here."

She smiled. "Is it all right for us to do what... you promised here?"

"There is no better place for it." He pulled her into his arms. His muscles were so strong.

Strangely enough, for all the attraction she felt toward him, in other ways, he unsettled her. He was overpowering and seeming above her on so many levels. He knew about a world she'd never know—schooling differences or not. She liked that she sometimes had control over a man like him, could break through his barriers as she had that first time they made love.

Her thinking though was going far beyond this time on the river beach. She had begun to wonder why the two of them could not have more, could not have a lifetime.

"Don't even think it," he said seeming to read her mind.

"Why not? You know I love you, don't you?" She had never said it, but she had known it from the day he had come to her home, maybe even when he had pulled her from the horse.

"Me? Or that man in another lifetime? I don't think you know."

"You are going to make me angry," she said as she pulled his head down and kissed him the way he had kissed her so many times by pressing her tongue against his lips and then thrusting into his mouth. When she released his head, she said, "You are treating me as a child."

He smiled, lifting his head to look down at her. "No, I'm not." He fingered her nipple through her shirt, as he teased it, leading to her whole body feeling as though it was swelling. "I am most definitely not treating you as a child. Even though, you are in some ways."

"I am not. I am a full grown woman."

His bent and took that nipple into his mouth, sucking on it and then the other, the thin fabric of her shirt and chemise not lessening how it stirred the rest of her body. "Yes," he whispered, "you are very much a woman."

Her breathing came faster as his hands went to her

buttocks and pulled her against him. "So are we only going to talk about it?" she asked beginning to unbutton his shirt.

To her disappointment, he stepped back. "What do you want to do?"

"I want you to take off all of your clothes." Her voice grew husky as she said it. "I haven't seen you naked enough recently."

He laughed but finished unbuttoning the shirt, throwing it to the sand. "Enough?" he asked.

"Not nearly but oh I do love your chest, Vince." He folded his hands over that muscular chest as she walked around him. She liked the hair that was sprinkled across his chest and then arrowed down to his belt. "Your gun must be heavy," she said smiling.

"You want it off. Take it."

She took her lower lip between her teeth as she untied the string that held the holster down. She took her time, handling his thigh as much as possible, and brushing the bulge above. The cartridge belt buckle was heavy and took time to unfasten. She set the belt and gun on the shirt and again looked at him. He spread his hands, offering her free access. She unbuttoned the first button of his pants, all the while, her gaze holding his. Slowly, she undid each one, watching as his eyes darkened. When she had finished, she pushed the pants down, taking her time again as she moved them down his thighs to his knees. He wore nothing under, which left him effectively naked all the places she most wanted to see and touch.

"You are to remain just like that," she said as she knelt and helped him pull off boots and then pants. Finally, when he stood naked on the sandy river bank, the breeze ruffling his hair, with that smile that had her heart beating faster, she rose and moved to stand where she could see him. She let her eyes roam slowly over his entire body.

"You do like to play." His breath quickened.

"With you, oh yes." When he would have reached for her buttons, she stepped into his arms, pressing her clothed body against his nude one. She ran her fingers down his buttocks, squeezing and loving the way he let his breath out in a groan. She felt him hard against her.

"You are so beautiful, Vince. Do you know how beautiful you are?" she asked pulling his head down for a kiss that lasted until he broke it off.

"Men aren't beautiful," he said huskily, and this time he didn't let her stop him as he unfastened her shirt, pulled down her chemise and then took her back in his arms, bare chests now pressed together. It didn't take long from there to remove the rest of her clothing, and have her down on the sand as he leaned over her.

She reached over for her britches and delved into a pocket before opening him the condom she had brought. Hungry now for the next step, she slowly, oh so slowly sheathed him with it. "Come into me now," she whispered as she kissed his neck and down his chest.

His smile was hard as he levered himself over and took her in one hard thrust. From that moment, she lost touch with what was around her, as they seemed to be one with feelings, which built until she exploded in a cry and climax that filled her whole body. She heard his groan and knew he was coming with her.

They lay together until they came to an awareness of the world. "You know I waited for you. I knew someday you'd be there, not consciously but unconsciously," she said with a sigh. "And I love you, Vince. I don't care if you believe me or not. I do. It's not the man from the dreams. I quit dreaming about him as soon as I met you."

"Dreams are only that. There are a hundred reasons it cannot be for us," he said as he sat up and pulled his cigarettes from his shirt.

"I don't want you to tell me any of them. I want to have this moment, and I want to have you know how I feel. I don't ask anything from you. Not anything."

He lit his cigarette. "I wish it could be otherwise."

"Let's not ruin what we can have with maybes or worrying about what cannot be."

He smiled. "You can do that?"

"Of course not." She rose and walked to the river, wading in to wash her body. The moment went beyond ecstasy, as she washed with the cool river water, red canyon walls soaring above, the sounds of birds as they soared overhead. She turned to see him watching her from the bank, her lover who was more ruggedly beautiful than any Michelangelo sculpture.

She had never imagined being with a man like him. If she never had more, she would consider herself blessed. Before she came to Tucson, all she had had were dreams. Now, no matter how it worked out for them, she would have memories. They were definitely better, somehow more complete, and there would be more memories. For this summer, there would be many more.

Tucson

Jeremiah and Jesse ate a quick breakfast and then walked to Sicillas Store. At the Pedrales, when he had asked about Vince Taggert or maybe John Damian, Delbert Sicilla had come to him and asked why he wanted to know. When he had said that was his business, Sicilla had turned to walk away. Jeremiah had stopped him. "Wait, I am worried about him, about someone out to kill him... and Sam Ryker." That had turned Sicilla around. He had then said to come to their store, told him where it was, and said to be there before eight the next morning. They'd have to talk to his wife.

Since Jeremiah had no idea what Sicilla's wife might know, he had agreed but still visited two other bars to ask questions. With no answers, Sicilla appeared his only hope. The more time that passed, the more chance that even if he found out where Vince was, he'd not have any chance to get there in time.

The store had been left unlocked, and they walked in only to see Sicilla leaning against a counter and an older balding man beside him. A trap?

"Jeremiah Taggert meet Ollie Oliver."

"Do I know you?" Jeremiah asked as he moved forward. He hadn't checked the load in his gun. He hoped that wasn't about to be a fatal mistake.

"Not direct," Oliver said. "We might've crossed paths a time or two."

"Don't keep me guessing."

"Would you gentlemen like some coffee?" a woman's voice asked from the other side of the store. Jeremiah turned to see a beautiful woman, but older woman, standing at the door to what must have been the back room.

"That would be nice," he said putting on his most mannerly voice, while he tried to figure out what the hell this deal was.

A few moments later, they were all seated at the table with coffee. "This is my wife, Mr. Taggert," Del said. "I already told Connie who you were."

"How do you do, Mrs. Sicilla."

"Please, Connie."

He smiled. She was not only beautiful but had the way about her that ladies had. He always appreciated a beautiful lady. "So why did you invite Mr. Oliver to join us?" he asked then turning back to Sicilla.

"Ollie is Sam Ryker's mother."

Jeremiah managed to avoid a double take. "I take it you mean figuratively, he said taking another look at the older man. He had a tough look about him, and he had not missed the way he was wearing his gun tied down. Interesting situation.

"It ain't figurative, you sidewinder," Oliver snarled.

"All right, gentlemen, may we start over?" Connie put out her hands for peace. "It seems we are facing a mutual problem." She gave Oliver a look that caused him to subside. "Please give Mr. Taggert an opportunity to tell us why he has come." Oliver's cold gaze never left Jeremiah.

Jeremiah considered what he should say. Only the truth would do. "I made a mistake. A big one. I accepted a deal from someone who came to my ranch. The request was not to commit a murder but to get Sam Ryker dead. I sent down the best man I knew with a gun to get the job done." At the angry grunt from Oliver, he put out his hands, palms up. "I said it was a mistake. Ryker had been a gunman and outlaw. I thought he still was." A minor lie. He actually had had no idea what the man had been today. He hadn't cared.

"Save the smooth talk," Oliver said. "We know about your crooked deal. Why are you here now? To finish what got stopped? And where in blue blazes is your other son?"

This was a sharp old-timer, maybe as sharp as he was. Jeremiah smiled, admiringly, even though he realized this was still a delicate situation. "That is where my problem comes in. Asa, along with two of my men, went north to kill Ryker."

"How did he know where he was?"

"Asa had run into a guy in the bar who said he knew. He offered to take us there if he could go along."

Oliver interrupted. "Who the hell was it?"

"Clint Madison."

"Whoa, this isn't making sense," Ollie said. "Madison went with them when they left."

"Until Vince fired him." Jeremiah tried but could not resist the grin. "Madison was a little vague on why." Not hard to figure it out for anybody who was a good judge of men, which clearly Vince was. He felt proud.

"Vince fired him? This don't make much sense to me."

"We are talking about what Madison told us, sir," he said with a sneer he couldn't stop.

"Why didn't you go with them then?" Oliver asked distrust dripping from his voice.

"I didn't feel I'd be needed." He debated how much to tell. What did he have to lose with the whole truth? "Also, after meeting the lady who offered the bounty, I was beginning to have second thoughts on the whole deal."

"You polecat. I oughta drill you right now," Oliver growled.

"There is more to the story," Connie said.

"It was only after they had left that I learned my mistake, and it was huge. Asa doesn't only intend to shoot Ryker but my son, Vince."

"And you'd care about that?" asked Connie. He looked over and saw her sharp gaze on him. Who was this woman?

"I would very much care about that. To be honest, Asa is going to try to kill me whenever it profits him. I had the feeling Ryker would take care of that problem for me." He gave a snort. "I never claimed to be a prize father. I would, however, do anything to stop Asa from killing Vince. To do that, I need to know where he is."

"Why should we trust you?" Oliver asked with a gimlet eyed stare that hadn't softened a bit. He had one hand on the table with his coffee cup, but his right was not far from his revolver.

"Because I am desperate to keep Vince alive. You tell me where they are, and I will do all I can, to keep Asa and the men with him from killing either. I swear it on my dead wife's grave."

He was shocked when he heard Oliver laugh. "Try another one, you skunk."

"Gentlemen, please," Connie's sweet voice cut through the heavy atmosphere. "You won't gain anything by fighting. If that happens, nobody will save anyone, will they?" She looked at Oliver who nodded reluctantly. "Would you gentlemen give me the opportunity to consult... higher wisdom?" She smiled.

Whoa, he hadn't figured on that. Was she a religious lady? He looked around the room for clues. No crosses, but that didn't mean much. He nodded and agreed to her doing whatever that was. He saw her watching him. "Mr. Taggert," she said.

"Jeremiah," he reminded her.

"Jeremiah. I am a seer."

He smiled then. Fraud? She didn't strike him that way. She also did not seem mentally deranged. "So what are you expecting to get that will help us?"

"Whatever someone over there wishes to tell us or feels we need to know. I can't guarantee it will happen, but I can ask."

Jeremiah looked at Oliver but saw no surprise on his face. Apparently, this wasn't new.

"You talk to the other side?" Jesse asked, surprising Jeremiah as his youngest rarely spoke in groups.

"Sometimes. Do you also?" Connie smiled at him.

Jesse didn't answer and looked away.

"Since time is of the essence, would you gentlemen allow me to inquire if anyone is around who wishes to share information with us?"

Jeremiah knew she was showing a lot of trust even to suggest she could do this. There were still places in the West where it could get a person killed to sound in league with the devil. He was glad Jesse hadn't answered her question. He worried enough about having his youngest son locked up for being crazy. If he admitted he talked to those nobody could see, his risk of being in a straitjacket would increase.

Since Jeremiah believed in nothing, he had no problem with whatever twaddle she wished, as long as it didn't take too long. He wanted to be out of town and on the road with a chance to get at least a half day on his way. Whatever would convince these people to let him know where he'd gone, that would be fine with him.

"First, I want to say that whoever comes through, that entity may contact any of us. I suggest you try to be open to the inner voice or what will sound like it. Now, either close your eyes or put your heads down. Listen for a message, perhaps even in a familiar voice. I ask that only what the white light permits comes through. We want nothing from the dark side."

Jeremiah smirked. That let him out.

Connie closed her eyes, her hands out in front of her, palms up. "Please help us. We must have insights and need them now. No one here has reason to trust anyone else. If there is help available, we are listening."

Jeremiah was unsure how many moments passed as he watched her. She sincerely seemed to be concentrating. Was she hearing something? He looked over at Oliver to see he was watching him. Only Sicilla had his eyes closed. Then he realized Jesse's were also.

Finally, Connie opened her eyes and looked at him before she turned to Jesse. "She came to you too, didn't she?"

Amazingly, Jeremiah saw tears in Jesse's eyes when he looked at her and nodded.

She then looked back at Jeremiah. "A being, who said she was Valerie came to me. You know the name, don't you?" He felt stunned. There is no way she should have known his second wife's name. Or might Vince have told her?

"She said to tell you she was sorry."

Now he knew she was wrong in what she thought she heard. "She had nothing to apologize to me for. She was as close to a saint as a woman could be."

"She said she wasn't. She had let you down. Not been there for you. She didn't understand though back then."

He didn't want to hear this. He didn't believe it. "She was a good woman."

"Yes, I felt her energy was good. Beautiful too, wasn't she in that lifetime, with blonde hair. The opposite of your darkness. She loved you very much, you know."

Now he knew Vince could not have told her that. He almost stood up. He didn't want to hear more. He tried to relax. He needed to know where Vince was. Maybe enduring this would convince them to tell him.

"Did she say you can trust me to tell me where Vince and Sam went?"

"She said you mean well. She thinks you have a good heart deep down inside. But that you have been wrong in some of what you've done."

He felt his breath coming faster. "Tell me where I can find Vince and let me be gone."

"Before we get to that, there is something more important that you must hear." She looked at Jesse. "She told you, didn't she?"

"Yes."

"What the hell."

"Let him speak. He needs to tell you this," Connie said.

Jesse looked up. He had a square face, his eyes were so beautiful. For a father, it was hard to believe such a handsome, beautifully made son had a slow wit. He hoped Connie understood that nobody could rush Jess. His boy needed time. If they didn't give him that, he'd never get it out.

"Asa... poisoned Mama."

"What!" he sputtered. "What the hell are you talking about?"

"Asa told me after Vince had been there. He got drunk, and he started bragging what a fool Vince was. He said Vince was stupid like me." Tears ran down Jesse's cheeks.

Connie got out of her chair. Standing behind Jesse, she stroked his hair back from his forehead, as a mother might have. "It wasn't your fault, Jesse."

"I thought she was sick but..." He sucked in a breath to get control of himself.

"What are you saying?" Jeremiah asked feeling broken. He couldn't get his head around it. He wished he had died before he'd heard it.

"Asa said he'd kill me if I told... I didn't mind that so much but figured it was done. Couldn't be undone." He looked up with those beautiful dark eyes. He was asking for something Jeremiah didn't have in him to give. He couldn't understand how it could be. And yet he knew it could be. Asa did have it in him to do such a horrible deed.

"No, you couldn't change it once it had been done," he said finally. "All right, I understand." He didn't. He didn't understand how he had raised such a monster in Asa. He had even blamed Valerie for all that went wrong, for Jesse's slowness, but it wasn't her. It was him.

He looked then at Oliver feeling a soul deep coldness. "Now, you tell me where they are." He gritted his teeth. He didn't care if he lived through this but Asa wouldn't, not if he had killed Vince or he hadn't.

Oliver looked at him but nodded.

Jeremiah looked then at Connie. "Thank you. I think you destroyed me but thank you."

"Valerie wanted to help. I think she will be near."

"I don't want a ghost traveling with me," Jeremiah snapped. "I got enough of those without her too." He then looked back at Oliver. "Now, where are they?"

"I will take you there. I ain't giving you no map, you polecat. I still don't trust you. You go with me or you stay here, makes no never mind to me."

Jeremiah managed a smile that he didn't feel. "Where do we meet you? I hope you are able to ride like the wind because it'll be no angel but hell that is going with us."

CHAPTER 20

Salt River Canyon

I t was almost six when Holly and Vince rode back to the camp. They were both relaxed and in better moods. Vince unsaddled their horses as Holly listened to the others talk about the falls and the beautiful rock formations. "There were a few lupine still blooming in one of the crevasses. So beautiful," Alice said. She had brought one stem back to press.

After a relaxing day in one place, Song was in a good mood too and quickly put out the plates and two cast-iron Dutch ovens filled with a savory smelling stew. There was also freshly baked bread, made thanks to the small stove they had brought.

"See any sign up there?" Vince asked Sam as they sat on one of the logs.

"Cougar but not recent. No human tracks... but with the rock and water, they could've been there and left no sign."

"Did you swim?" Holly asked Alice.

She laughed. "It was colder than I expected but maybe next time. The Salt is warmer."

"So what did you two find for tomorrow's camp?" Cole asked.

"I need to check the mule's hoof, but I am thinking we need to lay over another day."

"Reconnoitering for more campsites?" Sam teased.

"Could be. I was thinking though that maybe I'd send you and Abby off for that." He grinned at Sam's smirk. "We did see one possible site, but we didn't go up Canyon Creek itself. The question, where I'd like your opinion, is the best spot we get the wagons up the slopes and onto a likely level spot above."

"We did see a turquoise vein," Holly said. "We didn't climb up to it, but the color was unmistakable. What I am interested in there would be the type of turquoise, maybe a few small shards if the tribe will permit it. Then I can compare the colors to Aztec jewelry. Turquoise comes in many shades. If this color matches that found in Aztec ornaments, it would be possible evidence of connection."

"As in what?" Alice asked with interest.

"There are several possibilities. Traders could have visited both regions. But the Aztecs might've traveled here to mine it. Or they came from here and brought turquoise with them."

"You think there is a connection?" Gabe asked. "It's been a myth."

"Sometimes myths are there because of history," she repeated what he'd earlier said. "The other thing I was hoping is that tomorrow we can set up the camera."

"Camera?" David's ears perked up at that.

"I brought a box camera, David. It's a Rochester. Have you heard of it?"

He nodded. "I read about it. You really have one?"

"I do. Maybe you'd like to become our cameraman?"

"Could I do that?"

"Possibly better than me. There are things to photograph

that go beyond the ruins. The salt springs are beautiful. Of course, we could not capture the color, but I think they would still be exciting in photos with their shapes."

"You'd let me do that?"

"It would be a big help if you would. I could then concentrate on other things. I will need photos of the camp, then what we find. They might be used in articles later as validation."

"What is Canyon Creek like?" Sam asked as he lifted a whiskey bottle. "Who wants a shot?" Only David and Zian shook their heads.

Sipping his whiskey, Vince looked at Sam. "Keep your eyes open tomorrow."

Sam sat beside him as the others continued to talk about the camera. "You expecting trouble?"

"Jackson has had enough time to get to Pa, and they had enough to get back to Tucson."

"True." Sam sipped his whiskey thoughtfully. "Maybe I shouldn't leave camp right now."

"I've been doing some calculating. I don't see it possible that they'd be here for two more days. They have to find where we went."

"Madison."

"I likely shouldn't have fired him."

"Couldn't have him at your back."

"There was that. When we go downriver, we will set up two camps. One with the women, Cole, Gabe, Zian, and your youngsters."

"Your excuse being?"

"They are the archaeology camp. We are the security. Theirs will be closer to the site-- when we find it, of course."

Sam grinned. "Crafty devil, aren't you, but what if they hit them instead of us?"

"We'll be the ones they come to first if they come up from Tucson. Cole and Gabe though will be above."

"That would be Cole's brothers and pa. He was with them longer than you. Think he'd fire on them?"

"I'll talk to him. I don't know. Gabe would though." He glanced over at Holly as she was opening up the boxes with the cameras. "We won't tell them why. Only that there isn't room for us all together at night."

"Abby won't buy it."

"Maybe not, but she won't want her children endangered either. If I am blowing smoke, then it costs us nothing."

Sam nodded approvingly. "All right. Makes sense."

"I don't even know that Pa will come after us. The whole thing has seemed strange from the start."

"What do you mean?"

"Why would anybody put a bounty on you? I get why they'd go to a known crook like my pa, but why do it to begin? Buying the ranch doesn't sound like enough reason. There are lots of ranches."

"I've been thinking on that too."

"You come up with anything?"

"The will."

"The widow is mad at you for Marius leaving you the money?"

"There is a catch. I have to be alive to claim it."

"You haven't?" Vince turned to look at him. "Why the hell did you wait?"

"At the time there seemed no rush or reason. I wasn't sure I wanted it."

"Why?"

"Money doesn't always make people happier. We've been doing all right without it. I have enough for Dave and Alice to go to college or get them a start. What would the extra money do to our family?"

Vince saw the irony in what he was hearing. Money was one of the barriers between him and Holly. Not the only one but a big one. He could see that there was logic to Sam's reluctance to take what sounded like a fortune for how it might impact his children's lives.

"I see your point, but if you don't claim it where does it go?"

"I didn't get told that. But supposing it was the Breanna Osbourne?"

Vince let out a breath as he reached for his cigarettes. "That would be motive all right."

"I had no idea the money could prove as much a drawback if I didn't take it as if I did."

"No, you wouldn't." He lit the cigarette and took a long draw. "So no way to fix that right now. If you turn it down, maybe she'd forget the idea of killing you."

Sam reached for the cigarette and took a satisfying pull on it. "Not much I can do about it up here either way."

"You could go back down and take the will, end her reason."

"And leave you to face whoever might show up in a few days? No thanks."

Gila Crossing

"You did mean ride like the devil," Oliver said with a chuckle as they dismounted, unsaddled and let Jesse tend to hobbling their horses.

"You're in a better mood than I expected after riding so many hours," Jeremiah said rubbing his back.

Oliver was squatting as he built a small campfire. "I train horses, sidewinder. I am on them all day."

"The name is Jeremiah or Taggert if you favor it."

Jesse came back from settling the horses and laid out the bedrolls. He sat at the fire saying nothing. Oliver held out some jerky "Want some?" he asked the young man.

Jesse looked at him for a long moment and then nodded. Oliver handed them both a strip, then reached into his bag and pulled out a sack of biscuits. "I didn't plan food for three. You should have stopped and bought some supplies."

"There wasn't time." Jeremiah still felt a terrible urgency. He would get there too late. He chewed on the jerky and then reached into his saddlebag and pulled out a whiskey bottle. "You want a swig?"

Oliver reached for it. "Alcohol ain't got no family connected to it."

Without a word, Jesse also took a slug from the bottle and handed it back.

Jeremiah looked at Oliver. "You been with Sam a long time, I guess." He leaned back against a fallen log.

"Since he was a sprout. He grew up in a sporting house and left as early as he could. He was looking for a pard." Oliver chuckled.

"And you took him under your wing and taught him the outlaw ways."

"It was a hard time. I reckon you know about that. War tore the country apart. Not an easy time to keep eating even. We never robbed banks or trains like some." He gave Jeremiah a look.

"That world is gone now anyway." He sighed and wished for a cigar. He should have stopped for supplies. Maybe he could get some in Globe. His biggest hope though was that Asa would be in no hurry and still hanging around the bars there. He didn't believe it, but it was his likeliest chance to get to him before he got to Vince.

"You got any wanted posters out on ya?" Oliver asked with a smile.

"None that I know of. You?"

"Nah, we been honest ranching-- anyway since Sam hooked up with Abigail. A man meets a woman like her, and he straightens up or loses her."

"I would know about that one." Jeremiah felt sick at his own botched chances.

"So you do want to save your son," Oliver said taking another sip of the whiskey before handing it back.

"I've been a fool. I knew what Asa was but used it." He shook his head. "I ain't been a good man, Mr. Oliver."

"I knew that and call me Ollie. Whether we'd of been on the same side before, we are now."

Canyon Creek

It took a day and a half for the wagons to travel what amounted to five miles if one could have flown. One of the wagons contributed to some of the slowdown when it had a damaged wheel. Holly felt frustrated but also impressed with how Vince knew how to fix it. For a wagon to lose a spoke, she'd have assumed it was finished, but he had brought parts and tools. It was a few hours down, a lot of muscle from the men, but then they were again on their way.

They passed one ruin high on the cliff above the Salt. It looked nothing like the one she had seen in the dreams. The mouth of Canyon Creek broadened out in comparison to how the Cibecue had been. Sam had plotted a way for them to get the wagons up onto the first hills. Close to the Salt, there were only a few spots flat and wide enough for a camp. Vince explained they would divide the camps where she would take her main crew upstream to a higher plateau. He and Sam would sleep at night on the banks of the river.

She supposed it made sense, but something about the way he said it gave her doubts. When she asked him about it, he smiled and reminded her who the boss was. She had given him what she hoped was one of those looks that said she bought none of it, but he had walked off without further debate. That seemed to be his method of dealing with any disagreement. Irritating but in this case, she couldn't argue with him..

After unhitching the wagons, securing the mules, setting up their tents, and the stove at their chosen site, Vince came to squat beside where she sat on the ground. "I sent Gabe up the canyon today. He saw several possible ruins."

"Why didn't you have me go with him?" she asked sticking out her lower lip.

His smile seemed condescending. "I wanted to be sure there weren't any surprises likely. He's good at tracking. He saw no sign of visitors of the animal or human variety."

"We are all animals," she said trying for a superior tone.

"Oh, I do know that," he said giving her a quick kiss and rising with one easy movement. "Best you don't forget it either." With that he was off and leaving her frustrated again. She wanted them to sleep together-- not for the sex. In such close quarters, that was impossible, but she needed to be close, to touch. He seemed to have no such need.

With Song beginning to prepare the evening meal and having been told her help was not needed, Holly walked up to a little hill where she could see the canyon to the north. The lower hills, dotted with pinyon pines and junipers, had appeared rolling until they got closer and saw the crevasses and dips. The looming cliffs were the more promising locations for the ruins she sought. She felt excited at the prospect of maybe tomorrow seeing the structures that had been in her dreams.

"Can I use the camera today?" David asked arriving to take her from her musings. Her plan that he start with it earlier hadn't worked out.

"Wonderful idea. Let's get it out and set up the tripod. We need a spot for you to develop them also. I am thinking right below the camp where we can set up a tarp. Collect some poles and rig up a table with the wood we brought."

"I hope I can remember it all," he said as with Zian's and Alice's help, they began to construct the needed location for a dark room between two juniper trees with rocks to hold down the sides.

"Just read the instruction book again and again. I think it will help you in focusing. The real complication is learning how the shutter and aperture work. If we still have daylight, you can practice today with photos of the crew and camp site. Don't forget the notebook for recording the details of each shot. Every box of plates or batch of chemicals will work differently. This not a temperature controlled environment."

His smile broadened.

An hour later, the space was ready. One bucket of clear stream water would be filtered through a double layer of cloth. On a primitive table of sorts were brown bottles, the trays, and a glass measuring cup. A small candle holder hung from the ridge pole.

"You will take photos during the day," she said, "and develop them each night. Whatever doesn't come out, we will save for recoating. I have both tin and glass plates; so you will have quite a challenge in this."

"I can hardly wait."

"It will be hard work."

"I am strong."

She smiled. He was that, and if he could take the photos, it would take one weight off her shoulders.

David quickly got the knack of setting up the camera, focusing the shot, inserting the plates, taking the photo, and then pulling them out to put aside until he could develop them. With a big grin, he walked around the camps and chose views of the camp that yielded photos with different exposures as he got a feel for the work.

The one she most wanted to see was one he had taken of Sam and Vince talking over something they didn't want others to hear. They had laid out their bedrolls and built a fire ring, three hundred yards below the main one. It was above the river in a spot too narrow for them all. She noted it had good visibility all ways. She had no doubt it was for security but what worried her was against what. It meant that Vince believed whoever had come to kill Sam in Tucson was going to try again. He didn't want the women and children to be there when it happened.

She went to the wagon and dug into her own gear. Although she had shovels, picks, trowel and hammers, she also had her Winchester 73. She hadn't loaded it since she had come to Tucson. She did now. She practiced sighting it to the distant cliffs.

She was a good shot. Some of her friends had enjoyed target and skeet shooting. She'd had a good eye and a steady hand, and out shot most of her male friends. She had understood, before she came up here, that she might need to protect herself with a deadly weapon. She didn't like thinking it, but it was simple wisdom. She hadn't expected she would want to protect someone else.

When she heard the step behind her, she whirled, smiling

when she saw it was Abby. "You know, it doesn't do any good to have one if you can't use it in a crunch," her new friend said.

"What makes you think I couldn't?"

Abby shook her head. "I don't. Maybe I want you to be sure you can. Holding a gun makes you a target. Don't think you can bluff with it. If you ever put it to your shoulder and point it at a man, fire-- don't wait. That man won't."

It made sense. "I will remember."

"What made you get it out now?" Abby put out her hand to take the gun. "It has a nice feel, good weight."

"You seem to be good with a gun too."

"I had a small revolver before I met Sam and did know how to use it. I learned with the rifle after he and I got together. We don't exactly have a sheriff in easy reach." She handed the rifle back to Holly

"They expect trouble, don't they?"

"So it seems. If it doesn't come in a few days, they will have less concern."

Holly looked at Abby wondering how much Sam had told her about the threat to his life. If he had not, she didn't want to upset her. "Yes," Abby said with a smile. "I know. He has faced many dangers in his life. I am sure it will be all right." Her voice didn't sound that certain.

"If they do, then our being up here makes sense... unless we could help by having a gun above their camp and..."

Abby laughed. "You are a bit of an outlaw type yourself, aren't you? So that's why the gun?"

"Well, if I was above their camp. I noticed a stack of rocks that would make a good shelter. They wouldn't know I was there and..."

"Whoa," Abby said putting up a hand. "They have to know. My dear, do you want to be shot by the man you love when he doesn't know it's you above him?"

"I hadn't thought of that. I guess I would have to suggest it... sort of ask."

Abby shook her head and laughed again. "I like the idea, and I think they will go for it when we explain it. That keeps the others safe up here but gives them an edge down there... Right now, the moon doesn't rise until after midnight. That means night travel for anyone approaching us isn't likely."

"When did Sam say they expected them at best... or is that at worst?"

Abby stared off at the distant hills. "Before dark tonight or tomorrow. If they didn't lay over long between leaving Vernal, getting to Tucson, and then heading back up here."

"Vince tells me nothing."

"I have been married a lot of years to Sam. It's pretty hard for him to hide things from me."

"How would they have found out where we are? We kept those who knew to a minimum. Or do I have to ask?"

"I doubt you do." Abby moved to the front of the wagon and picked up a box of cartridges and the Winchester 94. "I will explain to Sam our plan." Abby smiled. "He can likely talk Vince into it."

"If he can't?"

"Short of tying us up, how would they stop us? Are you good with that?" She pointed to the rifle in Holly's hands.

Holly grinned. "Dead sure."

Abby laughed and headed off to explain the new plan to Sam.

CHAPTER 21

Rim above the Salt River

"Y ou want to break your horse's neck and your own, you go on down," Ollie said as he dismounted and led his mount to the level site he had said would be where he rolled out his bedroll.

"I give up. You're right," Jeremiah said reluctantly and slowly swung his leg over the pommel and dropped to the ground. He was physically beat but emotionally wanted to keep going. Although they had changed horses in Globe, he was satisfied with his gelding. Although not as well trained as his mount had been, the horse was bright and had learned quickly with an experienced hand on the reins.

Jesse took care of the three horses by hobbling them where dry grass offered fodder. He lifted the hoof of the one he'd been riding to examine it before he came back to where Ollie had built a fire and was heating up a can of beans. They had stopped in Globe long enough to get information and buy supplies.

"He don't say much," Ollie said, gesturing toward Jesse, "but he sure knows horses."

"Any animal," Jeremiah said.

"I seen that."

"I want to get there in time, and even with Asa laying over a night in Globe, it seems we will be too late."

"Maybe so. Maybe not. You are though assumin' Sam and Vince can't take care of the problem even if we are."

"I worry about bushwhacking."

"They won't be caught off guard. They knew before they left Tucson what was possible."

Jeremiah bit the tip off and lit one of his new cigars. "Archaeology? What the hell is that all about? I don't get why Vince even went on the stupid venture. Who goes into this country if he ain't Apache?"

"You can ask when we get there," Ollie said with a chuckle.

They had bought spoons and took turns eating the heated beans. It was filling but not great fare—still, better than the first two days when they had subsisted on jerky, biscuits, and water. At least they now had coffee and more whiskey.

Jeremiah knew he was being a fool. He hadn't pushed his body this hard in twenty years. Likely, he'd have a heart attack before it was finished. He only hoped not before he killed Asa.

When they finished eating, they passed around the whiskey bottle. The stars were bright overhead. One thing, to be said for sleeping out, was the stars. With the moon not rising until after midnight, the sky was inky black with bright dancing dots.

"You trust that seer woman, don't you?" he asked Ollie, his mind on more than Connie Sicilla.

"I do."

"Why?"

"She's a good woman, and she does seem to get something

269

from beyond. Did ya know she never charges anybody for those readings?"

He hadn't thought of that. He'd been too eager to head out that he hadn't thought to offer her money. Odd woman. Everybody did things for money. What other reason was there? He snorted. He wasn't doing this for money. Maybe everybody didn't.

"You believe what she told you about your wife?" Ollie asked as he laid back on his bedroll.

"I been thinking about that." He looked then at Jesse. "You told the truth about hearing her, didn't you?"

Jesse was sitting cross-legged in front of the dying campfire staring into the last flames. "Yes."

"It's hard to understand why Asa would have done it." Jeremiah felt as though his world had been torn apart. He was too old to learn new things. he had everything set in its place. But now...

"He was mad at her." Jesse didn't look at him, but Jeremiah knew there was more.

"Why?"

"Asa hates anybody stands against him. She did. Asa has to be in control." Jesse grimaced and looking into the flames.

"He hurt you, Jesse?" he asked not wanting to know and yet compelled.

"He used to." Jesse didn't look at him.

"But he stopped?"

Jesse looked at him for the first time with that smile he'd seen before. "Yes." So, he had been abusive until Jesse had too much strength. All the time, he had been blind to what was going on

Jeremiah felt like crying, but he never cried. He wished he had killed Asa the first time he knew what kind of person he had become. It was when he came on him beating one of their horses. He had yanked the whip from his sixteen year old son and asked him why. 'She didn't do what I wanted,' the youth had said. he had seen it then that Asa had liked hurting the mare.

He had never seen himself as a fool, but he surely had been. He had heard Asa angry at his mother, but it never once occurred to him that he would hurt her. Maybe him but not her. He ground his teeth.

"Can't go backward," Ollie said. "Only forward."

"If Asa kills Vince or Sam, either one, I can't go either way."

"What are you hoping to get out of this?" Ollie asked.

"If I'm lucky?"

"Sure."

"That I kill Asa before he kills anybody else. Then I die of a heart attack."

He heard Ollie's chuckle. "Man don't usually get out of it that easy."

Yea. Jeremiah grimaced. Lying flat, still smoking his cigar, he knew only one thing. Living with what he had to live wasn't going to make the years left, how many ever there might be, worth anything. Morning would find him where he'd know one way or the other what had happened. From what the town folk had said, they likely were on the river but no more than a mile or so west.

"You think he took Clint with him once he knew where they were?" Ollie asked.

"Good question." Jeremiah let out the smoke and watched it trail up, lit by the campfire. In the distance, he heard an owl. He remembered hearing them meant death. He didn't care one way or the other about Madison, but he supposed they should look for a body on their way. Stupid mouthpiece for trusting Asa. He hadn't been left in Globe; so he made it at least to the Salt, as they'd seen no buzzards circling. He didn't care, wouldn't have taken the time to bury him if he'd come across the carcass. He only cared about one thing. Seeing Vince alive.

Canyon Creek Archaeology Camp

"You want me to do what?" Holly protested.

He hadn't expected her to like it. "Right after breakfast, you take the crew with you to scout out possible sites. Don't take equipment but do take guns and food for a noon meal. Find the place if it's up there."

"And without you."

"Without me."

"Why should I?"

He blew the smoke from his cigarette away from her. "Because I am the boss, little girl."

"Don't call me that."

"Then don't act like it. I am a lot older than you, and those years were mostly spent learning how to stay alive. I know what we have to do now. And I want you to find out if this even is the right canyon."

"It might not be?"

"There is still Cherry Creek. There are abandoned ruins up there too. Only you can find out if this is the one."

"Who looks out for you?" That cute lower lip was stuck out again. He felt like kissing it, but that would only distract him from what he needed to do. He was right. He felt it deep in his bones. This was going to be the day. He didn't know when. He believed it would be settled before dark. The idea of killing his father and brothers was not a pleasing one. Being killed himself was even less so. He didn't answer her and instead took another long draw on the cigarette. She reached out and took the cigarette from his fingers.

"What are you doing?"

"Maybe I want to smoke too," she said taking a long draw on it before coughing and having to hand it back.

"It's an acquired habit," he said with a grin. She was a little girl in some ways, and yet he knew how much a woman too. He wanted her to find her answers. He wanted them both to stay alive. Not much to ask or maybe it was.

"All right," she said her tone no less resentful. "You stay alive."

"I aim to."

"Don't get hurt."

"Oh my list."

"Keep Cole with you."

"No, he goes with you."

"Why?"

"It's better that way." He had talked to Cole about the possibility of having to fire on his brothers and father. Cole had considered it in his way, nodded, and said all right. You can do that? he had asked. The answer had been that smile and a nod. Cole would be added security for her if his pa and the others got past him.

"And Sam?"

"He'll be with me." He trusted Sam in a fight. That's the only one he needed with him even if they faced five or even six men, some of whom were related to him. More and more he had the feeling he could trust Cole but that was one more reason to have him with her.

She gave off an angry huff but then grabbed his head and pulled him down to where their lips were inches apart. "You take care of yourself. I have plans for us."

"Will I like them?"

"You will. So, don't forget about that and don't take any stupid chances." Then she pressed her lips against his, delving into his mouth with her tongue. For a moment, he forgot he had a good reason for his plans. For a moment, only she existed.

When she released his head, he said, "You take care too. Keep that rifle with you today. Don't go digging in the dirt. Watch for what's around you as you ride."

"Why?"

"You are full of questions. Will you do it?"

She nodded. "I don't like it, but all right."

"Don't hurry back."

She let out an angry hiss but nodded again. Gabe had saddled her mare, and the crew was waiting, for riding north up the canyon and mapping out the location of dwellings. David had wanted to take the camera, but he'd been told next time.

Vince turned to Sam, and without a word they walked down to their own campsite. "Here's how it works," he said to Sam, lighting another cigarette.

"You figure to boss me too?" Sam asked with an amused smile. He pushed his hat back on his forehead. "No kiss is going to do it."

"I figured on logic with you."

"Might work. Try me."

"If Pa and Asa see you, they might shoot you before we get a shot at them."

"Bushwhack?"

"It would be easier. They won't shoot me at first sight, not 'til they know where you are."

Sam let out a breath and reached over for the cigarette. "You sure about that?"

"Asa will want to kill me face to face. I don't know

about Pa."

"How do you know about your brother?"

"He is a mean bastard. He likes to hurt things. I beat him in a fistfight. He will want satisfaction."

"Can he take you?"

"I guess I'll find out."

"How many you figure there will be?" He handed back the cigarette.

"I don't know. Three Taggerts, likely two extras, and Clint if he makes it this far."

Sam laughed. "That's definitely a question."

"He won't figure into it if he does. He's a coward. I think that's what's eating at him. He must have learned it in Cuba when he didn't fight. He might shoot a man in the back, I don't know, but he won't face to face."

"Nice fella."

"Anyway you stay back where nobody sees you when they come riding in. When they're here, and I can see it's all of them, then you come out. How does that sound?"

"All right. Yeah, it makes sense. If you are right, and they won't bushwhack you."

It was Vince's turn to laugh. "Yeah, if I am right."

On The Canyon Floor

"Horseman coming," Ollie said, pulling his horse to a halt. "Not fast. Only one."

Jeremiah put out his hand for Jesse to stop also, and they waited until the rider came into view.

"Madison," Ollie said. "Didn't expect to see you."

Madison's expression looked sick as he pulled his own mount to a halt. "I am lucky to be alive."

"That might yet change," Jeremiah said. "What are you

doing here?"

"Asa told me to leave, or he'd kill me. He didn't want me with him anymore. He didn't need me once he knew where they'd be." His mouth was down turned.

"Surprised he didn't shoot you," Ollie said his hand on his revolver.

"He took my gun."

"Pity," Ollie said. "I'd rather you had it."

"So I could fight alongside you?"

"So I could shoot you."

Jeremiah smiled when he looked over and saw the hard expression on Ollie's face. He clearly meant it. There was the promise of death on the older man's face.

"You wouldn't kill me, would you?"

Jeremiah laughed. "You might not be able to kill a man in cold blood, Ollie, but I could. You want? Wouldn't bother me at all." He drew his revolver and watched the shyster's face whiten further.

"No," Ollie said. "Noise would give us away. How far ahead of us are they?"

"I... I don't know."

"He's got nothing worth keeping him alive for. Want me to kill him with my Bowie?" Jeremiah asked grinning. "No noise."

"No, please. All right, we camped about four miles farther on; they left when they made me not go with them. I hadn't thought, but guess it's why they didn't shoot me."

"You weren't worth a bullet," Jeremiah said with a snort.

"If I see you again," Ollie said, "I swear to god you better be holding a piece. I will shoot you down-- one way or the other."

"We need to move fast," Jeremiah said as they rode past the shaking barrister. "I think we should have killed him though."

"Not worth it. Take too much time to dispose of the body."

"All right but..." He looked back to see the lawyer watching them and not moving. "He is a back shooter."

"Not without a gun."

Jeremiah didn't like leaving a skunk like him alive, but he couldn't argue. Only one thing mattered and that was getting to Vince. Clearly, unless Asa had a hard time finding him, it'd be too late.

Canyon Creek Camp

The sun was high in the sky when Vince heard the horses coming down the river. It might not be them, but he rose and moved to where he could see and be visible. Glancing back, he saw Sam rise and then put up three fingers. He remained in the shadows, his rifle in his right hand.

Vince had earlier made sure his Colt was loose in the holster. He stacked his rifle against a dead log, and waited. He'd been in enough fights to know what mattered now was to stay loose.

When the riders came in view, there were the three Sam had indicated. Vince saw Asa but didn't recognize the other two.

"That's far enough," he yelled.

He saw the grin on Asa's face. "Been a long time, big brother."

"Would've been better for you if it'd been longer."

Asa laughed. "Or you."

Vince shrugged.

"Looking for someone?" Sam said coming out of the shadows.

"Oh yeah, this is sweet. Just two of you?" Asa asked as he

dismounted along with the others. He took a few steps away from his horse, still smiling.

"Two's enough," Vince said.

"I wanted to kill you. Should have done it when you came back to Vernal."

"You could have tried."

"I killed Ma. Did you know that? The old biddy got what was coming to you. Now you get it too."

Vince clenched his jaw. He knew what Asa was trying to do. Say something to throw the other off their game. He smiled as he waited. It wouldn't be long. When he saw Asa's hand dart down, he had his own gun out and was firing. First shot went to Asa. He saw the shock on his brother's face, knew his shot had been true, as he shot again at the man on Asa's left. He heard other shots, felt the shock of a bullet to his left side but kept firing. It was over in a minute.

"You hit hard?" Sam asked after going to the three fallen men and assuring himself they all were dead.

"A graze is all. How about you?"

"Nothing."

"Pa and Jesse weren't with them. No Madison either."

"You think they might still be coming?"

"I don't know."

Sam put his gun back in the holster and unbuttoned Vince's shirt, pulling it open to look at the bloody gash. "Doesn't look too bad. We were lucky... unless more are coming. I better get something to tie this closed. You are bleeding."

Feeling the shock of the shooting, the deaths and his own injury, Vince sat on the log where his rifle was propped. Sam went back to their gear and returned with bandaging and a bottle of whiskey. "Brace yourself," he said as he poured the liquor over the slash before handing it to Vince to take a slug as he wrapped a cloth tightly around his torso to close the wound. When he was finished, he took the bottle and drank from it.

Before they could say more, more horses were heard coming fast down the river. Vince rose with the rifle in his hand as they came into view, then he heard Sam's laugh.

"Damnit, can't you stay away, and aren't you riding with bad company?" he asked as Ollie pulled his horse to a halt.

His pa was smiling as he looked at the bodies and then back to Vince. "You here for more shooting, Pa?" Vince asked as he looked then at Jesse. He had never seen his youngest brother as a man. He was powerful looking, taller with likely a longer reach. Lucky he hadn't wanted to fight him that day at the cemetery.

"Looks like you took care of the shooting for us," his pa said with a laugh. "Damn, good to see you standing but what's that blood?"

"Nothing much. Why are you here if you aren't with Asa?"

"Came to stop him once I found out what he was up to."

"Stop him from killing who?"

He knew that Ollie wouldn't be with him if he had come to kill Sam. His head felt fuzzy, maybe from blood loss or the shock of seeing his father. He sat hard on the log.

"I ain't proud of anything I done, son," his father said. "Jesse and I wanted to stop Asa. Ollie knew where you'd gone and agreed to let us come along once he figured I wasn't out to kill anybody but Asa, Brewster, and Boggs. Looks like the two of you took care of that."

Ollie walked over to examine Vince's side. The blood was barely seeping through the cloth. "You better lay down afore you fall," he said. "This all can be settled later."

"Likely not," he said as he heard more horses, this time coming from the direction the crew had gone. It was only moments later when Holly slid hers to a halt and was off and at his side.

"I told you not to get hurt," she snapped as she pulled his shirt back. "How deep is it?"

"A scratch."

She looked then at the dead bodies before she turned to look at the three new arrivals. "Ollie, I didn't expect to see you." Her gaze turned then to Vince's father and brother. "I guess I don't have to ask who you two are. You look a lot like each other. Since you aren't dead, I guess you didn't come with those three."

Vince's father chuckled. "This must be the reason you are here, son."

"We can talk this all out later," Holly said as she looked back at Vince. "You need to come up to the other camp. I gather your reason for being down here is gone."

He heard the exasperation in her voice and nodded, not willing to fight it out with her—if an argument was what she wanted. The pain in his side was growing as was his confusion over his father's presence. He let her push him to her horse and ride Princess up to the camp rather than walk. It seemed easier on a host of levels.

CHAPTER 22

After the excitement of finding the ruin Holly had sought, they had all heard the shots and raced back to the river. It was then that she had seen the carnage on the beach and Vince bleeding. An hour later, after she had him lying down and accepted some whiskey from Song, she finally quit shaking. Gabe and Cole had taken care of burying the bodies above where the river would unearth their graves. Whether there would be questions from authorities, she rather doubted. They didn't seem like the sort anybody would come with questions about.

Sam and Abby were watching David as he again set up the camera. They had had to convince him no photographs of dead men. Now he was interested in taking some of the new arrivals.

Vince's father was watching her. She finally turned to him and dealt with it. "You are Jeremiah Taggert, the leader of a deadly band of outlaws, am I correct?" She smiled with the look that usually had men at her feet.

Taggert grinned back. "No gang. Currently, I am an old man trying to figure out how I managed to live too long."

"I take it you want sympathy, Mr. Taggert?"

"Make that Jeremiah," he snickered. "Come over and sit by me and let me get to know something about this lady archaeologist who has entrapped my son."

"Oh and if I could only say I had." She walked over and sat on the log beside him.

"You and he seem an unlikely pair."

"He is only helping me for the summer." She wished it wasn't true, but repeatedly she saw it was how Vince saw it. On a ton of levels, he was so much more mature, more knowledgeable, and stronger, that she knew she could never be his partner. It wasn't her choice, but she accepted it was his.

"Is that so?" he asked with a smile that reminded her of Vince's.

"It is all he has committed to."

"And he keeps his promises."

"He does."

"Interesting addition to your foray up here, having killers come after you."

"It was not part of the plan, of course." It did open a door. "I have a question."

"I like answering questions asked by beautiful women."

He was quite the flirt. His son could take some lessons. "We assumed Clint Madison is why the killers could find us. Do you have any idea what happened to him, or were we wrong?"

"You weren't wrong. We saw him as we started down the river. He was running off and lucky to escape with his hide. Asa probably only didn't kill him because he saw him as of no account."

"I should never have let him come on the venture. I knew

he wasn't reliable, but he kept insisting. I didn't trust my own misgivings."

He chuckled. "Welcome to the crowd. I made mistakes with Asa that almost cost me my son. I kept knocking myself all the way up here. Thank God, it didn't end as I feared."

"You look to be consorting," Vince said as he startled her by coming up behind her.

"You were supposed to be sleeping," she remonstrated.

"Can't sleep." He sat on the log, beside Holly before he looked at his father. "I don't understand what you are doing here."

"Even an old fool can sometimes learn."

"Is that an answer?"

"Not enough huh?" His father grinned.

"No."

"You know I took the job to kill Sam Ryker. I sent Cole, Jackson and Brody to do it. When Jackson got back, he told me they'd failed."

"Too bad," Sam said from where he had also come up.

The older Taggert smirked. "I thought so at the time. I went down to Tucson to make sure it got done right. I took Jesse, Asa, and two new men... the ones you buried." He glanced over at Vince. "Jackson wouldn't come. Said you promised you'd kill him if you saw him."

"He was right."

"We got to Tucson and asked around. I also had arranged to meet our client, Mrs. Osbourne." He looked at Sam. "You know her?"

"Marius' wife but no, we never met. She left the ranch before I arrived. He was still hoping she'd return. When he realized she wouldn't, he went back to Boston hoping he could win her back."

Jeremiah snorted. "He was a lousy judge of women if not of men."

"I won't take that personal," Sam said as he sat on the log across from them. Holly could tell he was still trying to evaluate how much to trust a man who had ordered his death. Ollie coming with him was probably the only reason Jeremiah was still alive.

She realized she was sitting with three dangerous men. When Ollie joined them, she amended that to four. Again, she felt swamped by their power. They understood and had done things she never would. She was in love with one of them, but she saw again how she would never understand him.

"I met Mrs. Osbourne, figured her for a whore, maybe a high priced one but a whore. Whatever Marius Gray saw in her, he was wrong. The fact that she would order a murder didn't surprise me. I began to see though how I could solve an old problem by letting Asa do what he was hot to do as soon as he found out Madison knew where you'd be. He was hot for Mrs. Osbourne."

"Isn't she a little old for him or make that wasn't she?" Sam asked.

"Her money had the appeal. What Asa didn't know was she didn't have it. She told us she hoped to get Gray's wealth but then he left it to you. There was a codicil. Did you know that?" Jeremiah looked back at Sam.

"If I wasn't alive or didn't accept it, it'd go to someone else."

"Yep, it'd go to her. Asa figured he could get her reward, which I doubt she had, and her with the newfound wealth. He always did think ahead but never far enough. She'd have left him flat, and there'd have been no reward."

"You sent him anyway?" Vince asked reaching into his pocket for a cigarette.

"I am not an admirable man. You knew that, Vince. Valerie

284

knew it. I figured Ryker would kill Asa, who was becoming a problem for me, and I'd deal with Ryker whenever he got back to Tucson."

Sam shook his head but smiled. "You are an old crook."

"I am and a lousy father who screwed up one son, not sure about the others."

Cole had been listening from the shadows. "I knew I disappointed you with no interest in taking up the gun."

"I haven't known what to think about you," Jeremiah said. "Any good in any of you won't be to my credit. I am sorry, I did wrong by you all. I was furious when Valerie helped you get away, Vince. Yes, I knew she had. She told me later. That woman couldn't have lied to save her soul. Later, much later, I knew she'd been right. If you'd stayed, Asa would have either turned you or killed you like he apparently did Valerie."

"Wait a minute. What are you talking about?" Cole asked.

Vince took a deep drag on the cigarette. "Asa, when he was trying for an edge, said he murdered her."

"As best I know it now, he did," Jeremiah said. "I swear I never guessed it until we got to Tucson..." He stopped and shook his head. "During one of Mrs. Sicilla's readings, Jesse finally said that Asa bragged about it later. I think now that Asa hated everybody and you, Vince, most of all."

"I knew it but never why."

"You are all he wanted to be but never would is my guess," Jeremiah said. "Because you were older, he couldn't bully you. I think he needed to beat you at something. He was my mistake. I should've killed him years ago."

"He was your son," Holly said with shock she couldn't suppress.

"All the more reason. It was my fault he was what he was."

"I doubt that," Ollie said. "Parents ain't all of why a man turns good or bad."

"I suppose since you won't kill me," Sam said, "assuming you won't." He gave Jeremiah a steely look. "Then Mrs. Osbourne will send someone else."

"She will unless you settle that will. Take the money," Jeremiah said. "Even if you give it all away, take it. If you don't, she gets it. She doesn't deserve it. I guarandamntee you she won't do good with it."

"I brought the papers with me when we took in the herd up. I figured Abby and I'd talk to someone in Tucson about them. Then when this came up, I took them with us. I guess I'll have to do it. I was afraid what it'd do to my life, my family. Money doesn't always work to help people."

"Lack of it isn't so great either," Jeremiah said with a thin smile.

"Agreed." Sam groaned. "All right, I'll have to head back for Tucson to get this straightened out."

"Unless, ya wanta go back anyway, why don't you sign the papers," Ollie said. "I can take them back and get the work started."

Jeremiah nodded approval. "And I will guarantee Mrs. Osbourne will be out of town when you do return. I will tell her when the will is settled and what will happen if she's still there when you return."

Looking at Vince to see if he agreed, Holly saw the strained look in his eyes. "You need to lie down," she said with what she knew probably was a proprietary air, that she didn't have a right to, but she didn't care. He had been under heavy demands since they left Tucson. The wound was harder on him than he admitted.

He gave her a look and then his father. "Will you be here when I wake up?" he asked.

Jeremiah nodded.

Vince looked back at Holly. "Come with me. I want to hear

about the ruin you found." He stood and pulled her up with him. Tired or hurting, he had lost no strength. She was in no mood to argue anyway. She wanted to be with him, to feel his strong body beside hers. The day could so easily have ended another way.

Two hours later, the sun starting down, Vince woke. Holly was curled against his good side. He could hear the low hum of voices on one side and the rhythm of the river on the other.

"How do you feel?" she asked. She had been watching him but not moving to avoid disturbing his rest.

The wound hurt, but he felt more rested. "Like it's been a long day."

"We should redress your injury to be sure it's not infecting."

"Sam poured whiskey over it. It'll be fine."

He saw she didn't like that. "Tomorrow you can check."

"I brought carbolic acid, iodine, and hydrogen peroxide for what I thought would be scrapes or even burns. Connie threw in some assorted herbs of which I have no idea what they were for, but I guess they have instructions with them."

He smiled and moved to put his arm around her. "Now tell me what you found," he said.

"I think it's the one. It is up against the cliff. It takes a little climbing to get to, but with a ladder, which we can make, even I can do it. The grove of manzanita below seems like it has more trees, but it also looked like the dreams."

"How did you feel being there?"

"A little scared and excited. I'd have been happier if I hadn't worried how you were back here."

"I worried about you too. I didn't like you being up there without me, but didn't want you in the line of fire."

She sighed. "It's over now though, and we can concentrate on the ruins, right?"

"It seems that way. Pa isn't looking for trouble. I honest to God don't know what he'll do next. This deal broke him."

"He will recuperate and be his old self, hopefully without the robbing part." She reached up to kiss his neck.

"We'll see." He wasn't sure he bought that.

"What about Clint?"

"We'll deal with that when we get back to Tucson. Maybe if we are lucky, he'll have moved on. If he stays, he has to know it won't go well for him."

"I hope so."

"Is there room closer to the ruin to reestablish our camp. Together this time." He smiled.

"Yes, Gabe said there is a better location, with more room. There is a nice spring about fifty feet north of the ruins, a bit above that level spot. Evidently, rocks were thrown into it, but he says it can be dug out. That would give us fresh water."

"So you will soon have your answers."

"I already have them," she whispered against his neck.

After they had eaten the delicious meal Song had prepared, Jeremiah enjoyed sitting around the campfire. Sipping the whiskey, he said, "I'd like to see the ruin. Would that be possible that we wait that long before we leave?"

"I see no problem with it," Vince answered. Jeremiah still couldn't get over what a handsome and strong man his boy had grown to be. He regretted again the lost years, but maybe he could fix some of that with future ones. Or maybe not.

"I need to get back," Ollie said. "I was leaving Royce's care on Rose's shoulders. He's a good boy, but he's a handful sometimes. But one more day couldn't hurt. I'd like to see it too, so I can tell them about it."

"We could help you move your camp," Jeremiah suggested.

"That would be good," Holly said, who was sitting on the ground at Vince's feet. Whenever she looked up, she made no secret of her fascination with him. Why wouldn't she be? He had to be an extraordinary being in her world. She was a lady and from what he'd heard, a wealthy one. It reminded him of his own ill-fated love. He had tried to drag Valerie down to his level. He could feel some of Vince's resistance for fear of that happening to him.

Valerie's family had been solid farmers but not wealthy. They'd been no richer than Jeremiah. It was his fault for courting and marrying her, convincing her to move to Utah. She hadn't wanted to go. He should have left her with her kin, never married her. She could have done a hell of a lot better than him. He was surprised she had stuck it out as long as she had. Her reward was to be murdered.

He looked over at Jesse. "Did Asa tell you how he poisoned your mother?"

Jesse uneasily looked at the ground. He was sitting a little back from the others as was his wont. It was obvious he didn't want to talk about this, but Jeremiah couldn't let it alone. He needed to understand how his murderous son had managed it.

"He put it in her tea," Jesse said after a long silence. "The plant grew near our ranch."

"Are you sure Asa murdered Mama?" Cole asked

Jesse looked at him. "He bragged about what he had done after Vince came back that time?"

Cole sunk to a large rock. "I knew he was no good but... He poisoned her?" he repeated looking sick.

"A vine. Nightshade."

"Deadly nightshade," Abby said from where she was

seated next to Sam. "The whole plant is poisonous and it would be undetectable in flavor."

"She seemed to only be sick, throwing up, sweating." Jeremiah felt sick as he remembered. "Asa was so good to her then, even made her more of her favorite tea."

"Horrible that he'd do such a thing for his own mother," Holly said.

"At the last, she was seeing things. I had the doc come out," Jeremiah said, "but he couldn't figure it out. I never imagined..." He couldn't find the words.

He looked then at Vince. "I wrote you when she got sick. I thought you'd want to see her. Then she got bad fast. Died three weeks before you got there."

"Lucky the letter ever caught up with me,"

"I knew the name you were using, kind of kept track once I found out you were trading with the tribes. Even learned who your stores were in San Francisco. I know I cursed you out that day when you got to the ranch, but I was hurting real bad. I shouldn't have said what I did. I hoped someday you'd come back, but it was probably as well you didn't. Maybe he'd have poisoned you too. I wonder he didn't kill me."

"Where did he learn about the plant and its toxicity?" Holly asked looking back at Jesse.

He stared at her a moment as he worked out what she had said. "Mrs. Jeffers, the midwife, knew plants. I don't know if she knew how he'd use them," Guilt was written on Jesse's face.

Vince lit another cigarette. "It wasn't your fault, Jess. Nobody would figure a man would do something like that to his own mother."

"She was a good woman," Cole said shaking his head. "She tried with us all. I remember most her pretty blonde hair." He glanced over at Holly. "She looked something like you, Miss

Jacobs. Not as beautiful maybe but pretty and delicate. A real lady."

Jeremiah hated even hearing about her and remembered then what Connie had told him. "You folks know much about Connie Sicilla?"

"She's a good woman, who does seem to have a gift—hard as that is to understand," Holly said. "She contacts the other side, I believe."

"Some would say she's a witch," Jeremiah said. "She thought she reached Valerie or maybe that's Valerie reached her. She said Valerie would be with us as we headed north. I didn't want to think she would. I felt... Guilty would be the word and that long before Jesse told me about what Asa had done. Mrs. Sicilla said she told her, but she said Jesse heard her too." He looked at his son. "Do you sometimes talk to her or other dead people?"

Jesse sighed before he reluctantly nodded. "Not often. I don't say anything about it. People already think I am crazy."

"Why would they say such a thing?" Abby asked.

"Because I'm slow, can't even read."

"That's not crazy, Jesse, just different." Abby turned to Jeremiah. "Did he have a difficult birth?"

"Nearly lost him and his ma with him."

"If a baby doesn't get enough air when being born, that can happen, the slowness to figure things out. That may be what happened, Jesse." She looked at him again. "If you tried harder, took time, I think you could learn to read."

"I didn't learn until after Abby spent the time with me," Sam said. "I saw the words mixed up." He looked around then. "Where is Zian?"

"Helping Alice and David develop the plates that David took today," Abby said.

"Maybe I should go check on them," Sam said, rose and headed off to where they had set up a portable darkroom.

Abby smiled. "Alice has a crush on Zian." She looked at Song who was seated beside Cole. "Did you know that?"

"No, but that's not good," Song said looking worriedly toward where Sam had gone.

"It's natural though," Holly said. "He's a handsome young man, and she is a girl at the age to start noticing such."

"Not good though. Not good." Song looked concerned. "His grandfather not like it at all. Her father even more not like it."

Abby laughed. "He won't like any man that Alice gets interested in, but I think Zian is being careful with her. He is more interested in David as a friend."

Jeremiah poured himself another whiskey. "Whatever way it works between a man and woman, in the end, it's not good." He gave Vince a pointed look. At least he hoped it was. He didn't want to see his son hurt. He could see Holly was a good woman, but she should marry someone from her own station in life, someone far above Vince's. He might be a flirtation to her, but that was likely to be all.

Then he shook his head at his own foolishness at taking on that worry for a son who had run his own affairs fine for many years. Life went the way it went. Not a thing he could do to change the path for his son or himself. Actually, his biggest worry now had to be what the hell was he going to do?

CHAPTER 23

Holly had insisted she sleep beside Vince. She no longer cared what anyone else thought. She worried he would run a fever, minor wound though he claimed it was. With morning, after they ate, she convinced him to let her remove the rough bandaging and use some of the remedies she had brought. He hissed in complaint at the iodine and claimed it hurt worse than the whiskey.

"But it is also more effective," she argued as she used surgical tape and cotton pads to rebandage the injury. She was not immune to her usual reaction at touching his chest.

She had felt she was doing a good job of hiding it when he put back on his shirt until she saw Alice again watching her with curiosity in her eyes. She remembered how as a girl she had been curious about male female relationships of all sorts. It seemed Abby needed to talk to her about some important things—if she hadn't already.

Alice was so lucky to have a mother who could do that. Holly's own mother had always seemed in a bit of a haze, which she'd only understood later came from an overuse of opium. It appeared that she had been an unhappy woman with apparently no way to escape other than by drugging herself.

As she began taking helping to take down the tents, she forced the thoughts from her mind—other than realizing she needed to try to reconnect with her sister when she returned to Tucson. Their unhappy childhood didn't have to continue into their adult lives. Time to make some changes.

Breaking camp went smoothly. Her main concern, as they headed north, was for the photography equipment. It would not do to damage the camera before they got to the ruins for the only photos she had actually needed.

David offered the solution by packing it on his horse and walking beside it. He had taken a personal interest in the process-- a bonus to Holly as the photographs he had taken showed a gift for seeing the right angle, getting the settings for the best photos. He used the instruction book but added to it an eye that could not be taught.

Their next camp was not within sight of the ruin, but it was a short walk to it. From what she had seen from below, it looked as though it had seven rooms. They would easily build a ladder from the pinyon pines nearby. A twenty foot ladder would have them into the rooms from the accessible sandstone ridge.

Vince was doing far more than she considered safe for a wounded man, but there was no babying him much as she might want. At the site, he had shown interest but said little. She caught him looking around but more at the surroundings than the ruin itself.

As they ate the evening meal, the discussions ranged from the needed ladder to the tasks for the next day. The immediate concern was surveying anything on the ground below and then in the ruins.

"I would like to stay," Jesse said coming to stand in front of her.

"When I leave?" Jeremiah asked. Jesse nodded.

"We could use your help," she said, "but that will be Vince's decision."

Vince had been sitting with his back against a pinyon pine. "Seems fine to me."

"I wish I could stay too," Jeremiah said, "but I should get back to Tucson and deal with Mrs. Osbourne as soon as Ollie files the papers.

"Would you like to stay in my home until we return?" Holly offered.

"That's generous of you, Miss Jacobs."

"Holly, and it would be good for the house to have someone in it, so not totally generous."

"All right then, I would like that. I am not sure where I will go or when, so I can wait until you return."

"Perfect." She looked to see if Vince approved but could not tell. She imagined he was having a hard time getting used to so much family after years on his own. First Cole, then Jesse and a father who didn't appear to be the monster she had been led to expect. She wished Vince would talk about it, but it seemed he kept most of what he felt to himself.

"Besides proving your dreams were of something real," Gabe asked, his eyes intense on Holly, "what are you looking for?"

"There were several reasons that I funded this dig rather than look for a sponsor. One was to have the freedom to explore the reality of my dream—or its unreality. The other though was a belief where I don't think museums are the best place for antiquities, not given their current inability to display them with meaning."

"And that means?"

"My interest is in revealing who these people were. The objects we find, what is next to them, might someday tell future researchers far more than can be determined now. More importantly, I recognize my own limitations or even the limitations of science today. We have learned so much, but more may yet be possible. What we will do this summer is photograph, draw and write notations as to what we see and where it was found. That includes burials.

"It won't only be what is in the rooms, but there is where we may find more evidence of how long the rooms were occupied. This can show up in their garbage. The indigenous people, who have avoided the ruins, have helped this be possible. Until the pothunters learned what collectors and museums would pay, these places were left undisturbed. We want to leave ours that way when we go."

"So what will we be doing?"

"I had thought we could thoroughly investigate only two rooms. To do this, we dig narrow trenches and measure the soil layers as we go down. Any objects we find will be recorded at which level. When we are finished, they will be left where they were found."

"What are you expecting to find?" Alice asked. She was sitting at the edge of the circle with her knees tucked up to her chin.

"Skeletons are possible."

"I thought you said that the body was buried under the trees somewhere," Vince said.

She nodded. "But there may be others in the rooms. Sometimes family members were buried in the room where the family lived."

"Then they did not have the superstitions of the chindi," Vince said. "The Navajo won't enter a hogan again if someone dies there. It is abandoned."

"Why?" Again, it was Alice with the question.

"Chindi is some part of the dead that is left behind," Vince said. "It is the bad part. Supposedly it can create problems for the living."

"We don't know what these people might have thought," Holly said nodding. "The interesting part is how their burial practices changed with cultural influences. In some communities, I have read that they buried their dead in their refuse piles."

"They saw them as garbage?" Song asked as she had joined the circle to listen.

"Or they didn't see the body having value once life left," Holly suggested.

"I admit that I am surprised you do not want to take pots and such for museums," Abby said. "From what I have heard of their value, it could more than pay for this expedition."

"I heard a lecture from Dr. Petrie, who is a famed Egyptian archaeologist. He said museums are full of murdered evidence where the dry bones of objects had been placed with no context to what they meant to the people. He has little use for grave and site robbers who then try to call it a science."

"Intense fellow," Abby said with a grin.

"Yes, he has strong beliefs. There is no way to protect a site like this one eventually from pot hunters. Our record might be the only one of a site which could yield information regarding who these people were, what mattered to them, how they lived."

"You are passionate about your subject," Gabe said with approval.

"I do love archaeology, studying how people once lived. I think we can learn from that. But, of course, I have a personal interest in this site. Perhaps I once lived here in another body."

"Maybe I did too," Gabe said. "The Yaqui don't believe or

disbelieve in returning to life after life. At least, before Catholicism got a hold of them." He smiled broadly.

"Maybe there are ghosts," Alice suggested looking into the darkness beyond the campfire.

"Life is a mystery at the least," Holly agreed. "I only want to satisfy one mystery for myself, but if I can contribute information about who those were who built these wonderful structures, well that matters to me also."

"Will you only write about the findings that are physical or about the dreams?" Abby asked.

"I will stick to science. The other is personal except for you all."

Abby looked toward the cliff. "It's hard to even imagine the difficulty they must have had to build them in these places. We will have work to get up to them, let alone what they had to do in building their homes. Imagine hauling the rock up there."

"Some argue they made a peaceful life here with agrarian practices," Holly said, "growing corn in the valley below and living in the rooms above, but it's hard to believe they would have built them in such places, if they hadn't feared someone or something."

"You aren't likely to settle that one," Gabe said.

"No, I won't. Except for my own mystery—if I am lucky." She smiled but tried not to think of her fears regarding what she might find. Even worse was to imagine Vince being killed. In the dream, the background had been vague. She had not seen the exact site, but she still wished he would go back with his father. Maybe he would consider it now that the danger he had believed stalked Sam was behind them.

An hour later they let the fire go down and had all laid out their bedrolls. Song and Alice still preferred the tent, but Holly had laid her bedroll by Vince's. "I hope you don't mind," she said as she stretched out.

He had taken off his shirt and boots and sat on his blanket smoking the last of a cigarette. "Would it matter?" He sounded edgy.

"Of course. If you prefer, I'll move." Before she could sit up, he had twisted and pressed her back.

"You know I don't mind."

"Well," she said smiling and watching his face with the firelight reflected on the planes and angles. His cheek had a deep line that the light caught to make him look even tougher than usual. "Do you like the idea?"

She needed reassurance. She ran her fingers down his back. She loved the strong muscles that flexed with his movement, but a bullet, spear or arrow could kill even a strong man. His recent wound had illustrated that. A few inches and it could have killed him.

"Ah so you want words?"

"Of course. All I can have."

"I want to be with you." He stubbed out his cigarette and pulled her back into his arms. "I like waking up next to you too. I never did that before."

"I know you didn't come to me without experience with women. That was obvious."

"Oh, it was, was it?" He smiled against her hair. "Well, what I said is-- I never woke up next to a woman and that is true. I didn't know if I'd like it. Found out in Tucson it wasn't bad."

When she would have pulled away, he laughed and drew her closer. "All right," he said, "I found I liked it. It could even become addictive. That though is bad for a man like me."

"Why?"

"You know why. It can't be for us. When the summer is over, it will be."

"You don't have to go to Vernal now."

"No, that's finished. But I will have to hit the road to trade."

She didn't like that, but she wouldn't argue with him. Not yet anyway. The summer lay ahead. "Do you like your father?" she whispered against his chest as he had cradled her to him.

"More than I expected. My memories haven't been good ones, but when I think about it, he was gone a lot. Maybe they were colored."

"By your stepmother?"

He nodded. "She didn't like what he did. I think she loved him, but what he did was hard on her. It was why she wanted me out of there. I have yet to figure out why she didn't try harder to get the others to leave. Maybe she did, and they didn't listen."

"Maybe you are the one now who should listen."

"To what?"

"That you should go back with your father," she said.

"Why?"

"You know why. You came to be sure Sam would be safe. Now he will be."

"You are still afraid of the dreams."

"I am."

"Beautiful, they are only dreams."

"What if they aren't? What if they are warnings?"

"I am not going to run from them, and you shouldn't either. Didn't we talk about living past them."

"You don't even believe in them." She tried to stop the tears but knew she was wetting his chest with them.

"I also don't disbelieve in them. I have lived a life that has had a lot of danger in it. You know that. I could have hidden somewhere and had a tree fall on me."

She lightly slapped his chest. "I don't want you dead. You could stay with your father at my house until I came back."

"Hiding under your bed," he suggested with a smile she could see in the dwindling light from the campfire.

"Would that be safe?" she teased.

"Might be a scorpion under there."

She put her fingers up to run over his cheek and touch his lips. "I am being silly."

"You are, but I like it. You can stomp the scorpion for me, keep me safe." He brushed away her tears.

"I would do that... if it's not a spider." She smiled against his fingers.

"Don't like them much, huh?"

"They have wicked little mouths. Haven't you noticed that?"

He chuckled. "Sounds like a deal. You stomp the scorpions, and I'll get the spiders." He positioned them where she could lay her head on his shoulder.

She tried to sleep, felt when he did, but she kept remembering the dream. It was foolishness. There wasn't any real danger out there, at least nothing more than there always was with life. She had to put this aside and do the work that she had come to do.

In the morning, after breakfast, Sam handed Ollie the signed papers to take back to Tucson as the two men saddled their horses. Jeremiah looked at his three sons as they stood to one side. They were all mature, dark haired, strong men whose features resembled his.

Nothing in Jesse's face showed his limitations—a gentle giant. Cole had stayed with Jeremiah, kept the ranch working, and was always there for a chore. Then Vince, probably the most intelligent, forceful of them all, and the daring son he wished he had some credit for the man he had become. The three owed him nothing as a father. He owed them so much. He could not undo the past, maybe not even fix the future.

He walked over to them. "I want you to know." He moved his gaze from one to the other, "That I do love you all. I have not been a father like I wish I had, but I am proud of the men you became despite me."

"There is always the future," Vince said reaching out and pulling his father into a masculine embrace. Jeremiah hadn't hugged his son since he had grown out of childhood. He heartily returned the hug to Vince's wince. "Sorry, forgot about your wound."

"It is all right."

Jeremiah than hugged the other two. Holly was watching and smiling. He turned to her. "Can I hug you too?" She grinned and stepped into his embrace. "We will see you before summer ends."

He nodded, mounted and turned his horse toward the Salt and away from the only family he had. No, that wasn't true. He rode past the grave of his dead son. He had to fight back tears. He had failed Asa too—there was no fixing that. He felt sorrow at that.

"Can't look back," Ollie said as he caught up with him.

"I pretty well wasted my life."

"Don't waste the rest of it."

"It's a little hard to start changing at sixty-one."

"What's your choice?"

Jeremiah laughed as he looked over at the salty old man. Well, younger than him but with many of the same experiences. "Can't argue with you about that." He had no idea how to do it, but he didn't have a choice either—at least if his past didn't catch up with him.

Tucson

Four days later, with the key to Holly's home, Jeremiah settled in and waited for Ollie to notify him that the legal papers had been filed. When he knew the widow Osbourne could no longer benefit from killing Sam Ryker, he would pay her a visit. He had learned she was now at the Continental Hotel. With her limited funds, he doubted she had arranged for another paid assassin, but he would feel better about the whole thing once he had talked to her.

Ollie's knock at the door came two days after they had arrived. "I made some coffee, want some?" Jeremiah asked. The old-timers went into the kitchen.

"It's finished," Ollie said as he took his cup. "Angus got 'er done. He said the other lawyer hurried through his end. The money was waiting and has been transferred to Sam's banks. There was shore a lot of it."

"I'll talk to the widow then today. The sooner the better."

"You make a good cup of coffee." Ollie smiled. "Come on up to my home, meet my wife. Rose loves feedin' folks. She's a danged good cook too. You can meet my grandson. It's what you might call evidence that a man can turn his life around."

"I'd like to meet your family. I still have no idea what I am going to do other than wait until Vince and Holly return."

"Men change their lives all the time in these parts—for good or bad."

"I've been thinking on that. If I don't have to, I don't want to go back to Vernal. It'll drag me the wrong way. I'm too old for the outlaw trail. This is a hot miserable climate at times, but it's new. Maybe there is a chance here."

"Something else come up," Ollie said as he rose to pour himself another cup of coffee.

"Doesn't sound like good news."

303

"It ain't. Madison hasn't been seen in Tucson since he left."

Jeremiah took his cigars, offered one to Ollie, who refused. "People asking about him? He was fine last we saw him."

Ollie shook his head. "Nobody much seems to care, but it makes me wonder where he went after we saw him."

"Hmmmm." Jeremiah bit off the tip and lit his cigar. "What are you thinking?"

"Several possibilities. He might've died. Greenhorn like him. Horse falls, he ends up in the Salt. No buzzards. No sign. He might've taken off out of the country, which means head north, since he hadn't been back to Globe when we rode through."

"He'd have no reason to go to Canyon Creek, or even know they were there."

"No, he wouldn't. Not a sensible one anyhow."

"Not much we can do about it unless you were thinking of riding north again?"

"Nah, I can't be gone again. I train horses. I already have two clients mad at me. I wouldn't do it unless you was thinkin' he'd be a danger to them."

Jeremiah considered that. "I don't know. Don't see how we can know, but Sam or Vince will shoot him on sight."

Ollie nodded. "More or less how I was thinking. When I wire Sam about the money, I'll let him know at least. Just bothered me some—him not back here."

When Ollie rode off, Jeremiah considered it. It bothered him too. Still, it was a long ride back up there and most likely a wild goose chase. He'd deal with the widow first and then think on it some more.

An hour later, Jeremiah had arranged for her to meet him at

the Rainbow cafe. He'd be stuck paying for her coffee, but he figured best to meet her in a public place. He didn't trust her.

"How did your business go?" she asked. "I thought Asa might be back also," she added. She signaled to the waitress that she would also like a sweet roll with her coffee.

Jeremiah figured he better make this quick, or she'd be ordering a full meal. "It turns out your reason for wanting Ryker dead is finished. He took the money. There is no more estate you could get even if something happened to him now."

Her face whitened. She stared at him and then out the window. He might have felt sorry for that stricken look if he didn't know what a viper she was.

"You are sure?"

"I am. I am also sure that when Ryker returns to Tucson, you need to be long gone. I don't know that he'd hurt a woman, but his wife would tear out all your hair—at the least." He smirked as her face fell even further.

"I guess... Except, I don't have the money to leave. I can't even pay for my hotel room. I am broke. I guess you figured that."

He had. "I will buy you a ticket to get as far as Dallas. From there, it's up to you."

She nodded. "You are sure about..."

"I am dead sure."

"What about Asa? I thought he was... well, interested in me and maybe."

"Asa ain't interested anymore. You get on that train. Sneak your bags out of the hotel. You know all about how to do that, don't you?"

She sighed. "I do."

"I will meet you at the depot. I checked. In an hour and a half, there is a train due in and heading east when it leaves.

305

You best be on it. Ryker has friends in this country. It won't be healthy for you once word gets out what you tried."

"How would word get out?" She stared at him and then looked down. "All right. I will meet you at the depot. And... thank you for the ticket."

"My pleasure."

Two hours later, he watched the train leaving the station with the widow on it. For the first time he felt a sense of relief.

CHAPTER 24

Aﬞter a week's work, which had included building a ladder to get them to the rooms, Holly was happy that, in room one, they had found some artifacts and were able to establish their distance down and apart. Nothing was earth-shaking, but the method of digging the narrow trench, studying the layers, had given her a rough idea that the recovered items appeared to be from as much as a thousand years earlier and established a long period of occupancy. There had been the expected pots, tools and a well-crafted chert knife.

Using ropes and protective pine branch baskets to pull the camera up, David had taken photos of the rooms using the combination of reflective panels and natural lighting. Each night he had been developing the plates, and she was delighted with what they had recorded. Alice had proven to be an excellent artist and several sketchpads were full of drawings of artifacts and the structure of the rooms.

Room one had a small room behind it, which, with the tin plates, they had enough light to investigate. In baskets, the dried food included corn cobs, pine nuts, roots, leaves, mesquite beans, cactus fruit, and even a pot containing dried meat, which might have been venison or rabbit. Finding such items told her something about their diet, but not why the food had been left. Perhaps they had been left after a hurried departure or for a hoped return.

She climbed back down to where Vince worked in the midden. He had opened his shirt. "Bones of deer, rabbit, but no human. There were pottery pieces and a broken knife," he said as he stopped to point out the few findings. His skin glistened with sweat. "How'd it go up there?" he asked as she slumped onto a rock.

She handed him her canteen. "There is only one room left to investigate for the corner with a pot."

He took a drink. "Then that's where it is."

"I thought I'd recognize the room when I was in them, but they look alike. The doors, the walls. They are all like my dreams."

"You saving the remaining one for tomorrow?"

She nodded. She both wanted to find that pot and dreaded it. If it wasn't there, then her dream wasn't what she had thought. In a way, that was a relief—except then why the dreams. But if it was... She looked up as Vince handed her back the canteen.

"I'll go with you tomorrow," he said.

"Would you do that?"

"Sure. Want to go looking for the grave now? It'd be cooler in the trees."

"I am almost afraid to find that."

He shook his head and smiled. "My brave little explorer suddenly afraid. Hey, I have a shovel in my hand. Let's go looking."

"I won't recognize any of what was in the dream for the

trees. It's obviously changed a lot since then." She picked up a trowel.

"Graves are not so hard to find as you might think. Especially not if they are shallow." He started toward the manzanita, and she followed.

"It's been a lot of years. Trees might come up over it. Then we aren't likely to find it."

"We can look anyway."

She was surprised he was showing interest in what might've been his own grave. "Aren't you worried about ghosts?" she asked as the reached the grove of trees.

"If you are right," he said with a laugh, "I'm my own ghost."

"I suppose. Well, what about the chindi?"

He smiled at her. "Any spirits are likely up in the rooms trying to foul up your discoveries. Not likely interested in this." He studied the ground. "If your people were looking for soft and easy places to dig, they'd have avoided the clay. They are also unlikely to put bodies near the spring."

"In the dream, the grave seemed to be a clearing."

"That's a help. Some soil is wrong for trees. Let's start with there." He walked toward the right and then back.

"What are you doing?"

"Looking for sunken ground. A body becomes part of the soil eventually, but it takes the bones longer. Most burials are west to east in our culture but wasn't that way back then, nor for the pueblos now. At least when they aren't influenced by Catholic rituals. Northeast is the way they face their bodies. That's the angle for us to look for a long depression."

She should have remembered the sunken ground. "Their burials were shallow," she told him. "Like only two or three feet in depth. And I am just remembering that the human body is alkaline. Any wildflowers growing over them might be ones that like alkaline soil." As she walked and looked, she tried to remember which ones-- poppies, pensternon, mallow, yarrow were most likely.

"Come here, Holly," he said. He was kneeling by a faint depression. The earth was an inch or even two below the surrounding ground. "Let's try this spot first. Except, only finding bones won't mean it's the right one, will it?"

"In the dream, he was buried with a small pottery figure, four small pieces of garnet, a bow, and one arrow." She clenched her jaw as she remembered the last item. "There would also be a knife, different than expected here. He was buried with it." She felt numb as she remembered the last proof. "The spear that went through his heart, the shaft was broken off but the head not pulled out. It had gone through his breast bone."

"Good." She wondered why it didn't bother him to imagine the agonizing pain of a spear piercing what might have been his own chest.

"How about we find out what's down here." He dug carefully, removing a shovelful of soil at a time. Their activity had drawn Gabe and Sam. "This a grave?" Gabe asked.

"Looks like it."

Vince carefully dug down around the roots of some of the plants. Yarrow and pensternon were set aside for replanting. Going deeper, he worked a little faster. Gabe yelped. "I see bone."

Now they worked with trowel, shovel, and their hands. A big rock was pushed aside and in less than half an hour, a skeleton had been fully revealed.

"It'd have been six foot, way taller than the expected here; so most likely a male and from elsewhere," Gabe said as he studied the bones. The spearhead in the chest was enough to cause Holly to sit to avoid collapsing.

"The rest is here too," Vince said as he pointed to the bow

and arrow, somewhat deteriorated but still recognizable. At the skull were garnets. The knife at his other side had a blade of bone. Most likely of whale bone.

"You have your proof," Gabe said as he stared at the grave.

She began to cry unable to stop the tears.

"I think we should close it back up unless you want something from the grave," Vince said. Again, his face gave her no clue what he was thinking.

"Yes, but... could I have a few moments... alone with him?"

"Of course."

When they had gone, she put her hand over the skull. She closed her eyes, tears running down her cheeks. She could feel all the pain that had been felt that day when he had been laid in this narrow trench. The objects he had loved had been put beside him. The small clay figure had been what she had wanted him to have. Or... the woman that day.

She didn't try to think it through, what had happened, whether it had been her. She just let the feelings soak in and more memories return. She was well aware that such memories could come from many sources. The tears were all hers.

It was an hour later when Vince returned. "I think we need to close it up," he said putting a hand on her shoulder.

"Yes," she said. She had stopped crying. "Let me help."

She took the trowel and pushed in the dirt to go around the skull and then torso as Vince added shovelfuls of dirt. When the grave was again enclosed, He replanted the flowers he had removed. He left and returned with a bucket of water. "They might make it if the storms come soon enough."

He hunkered down beside her. "Are you all right?"

She nodded. "It was real. The dream had real substance." She looked up at him. "Do you remember any of it?"

"No. Maybe it wasn't me." He smiled at her.

She smiled, convinced it had been him, but maybe he

didn't need to know. "The last room will have the pot," she said as he helped her rise.

"It seems likely. What will be in it?"

"Items that belonged to him. I think a hide jacket, sandals of yucca. He had given me gifts. I left them there also."

"Why not take them with you? Were you leaving?"

"I don't know, but I wanted to protect them. There was a necklace carved of bone with a rawhide cord. It's the only thing I want. He had worn it until the day he put it around my neck."

"It was in the dreams?"

She nodded. "I do remember life here and things the dreams never had in them." She pursed her lips. "Was it me though? Or I am feeling her now, and it's her memories I have? I can't prove any of this. I thought I would be able to, but I can't, can I?"

"No, you can't."

Back at the camp, the others were excited about the grave. "Should I have photographed it?" David asked.

She shook her head. "No, not that one." The men walked back to look at the site to see if there were any other likely looking graves.

Abby came to sit beside Holly on the fallen log. "Are you all right?"

"I will be. It was a shock. Despite believing it was there and real, I wasn't sure."

Abby put her arm around her. "There is something more about this, isn't there?"

"You already know, don't you?"

"That you believe the man who occupied that skeleton had once been Vince? Yes, I do."

"Do you believe in reincarnation?"

"How else can we explain some things? From the moment,

I saw Sam, I felt I had known him, and yet, of course, I had not. I had no reason to trust him, not given who he was back then, but I did in the deepest place. Of course, I had to learn who he was in this lifetime, but yes, I believe in reincarnation and mates who are together through more than one lifetime—not always in a positive sense." She smiled at that.

Alice and Song had come to listen to them. "Buddhism also believes we reincarnate, even sometimes as an animal." Song smiled as she said it. "The soul returns again and again until it achieves moksa and can enter nirvana."

"Do you remember past lives, Song?" Alice asked.

Song shook her head. "When I was a little girl, I thought I remembered something-- how I had died, but then the memory, if it was that, faded as I grew past that age. Now I don't even remember what it was, only that once I had thought it."

"I have never been religious. Perhaps that is why that I never looked to a religion for the answers to the why of the dreams," Holly said. "I looked to science. I am still trying to decide if they had real meaning. They were persistent and now did follow through to an actual historic event. I can know just that much."

Abby shook her head. "Searching for meaning in anything in life is where we all find ourselves struggling at times. Maybe it was to lead you to become an archaeologist."

"That might be. It would have been easier to be a banker or even lead an indolent life. Money and opportunity were handed to me. Even being able to attend a college came on the backs of the struggles other women made to get an education. I suppose coming to this place was the first real struggle I had to go through, had to work for. Maybe I needed it to become stronger and more confident in myself."

She felt tears again and brushed them away. The dreams

had been hard, frightening but maybe they were to lead her to a life work. Maybe they weren't warnings. Why would a warning draw her to the place it could be relived?

That night after they had eaten their evening meal and helped Song clean up, they sat around the campfire quieter than they had been. Vince supposed that was to be expected. The more practical among them, which meant him, hadn't expected to find a grave or any of what Holly said she had dreamed.

"What are you thinking?" she asked. She was sitting at his feet, her arm resting on his thigh. The intimacy of the moment, the sense of belonging only added to his feeling of strangeness.

"Today was a surprise for me." He looked down and saw her smiling.

"I knew that."

"Not only today. This whole journey, including my father, my brothers. I might have thought someday I'd have to kill Asa but never that Jesse and Cole might be real brothers if I gave them half a chance. I'd put the idea of family away from me, behind a barrier."

"You have a lot of barriers, Vince. Do you know that?"

Yes, he knew. He looked across the fire at where Cole and Gabe were talking and laughing while Jesse watched and smoked. He had walked off from the family because he had felt he needed to do it. He hadn't thought about what he had left behind, hadn't thought any of it was worth going back for-- except his stepmother, and he hadn't even done that. He hadn't felt guilty about that part of his life, not until his father had showed up wanting to help. Damn.

"You can remove barriers—if you want," she said looking up into his eyes.

"You are an optimistic little thing, aren't you?" he said trying for a light tone but unsure he had succeeded.

"I could only wish. She rose and took his hand, pulling him to the spring, which the crew had restored by a combination of removing the big rocks and digging it out. "I wish you would go back to Tucson."

"You still fear the power of that dream?"

"I do."

"Let me tell you about something I have learned." He sat on one of the big rocks and drew her to sit on his lap.

"Will I like it?" she asked as she brushed his bristly jaw with her fingertips. He liked her fingers on his skin but reminded himself to shave in the morning, as he didn't like how that bristle marked her skin.

He smiled. "I am not sure. Here it is anyway. The only way somebody could kill me would be to bushwhack me. No man can protect himself against that. But it could happen if I was to ride down the Salt or even got back to Tucson and a stranger hid in the shadows, maybe a relative of someone I killed."

"You are a fatalist." She ran her fingers through his hair.

"Maybe that's what it is. But it's what I have seen with life. You can't run away from fate. It's not so much luck but more that your time is up. If mine is, I will be killed somewhere by someone. If it's not, nobody can kill me."

"That sounds religious."

He pulled her fingers around to where he could kiss them. "I was a parson."

"And you believed it."

"I did. I guess I still do. It's like in the Ecclesiastes."

"I am not knowledgeable about the Bible."

"'To everything there is a season, and a time to every purpose under heaven; A time to be born, and a time to die, a time to plant, and a time to pluck up that which is planted.'

There is more but the gist of it is we don't determine as much of our life as we think."

"You are religious." She felt a little shocked but supposed she should not.

He smiled. "You think because I have killed men, that it doesn't fit."

"Perhaps I had thought that."

"Because I don't live it, doesn't mean I don't believe it. I am not in a religion anymore, but I believe there is a right way to live life and part of that is to accept death. I believe there is more to life than we can see."

"I don't want to accept your death."

"I don't either right now." He drew her down and lightly kissed her lips.

"All right, I think I understand, but you are being careful, aren't you?"

"You better believe it. I watch the hills, look for metal shining where it shouldn't be, movement where it doesn't belong. I though won't live with fear."

She sighed. "I don't want to lose you."

"You won't—not that way."

"I feel I did before."

"That's still a dream, beautiful. Maybe you lived it or maybe you connected with someone else's story."

"I knew your eyes that first day in Tucson when you came to the house."

"And I knew your body." He smiled. "They call that lust."

She gave him a little slap. "They do not!"

"All right, they don't. Look, it will be all right, and tomorrow you will find that necklace and the pot."

"You do believe in it now."

"I believe it's there. I don't know how you knew it, but I

think you will find it. There is a question though that has occurred to me."

"Go ahead."

"You know what happened to him. What happened to her?"

Her dreams had always stopped before or with the burial of her beloved. Why had they stopped there? "I don't know," she said. "Maybe there is something in that pot. These people didn't leave a written history, only pictures carved on walls. I haven't yet seen any of those here. They might not have told about her anyway. I have also wondered."

"There were two other graves near his. They were in a row with only a big rock above them. If they left any markings on the rock, they were weathered off."

"I suppose we should see what was in the other graves." She felt strangely reluctant to do that.

"Explorers of anything, whether physical or emotional remains should want to find out."

"Maybe I have been afraid to know. Maybe she married again."

"You were that sure she married him?"

"So far as I know, there is no evidence of these people's marriage practices. If they were influenced by or influenced the Aztec, their marriages were more clan business than an attraction between two people. The prospective groom had to go to the council. The old women arranged much of who went with whom. The night of the marriage, an old woman, an elder, would carry the bride to the man's clan for the ceremony. Both parties would be dressed in white robes. When the marriage was confirmed, the robes would be tied together by the old woman. The strange part to us is that, when the consummation occurred, it might not even be the groom. It could as well have been the bride's brother, father, or uncles."

"Interesting people," he said with sarcasm. "For being up here for your exploration, you do know quite a bit about the Aztec."

"It has been my belief that they are connected but exactly how is the question. Some think the ancestors of the Hohokam came from Mexico. Others that Hohokam, and the others in these regions, went there when they left these homes for unknown reasons."

"You know the Pueblo and Hopi people believe those living here were their ancestors."

"And that might well be true. Either way, there seems to be a strong cultural tie. The ball courts would be one example wherever they were possible. The courts look similar to those found in Mexico and Central America."

"Men do like to compete."

"Sometimes it was for life, to survive. Rather like the Romans with the Gladiators."

"Also human nature."

"The greater question for places like here is why build their homes in places so difficult to access."

"Defense is the obvious answer."

"And yet from what I have read, few violent deaths have been evidenced. Now, with this grave, I wonder if they weren't buried like others because of the violence."

He brushed his fingertips down her cheek. "Or they were left where they fell and the scavengers took care of the bodies. I figured that'd be my end someday in a lonely canyon where I didn't see the danger in time."

"I hate it when you talk that way."

He smiled. "It is a possible reason for no archaeological evidence left a thousand years later."

"It's possible." She gave his cheek a little slap. "On a more positive note, what we find will be nothing to what they will someday be able to determine regarding a place like this. There will be improved scientific methods that will link one people to another, tools we can't even imagine now."

"You have a lot of faith in science."

"I do. I think it's the hope for a better world."

He tried to resist the cynical smile. He had little hope for a better world. Man's nature was what got in the way. "When you saw this man killed, what did you see beyond that?"

"Like?"

"Were the killers strangers, a lot of them?"

She shook her head. "I don't know that the attack came from outside the tribe. Parts of the dreams were vague images. Maybe it was from within the clan itself. Her relatives. Maybe the trader threatened them or perhaps their love did."

"We can at least open the other graves."

She didn't like that idea, but he was right. "I suppose we should also have David photograph the placement of the bones in them. it could determine tribal connections. Also, while we know why the first man died, who knows about the others."

"They will be easy to access."

"Tomorrow. I will go up and see if that pot is at the back of the seventh room."

"Which place do you want me?"

"With me." She smiled. "I always want you with me."

He knew that desire would fade. Holly Jacobs could do far better than a man like himself who had used up more than half his life and had little to show for it. However, he would enjoy what she offered while it lasted. "Then that's where I'll be." He pulled her back into his arms.

CHAPTER 25

Morning saw the crew divided. Gabe, Sam, David, and Abby went to the graves. David took the camera to record the position of the bodies if there were any. The others resumed their work in the room they had been excavating, while Vince went with Holly to the seventh room.

The room had a small door, which required even Holly to scrunch down to get through it. Once inside the room, Vince still could not stand upright. "They were a small people." He didn't like the claustrophobic feeling it gave him. If he had to live in such places, he'd sleep outside a lot.

She moved to the far right corner and with her trowel, began digging down. After awhile, he took it from her and carefully loosened the packed floor. When he felt something hard, he stopped. "It might be here."

Even in the dim light, he could see that her face had whitened. He handed her the trowel. Soon she had uncovered what appeared to be a red clay plate. More soil removal showed the edges of a pot that was probably a foot or more in diameter. The plate had been to protect what was within it. It had been put into hollowed out sandstone. It took careful work to reach down and lift it from its hole. It was red ware with no designs, round without a crack or knick. He knew from the weight as he pulled it out that it was not empty.

"Where do you want to investigate what is inside?" he asked.

She stared at the pot. "Below. Is it too heavy to carry? I... I want to get out of this room."

He lifted it and carried it out. At the ladder, he stopped, stepped onto the rail and then reached back for the pot to climb down. When he reached the sandstone shelf, he set it on the rock to help her down the last steps. Without a word, they walked back to the camp where he set it on the tail of the wagon.

Holly reached into the pot and brought out a leather shirt. Too small for Vince, it had obviously been worn by a large man. It was not damaged or stained. If she was right about it belonging at one time to the trader, he'd not been wearing it when he was killed.

She carefully laid it beside the pot and brought out a bone necklace. He felt of the delicate carving. A whale. He had seen others like it in San Francisco. This man could have come from whaling cultures, which meant far up the Pacific Coast. Haida maybe.

When she had everything out, there were yucca sandals, in perfect condition, even what looked like deerskin moccasins. Remembering the bones of the man had had no sign of garments, it told Vince that he had been placed naked in the grave. Either he had been disrobed before burial or killed when stripped. If the latter, it might have been an execution not an attack.

He saw Holly was upset, but he had questions for her.

Maybe now would be the one time she would have the answers at the shock of seeing her dream come to life.

"Where did you see yourself in the dream when you saw him being killed?"

Tears were running down her cheeks as she fingered the leather shirt. She closed her eyes. "Beside him. I screamed. I don't know what happened after the life left his eyes."

He saw her upset-- better to let it go for now. "We've done enough with this for today. Will you want David to photograph it?"

"I had permission to take it with me but... now I am not sure I want to. I..."

"Take your time thinking about it. No rush."

He was curious now about the other possible graves. "Why don't you stay with Song and have some tea," he suggested. "I want to see how Sam, Gabe and David have done."

She stared blankly at him but nodded. He realized what this had to mean to her-- years of dreaming and then revelation. It wasn't hard to understand how she must feel. He wanted more answers though and after he got her settled with Song, who had been preparing the evening meal, he headed for the gravesite.

Sam and Gabe were squatting around two holes when he got there. Cole, David, and Jesse stood back. "And?" he asked as he looked at the bones. He lit a cigarette.

"This one is a woman... with a baby still in her womb," Sam said. He rose and took the cigarette as soon as Vince had his first long draw on it. "From the position of its skeleton, down so far into the pelvis, I'd guess it could not get out and she died in childbirth."

"And the other one?" He glanced toward it with a vague feeling of repugnance.

"Another male, I think, from the shoulders the narrower

pelvis but I can't prove it. It's taller than the woman but not big like the other man."

Vince walked over to look down at the third skeleton. "Is that a broken arm?"

"And crushed skull," Sam said taking back the cigarette.

"This is a tragedy from beyond the grave," Gabe said standing beside them before he also took the cigarette. "The story though is unknown."

Vince turned back to look at the woman's skeleton. The tiny bones of the baby were perfectly formed and not deteriorated as one might expect after maybe a thousand years. Evidently, this soil was kind to bones. Despite his wishing she had stayed away, Vince looked up to see that Holly had come to look at the graves.

"I suppose this is why I didn't remember before," she said in a quiet voice.

"You do now?" Vince asked.

"Ka-tah-yang was attacked because we weren't supposed to be together. I had been long promised to another. I was pregnant with my lover's baby." She stared at the tiny form. "I hid it as long as I could but finally it was impossible. They would not let us marry. This one." She pointed to the third grave. "He had been promised me. He tried to kill Ka-tah-yang. The fight ended with him dead. The clan did not accept that it was self defense. They held Ka-tah-yang and drove the spear through his heart. I watched him die." She didn't cry, but her face was pale. "I took his things to the pot where I buried them to protect them so no one would have them. I am not sure how much later, but I went into labor with our child-- only it wouldn't be born. I tried but... After... a long time, I quit trying and died. I was filled with sorrow for our child but glad I would see Ka-tah-yang again."

"And that's why you never remembered it all," Vince said reaching out and pulling her into his arms.

She nodded and then the tears came. "I guess I couldn't handle the whole tragedy. The dreams were hard enough as they were." She managed a smile, for which he gave her full credit as he saw how hard it was for her. "There is one plus. Their story is now out. Maybe I won't have the dreams anymore."

"Shall we close them back up?" David asked, "Or do I take photographs first?"

"I think photographs," she said. "And if you wish, you can of the first one too. I was not behaving as a professional when I stopped you." She looked at the woman's grave. There had been no ornaments put beside her body. "Before you close it, I have something that should go in it."

She walked back to camp only aware when almost there that Vince had followed her. "Do you want the pot put back in the room?"

"Yes, except for." She took the necklace. "This belongs in the grave with her."

He smiled and pulled her into his arms. She felt so small, so vulnerable. "Maybe now it'll all be about archaeology," he whispered as he kissed the top of her head.

She gave a little laugh. 'Yes, now it's science. I just... I wish I understood the reason for the dreams."

"Everything in life doesn't have a reason. Some simply is."

She gave a little sniff. "All right, be that way, just when I want to create a grand scenario of life."

"There might be one," he agreed. "But, we may never see what it is."

By evening, the three skeletons had been photographed and

the necklace placed with the woman's bones before it was closed back up with the others. "In some ways," she said, as she and Abby walked back from the brief ceremony, which Gabe had conducted, "I wish the other man wasn't there. He didn't deserve to be there."

"Why do you say that?"

"He ruined it for them."

Abby smiled. "Or they ruined it for him."

"You are too understanding." Holly laughed. "I guess most things can be seen both ways."

"We'll never know."

"Not even with our own lives."

When they got to the camp, Holly realized there were three strange horses tied to the trees below the camp and three men were standing talking to Zian and Song. They turned when Holly and Abby arrived.

"What you folks doing up here?" the fatter of the three asked.

"It's a scientific excavation. May we help you?" Holly asked.

"Got any grub to spare?" the tallest asked.

"Very little although you are welcome to eat with us this evening," she said wondering if there would be enough.

"You digging in that ruin up there?" The one with the big belly asked as he took a cup of coffee from Song.

"I guess that's obvious."

"Feisty little thing, ain't you?" the tall one asked and for the first time Holly had some concern as to who these men were as one used a slur to describe Song and Zian. "Pretty women like you should have better sense," he added with a leer.

"I rescind the dinner invitation," Holly snapped. "You do not deserve to eat with us"

The tall man looked around. "Us? Who is us?"

"How about me?" Vince asked. He had walked in without

325

Holly hearing him. She looked back at the three, heavily armed strangers. She knew Vince was wearing his revolver, but was that enough against three men? Zian was unarmed, as he had been helping his mother cut up the deer Sam had shot the day before.

"You folks looking for Coronado's gold?" the fat man asked.

"Get on your horses and ride out. Don't come back," Vince said approaching them too closely for Holly's comfort.

"Says who?" the tall man asked.

"Him and me," Sam said as he now backed Vince. He also was wearing his usual sidearm.

"You had been invited to dine with us," Holly said, "but you insulted us. Now we would like you to leave without more unpleasantness." She thought she said it politely, although she was both angry and frightened.

When the tall man stepped forward and reached out with a fist, Vince slammed him back with blows so fast that she only saw the impact as the man crumbled to the ground. "You heard the lady," he said, not even out of breath from the exertion. "Get out. Don't come back."

The man who hadn't spoken moved to his horse but before he had the reins, he had turned with a gun in his hand. With a swift kick, Vince slammed his boot into his wrist, sending the gun flying. "Don't pick it up. For that matter, drop your guns—all of them. We'll throw in the Salt. Any other stupid plays, and there'll be the three of you with it."

The men grumbled, but they threw down their weapons, mounted their horses, and rode back the way they had come.

"Will they be trouble?" she asked shaking.

"Not unless they can afford to buy new guns and come with friends," Vince said. He looked down at one of the revolvers and picked it up. "Not bad, a Colt 45. You were talking about getting a better gun, Zian." He handed it to the youth.

"For me?"

"Why not. He won't be back for it. It's a nice gun. You know anything about shooting?"

"I have done some, but Mother objected to the noise."

Vince looked at Song. "It's better he learns the right way than to pick it up on his own."

"All right," Song said shaking her head as she looked from the grinning Sam to Vince and then back to her smiling son. "I guess you are right. Don't do it near me, or I might ruin your supper."

"We wouldn't want that," Sam said. "We'll take him down toward the Salt, where we will throw away the other guns, and at the same time make sure those jaspers left."

The three of them headed off to make noise and break things. Holly sat on the log. "I am definitely thinking I don't understand men."

Alice had come down from the rooms only to hear the last of the altercation. "Was there wisdom here about men that I should know?"

She smiled at her mother's look of exasperation. "Not quite yet," Abby said. "I hope. I don't want your father having a heart attack."

For the crew, the next two weeks flew by. Vince saw Holly blossoming as she had put the past behind her, and now it was all about assessing what they were finding. If she still had concerns regarding past life curses, he and she had little time to discuss them. It was all about putting together as accurate a picture of the ones who had lived here and their life as possible. More burials had been found in the rooms. It began to look as though a violent death or some kind of disgrace had landed the three off by themselves.

With Alice so good at sketching and David taking over the photography and developing, it enabled Holly to spend her time writing in her notebooks dimensions, details of placement, and from those findings, her own conjecture as to what life might have been like in this small community. While it seemed hunter agrarian from the midden and storage rooms behind their living quarters, it was impossible to forget the violent end to two of them. Any evidence of wars being fought were likely going to be impossible to find—other than the homes so high on the cliff.

Sam made one trip to Show Low, taking Zian where they brought back a packhorse loaded with fresh supplies. When he returned, he opened a new whiskey bottle and drew Vince aside. "That lawyer was there for awhile."

"Madison?"

Sam nodded. "Ollie's wire told me the will had been settled. I called him, and he said Madison never showed up back in Tucson. I asked around Show Low. He was gone but had been there for two weeks or more."

Vince put out his cup. "Interesting," he said as he took the first sip of whiskey.

"People were vague on when they stopped seeing him. Not like he had friends there. He isn't likely to go back to Tucson. Ollie said a little asking there told him and your pa that Madison didn't have much of a practice. He was broke and in debt."

"How'd he manage in Show Low?"

"My guess is a little gambling, some borrowing before the folks got onto it that his smooth manners and talk didn't mean he was worth anything."

"This doesn't have to impact us," Vince said as he weighed

the possibilities. Maybe the shyster had headed north where he wasn't known. He had not, however, forgotten his impression of the man as a back shooter.

"Not necessarily," Sam said lighting a cigarette.

"All right, give it to me straight. What do you think?"

"Where it comes to that one, there is no straight."

"He had his guns taken. Did he buy one?"

"Not at the mercantile, which doesn't mean he didn't buy something elsewhere or steal one."

He stared at the circling raves as he considered the few facts. "Not much we can do about it."

"True. By now, there'd be no way to track him. Something about it though doesn't smell right."

Vince took the cigarette from him for a few long draws. "We'll stay alert, not that we don't anyway."

"Yep. Otherwise, Ollie said Osbourne took off for Dallas. Your pa bought her the ticket."

"Good for him. Hope she stays gone."

"She has nothing to gain by hanging around or hiring someone else."

"You thinking of heading back soon?"

"No need. Cattle graze the hills in the summer, not time to brand. David and Alice are loving this and learning a lot about history from Holly."

"Originally she thought it'd be the summer, but once the monsoons start, end of this month, she might see it otherwise."

"It would make it tougher for taking wagons back."

"I'll talk it over with her. Unless she decides to start a new excavation, we might have all we are going to get from this one."

"When I came back from Show Low, there were three ruins possible up Canyon Creek," Sam said. "They're like this one though for the number of rooms, set into the canyon walls. I am not sure how much she'll learn there that she doesn't already know."

"Cho Nah told me there is a big one farther up. He said it was hard to see unless you knew where to look. Guess I should take her up that way to see what she thinks." He handed back the cigarette.

Sam got a sensual smile. "You think that's a good idea, do you?"

Vince chuckled as he finished his whiskey. "Overnight maybe."

"Oh yeah, I can see the advantage of that." Sam laughed.

"Just trying to help... science along."

"When she does head back to Tucson, you staying with her?"

"For what?"

Sam snorted. "You know for what."

"She's not for the likes of me."

"For you or not, you're in love with her."

"That doesn't count for much in the world."

"For a padre, you don't have a lot of insights into life, mi amigo."

"Maybe too many."

"From the wrong side."

Vince shrugged. "I can't argue with that."

"Give her a chance."

"I am trying to give me one to be able to walk away from this and go on living without her. The longer it lasts, the harder that will be."

"Which is why you want to go off-- the two of you, alone," Sam said with a humorous snort.

"All right, so I am not using my head on that."

Sam laughed. "I'd address that, but here comes David, and

I have hoped he'll stay innocent a little longer—that is, if he is."

The next morning, Holly was delighted to take Vince up on his suggestion. For her, it was not so much to see more ruins but to have time alone with him. The close quarters of the camp made it difficult even to have a private conversation.

"How far were you thinking we'd go?" she asked when the trail widened enough to ride side by side.

"The one you might find interesting is about ten miles from the Salt. From what I was told, it had more rooms but also some structures that might be of interest like a ball court."

"Who told you?"

"Cho Nah."

"Is he still alive? I mean could I meet him?"

"He was last time I was at Fort Apache. He's maybe sixty-five or so. We won't be going that far today."

"I know. I was thinking maybe sometime." She knew he never talked about a future for them, but she kept hoping he would come around to seeing there should be one.

"Sam told me that Madison had been seen in Show Low."

She felt a shiver go up her spine. "He wouldn't try to cause trouble again, would he?"

"He didn't seem to be much of an outdoorsman; so I don't see it being out here, but whether he would in the future, I don't know. He's an odd bird."

"Why do you say that?"

"It took tough and qualified men to be taken into the Rough Riders. How did he get in there with his lack of physical skills?"

She considered that a moment. "His legal ones?"

"Have you ever actually researched those?"

"Well, no."

"Ollie told Sam that not only did Madison not return, but his practice is practically nonexistent. Pa said his office is run down, no secretary. You didn't use him as a lawyer, did you?"

"No, I used James Angus. I did not have a good feeling about Clint. I learned Grace had removed her affairs from his office also."

"It appears your guess as to what he wanted with you may have been right. He's in debt and no income." His eyes scanned the distance.

"What is it?" she asked feeling a fear surge through her.

"Nothing. I thought I caught a shine where it shouldn't be. Nothing now though."

"You are scaring me."

"If I believed there was any danger up here, I'd not have suggested we do this." He smiled at her.

"Ah, are you sure? You are somewhat of a risk taker."

"Not where it comes to you."

"So, then this is all about furthering science?" She raised her brows and watched for his response.

"I am not that generous. I thought it would kill two birds with one stone."

She laughed and felt a joy that seemed to fill her. He did care for her. She knew he did. He had to.

CHAPTER 26

As they rode through the sparse pinyon pine and juniper, they saw several small ruins under the edge of the cliff. None seemed significantly different than the one they had been investigating. it was beyond what he took to be ten miles from the Salt that he saw the big one and pointed. "There."

It almost vanished into the red rock, until looking more closely and seeing the definite shapes. It had one large, rounded structure that looked to be three stories tall. Along both its sides were more structures with doorways and windows. It was not high on the cliff and would be easy to reach.

"It's a fantastic site," she said as they rode close enough to make out the fine rockwork. Circling over the rooms were the usual ravens, squawking at the disturbance of strangers. For whatever reason, they were often near these old dwellings.

He pointed to a flat area about one hundred feet from the buildings. "Maybe your ball court." She saw it then with the low wall and two openings. The court itself was relatively free of vegetation. Sunflowers bloomed at the openings.

"This is amazing," she said as they rode to where a small spring ran from a crevasse. Dismounting first, he helped her down and then hobbled their horses in a grassy spot near the spring.

She turned and from the ridge, she could see across the valley to distant cliffs. The colors were red, black and even some blue that might be turquoise. Beyond, she saw taller mountains.

"What a wonderful place to live."

"It would be possible to protect. I don't much like the grove of pine and juniper so close, but otherwise, it's good. They could be cut."

"You do think like a warrior."

"The day I don't, it could all be over."

"I wish you wouldn't say things like that."

"Sorry, it slipped out." He smiled then. "Want to take a closer look?" Of course, she did. "Take your rifle," he said.

"Why?"

"Good habit." He drew it from the scabbard and handed it to her. "You do know how to use it?"

"I do."

Reaching the first floor only required working their way up the gentle sandstone slope. There was even a ladder, which would enable them to reach what looked like an upper plaza of some sort. "The rooms are larger," she observed as she ducked into one of them. It not only had a window but an air vent above. "Maybe the rich or priests lived here."

He followed her in. In one corner was a large clay pot, the typical red but with some lines across it.

"I wonder if there are petroglyphs near this one," she said. She had been disappointed none had been found near the ruin they had investigated.

"We can look."

They ducked back outside and looked at the cliffs beyond. On one, somewhat protected from the wind, he saw etchings in the stone. She pointed to the man with the bow and arrow. "Maybe they used those more than some believed."

"Traders changed a lot of things," he agreed.

"A trader has changed my life," she said smiling at him. She would have liked a smile back, but he had moved down to look at more petroglyphs, which were of hunters. There was a male figure playing a flute and then some animals. A spiral was higher than either of them could reach.

They went back to their horses and removed the saddles. They had brought blankets, food, as well as one change of shirts for each of them. The first clouds of the coming monsoon had been filtering through, but Vince assured her that the likelihood of rain looked slim.

Their lunch was simple, as Song had put together some slices of bread, venison and one of the fresh tomatoes Sam had brought back from Show Low. When they finished, she moved to sit on his lap. "Do you mind?" she asked as she bent and lightly kissed his lips.

"You know I brought you out here for this reason."

"I wondered if you had tired of me. You haven't been close often."

"It's not out of desire but trying to do what is smart."

"Now it's smart?" she asked kissing his brow.

"Likely not." His smile took away the sting.

"Could we make love up there?" she asked pointing toward the ruins.

He laughed. "Would that be bad luck?"

"I don't see why. I'd like to make love in one of those ruins as women and men had done centuries ago. It's not particularly feasible at the one we've been investigating. Here, nobody would care."

"Sounds good to me." He lifted her off his lap as he stood. "Bring the blanket and your rifle."

"Surely you don't think I will need it against the ghosts," she teased.

"You never know. Take it."

She picked it and the blanket up and walked ahead of him, entering the room she had chosen. "Leave your weapons outside," she said in the most proper voice she could manage. "I am a woman of peace," she added.

He stopped and she heard him unbuckling his belt and then dropping it beside the door. He bent to come through the doorway when she heard the crack of a gunshot. Vince stumbled and fell to the floor. Getting past the shock, her first thought was to find out where he had been hurt. "God, please don't have him be dead," she begged as she simultaneously realized the shot meant a shooter was out there. She heard the sound of footsteps below the sandstone. Reaching for her rifle, she levered in a shell and came to the opening, half kneeling over where Vince had fallen.

Clint Madison was walking confidently toward her. "To the victor go the spoils," he said with a huge smile on his face. Quickly, she lifted the rifle to her shoulder, sighted it on the center of his chest, and pulled the trigger. The look of shock on his face was quickly replaced by a grimace. Before she could be sure he had been hit hard enough, she fired again, this time at his face. That shot toppled him backward to lie still. She didn't have to look to know he was dead.

Turning back to Vince, there was blood on his back, a little above his belt on the right side. "My God," she cried, trying to control her panic. This was no time to be missish. She tore off her shirt and pressed it to the bullet hole, turning him over to see that more blood was on his belly where the bullet had exited. It was closer to his side. Maybe, maybe this hadn't been a killing shot.

Quickly, she stripped off her chemise and used it to press against the second hole. She took the holster from his cartridge belt and lifting him enough to get it under him, she used it to roughly hold the two pads in place as she tried to remember her lessons in biology. What lay between the entry and exit wounds?

She hadn't brought medical supplies with them. As many miles as they had come and the way the canyon bent, no one back at camp would have heard the shots. She looked then at his face. His eyes were open. "Don't be dead," she begged as she brushed her fingers over his forehead.

"Not yet." He groaned. "You were my Delilah though." He managed a smile.

"I am not either." When she saw he was teasing, she fought for a smile. "How badly are you hurt?" she asked knowing it was a stupid question. She could see for herself that this was no minor wound.

"Bad enough." He tried to lever himself up, but she pushed him back. "I need to get you to the blanket." Before she could attempt to drag him, he said, "No, I'd make love to you in there, but not going to die there."

"Then all the more reason for me to get you there. I don't want you to die."

"No. I need to get back to the trees. It's not just superstition." He groaned again as he managed to lever himself to a sitting position. "Fresh air and the earth under me."

"Not much is holding those pads in place. Walking there could get more bleeding going."

He reached down and felt the belt, smiling at her. "Who shot me?"

"It was Clint."

"Did he get away?"

"He walked toward us, said something insane. I killed him."

He looked into her eyes. "Are you all right with that?"

Gritting her teeth against any weakness, she said, "I shot him twice. I would have shot him again if he'd moved."

"I am sorry. It's my fault... I..."

"It's not your fault. If it is the fault of anyone, it was me, for ever letting him come on the trip at all. The bastard." She pressed her lips tightly together. "Are you sure you shouldn't stay up here? If it storms..."

"Not here." He staggered to his feet, using the wall for support. "Bring the rifle and my gun."

She grimaced but went back in for the blanket also. It wasn't a long way back to where they had decided to camp, but she saw it was going to take all he had to get himself there. She put her other arm around him to steady his way.

When they got to the grove, she dropped the gun and spread the blanket. He slowly lowered himself to it. He watched then as she went to the saddlebag and pulled out a shirt. "I liked the view better without that," he complained as he watched her button it up.

"You do, do you?" She worked for her smile as she knelt beside him. "We need to do something more for that wound."

With her help, he unfastened the cartridge belt, sat up, and shrugged out of his shirt. He groaned as he lowered himself down and tried to get control of the pain. She got the canteen, encouraging him again to drink when his eyes opened.

"Cut my extra shirt into strips for bandaging." He handed her the knife from his belt. "And don't cut yourself."

"Hey, I took biology in college. I know how to cut things up with a knife," she tried to tease and had to work hard for a smile.

"Just what you went to school for," he said as she did it. "Good. Now, find the whiskey flask." When she was done, he said, "Pour whiskey over the wounds. First on front, then I'll try to roll over. If I lose consciousness, turn me and pour some over the back wound."

"That will hurt terribly when it goes in."

"I remember. Infections are worse. If I lose consciousness from it, tie the wounds up with the strips." As soon as she poured the whiskey over the first wound, he blacked out.

When he came to, the sun was going down. He had been out for too long. He put his hand down and felt of the smooth bindings around his torso. It felt tight. He wasn't sure what his odds of survival were. He'd seen gut shots like his. Sometimes something else set in, infection, and death was only a few days away.

"How do you feel?" she asked as she again brought the canteen to his lips.

"Not good enough to stay on a horse right now. You'll have to ride back to camp. You can make it if you stay close below the cliff and..."

He felt her fingers on his lips. "I won't leave you. Tomorrow they will come looking for us."

"Not right away."

"We have food, water and this forest as shelter. I have the guns besides us. I... I couldn't bury his body, but I did drag it down the slope to be away from us if predators come."

"You have to get back where it's safe." He saw from the set of her lips that she wasn't going to leave him.

"No. I have the rifle. You have the gun. I won't light a fire because I don't want to draw anyone or thing to us, but I think we will be fine here. Maybe tomorrow you will be stronger and able to mount your horse."

She was a dreamer, asleep or awake. "IF wishes were

horses, then beggars would ride," he said managing a smile.

"Your mother taught you nursery rhymes too."

"Some. That one stuck." He had thought of it many times, the uselessness of wishes or hopes.

She brushed his hair back from his forehead. "Tomorrow you will be able to get on your horse... or we will wait right here. Sam will come for us. You know he will."

He did know that. He also knew he didn't want her out here exposed to who knew what all through the long night, while he was virtually helpless to protect her.

"I know what you are thinking," she said. "I see it on your face. You have been strong for everyone else, all your life, Vince. Now let someone else be strong for you." She again put the canteen to his lips.

He let out a breath. Like he had a choice, but he nodded. He couldn't force her to go. He looked around then to assess their position for defense against wolves, cougars... or worse, human predators. He tried to get his elbows under him again, but nothing was working. He felt the world falling away. When he woke again, the moon was huge, as it rose above the canyon rim.

"It's beautiful isn't it?" she whispered where she was cuddled against his good side.

"Bright at least," He said after she again got him to drink water.

She brushed her fingers over his chest. "There is a nicer Aztec story about the markings, I mean than body parts."

"And you know it."

"Fortunately, for you, I do. The dark markings are actually the shape of a rabbit. The gods were teasing the moon and flung the rabbit up there. Some say the rabbit came back down, but the markings were left. It does kind of look like a rabbit doesn't it?"

He heard a coyote howl and then another answer. "If you say so," he said.

The next howl was of a wolf.

"Where is it?" she asked nervously.

"Miles away." Then he heard, from a distant ridge, the answering wolf call. "Maybe its mate," he said.

"It's melodic, more than the coyotes. Where do you think they are?"

"Higher on the mountain. Maybe as much as thirty miles from here. Canyons make it harder to tell as they bounce sounds."

"Do you want more water?"

"No, but some whiskey would go good."

She lifted his head, and put the flask to his lips. After he took a couple of sips, he said, "You have some too."

"I haven't been much of a whiskey drinker."

"It'll help you to sleep." It wasn't doing much for his pain, but he hoped it would for her sleep. He didn't want to sleep. He wanted to stay awake through the night to be sure nothing else went wrong.

She took a sip, coughing before she screwed the lid back on. "Just being with you helps me sleep," she said as she settled back against him. "I like feeling your muscles, stroking down their ridges." He could hear the smile in her voice.

"For a gal raised in a mansion, you are remarkably tough."

"It wasn't all that great a life. Money doesn't solve all problems."

"I remember you saying you didn't want marriage because of your family."

"That was true." She kissed his chest above the bandaging. "My mother was not treated well by my father. For that matter he wasn't that good to my younger sister either."

"You haven't talked much about her." Hearing her voice helped him forget the agony that surged through his body.

She left him for a minute and came back with a cloth that she must have soaked in the spring. She used it to wash his skin. He realized he was running a fever. He felt a little strange in the head. "What's her name?" he asked trying to stay lucid.

"Lily. Holly and Lily. She's dark-haired where I am fair."

"What did she study in college? Being a doctor?" He gave a little laugh, then wished he hadn't when it made the pain worse.

"She didn't go. Lily is an artist. She paints. Beautiful paintings of people and nature, anything she sees. Father never appreciated her gifts though. He put all his hopes on me, I guess. Now she's free, and so am I."

"Because he's dead?"

She nodded. "I didn't wish him dead, but he ruled everything with an iron fist. You know the fortune had come from my mother. Maybe that's what made him like he was, that he couldn't do more than her father had done."

He tried to keep with her, but his thoughts drifted away. He couldn't hold onto them before darkness took him again.

As the sun came up, Holly woke. The heat in Vince's body was greater. She again washed his skin. She could never manage to get him over a horse, nor would she leave him. She wondered how long before Sam would come for them. The food they had brought was more than enough for her since she could not tempt him to take so much as a bite. She got him to take a few sips of water, but he was barely aware.

She wished again that she had the iodine. Some claimed it would fight all infections. She thought briefly of riding down to the camp, except she wouldn't leave him when he was unable to defend himself—not with the metallic scent of blood in the air. She would wait. Sam would not take too long before he would know something had gone wrong and come.

With the sun high in the sky, nearing what she guessed to be noon, she saw three horsemen riding up the canyon and recognized the one in the lead as Sam. The other two were Vince's brothers. She stood and waved them to her. When Sam reached them, with a leap, he was off his horse. "What the hell happened?"

"Clint shot Vince in the back."

Sam knelt at Vince's side. "I saw the body. He shoot Madison?"

"No, I did that as he was coming toward us."

He gave her a look of surprise before he smiled. "Good girl."

"Vince has been in and out of consciousness since it happened. His fever is too high."

"All right, we'll get him back to camp." Sam stood and looked down toward Madison's body where Cole had gone.

"Did he have a horse?" Sam asked as he looked beyond the body toward the creek.

"I never saw him with one," Holly said.

"Maybe a stable horse," Sam suggested. "If he is, he'll head back to Show Low. I don't think anybody will come looking for this jasper. We can't leave the horse tied down there by the creek in case that's what he did."

"Want I should bury Madison?" Cole, who had come to look down at his brother, asked.

"The varmint doesn't deserve burying, but it'll save questions later if we do. I didn't think to bring a shovel though."

"I will ride back to camp for one. Bury him right where he is in case there are questions later," Cole said. "When I get it done, I'll look for a horse."

"Sounds good."

Cole mounted, nudged his mount in the side and took off at a fast run.

Sam looked down at Vince. "Fever's what's got hold of him now."

"I can't lose him," Holly said fighting back tears. This had been nothing like her dream, but the thing she had feared most had happened.

"You won't." Sam, with Jesse's help, set to cutting some pinyon pine poles, scraping off the branches and then rigged a travois with the blanket, which they secured by ropes to Vince's horse, who was surprisingly obedient or maybe this wasn't his first experience with such a rig. Jesse picked Vince up as though he was a child and laid him on it. They used rope to secure him in place.

"Can you ride?" Sam asked Holly, who knew she was shaking, still feeling stunned.

She nodded. Jesse saddled her horse and lifted her onto him. "My brother will be all right," he said as he handed her the reins. "I know it."

She wished she did, but she was scared. She had never seen Vince like this. He had always seemed so vital, so able to take care of anything. Now he was helpless and dependent on others to keep him alive—if they even could. She understood the dangers of wounds where Vince's was.

"Easy, Zeus," Sam said as he leaped into the saddle and then took the reins to Vince's horse. The stallion didn't like the smell of blood, but he soon settled down.

Sam looked over at Holly. "I know it looks bad, but Vince will make it."

"If he wants to," she said biting her lip and staring into Sam's eyes for reassurance.

He let out a breath. "Yeah, if he wants to."

CHAPTER 27

When they got Vince settled on a bedroll at camp, stripped off his clothing and boots, he was barely conscious as a blanket was pulled over him. Holly removed the crude bandaging, poured first the hydrogen peroxide and then the iodine on the open wounds. "Worse than the whiskey," he groaned, as he tried to twist away from the hurt.

"More effective too," she said with set lips as she placed cloth pads over the wounds and then used the surgical tape to hold them in place.

"Hand me the whiskey." He managed an attempt at a smile, which likely came out more a grimace. She put it to his lips. When she laid him back down, he looked up at her. "I am sorry."

She pursed her lips and sat back on her heels. "You said that before. It wasn't your fault, not any of it. I blame myself for it."

"I should have seen him. Better yet, killed him in Globe."

"You don't kill when you don't have to. You couldn't shoot him for what he might do, and you don't have eyes in the back of your head, remember?" With difficulty, she smiled. "Now you have to let your body heal."

"Beautiful, where I got shot may not work out that way. I've seen men die who were gut shot. Not right away but within a few days."

"I am pretty sure that you were shot in your liver," she said, working for a better smile, as she touched his bare shoulder. "It heals itself. Give it time."

He snorted. "Leave it to a college girl."

"Not a girl... a woman. Vince Taggert's woman." She met his gaze with as fierce a look as she could.

"It won't work."

"Let's argue it out when you are on your feet."

She realized then that Song had come to kneel on her other side. "This tea will help him sleep. He needs lots of sleep now."

Holly lifted his head and helped him take a sip. "My God," he said when he had swallowed. "What the hell is it? It tastes terrible."

Jesse had come to stand on his other side. "I can hold him down if you want. He'll drink it or choke." His small smile had Vince smiling but he drank the rest of the tea.

As she watched him sleep, working to get him to eat a bit, as one day stretched into the next, Holly realized something. Through this horrible experience, she had discovered something important about herself. She had seen him weak for the first time, and she'd had to be the strong one.

She had never seen him as someone, to whom she could be a helpmate. She had been afraid she was too weak to walk at his side. In Vince's weakness, she had discovered her own strength. She was stronger than she had known. He would get well, and they would work this out to be together. One way or another, they would find a way. She believed in that. Better yet- - more and more, she believed in herself.

For three days, Vince drifted in a world filled with delusions and places where he knew nothing. His bodily needs were all taken care of by others. He cared little what they did to him, as he seemed to be sinking into a dark place from which he wasn't sure he wanted to return.

When he finally woke, lucid but weak, he decided he was going to live. He wasn't sure he was glad about it. Despite his brothers doing everything they could to help him through this healing, the tea that Song brought him regularly, some which tasted better than others, despite Holly's attentiveness, he had been careless, and it could have cost Holly her life. He had been the one to kick Madison off the crew, although he had little doubt the man would have been a danger whether with them or sent home.

"You want to go for a walk?" Sam said as he interrupted his feeling sorry for himself. He needed to get up, to get his strength back, so he nodded. With Sam's help he pulled on pants. Not the boots yet though. The pain was bearable.

"Where's Holly?" he asked as Sam put his arm around him to steady him. He took some steps, feeling weak as a kitten.

"She's fine. It's my shift. Ever been shot hard before?"

"Once in the leg."

"Then you know, it takes awhile. A shock to the body. The hard part is you got to let go of thinking you could have changed it."

"I shouldn't have turned my back like I did." His breath was coming with more difficulty. Sam turned him and then helped him lie back on the bedroll.

"You know as well as I that when a man wants to shoot

another from ambush, it's only luck that makes a difference. What happened wasn't your fault nor Holly's, though you both want to blame yourselves."

He was grateful when Sam pulled out a cigarette and lit one for him.

"What'd you tell the others about the shooting?" Vince asked as he smoked.

"Just that you got shot. We figured it didn't matter and the fewer know, the better."

He hadn't been thinking much about anything but dying. Now back in the world, there were complications. "What did you do with Madison's body?"

"Cole took care of it. Buried him where he fell. He said he kept it from being seen as a grave and put him deep."

"I guess that's for the best. Not like we could take the carcass back to Tucson. I suppose I'll have to talk to Adams about it when we return."

"It's your choice but might be best to say nothing. He could've fallen off his horse and died in the hills been eaten by coyotes. Who's to know other than your brothers, Holly and me?" Sam took the cigarette.

Maybe that was best. Offer no more information than needed. "You didn't tell anyone here who shot me?"

Sam shook his head. "Bushwhacker. No idea who." His smile was the cold one. "I have learned a few things in life, compadre. Be careful what you say. It saves a lot of hassle."

He chewed on that. "Might be you're right."

"Holly say anything about whether she wants to go onto another site or turn back to Tucson?" Sam asked.

He shook his head. She hadn't had much to say when she sat by him, wiping his brow or helping him eat. He saw she was deep in thought but she wasn't offering him any clues about what. Had the shooting bothered her more than she'd admitted?

"She'll either go soon to beat the monsoons or have to wait for September," he said.

"I think it should be soon," Holly said as she walked up.

"You ready to go?" he asked as she knelt beside him and felt of his forehead.

"Yes. I don't want to excavate the big site, not now anyway. I learned all I can from this one. We should go back to Tucson."

"Good decision," Sam said as he headed off to tell the others.

"You can ride in the wagon," she said, "and in Tucson there is a doctor."

"Don't be leaving for me. I will be all right now—here or there."

"It's time to return. I thought it might take all summer, but we learned a lot in four weeks. The photographs David has taken and developed look wonderful. I want to get the where I can print them."

"Maybe he'll be a photographer," Vince said edging himself to sitting. She moved to where he could lean against her. It seemed strange to realize he was relying on her strength, but he had since he'd taken the bullet. Without her courage, he'd have been a dead man. She was a stronger woman than he had guessed the day he'd met her.

"What are you thinking?" she asked as she brushed the hair back from his forehead.

"You ask that at the worst times."

"Oh good, so what was it?"

"That I owe you my life."

"Then we are even." She kissed his neck.

"How do you figure?"

349

"That first day, when you pulled me from my runaway horse. I thought then I would easily have been killed."

"I suppose but more likely gotten a bruised rump." He smiled. Having walked, feeling the pain diminishing, he thought it was his first real smile in long time. "How long ago did I get shot?"

"It was the full moon. June second. And this is the... hmmmm the sixth, so I guess that means four days. Considering how bad the wound was, you have made remarkable progress."

"Sam thinks we should tell nobody about Madison's end."

"To protect me? I am not sorry I did it. I believe it'd be seen as self-defense.'

"Sam's view as there is no reason to tell someone and maybe lead to later complications."

"I guess... I don't know. I'll trust you both on this. Maybe Sam is right. The whole thing was so strange, his mannerism as he came up the slope to us. I never trusted him but never imagined he'd try to murder anyone."

Vince didn't answer that. He had seen men go crazy when they couldn't meet their own expectations. Madison ended up like so many in the West, those who drifted from place to place, and disappeared with no one caring. It had been the path for his own life—and his own likely end-- if that is he was even buried.

"You will stay with me in Tucson until you are fully healed, won't you?" she asked. When he looked into her eyes, he saw she had been more intuitive as to what he'd been thinking than he would have liked.

"You will have Pa there too. Make it kind of crowded."

"The house has room for a week or two, and you are making excuses," she said giving him one of those smiles.

Sam returned. "I need to talk to you," he interrupted before Vince had to answer her.

"About what?"

"Do you want me to leave?" Holly asked.

"Stay if you want." He squatted on Vince's other side. "It's about the money I now have."

"I don't know much about economics," Vince said, "But I think you'd be smart to hold onto it for awhile and decide slowly. It's a big change."

"You have no idea how big. You never asked how much money Marius left me."

"I figured it was your business."

"Ollie told me when I called from Show Low. The original paper had said his estate. It didn't go into specifics. When Angus filed the papers, he got an accounting. It involves property in Boston, a home, businesses, but in cash alone, it is a little under three million dollars."

Vince let out a whistle. "Guess that's why he didn't care if he got much for the ranch."

Sam nodded. "It was nothing to him. It also explains why Breanna was willing to have me killed to get it."

"You should not make any quick decisions about it."

"I won't, but I have been thinking on it, talking it over with Abby. It will be invested. It's what my sister-in-law has done with her money. Money setting doesn't help anybody. I can do good with it. We sure don't need it to live on."

"Good luck with it."

"One thing I want to invest in is you, Vince."

"Me?"

Sam nodded. "I can help you now with your trading business or whatever you want to do."

"I don't want your help, Sam."

"Like I am going to ask your permission." He snorted.

"You can't force it on me."

"What to bet." Sam laughed and rose. "Just thought I'd tell you, and you can start thinking what you want to do with your piece."

"You keep your money and invest it elsewhere." He was frustrated, when Sam walked off whistling.

"You don't want to take anything from anyone, do you?" Holly said, sitting back on her heels and looking at him.

He pulled out a cigarette and lit it. "It has seemed better to owe no one anything."

She shook her head. "I feel sorry for you. I thought I had had a rather cold life, but yours has been frigid. You have denied yourself any pleasure; any joy, any love, and the barriers you put in place are all of your own making."

He didn't look at her as he smoked the cigarette. "It's not about that, it's..." He stopped. He was no longer sure what it was about. Safer he'd been about to say. Had he gotten shot because he had been about to make love to Holly or was it one of those things. It hadn't been his time to die, but nobody put out guarantees about a time to be hurt.

She rose and walked off in what sounded like a huff. Well, maybe that was for the best. He was not taking help from Sam, and he was leaving Tucson as soon as he got back or at least was in fit shape to do it.

Although Vince was unable to help the crew in packing the wagons, he was determined, that he would ride his horse. Despite Holly's arguments, he mounted Jupiter slowly and with only some discomfort. Once in the saddle, riding wasn't more difficult than sitting in a bouncing wagon.

With the experience, they all had of working together, even minus help from him, the trip back to Tucson went smoothly.

Six days after leaving the Salt River canyon, they were in Tucson.

At Holly's home, exhausted, Vince dropped into one of the wooden lawn chairs in her backyard. How spent he was, was evidenced when he didn't argue when Gabe offered to take care of Jupiter. One good thing about the weeks they'd been through, he was used to the heat.

Jeremiah arrived at the house as Sam and David were carrying in the last of the equipment. Holly's concern had varied between keeping a watchful eye on his health and making sure the camera and its plates were safe. They stowed them in the small room off the kitchen.

"I'll get out of your way and take a hotel room," Jeremiah said.

"Nonsense," she said. "You took wonderful care of the house. Stay right where you are. David, how would you feel about staying here also before you all head back to the ranch? You could help me make the prints."

He looked at his father. "May I?"

"I don't see any reason why not. I have some business also that I need to take care of. We'll be up at Ollie and Rose's. In a week, we will leave for the ranch. We can talk more about what comes next when we get back there."

"Would there be room for me to stay here too?" Alice asked Holly. "I'd like to organize the sketches I made, add some notes, and I could help you put away equipment."

"Perfect. That would be a big help. David, you take the room opposite Jeremiah's, and Alice, you can sleep upstairs in the other room there."

An hour later Abby and Sam rode off without their offspring.

"What about Vince?" Jeremiah asked looking toward where Vince was still sitting on the outside chair looking totally spent after making a ride he never should have so soon after a major wound.

"He'll sleep with me, of course." Holly laughed.

"You aren't married," Jeremiah said.

"You are surprising me, Mr. Taggert. I never figured you for a moralist."

"Well, I am not but..."

"I don't care what others think. He will be sleeping in my bed and that's all. He's not remotely in shape for anything untoward if that was your fear." She gave him one of her smiles that had him smiling back.

"Of course." With that, she headed back inside to Alice and David and an attempt to get some order out of the chaos that had descended on her home.

Through the open window, Vince heard Song telling Holly she was heading home.

"That is fine, Song. And if you are tired tomorrow, wait a few days. I'll manage."

"You don't have to pay us," Alice said as boxes moved around inside and he felt he should be helping but instead, he sat and listened.

"You worked hard and deserve a wage. I will pay you. Tomorrow I'll visit the bank for the funds. I also appreciate your help in getting some organization into what we brought back."

Jeremiah settled into the chair across from Vince. In moments, Holly came out with a tray and three glasses. "No lemonade yet. This is white wine and it's cold."

Vince and his father each took a glass.

"You look exhausted," she said as she took the last one.

"What I need is to get down to the hotel for a bath and then a shave and haircut," Vince disagreed.

"You are staying here," she said taking a sip of her wine.

"That's settled. You can get all of that right here including having someone to look after you. You would insist to ride all the way here. I am sure it wasn't good for you."

Jeremiah chuckled. "Better do what she says, son. She looks like she means it."

"A shave and haircut?" he asked sounding half amused and half annoyed.

"I can bring someone in."

"Ah the benefits of wealth." He knew his tone was derogatory.

"Yes," she retorted without taking the offense he had expected, "including hire someone to tie you hand and foot and carry you upstairs if required—after your bath, of course." He looked up and saw by the glitter in her eyes that the minx liked that idea, having him naked, bound, and dropped onto her bed. He lost any righteous anger he'd been trying to hold onto as he smiled against his will.

"Shall I send for a barber?" she asked rising and taking their empty glasses.

"What about the bath?"

"Downstairs in the lavatory, there happens to be a tub. I shall call for the barber and start filling it." She walked into the house without looking back at Jeremiah's chuckle.

"You better marry that gal," Jeremiah said as he got Vince settled into Holly's bed. As she had promised, Vince had been shaved and had his hair trimmed, even had the bath although due to his wound, not a full soaking and she had taken care of his back. It wasn't as though she hadn't seen him naked plenty of times. This seemed different, but he wasn't sure exactly how.

Naked in her bed was giving him plenty of ideas, none of

which was he probably up to. The one point on which he had refused to give into her was his revolver. It was placed on the table alongside the bed.

"I can't marry her, and you know why," Vince said with a renewed surge of frustration.

"She doesn't see it that way."

"For now. How well did it work out for you with mother—either of my mothers?"

He glanced over to see the sad smile on Jeremiah's face. "You aren't a fool like I was. I thought I had to do things a certain way. Speaking of family, where'd Jesse and Cole go when they got to town."

"As best I know, they rode ahead when we got to Oracle for a room at a hotel and the bar. I didn't talk to them about their plans." He hadn't had the energy to talk to anyone.

Holly came into the room with a fan. "Even with the thick walls, it gets hot up here, but this helps." She set it on the dresser and plugged it into an electric outlet. The moving air did help. She sat on the other side of the bed. "What do you feel like eating tonight?"

Before Vince could open his mouth, Jeremiah said, "I am cooking tonight. I bought some steaks when you folks called from Globe. Still can't get over how good it is to have these tel-e-phones. That and some potatoes I'll roast. I can do it all outside. Maybe some salad. The garden has some needs to be used before the heat spoils it."

"Sounds wonderful."

When Vince nodded, Jeremiah went downstairs to get it started.

Holly reached over to touch his forehead.

"No fever," he said.

She smiled. "Good." She shifted then to where she had her

feet on the bed and her back against the headboard. "Want a massage?"

"You know how to do that?"

"Turn over and find out."

When he did, she flicked the blanket from him leaving him totally uncovered. "What about Alice?" he asked.

"She's busy downstairs but..." She got off the bed long enough to close their door. When she came back, she straddled him and began working the large shoulder muscles. Avoiding the bandages, she worked down his back and then shifted lower on his legs to massage his buttocks. Off his legs, she finished with his thighs and calves. Pain seemed to have vanished. He felt relaxed and sleepy.

"Turn over and I'll do your front."

He gave a little laugh. "Not now you won't, but when I get to feeling a little stronger, I might let you."

She smiled, gave his rump a little slap and pulled the sheet up to his waist. "Then you better get strong fast." With that, she was gone.

CHAPTER 28

Vince knew he should leave Tucson, get away from the temptation that seemed to grow every day. The Rykers had gone back to their ranch, but not before Sam had deposited money in an account in Vince's name. Vince had said he'd not touch it, but Sam had only laughed. "Then you'll never know what you have there." With that, he had ridden off with that daredevil way he had on a horse.

Sitting on the wooden chair in Holly's yard, Vince watched as a cardinal flitted from one branch to another on the cottonwood tree. Soon he heard the melodic cooing of a pair of doves. The air was growing hot, and he unbuttoned the top two buttons on the new white shirt that Holly had bought him. Only the shade made it still tolerable to sit out in the afternoon.

He remembered the first time he'd been in this yard and Holly with her camera. He'd never seen how those photos came out, but the memory of their lovemaking was vivid in his mind. He only wished he could forget it. Maybe riding a thousand miles from her would help.

He deliberately had not made love to her even though they had slept only inches apart, generally with her cuddled against him by morning. Before Alice had left, there had been that excuse, but then it was his reluctance to take any risk on getting her pregnant. More than that it would only make it harder to leave—and leave he must.

With the Rykers gone, Jesse and Cole had moved into Holly's home, but they slept downstairs leaving the upstairs for them. He supposed they thought they were helping him. It wasn't helping. He wanted her so bad he ached, but it wouldn't work.

She hadn't done anything to make him know she even wanted him to make love to her. Maybe that meant she had also come to see he was right. It had been a beautiful interlude —well except for the getting shot part. But, interlude is all it was ever meant to be.

Hearing the backdoor open, he turned to see her with a tray and two glasses. "Lemonade?" she asked as she put it on the table beside his chair.

He took the glass. "Thank you."

"So polite." She smiled. "Have you ever looked at the prints of the photos that David took on Canyon Creek?"

"No, should I?"

"I think you'd like them. I sent copies with David. He may have found a career for himself."

"Photo studio?"

"I think more than that. There are those who travel around the world taking photos of beautiful places. Others of the Western life as it's been but may not last much longer. People buy them. I think he has that kind of gift if he wants to use it."

"His Pa wants him running the ranch."

"Sam is a long way from too old to do that for himself. Maybe if David has some time doing the one, he'll want both."

"Maybe." He had his doubts.

"Did your father talk to you about the house he is thinking of buying on the edge of Tucson for you all to live?"

"He mentioned it. I won't be staying there. I am leaving soon, Holly."

"You promised to tell me before you went."

"I should have myself together enough to leave by Sunday."

"So soon?"

"I need to get back on the road, and I'm healed enough to do it."

"You could relapse."

"I'll take it easy."

"All right. Which way will you go?"

He had expected more argument. "I think I'll head for San Francisco and see what is wanted now. No point in visiting the reservations when I don't know."

"Tell me about San Francisco."

He sipped his lemonade as he considered that. "It's bustling, fancy buildings, streetcars, a lot of stores. It's on the bay with the ocean just over the ridge."

"I've never seen the Pacific Ocean."

"Well, I've never seen the Atlantic nor Europe."

"I was in Europe. The grand tour with some friends."

"Do you want to go back?"

"Not particularly."

He knew they were talking to fill space. Nothing that was on his mind was safe to talk about. He forced a smile. "I will never forget you," he said knowing that to tell her the rest of what he felt wasn't safe to say.

"Good." She smiled. "Supper will be ready in about an hour. Do you want anything else before that?"

He shook his head.

"There is brandy in the kitchen and a good whiskey."

"No, only makes the heat harder to take."

"All right then. I'll let you know when Song has dinner ready."

When she was gone, he felt an emptiness. Would that be there the rest of his life? It didn't matter. He knew what was best. He could do it.

An hour later, Del and Connie walked into the yard. "What you doing out here, cowboy?" Del asked as he took the other chair and Connie headed into the house.

"Enjoying the breeze," he said.

Before Del could respond with how little sense that made, Holly was out with a bottle of whiskey and two glasses. "We'll give you a holler when it's time," she said disappearing again into the house. She was humming. Definitely in a good mood. Another proof she didn't want a life with him. It was not only he, who saw it as a mistake.

"How's the store business going?" Vince asked as he poured each of them a shot.

"Got some competition. Bigger store opened up a block down, pretty much same merchandise as ours."

"I guess that's the nature of business."

"I am thinking of making a change."

"Moving?"

"Nah, Connie loves it here. I was thinking of selling Native crafts."

"Nobody's done that in Tucson. Is there a reason?"

"Just haven't caught up with the times. What do you think about supplying us? We are going to enlarge, do a little upgrading."

"I guess I could do that." He was a little surprised if they weren't doing well that Del would be enlarging the store.

Del grinned. "I saw that look. Sam invested some money in Sicillas. It was him who gave us the idea. I think he's onto something, and if we had a good trader to help us get the best merchandise, it'd work for us and save you going all the way to San Francisco so often."

Now Vince wondered if this explained Holly's good mood. She expected he'd be back off and on. He could be her casual lover until she found someone permanent. He clenched his jaw as he thought about her with another man.

"What do you think?" Del asked taking another sip.

He forced his mind back to Del. "I could get you quality merchandise." It wouldn't even take coming to Tucson. "I think it's a good idea. You can at least try it."

Del grinned.

"How you doing, boy?" Jeremiah asked as he, Cole and Jesse walked into the yard.

"You here for dinner too?" he asked. A going away dinner maybe, but she hadn't known when he'd leave until an hour earlier.

"Holly said we needed to be here."

"A family gathering." Vince took another sip of his whiskey ignoring what he'd said earlier about it making the heat harder to take. Holly came out from the house with more glasses. "Ten minutes," she said with a big smile before she was again inside.

The dinner was delicious as was everything Song cooked. Holly had also invited Zian. Conversation flowed easily but nothing that Vince even remembered when Holly said, "You gentlemen can go back out into the garden. We'll be out after we clean up."

Vince saw the beads of sweat on the faces of Holly, Song,

and Connie. They had cooked the meal. It was how it always had been for women to cook and clean up, but it wasn't right. "You ladies cooked," he said rising. "We will clean up."

"I clean up at home," Del said with a big smile. "Ladies outside, and we'll get this whipped in shape in no time."

"I'm good at washing," Jeremiah said carrying over plates while the ladies disappeared with the brandy bottle and glasses to the cooler night air. He filled the dishpan with soapy water that had been heating on the stove, adding enough cool to make it bearable. It was only fifteen minutes later when the kitchen was back to rights, and the five of them went out with their glasses to refill.

"When you leaving, Vince?" Cole asked from where he settled on the porch.

"Sunday. Less people on the road."

"Want me to come with you?"

"You can't do that," Jeremiah said.

"Why not?" Cole frowned.

"You have to go back to Vernal and sell the ranch. You know its value better than any of us."

"Don't you have to do that?" Cole asked.

Jeremiah shook his head. "A year after Valerie died, I put the ranch in your name."

Cole let out a breath. "Why?"

"Who else would I want to have it? Jesse couldn't manage it. Asa was as like to kill me as look at me. Vince was gone. No man worked harder to bring in money from it. You think I didn't notice?"

"To be honest—yes."

Jeremiah chuckled. "I'd like a share of whatever you get, but that's up to you. You have the right to it all if it's what you want."

"No, I'll head north tomorrow. If it sells for anything, we'll all divide it."

"Well, do your best."

"Ollie offered me a job," Jesse said. "Helping him train horses. He said when we were traveling north together, he saw I had a good feel for them. I'm going to take it."

"That's good, Jess," Vince said.

Holly was quiet, not saying much until everyone got ready to leave. When Vince and she were alone, she said, "I moved your things into the room Alice used. I think that under the circumstances, it is best, don't you?"

He nodded. It was best. He didn't like it, but it was best.

Saturday went by fast for Vince, as his energy level still wasn't all it had been. It took longer to get jobs done. He checked on Jupiter, made sure he was trail ready. He stopped by Sicillas and bought jerky, hard biscuits, another bottle of whiskey, a spare shirt, and new scarf. It wasn't as though he'd be traveling where hotels weren't possible. He had some money.

When he got home, Holly was sitting in the kitchen studying a book. "Hi," she said with a smile. "Leftovers tonight. Is that all right?"

He nodded. It would be their last night together. He wished she showed more regret, but then what should he expect. It was his choice to leave. The thing was what would he have staying here? Nothing. He hadn't bothered to stop at the bank to see what Sam had given him. He was not going to take it. Sam would eventually come to understand.

"I've paid everyone else off. The money there is yours," she said pointing to several bills on the counter. "It's the fee we agreed on for you to help me make the excavation happen— plus covering the rifles and what you bought before we left."

He took that. He had earned it. "Thank you," he said as he pocketed it.

"I am very grateful you came with me. You made it all possible." She smiled, the warmth in her eyes as it always been, but she didn't invite him to share her bed for his last night.

Restlessly, lying in bed by himself, knowing she was across the hall, he reminded himself again this was wise. Being wise and feeling good were two different things.

Sunday morning, Vince rose before light and walked out the door closing it softly. He headed down to the stable and collected Jupiter, tied his bags on back and stepped in the saddle. It used to feel better.

He rode out of town on the road north. He planned to pace himself slowly to begin. He could sleep in the foothills of the Picacho Mountains the first night. He had brought oats for Jupiter and carried enough water to get them to the Gila.

The road was busier than he had expected with wagons and riders traveling both ways. Arizona was developing too fast. He stopped briefly for a lunch break but kept on to get himself as far as he could from Tucson-- no tempting himself to turn around. Although he was heading toward a life he no longer wanted, it was all he knew. He was doing the right thing. If it hadn't happened now, it'd have happened later. He and Holly were not meant to be together—whether that soul thing was true or not.

When he saw a wash that he had remembered, he turned Jupiter down it and found a likely spot for a night camp. After unsaddling and securing his horse, he gathered sticks and lit a small fire to make coffee. It was only then that he saw the rider coming toward him. The sun was almost setting in the west, and the glow settled over her as she looked down at him from her horse.

"Got enough for two?" she asked.

For a moment, he worried that he was delusional. Maybe it would have been better. "What are you doing here?"

"Where else would I be? I'm your partner." Holly dismounted and led her horse to where Jupiter looked up with interest from the grass. Competently, she loosened Princess' cinch, hobbled her front legs, took off her bridle, and gave her a few pats before she returned to Vince.

"Are you out of your mind?"

She put her arms up around his neck. "I am. I am totally a lost cause. There is no hope for me." She smiled then as she pulled his head down for a kiss. "I have some of Song's biscuits. I brought a can of beans but not sure how you open it," she said when she released him. "I should have bought a can opener maybe."

"Holly, you can't come with me."

"Of course, I can. You said you cannot fit into my life. Fine, I accept that. Therefore, I will fit into yours. I know a lot about artifacts. We'll make a terrific team."

He sat down on the large boulder by his fire-- finding his breath coming faster. She went back to her horse and removed her bedroll. "You sure a wash is safe for sleeping?" she asked as she returned. "I hear flashfloods come down them."

"In the season." He stared up at her. She was wearing boy's pants, a white shirt and even had a cartridge belt and gun at her waist. "You are crazy," he said.

"You already said that, and I agreed." She pushed his legs together and sat on his lap. "I know it too. I am madly in love with you and not about to let the best thing that ever came into my life get away. You are stuck with me, partner."

"I am too old for you."

"All right, let's get this all out. How old are you?" She brushed his cheek with her fingertips.

"Forty-one."

"So ancient."

"It will be."

"So will I someday if both of us are lucky. Do you know how old I am?"

"A girl."

She laughed. "I am twenty-five, hardly a girl, but maybe I am the one who is too young for you."

"You're being silly."

"No, you are. You already know how much I desire you, how avidly I covet your body. You know age isn't the issue."

"All right, but this is. I don't have any money."

"If my money is a barrier, I'll give it away."

"That's foolishness."

"Not if it stands between us."

"You're a college educated woman and want a smarter man."

"Silly. You are smart enough for me and know things I never will."

"You'd have no home."

"Just you." She smiled then and kissed the tip of his nose. "Listen to me, Vincent Taggert. I do love you. I believe you love me too. We will make a great team. I can cajole the stores while you deal with the tribes."

He felt something give in his heart, as though a dam had burst and feelings surged through his body. "You can't go with me," he said as he put his arms around her and drew her more tightly against him.

"Why not? You do love me, don't you?"

"More than anything I've ever known in my life. Yes, I love you."

She laughed and kissed his lips, pushing his hat off his head and running her fingers through his hair. "Then I danged well, as Ollie would say, can go with you."

"No, you can't... "And suddenly he knew it was true. He wondered how far he'd have gotten if she hadn't followed. "You can't come because I am going to go back to Tucson with you... that is if..."

"I don't want you to give up your dreams for me. I can live with you on the road. I know I can." She stopped. "What is the-- if?"

"If you'll be my wife."

She let out a sigh and then tipped his head up for another kiss. "I would love to be your wife. But why can't I be the wife of a trader?"

"You could, but I'd rather be the husband of an archae-ologist."

She laughed then. "Seriously?"

"I never meant anything more-- other than that I do love you. I would like to help you do those explorations, learn those things about earlier cultures. This time without the past life karma."

She began unbuttoning his shirt and pushed it from his shoulders. She ran her fingers down the muscles on his arms, kissed his nipples, then looked up. "You do know we had more than one past life together."

When he groaned, she laughed and stood up. "But I am satisfied with this one that is if..." She began unbuttoning her shirt. "You will make love to me right now and as often as you can before we get back to Tucson, gather your family, my friends, and find us a parson."

"I think I can handle that."

And he did.

To review this book, please use the link below to access your sales channel.
http://romanceswithanedge.blogspot.com/2015/07/echoes-from-past-links.html

Sign up for new release notifications at
http://raintrueax.blogspot.com

AFTERWORD

More
Rain Trueax stories

Evening Star
Bannister's Way
Second Chance
Hidden Pearl
Her Dark Angel
From Here To There
Montana Christmas
Luck of the Draw

Fantasy - Paranormal
Diablo Canyon Trilogy
Sky Daughter
Enchantress' Secret
To Speak of Things Unseen
A Price to be Paid

www.ingramcontent.com/pod-product-compliance
Lightning Source LLC
Chambersburg PA
CBHW070759180626
46818CB00001B/21